Birthright

By Ethan Jones

Prologue

A fierce attacker is prophesised. A warrior of courage, strength and of noble birth. A leader of men, a man of vision who will deliver his oppressed people from their foreign oppressors. He, who will come intent on onslaught from across the sea. Despoiler is his name for he will despoil many.

Those words were spoken long ago, long in our people's history. They are the words of the great Myrddin, bard of the Britons. My mother would recount Myrddin's prophecy to me daily throughout my childhood. She would tell me tales of why I had been born and reared in exile across the sea in the lands of the Irish. She would tell me of my father, Cynan, who was betrayed by those close to him and forced to flee across the sea to seek the protection of the Irish and die in shame. She would tell me of the foreign tyrants oppressing my people and cheating me of my kingdom, of my birthright. My name is Gruffudd son of Cynan and I am all that is left of the royal house of Aberffraw which had ruled over the lands of Gwynedd until the murder of my grandfather, Iago, and the betrayal my father suffered. God bless her memory, but she set me on this path. I believed in Myrddin's prophecy and believed that, with God's grace, my actions would see the great bard's prophecy realised. I was determined to regain my family's honour and to claim my birthright from the usurpers.

As you sit here with me now my bones ache, my scars throb and my sight weakens by the day. My body is a far cry from that of my youth, from when I set out to reclaim my birthright. I was reared in exile and burdened by the shame which came with it. But there was a fire in my heart that would never be extinguished. By my sixteenth year I was a blooded member of my foster-father Sitric's warband, had stood in the shieldwall for the first time and my blade had tasted blood. Sitric was in the service of King Muirchertach, who was the son of Toirdelbach the High King of Ireland, and who ruled over the Kingdom of Munster in his father's name. Young warriors are always determined to prove themselves and I was no different. My desire to win a fearsome reputation on the battlefield had earned me a fierce reputation and a small amount of plunder to go with it. I knew the blood lust of battle and craved it, carving a bloody swathe through the enemies of my foster-father and Muirchertach.

My mother was Ragnhild, daughter of the late Danish king of Duibhlinn, the great Sitric Silkbeard who, they say, could trace his lineage back to the old Pagan gods. When Sitric Silkbeard died my mother and her family were forced to flee. The men of Duibhlinn cheated my mother's brother, Sitric Sitricsson, out of his right to the kingship in favour of a petty tyrant, *Jarl* Gofraid. Like my father, they were forced to flee like common thieves in the night. Sitric was a *Jarl* in his own right and pledged his sword to King Muirchertach. The Irish found a useful ally in Sitric. His talent as a war leader had turned him into Muirchertach's right hand man despite being what the Irish called a *dubh-gaill,* a "black foreigner" due to his Danish ancestry. So, my fate was set. I would have to follow in Sitric's footsteps. I, too, would have to pledge my allegiance to the Irish in return for their support and, even at an early age, I knew that day would come.

I was an infant when my father died and my mother was taken in by her brother Sitric. At an early age my mother entrusted me for several years to the church. Although we spoke Danish and Irish amongst ourselves she wished that I be schooled in Latin, the language of diplomacy. She died in my tenth year and it was then that Sitric became my foster father. He had always taken an interest in my development and soon saved me from the monks, insisting I learn the ways of the warrior. My natural skill was obvious from an early stage; I will not deny it with false modesty. My ferocity and natural skill at arms had earned the respect of Sitric, who had raised me as one of his own. Sitric was old, but he was still a hard man and I loved him as a father. His son, my foster brother, Cerit was the same age as me and Sitric ordered that we learn the ways of the warrior together under the watchful eye of our old tutor Wselfwulf. The old Saxon was a tough bastard, powerfully built and battle-scarred. He pushed us to the limit and beyond. He said that his name meant the slaughterer of wolves; it was fitting. His guidance did us no harm; the tricks that he drilled into us have saved us both on more than one occasion. It was on Wselfwulf's recommendation that Sitric made me stand in the front rank of the shieldwall for the first time. The old bastard wanted to see me fight, see if I could stand when it came to it. He was not disappointed. Since that day my reputation soared amongst Sitric's warband and Muirchertach's court. By my nineteenth year such was my reputation that Sitric, with Muirchertach's approval, released me from his service and granted me permission to raise a warband of my own.

Just as Sitric had done years earlier, I too pledged my blade to Muirchertach in return for his future support when the time came for me to return to Gwynedd. It was no secret who I was in Muirchertach's court; everyone knew my pedigree and Muirchertach seemed to promote it to anyone who would listen. So, it was of no surprise that men came to join my warband hoping to benefit from my growing reputation. Although my reputation had risen, my wealth had not. Sitric had granted me an old hall and lands, which were part of his estate. It was not much, a small piece of wooded land near Loch Garman in Muirchertach's Kingdom of Munster, with an old dilapidated hall. But that did not worry me much. We all knew war was brewing with the men of Duibhlinn and that was enough to keep my small warband happy. My warband numbered few in those early days, but they were wolves whom I knew I could rely on when war came. All manner of men had come to join my warband. However, I could only keep half a ship's crew and a handful of thralls fed. Within seven days I had twenty four men who had sworn themselves to my service, all of whom were either Irish or Danish and all as desperate and fierce as the other. They were cut-throats, rogues, thieves and warriors all. I could sense this was the beginning, the beginning of my journey back to Gwynedd, but I would have to earn Muirchertach's favour first. I set about training those men with the energy and ferocity of a fierce storm and had them battle ready in good time. I had made Bjorgolf my second man; he was the hardiest and most ferocious of the lot. Bjorgolf was an outlawed Dane from Duibhlinn. He had been outlawed for killing his woman's lover before turning his blade on her in drunken fury. He had fled Duibhlinn several weeks ago to drown his sorrows and then came to my hall to pledge his sword and take his vengeance on the men of Duibhlinn. The man was as hard as they come, with a vicious looking scar down his left cheek which made him look all the more fearsome. I was satisfied to have the oath of such a man. I judged him as one I could rely on to follow me without hesitation.

It was well known that Muirchertach would be ordered by his father to overthrow the tyrant Gofraid and take his lands back into Irish ownership. Duibhlinn lacked strong leadership, we all knew that. Gofraid was ageing, he was no use as a warrior and, it was rumoured, was afraid that his own shadow would one day kill him. It was common knowledge that Muirchertach had met many dissatisfied *bóndis,* land owners who were looking to see Gofraid removed for their own personal gain. It was also rumoured that Muirchertach had come to an agreement with several of Gofraid's *Jarls*. Although the men of Duibhlinn lacked a strong ruler they did not lack courage and those still loyal to Gofraid would resist, we were sure of it. Sitric was certain the men of Duibhlinn would follow Gofraid's henchman, *Jarl* Gunnald the Red, into battle. Gunnald was fiercely loyal to Gofraid, as he owed all he had to Gofraid's rise to power. Gunnald's reputation was fearsome indeed and his talent as a warrior was unquestionable. However, Sitric had a plan.

We received Muirchertach's summons the next day and marched north the following morning. Muirchertach was mustering his army on the borderlands of Duibhlinn. The night we arrived Sitric summoned me to his tent. Cerit and one of Muirchertach's lords, named Faelan, were also present when I arrived. Sitric greeted me and informed me that we would not be attending Muirchertach's council of war. He continued that he had met with Muirchertach earlier to suggest his plan to lure Gunnald out into the open and Muirchertach had accepted the plan. The men of Duibhlinn had elected to follow Gunnald the Red, exactly as Sitric had predicted. Gunnald was a giant of a man with a fearsome reputation and the temper to match it. Sitric was gambling that Gunnald's temper would be a fatal weakness. Gunnald was no stranger to Sitric; the two had a blood feud. Years earlier Sitric had killed Gunnald's brother when fleeing from Duibhlinn. So, it was our task to provoke the red-haired giant into a foolhardy attack and kill him before he could arrive in Duibhlinn to lead Gofraid's army. Gunnald held the lands of Sord Cholmcille a short march north of the port of Duibhlinn itself. The plan was daring and, if we were successful, our deeds would make an excellent saga tale.

Muirchertach informed Sitric that his spies had reported that Gofraid's army was mustering in the port of Duibhlinn itself whilst Gunnald was still at his homestead. He was believed to be with his warband whilst he rounded up the *ledungen*, a levy, made up of the freemen of his lands. If we were successful Sitric was to reap a handsome financial reward whilst I would gain Gunnald's lands of Sord Cholmcille and, with it, the wealth to raise a strong enough warband to aid me in my claim to Gwynedd's crown. If we moved that night, we would be there by morning. And so it is in the year of our Lord 1074 that my story of revenge begins.

Part One

Index of Placenames

Throughout the novel I have chosen to use the contemporary spellings of place names as they appear in the historical text, *The Life of Gruffudd ap Cynan*. Where the contemporary place names, which I needed to use, have not been available I have used the modern Gaelic or Welsh spelling. For some place names there have been several contemporary spellings such as that of Dublin (which I have seen appear as Dyflin, Duibhlinn, Duib Linn, Dubh Linn and Dulyn) I have opted for the one which simply read better in my mind.

Aberdaron - Aberdaron, Gwynedd, Wales

Aberffraw - Aberffraw, Isle of Anglesey, Wales

Aber - Abergwyngregyn, Gwynedd, Wales

Abermenai - Abermenai (Nr. Newborough Warren), Isle of Anglesey, Wales

Bangor - Bangor, Gwynedd, Wales

Braich-y-Dinas - Penmaenmawr Quarry (Nr. Penmaenmawr), Conwy, Wales

Bron yr Erw - Nr. Penrhyndeudraeth, Gwynedd, Wales

Carn Madryn - Madryn Castle (Nr. Dinas), Gwynedd, Wales

Castell Tomen - Tomen-y-Mur (Nr. Trawsfynydd), Gwynedd, Wales

Cemais - Cemaes, Isle of Anglesey, Wales

Clynnog Fawr - Clynnog Fawr, Gwynedd, Wales

Cruach Brendain - Mount Brandon, Co. Kerry, Republic of Ireland

Degannwy - Deganwy, Conwy, Wales

Deudraeth - Penrhyndeudraeth, Gwynedd, Wales

Dinorwic - Dinorwig, Gwynedd, Wales

Dissard – Dyserth, Denbighshire, Wales

Duibhlinn - Dublin, Co. Dublin, Republic of Ireland

Eryri - Snowdonia, Snowdonia National Park, Wales

Gwaed Erw - Dyffryn Glyncul, Gwynedd, Wales

Lleyn Peninsula - Llyn Peninsula, Gwynedd, Wales

Loch Garman - Wexford, Co. Wexford, Republic of Ireland

Mathrafal - Nr. Welshpool, Powys, Wales

Nevyn - Nefyn, Gwynedd, Wales

Rhuddlan - Rhuddlan, Denbighshire, Wales

Segontium - Caernarfon, Gwynedd, Wales

Sord Cholmcille - Swords, Co. Dublin, Republic of Ireland

Ynys Enlli - Bardsey Island, Gwynedd, Wales

Ynys Môn - Isle of Anglesey, Isle of Anglesey, Wales

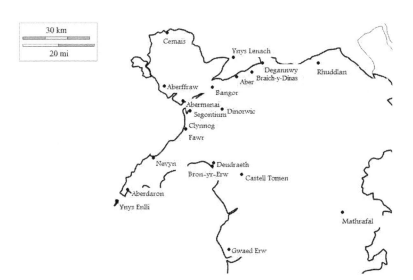

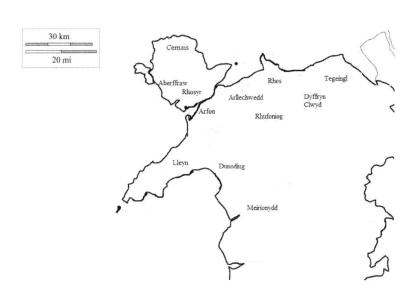

I

My heart was beating like a drum beneath my mail, it was cold yet I was sweating under my war gear. I could feel the familiar sinking feeling in my stomach and my knees beginning to weaken as the thunder grew louder. "Gunnald has taken the bait then," Cerit muttered to my right. "Those pirates don't half make a bloody noise."

The enemy chanting was reaching a crescendo as they thumped their shields. I could sense the unease in my shieldwall. I cannot show my fear - lead by example, I remember those words blowing round my head like a high wind as we peered into that God awful mist. The mist was made worse by the smoke as nearby one of Gunnald's tenanted farms burned intensely. I swallowed hard and shouted to be heard above the din. "Steady men, they do not yet know who they face. So let the scum know!"

As one the line roared Sitric's war cry. "For Sitric, for God!"

Bjorgolf was driving himself into a frenzy to my left. "Come on you pig humping bastards, come and die on my blade!"

The whole of my shield wall took up the rhythmic thumping of their shields and repeated Sitric's war cry to lure Gunnald in further. "For Sitric, for God!"

Then they appeared a shieldwall out of the mist a hundred paces to our front. The enemy began to beat their shields with renewed vigour as they approached our position across the saturated turf. I could vaguely make out the banner, a black axe on a red field and a giant of a man under it. He is their leader; he is the one I must kill. "The ground has been picked well brother," Cerit shouted above the racket. "The bastards are walking straight into it."

I knew Cerit was right; Sitric had picked the ground well. We stood atop a small grassy verge and a copse of woodland, where Sitric and Faelan's men were concealed, protecting my left flank. "Sitric knew this tree line would do the trick, give the bastards a sniff and he knew they would come to us," I replied with a wink. "So long as Sitric and Faelan hit them at the right time, they will be ours."

I sounded more confident than I felt, I remember that. Sitric had trusted me to be the bait of his battle plan. This was my first test as a leader of men in war. The weight of expectation burdened my shoulders, I could not fail or we would be dead. My twenty four wolves were bolstered by twenty of Sitric's men along with Cerit, under my command. We were heavily armed and would, I hoped, be more than a match for Gunnald and his warband.

They were seventy paces off now and I could start to make out the individuals in Gunnald's advancing shieldwall. A disciplined cluster of around sixty well-equipped men were concentrated around the enemy banner, which seemed to be heading straight towards me. They were flanked on their right by fifty or so ragged men; these must be Gunnald's levy. They were confident. Gunnald's warband approached in three disciplined ranks, whilst the levy was in an ill-disciplined formation on the flank. Fifty paces now - they were committed - they were coming for us. I could make out the leader's red plaited beard, long red hair and shining helm - there was no mistaking him, Gunnald the Red. He's mine, I remember thinking, and if I kill the bastard Muirchertach will have to help me claim my birthright.

I shouted to Cerit, "Gunnald is mine; I have to kill the bastard!"

Cerit laughed, "Your wish to make a name for yourself will be your death, brother. I will be here to save your royal arse if he gets the better of you," returning a wink.

"As will I, the cur has it coming," Bjorgolf growled.

No more than thirty paces now, they had passed the copse to the left of my line. I shouted the order. "Shieldwall!" Bjorgolf repeated the order at the top of his voice and as one the shields smacked together along my line. Suddenly the levy checked for a heartbeat as they were confronted by a formidable wall of shields. Gunnald's warband continued unperturbed towards my position as they shouted their war cries and jeered my waiting line. It was plain Gunnald believed he could win; he would march his shieldwall to mine and knew his superior numbers would count.

Come on Faelan now, now, hit the bastards now. Then I heard it, Faelan's Irish streamed out of the tree outcrop, screaming their fury, and smashed into the levy on Gunnald's flank. The enemy line faltered and immediately a roar came from behind Gunnald's unsettled men. "For Sitric, for God!"

Gunnald bellowed orders. I judged that now was the time for me to charge, whilst the enemy was panicked. My heart quickened and I felt the blood lust of battle flow through me. I charged forwards screaming. "Now you whoresons, now!"

The whole line charged as one behind me roaring their war cries. My whole world slowed as I sprinted towards my enemy, my heart pounded in my chest and my muscles tensed as I braced for the impact. Then I hit the first man with all my force as we crashed into the disorganised enemy shieldwall. I recovered first and smashed the hilt of my blade into his nose, crushing the bone as blood streamed down his ruined face. I pushed on as he fell and Cerit finished him off with a thrust into his unprotected neck which was rewarded with spray of blood. I took a blow on my shield from the left and hacked at an unprotected thigh to the right, feeling my blade cut through flesh and bone. We had broken through their shieldwall, we were amongst them now. Bjorgolf was there on my left and rammed his blade underneath a man's shield, doubling him over before dispatching him with a hack to the back of the neck, near severing the head.

I could feel Gunnald's line shattering as panic started to spread like a disease. For the love of God they must be breaking! Suddenly Gunnald's line crumbled, his men began to look about in desperation as the cheers of victory sounded on the left flank. Faelan's Irish chanted their lord's name and cheered in victory. A blow hammered against my shield and that brought my thoughts back to the task in hand.

Bjorgolf hacked down on a shield and a man in my second rank smashed his axe into the unprotected chest of a huge bear of a man. As he fell we hit the rear rank of Gunnald's line who had their backs to us. Sitric's men had closed the trap by hitting Gunnald's warband in the rear. With some of Gunnald's men having their backs to us, it was easy. I rammed my blade through the back of a short mailed man's head, before hacking my blade across the shoulder blades of another. A blow hammered my shield to the front as we met Sitric's line and I cursed. "Watch your damn blows you stupid bastard! We're on the same side you bonehead!" I screamed into my attacker's face. The man's eyes widened in surprise and as he grasped that what I spoke was true he laughed as I joined in.

But it was not over. Sitric's men had torn through Gunnald's line and to my right there was chaos. I noticed a mêlée twenty paces to my right, where the sound of battle still ruled. I pushed my way through my men, who plundered the dead. I cursed as I neared the source of the commotion. I could see a group of mailed men grimly fighting their way clear through my right flank in disciplined order under the red banner. Gunnald was breaking free.

I shouldered my way through to the front rank, with Bjorgolf and Cerit still beside me. Men threw themselves at Gunnald's retreating shieldwall in an effort to prevent the red haired giant escaping. Gunnald cut one of my men down with a powerful blow. A jet of blood and gore escaped from his smashed skull as the man died instantly.

"Gunnald! I'm coming for you bastard!" I screamed. The giant smirked at my words before hacking down one of Sitric's men in a flurry of brutal blows. Our line was faltering as the casualties began to take their toll. Then there was breathing space; Gunnald's men had broken clear as my line faltered. I had to do something, lead by example, those words went through my head again and I acted.

I broke clear of the line and hurled myself against Gunnald's retreating shieldwall. A dark blur to the left caught my eye and I raised my shield dropping to one knee, as Wselfwulf had taught me years ago. The spear thrust glanced off my shield before I rammed my blade at the shins of the man to my front. He went down and fell towards me, taking me down with him. We fell almost like lovers, in a deadly embrace onto the saturated turf. I hammered my sword hilt twice into his face as we fell. I can still hear his screams and remember his foul breath, cracked teeth and blood matted beard as his life blood seeped out of him and into the mud.

The attacker to my left grunted as he thrust down with his spear. I took the blow on my shield and the weapon stuck fast. I kicked out, swiping his legs from under him, discarding the useless shield and went for his throat as his body smacked into the sodden earth. I was on top of him as we grappled, smashing my fist into his unhelmeted head, dazing him before removing my helm and slamming it down, as hard as I could. His face crumpled into a mangled mess of blood and grey gore, which protruded from his shattered skull. The blood and grey matter blinded me as he went limp. I rolled over wiping an arm across my bloodied face in an effort to clear my vision. I was vaguely aware of Bjorgolf and several of my men standing over me, fending off blows from Gunnald's men.

Then I heard Sitric's voice boom across the battlefield. "It's over Gunnald. There is no escape, we end this today!" As my vision cleared I could see Sitric and Faelan's forces joined by my men surrounding Gunnald's depleted warband.

Only sixteen of Gunnald's men were standing and the giant himself carried a wound to his left shoulder. The huge red haired warrior pushed his way past two of his men. "You are right, it ends today Sitric you nithing. You killed my brother, let's finish this between us. When I have killed you I will kill your whelp of a son and that runt of a Briton who claims to be a royal. Then I will kill your men one by one." A defiant cheer went up from Gunnald's men;

even facing certain death the man's arrogance still radiated off him.

"You will face me you bastard," I heard myself shout.

Gunnald made a rumbling noise, which obviously passed for laughter as his men joined in. "See men? Sitric the whoreson would rather a youth fight in his place!"

Bjorgolf passed me his shield as I stepped forward, "I've given the piece of shit a knock for you," Bjorgolf muttered. "Work the arsehole's left shoulder."

My heart was racing and I could feel it thumping against my rib cage. My muscles ached and my soaked clothing weighed me down as I approached Gunnald. But the bloodlust was still running through my veins. I could not fail. I could not let this cutthroat kill me or Gwynedd would be lost forever and the bloodline of the ancient house of Aberffraw would die with me.

"Come to die, have you boy?" Gunnald rumbled through a near toothless grin. "I shall show you how a true warrior fights. This will be your first and final lesson. Tell me, boy, who dares face me?"

"I am Gruffudd son of Cynan and the bringer of death," I shouted back and winked at him. The men laughed. Gunnald was clearly taken aback by my confidence. I had planted a seed of doubt in his mind and I struck.

Gunnald deflected my strike well, before attempting a backhanded hack aimed at my neck. I ducked and shoved forwards with my shield, forcing the giant a couple of paces back. He struck like a hammer blow before I could recover, bringing his blade down towards my shoulder. I reacted just quick enough to catch the strike on the rim of my shield. The impact jarred my left arm as his blade splintered through inches of my shield. As quick as he had struck he removed his blade, with a shower of splinters.

He rained a flurry of blows as I desperately fended him off with my shield. His final strike hit the boss of my shield, forcing me back. I cursed as I lost my footing and slipped in the treacherous mud. I splattered into the sticky earth and rolled out of danger.

His men were cheering as mine shouted encouragement. "Work his fucking shoulder!" Bjorgolf roared above the crowd. I desperately tried to catch my breath as we circled each other. Gunnald was good, but I was quicker and I prayed that would be my advantage. I hoped his hulk of a body would tire soon, as my arm muscles began to protest and my whole body ached.

"I've got you, you little shit of a Briton," Gunnald rumbled as we circled each other.

"You move quick, for an old man," I retorted, between breaths, and Gunnald's face flushed as he roared in anger and darted towards me. I was quicker, deflecting his blade with my splintering shield. As I sidestepped to the left I brought my blade across his sword arm, ripping through mail and flesh as Gunnald's momentum carried him past me.

He cursed in disbelief at the gash on his upper arm. My men cheered as Gunnald roared his anger. "You bastard Briton, I'm going to gut you and you will scream for your bitch of a mother!" Again he plodded forward, like a troll from legend, much quicker than I expected swinging his blade in huge butcher's strokes like a madman.

I caught his first blow on my weakening shield, as splinters of wood flew across my face. Another blow hammered on to my blade before I thrust at his exposed shoulder. He brought his shield across in time and my strike glanced off it. Gunnald grunted at the pain in his wounded left shoulder as the impact jarred his shield arm.

He attempted to hack at my left thigh, but I swiped my shield across hitting his sword from his grasp and cursed as my shield disintegrated into kindling. The leather thong, tied about the wrist, on Gunnald's blade prevented him from losing it as the impact drove him down. I discarded my useless shield and rained blow after blow down onto the floored Gunnald, who had desperately brought his shield across to defend himself. My blows splintered Gunnald's shield and he roared in anger and fear. I stepped back to allow the giant up. I must put on a show I remember thinking. I could not kill Gunnald badly; he must be killed holding his sword in the way of the warrior. I wanted bards to sing of this fight, I wanted men to remember it and raise their drinking horns in memory of it. No, I could not kill Gunnald like the animal he was, I had a reputation to build.

Gunnald dropped his shield as he regained his footing. We were both covered in the dark sticky mud as we circled each other. Rain began to beat down and I could see I had wiped the grin off Gunnald's face. The giant was worried, he was panting as the rain water streamed down his flat nose. He was bleeding freely from the wounds to his left shoulder and his sword arm.

"I have to let an old man catch his breath." I smirked at him, though my heart was racing beneath the weight of my war gear. Gunnald blinked back his anger as I goaded him further. "Gunnald the Red, beaten by a Briton. Bards will sing of your disgrace you whoreson."

Then he lost what little was left of his self control; in a deafening roar of defiance he came at me, bringing his blade down in a wild swing which was intended to split my skull. I side stepped smartly and brought my blade back across his unprotected right hamstring. The giant let out a gasp of pain as he went down on one knee. I turned as he tried to stand and face me, thrusting my blade into the wound on his left shoulder before the steel grated against bone. I withdrew the blade with a gush of blood and shattered rings of mail. The giant desperately tried to hack at my leg, but he was done, I was too quick for him. I batted his blade away and kicked him in his groin. And there was total silence.

He brought his head back up to face me as I rammed my fist into his nose, breaking it; I stood back; there was acceptance in the giant's eyes. Blood streamed from his nose into his graying beard as he sagged forward on his knees. I stopped his fall and held him upright; there was a deathly silence as I looked into those cold blue eyes. I remember it still. "Well, you have made your reputation today boy," Gunnald rasped as a trickle of blood escaped the corner of his lips. "Men will sing of Gruffudd who killed Gunnald the Red. Let me die well." I swear a single tear streaked down the giant's blood stained face as he held my gaze.

"Grasp your sword," I muttered harshly as I stepped back two paces. As he grasped his sword's hilt I brought my blade across his neck in a spray of bright blood. I still remember those cold blue eyes holding my gaze as I took his life. Gunnald fell to the side and splattered into the quagmire we had created. His eyes rolled upwards into his skull as his life blood poured out of him in a river of crimson. There was deathly silence as men stood still in amazement. Gunnald's blood streamed freely through the mud, forming little puddles as it mixed with the rain water. I knelt near the dead warrior and took the wealth from his corpse. I took his blood encrusted, filthy helm. It was a work of art, beautifully crafted with a figure of a boar on top; I thrust my arm up with it above my head. The men cheered and shouted my name as they put Gunnald's remaining men to the sword. I was Gruffudd son of Cynan and I had made my name.

II

Those grey eyes stared intensely at me. Sitric looked old. He had taken a blow to his shoulder during the battle, which had broken his collar bone. He grimaced as he tried to flex the sore muscles of his left arm. He bit back the pain and glanced ruefully down at his shield arm which rested across his chest in a sling. "You did well today Gruffudd," he finally said. "Gunnald is dead and his army defeated, we have dealt the enemy a heavy blow."

"Thank you, father," I began.

"Don't thank me yet," Sitric cut across me. "The war is not won. Tomorrow we must march on Duibhlinn and that tyrant Gofraid must be dealt with. Today Gruffudd, you showed me that my days in the shieldwall are over. Gunnald would have killed me; I have no doubt, especially with this useless arm." For once Sitric looked all of his fifty-two years. His grey eyes looked down to the rush mat on the floor of his tent as he spoke. He spoke quietly, as if he struggled to say the words. "Gunnald was mine to face, you had no right to take up the challenge." His eyes locked with mine and, to my shame, I could not meet his gaze. I sensed Wselfwulf stiffen at Sitric's words. "Now go, my boy. Leave an old man to his thoughts," and then those heavy grey eyes looked away.

As I left his tent and trudged out into the blackness, towards where Bjorgolf and the rest of my men were camped, I could not help but feel I had somehow betrayed Sitric. His words stuck in my mind as I sat on a damp log, not far from the camp, but far enough not to be disturbed. The smell of boiling stew floated across the camp, as men drank and boasted about their exploits during the battle. The rain had subsided, but the ground was still waterlogged. A mile to the west the remains of the farm buildings still smouldered in the dark, giving off an eerie glow through the mist which had again descended upon us.

I heard movement behind me and as I turned a familiar voice rumbled out of the darkness. "He did not mean to hurt you lad." It was Wselfwulf. The old Saxon sat next to me and mumbled a curse in his harsh native tongue as he forced his stiff muscles into action on a cold night. "You did well today, lad. You made one old warrior proud," the Saxon rumbled through a near toothless grin. His scarred face looked menacing in the dim light. "I thought that red haired bastard was going to have you for a minute when you were on your arse."

"I did too, I thought I would die. But, I am alive and he is not," I managed to say. "Is my father's wound bad?"

"No lad, I've seen him take worse and live. He's old, I'm old, we're not as young as we once were and it hurts his pride." Wselfwulf looked away and muttered a sentence in his native tongue before translating. "Age comes to us all." He looked back to me. "Men will come to you after this you know, so long as you don't do anything stupid in Duibhlinn. We will go to Gwynedd with you when the time comes, I am sure of it." His dark eyes fixed on mine. "In the morning we will pass Gunnald's homestead, your new estate. But you cannot stay for long; we must be at Muirchertach's camp before nightfall tomorrow. I will task some trusted men to hold it safe for you whilst we go on to Duibhlinn. There, Gruffudd son of Cynan, you must win Muirchertach's approval. I am confident you will."

"I will," I murmured as Wselfwulf rose to his feet.

"Don't dwell on Sitric's words lad. He did not mean them and will regret them by morning. Go and have a drink with your men and savour your victory." And with that he went back towards Sitric's tent. Moments later I got up and went over to join Bjorgolf and the men around the campfire. *Your victory*, those words came back to me, Wselfwulf was right it was my first victory. I grinned at the thought and I knew this was the first step to earning Muirchertach's support in my quest to claim my birthright.

My fourteen remaining men were drinking heavily around the fire, laughing and jesting. They raised their drinking horns at my arrival and cheered my name before downing the contents. Ronan rose and handed me a drinking horn brimming with ale which I drank from greedily. The bearded bush, which passed for a head, nodded at me whilst I drank and I returned the nod with a friendly grin. Ronan and his brother Ruaidri had joined my warband on the same day as Bjorgolf. The two were the sons of a tenant farmer on the lands Sitric had rented me. Ronan was a large man with a heavily deformed face. He had been kicked in the face by a horse as an infant and grew the wild beard and hair to hide it. He was a man of few words, a contrast to Ruaidri who always had something to say. Ruaidri was a trustworthy man in war but I would not trust him with my silver. The man was a rascal but good company as he could raise the men's spirits, not that they needed raising that night.

Ruaidri was in the centre of the small warband, dancing round the fire reciting the tale of my fight with Gunnald. I laughed along with the men as Ruaidri mocked me falling on my arse as the imagined Gunnald came at me. As the tale grew in fantasy and humour I left them to it. I walked twenty paces or so to my left away from the men.

There I found Bjorgolf who was hunched over my one and only wounded wolf, Ljot. Bjorgolf turned as I approached and Ljot sat upright, they both nodded a greeting.

"How's the arm Ljot?" I asked through a smile. I liked Ljot. He was a short stocky man in his twenty-fourth year and had fought well, taking a spear thrust to the shoulder during my desperate attempt to halt Gunnald's escape.

"It will heal, I shall be back in the shieldwall before long," he responded through a wince. "I will be of use to you in Duibhlinn," he insisted. I looked at Bjorgolf who silently shook his head. Ljot, sensing Bjorgolf's gesture spat a curse and looked away. He was a proud warrior and did not want to miss the battle that was to come.

"Rest your arm and we shall see how you fare tomorrow," I told him as I rose and gestured for Bjorgolf to follow me away from the men and out of earshot.

"I haven't told you yet, but you did well today. Bards will sing of that fight for years to come, I am sure!"

"Well, not as poorly as Ruaidri over there, I am hoping," I responded and we both laughed. "Let's hope it brings me more men and money then," I replied seriously. "The men did well today."

"That they did," Bjorgolf stated through a broad grin. "It was not just them, but who led them. Shame we lost nine in the fighting and Ljot is our walking wounded." Bjorgolf shook his head as he continued. "The lad won't be any use in Duibhlinn. If he doesn't't get himself killed, he will get someone else killed."

I nodded my agreement, "I am to have Gunnald's estate." I could not resist a smile. "We pass by there

28

tomorrow on the way to Duibhlinn. I shall charge Ljot to keep it safe for me, he will be more use to me there than as a corpse after the fight."

Bjorgolf mumbled his agreement before clapping me on the shoulder. "Gunnald's hall is a grand building. I was there once, a few years back." I fixed Bjorgolf with an interested gaze. He noticed my curiosity and decided to explain, "It was when I was in Duibhlinn's garrison. My captain was sent on an errand there by the commander of the watch. Gunnald was a bastard true enough, but the man had good ale." Bjorgolf grinned back at me. "You will gain a fair bit of wealth from the farms on the estate as well, which is what you are interested in most, I am thinking," he continued. "Better than that shit heap you currently have by Loch Garman," Bjorgolf winked at me and chuckled as I laughed.

"That's good to know," the news had pleased me. "I am thinking that I will be ready to sail to Gwynedd next summer, Bjorgolf. Then I can retake what is mine by right." As I took a sip from my drinking horn my thoughts were focused on how I would claim my birthright and kill the usurpers, Cynwrig of Powys and Trahaearn the Lord of Arwystli. That time would come soon enough.

Bjorgolf must have read my thoughts. "Don't get carried away just yet. You may have forgotten, but Duibhlinn must be taken first." He fixed me with a knowing look. "And you must distinguish yourself yet again, I am thinking." I nodded and Bjorgolf continued, "Duibhlinn's defences may look formidable from a distance but when you get up close, they are not that impressive. The defences are weak and an assault would easily get through them. Be the first over and Muirchertach would have to give you whatever you want as a reward, I wager."

I nodded and smiled at Bjorgolf, "I hope you are right my friend," and with that we both returned to the camp fire where Ruaidri's saga tale was still in full swing.

Ljot had rejoined the men and turned as we approached. "You are just in time," Ljot said through laughter, "Ruaidri's saga tale is nearing its end. Bards will be in awe of him!" I and all those in earshot laughed at Ljot's jest, as it seemed Ruaidri wasn't as talented an actor as he believed. Most of the men were laughing at Ruaidri's acting skills. As he reached Gunnald's death and ended the saga tale in a dramatic action, he bowed at the men as if they were royalty and almost stumbled over.

"It seems the man can't handle his ale," Bjorgolf declared and, as if on cue, Ruaidri took another deep bow and fell flat on his face. The men laughed as Ruaidri struggled back onto his feet and just then Ronan stepped forward.

The big Irishman threw his drinking horn at Ruaidri and it struck him on the head. "That's for your piss poor acting!" he shouted. The men wailed in laughter and I joined in as Ruaidri rubbed his scalp and cursed in Irish before stumbling towards Ronan. Ruaidri swung a clumsy fist at the bushy haired giant who deflected the blow before striking Ruaidri in the jaw. Ruaidri fell to the damp turf and was still. "That will give us some peace and quiet, so it will," Ronan grumbled. "Giving me a bloody headache, so he was." We were all laughing as Ronan wrapped Ruaidri's cloak round his unconscious body before settling down for the night himself.

I drank long into the night with the men and outlasted all but Bjorgolf and Ljot. Cerit had joined us for a while before returning to his men in his usual high spirits. The hour was late and the sound of an army asleep carried across the camp as I stumbled behind a tree to relieve my bladder. Just then I froze as I heard a stick snap in the woods behind me, maybe fifteen paces away. I could not be sure as my mind swam with the effects of the ale. I tied my breeches quickly and dropped into a crouch and listened. At first I could not hear anything and, just as I was about to relax, I heard another noise faintly in the distance. It sounded like a voice, but I could not be sure. I crept through the undergrowth and took great care not to make any noise. I paused and listened again, the effects of the ale were quickly beginning to wear off as I drew my dagger silently from my belt. There it was again, twenty paces ahead. It was definitely a voice, no, two voices.

As I crept forward the undergrowth began to give way to a small clearing near a stream which was swollen with rain water. I could make out two men in the clearing fifteen paces to my left, but no more. I could not tell who they were; I crept to my left through the undergrowth to see if I could recognise either of the two men. They were talking quickly and quietly; the two were in serious discussion. I made out a word, then another. My God! They were not talking in the Danish tongue nor Irish, it was in the tongue of the Britons, the language of my birth. I made out another word, then another, my ears were straining as I tried to make out what was being said. I heard one word several times, "tomorrow."

A bush rustled violently to my right and then again as a boar made its way into the clearing. The two men quickly finished their discussion and walked in opposite directions, one to the east and one back towards the camp. The boar stared at the scene through its small eyes and then disappeared into the undergrowth the other side of the clearing.

I stayed still for a few heartbeats and then retraced my steps, hoping to catch a glimpse of whoever the man was who had headed towards the camp. But there was no trace, the man had vanished. As I returned to the dying camp fire around my warband, both Bjorgolf and Ljot were still drinking but I had no appetite for more ale. I had consumed a vast amount of ale, could I have been mistaken? No, I definitely heard the two men talking in the tongue of the Britons, the tongue of my people. I played the scene over and over in my mind, what was the significance of tomorrow? Something was definitely being planned. Why else would those two men meet in the woods like that; something was afoot, something dangerous. Those were my last thoughts as sleep finally took me.

III

My head pounded as we trudged along the muddy track which cut through the woods where we had camped the previous night. Damn, but I should not have drunk that much ale. My head seemed to pound harder with every footstep. Bjorgolf laughed at my discomfort. "The youngsters always feel the worse for wear in the morning." A few of the men in earshot chuckled at Bjorgolf's words, but his words did not amuse me. The weather did little to raise my spirits; in fact it reflected my mood exactly. The rain had started again before we struck camp and had beaten down relentlessly on our marching column ever since. The going was slow, as men tried to keep their footing on the treacherous mud which passed for a road. Gunnald's helm was tied to my belt and was uncomfortable, adding to my bad mood. The scene from the clearing played over and over in my mind; something was planned for today, but what? What in God's name were two Britons doing meeting so close to Sitric's camp? As far as I knew there were no other Britons in Sitric's force. Something was going to happen if what I had heard was right, and it gave me a deep feeling of unease.

Bjorgolf was disappointed that I had not responded to his jest and fixed me with a worried expression. "What troubles you lad? I am wagering that it is not your sore head either."

I was in no certain mind to share my worries with Bjorgolf, in full earshot of others. I shook my head. "Nothing Bjorgolf, hopefully my head will clear soon enough. The sooner this damn rain stops the better."

Bjorgolf looked as though he would press me further but decided not to and continued to march forward in silence. As the trees began to give way we marched across a flat landscape where thralls working the fields did their best to hide themselves as we passed. We were not interested in them; our fight was with their masters who still supported Gofraid. I was impressed with the lands we passed throughout the morning and Bjorgolf eventually raised my spirits.

"This is all yours now you know?" He laughed at my obvious surprise. "Soon you will be very wealthy Gruffudd son of Cynan." The men were just as surprised as me and Bjorgolf was clearly taking pleasure in the surprise he had caused.

"I hope you are right Bjorgolf," I managed. "You will all be rewarded for your bravery as well men!" My small warband let out a cheer which caused Sitric to turn in his saddle and shoot me a scowl. As the commander of our small army Sitric rode at the column's head with Cerit and Faelan. At this time I could not afford a horse, not that it bothered me much. A leader's place was in the front rank of his men in my eyes.

We continued to follow the road until midday, when we advanced over a crest and came upon Gunnald's hall. "There it is lads," Bjorgolf shouted. "Gruffudd's new estate, not bad, eh?" I stared in surprise at the size of Gunnald's hall and its outbuildings. The hall looked grand, even from this distance, and the land fertile. It was clearly a prosperous estate and I smiled inwardly at the prospect of how much these lands would fill my coffers. A small village, which must have been Sord Cholmcille, lay a half mile ahead, nestled near a stream, but my interest lay with the imposing hall and its lands.

I continued to marvel at the sight as we approached along the muddy road. The hall lay a hundred or so paces from the road, with a small track leading to it, and Sitric called a halt. We had been marching since before first light and the men had had little rest the previous night, so were pleased for the respite. Sitric and Faelan's men dropped out of the column and sat in groups on the track's edge. Mine followed suit as Sitric trotted his fine mount a short distance down the track towards us.

"I suggest you charge one of your men to keep this place safe for you, Gruffudd," Sitric stated formally. He seemed uncomfortable as he continued. "I shall leave ten of my men to help safeguard the place for you" he continued. "They all carry injuries, but will be more than capable of the task at hand." He nodded at my thanks and turned his mount back up the track.

"He's colder than usual this morning," Bjorgolf declared and the men nodded their agreement. "Still, I hope Gunnald has plenty of that ale stored away." The men smiled at that and talked amongst themselves.

"There is no time for ale," I stated firmly. "We shall have to get moving again shortly. We must reach Muirchertach's camp outside Duibhlinn before first light tomorrow." Ronan murmured his agreement with a couple of others, but Ruaidri spat in disappointment at my orders, earning a cuff on the back of the head from Ronan, which I pretended not to notice. "Bjorgolf and Ljot you will follow me, the rest of you are to stay here."

With that the three of us walked down the track to where Cerit waited with the ten men Sitric had granted me.

Cerit beamed one of his customary smiles at me. "A fine hall by the looks of it, brother," he declared. "I hope you won't forget who helped get you it," he said with a wink.

I laughed at his jest. "There will be plenty of drinking and feasting to come, I am sure." Cerit let out a mock cheer and, with that, we turned off the track and headed towards the impressive hall.

As we approached the hall and its outbuildings the thralls, who had not fled already, quickly scattered into the fields. We passed the first outbuilding and faced the grand hall as the doors creaked open. A short, skinny old man stepped out into the rain and stood defiantly outside the entrance. "He looks like he means business," Bjorgolf joked to my left. "Want me to teach him a lesson?"

"No, Bjorgolf, we shall see what he wants. He does not seem armed." The man stared straight at me as I neared him. A few stray chickens cackled their fury and fled from my path as I approached. I met the man's gaze as I halted ten paces away from him. He had neatly cropped grey hair, which had clearly once been black, and a well groomed beard. He was wearing a dark blue robe, expensively tailored, with long sleeves. He sported a long, slim scar which stretched from his forehead down the side of his head to the jaw; it reminded me of a crescent moon. He puffed out his chest in a gesture of defiance. "Who are you to come across *Jarl* Gunnald's hall unannounced?" The man demanded with a commanding voice in accented Danish. The man was clearly educated and used to being obeyed; his whole character was unsettling for he seemed completely out of place.

I spoke through a wicked grin as I tried to unsettle the old man. "*Jarl* Gunnald's killer." The man seemed completely unmoved as I threw Gunnald's blood crusted and dented helm at his feet. "He died well; his lands and property are now mine by the order of King Muirchertach. I am Gruffudd son of Cynan, son of Iago who used to rule the lands of Gwynedd across the sea."

I detected a flash of surprise on the man's face, which was gone as soon as it appeared. His dark eyes did not falter as he met my gaze. A sly grin creased his features before he let out a sharp laugh. He looked at me maliciously, prompting Bjorgolf to stir at my shoulder. I was about to push my way past him and into the hall but, before I could, the man began to speak, to my surprise, in the tongue of the Britons,

"I know those lands of which you speak; I am steward to *Jarl* Gunnald of Sord Cholmcille. You are truly the last of the line of Aberffraw?"

"I am," I replied. "The last of the royal bloodline and the rightful ruler of Gwynedd. One day soon I will reclaim my birthright." The old man simply smirked a sinister grin as I stared coldly at him, suppressing the urge to strike the man's pompous features.

To my anger he laughed again and continued in the tongue of the Britons. "A bright eyed youth to take the throne of Gwynedd? The killer of *Jarl* Gunnald? I do not believe it."

Bjorgolf tensed and grumbled for the old man to stop his rambling and hold his tongue for he would soon lose it if he continued. "Silence you old fool," I threatened in Danish so all could hear and understand. "Gunnald thought the same. He thought I was but a stripling. He is now dead. My blade took the bastard's life. I stood over him as his life blood seeped from him. I shall do the same to the usurper Trahaearn and his puppet Cynwrig of Powys."

The old man shook his head slowly and locked me with a penetrating stare. Had I seen him before? His voice sounded oddly familiar. His whole manner was peculiar and he seemed very well kept for a steward but, as I had no time for such puzzles, I strode forward and shoved the old man to one side, pushing the heavy doors completely open. The old man lost his footing and fell. I strode in with Bjorgolf and the rest close behind. One of the men must have given the old man a kick as I heard him yelp like a struck dog, bringing a satisfied grin to my face.

The hall was well built and was big enough to play host to a royal visit. These lands and this hall will see my income improve I thought, perhaps enough to fund two to three ships and the men to crew them.

"What was that old bugger rambling about then?" Bjorgolf demanded as the rest of the men and Cerit explored the hall. Ljot moved over to where the old man was now standing, to make sure he got up to no mischief.

"He thought I was a bright eyed youth who stands no chance in reclaiming my birthright." The anger still burned in my chest as I spoke. "I will rain death and destruction on Trahaearn the usurper and those who stand by him mark my words. But first we must kill that mad bastard Gofraid and take Duibhlinn for Muirchertach"

Bjorgolf met my gaze and lowered his voice so none could overhear. "You have the truth of it. But it would not serve you well to show the men that the words of one mad old cur make you lose your head."

He was right and I knew it; my face flushed hot with the embarrassment. Luckily none of the men noticed, or at least they had the sense not to show it. I cannot allow my temper to visibly get the better of me in future; I remember thinking for I was young and still learning.

"So then, I think it is time," Bjorgolf said nodding in the direction of Ljot. "He's not going to like it, but I am sure he will see the sense in it soon enough." I grumbled my agreement and made towards Ljot. His wound meant he would be no use in the shieldwall and would more than likely get himself and others killed in the fighting to come. Ljot nodded a wary greeting as I approached. "How is the arm Ljot?" I asked.

"It is healing well, for sure, I will be able to take my place in the shieldwall in the days to come," he sounded confident but his eyes betrayed him.

I shook my head sadly, I did not wish to crush the man's hopes but I knew it had to be done, so I took a deep breath. "Ljot, I cannot allow it. Your wound will slow you down and it could get you or someone else killed on the battlefield." His eyes dropped away from mine and he could not meet my gaze as he absorbed what I was telling him. "You have already proved your worth to me and it is for that reason that I am trusting you with keeping this estate safe. You may use whatever livestock and stores you wish. I know I can rely on you to do this task for me." Ljot did not meet my gaze as I continued. "There will be more battles to come, I know it, and you will be there at my side when we go to Gwynedd."

He looked up at my final words and nodded his acceptance, before turning away without saying a word. He saw the logic in it, I knew, and he had the good sense not to argue. Ljot moved over to the far side of the hall as a cheer rang out and a huddle of men encircled a victorious looking Bjorgolf, who had ferreted out a barrel of Gunnald's ale.

Cerit was still in high spirits as he stood in the centre of the hall admiring the craftsmanship which had gone into its construction. I was still troubled by the scene I had witnessed in the clearing the night before. I nodded to myself, my thoughts were becoming a burden and I would have to discuss them with someone else. I was about to confide in Cerit but, before I could, he turned and frowned. "What the hell does that old goat want now?"

The old man was walking calmly towards me. He carried himself like a monk, with his hands concealed in the long sleeves across his front. I moved towards him and showed him an expressionless face. "I am tiring of you, old man," I threatened. "Do not test me further."

The man smiled maliciously. "King Trahaearn sends his regards." The man smirked as he came within striking distance. It was then his arms came free from the cover of the sleeves and I noticed the wickedly shaped dagger in his right hand. There was no time to draw my blade as he thrust the knife at my chest. Youth was on my side and I had the speed to sidestep his thrust and cuff him across the back of the head as he moved past me. The old man stumbled and fell into the ash of the cooking fire in the centre of the hall. The men dropped what they were doing and looked at the source of the commotion.

I did not want to kill the old man; there were too many unanswered questions. Was he one of the men I had stumbled across last night in the clearing? He struck towards me again with surprising speed. This time I struck before he could. I tackled him round his chest and hooked

40

his legs from under him, slamming him to the floor. He shrieked in pain as his brittle old bones cracked on impact. The men were silent now as the old man shrieked an inhuman sound.

He writhed on the floor as blood pooled round his breeches; he had unwittingly stabbed himself in his thigh as he went down. Blood was pumping out of him like a waterfall, and I knew he must have cut the main artery in his leg. The shrieking stopped as I stood over him and he opened his eyes, which were deep pools of brown. The colour had drained from his face so that he looked like a corpse. The crescent scar was oddly highlighted on his pale face, giving him an un-Godly appearance. He raised an arm, still clutching the knife which had killed him, in his bony right hand. The knuckles in his left hand cracked as he made a fist and then he pointed at me. The men were deathly silent now as I held the old man's gaze as the breath rasped in his throat. "The bloodline of Aberffraw is cursed Gruffudd son of Cynan, son of Iago. Your blood line is cursed; you and those who follow you to Gwynedd will be washed in blood. You bring death and despair Gruffudd son of Cynan. All you will bring to Gwynedd is blood and the drum of war."

At that moment all eyes were fixed on me as men crossed themselves and a couple of Sitric's men touched their hammer amulets. The old man's arm fell and slapped the floor as his eyes rolled back up into his head and he writhed one last time before wheezing out his final breath. I did not cross myself or mutter a prayer to show my weakness, but the old man's words hung in the room and I could feel the dark arts at play in the grand hall. He had spoken in the tongue of the Britons so only I would understand, but the men had the feel of it as they stared open mouthed at the bony old corpse.

"Bury the body quickly; make sure there is a cross to keep his spirit below ground." I ordered as I turned to exit the hall. The man's final words troubled me and I did not want to risk his un-Godly soul roaming my new lands. I paused as I neared the door and called over my shoulder at my stunned men. "Quickly now! We leave shortly."

"Well don't just fucking gawp like a bunch of virgins, get rid of that old fucker," Bjorgolf shouted behind me.

The whole scene had unsettled me. The rain had finally stopped, which was a small blessing, but my thoughts were more troubled than ever. That man was certainly no steward. He was well spoken and had concealed his dagger expertly; he was a trained killer sure enough. But was he one of the men I had come across in the clearing last night? He must have been, as his voice had sounded vaguely familiar, but perhaps I was imagining that. I could not be certain. This must have been what was planned for today, when I overheard the word "tomorrow" repeated several times in the clearing. But how would that man know I would be here today; only Sitric and a few people were privy to that information. That meant the other man from the clearing must be with Sitric's forces now, but who? Trahaearn clearly had agents at large; I could trust no one.

IV

My head had stopped pounding shortly after we had left my new hall, but that was little consolation. The assassination attempt played heavily on my mind. Sitric had summoned me to the head of the column after Cerit had informed him of the incident. Sitric's earlier awkwardness had disappeared at the news and he showed nothing but genuine concern. Faelan, the Irish nobleman, seemingly could not have cared less. The man's face was dominated by a long, drooping moustache which quivered every time he spoke. He was a wealthy lord of some shit hole in Munster and thought highly of himself. He seemed to harbour an intense dislike towards me, probably borne out of jealousy. He had laughed at the tale and wondered aloud why someone would waste their time sending an agent to kill someone of 'minor royalty.' I would give the pompous bastard his comeuppance one day, I thought, and that brought a smile to my face for the first time that afternoon.

Bjorgolf noted my smile. "Cheered up at last have you?" He grinned at my glum acknowledgement. "So Trahaearn sent someone to kill you; he must be worried," I nodded my agreement to that statement. "Still, that is no bad thing," Bjorgolf declared through a broad smile and laughed at the scowl I shot him.

"No bad thing, eh?" I questioned. I was in no mood for jests. "How the hell do you figure that one out then?" I demanded.

"Well, if he has sent someone to kill you then he must be worried. His position in Gwynedd cannot be all that secure if he feels he has to do away with you. Besides it's common sense to do away with someone that has a better claim to the throne than you." Bjorgolf smiled as he spoke. "Made quite a reputation you have, this is what comes with it if you want to be a king."

"I suppose you are right," I replied. "We shall carry this conversation on later." I did not want this conversation in earshot of the men, for I still did not know which of them could be trusted, but I could trust Bjorgolf, of that I was certain.

"Suit yourself," Bjorgolf grumbled at my evasiveness. "Just voicing my opinion. If you have Trahaearn worried it is not so much of a bad thing." He belched loudly before continuing enthusiastically. "Danger just comes with it. I bloody love danger. I'll be watching your royal arse, don't you worry."

I smiled at Bjorgolf's words. Trahaearn still had one man out there, at least, and I would have to be careful.

The hours slipped by and the countryside descended into darkness as we marched on and on through the ankle deep mud. A few miles ahead, the sky glowed as Muirchertach's army besieged Duibhlinn. We advanced further along the track until we forded a swollen river. The river had a strong current and, in places, came above a man's waist. Bjorgolf cheerfully informed us the river was known in Irish as the An Tulcha. The An Tulcha was only a few miles from the An Liffe which we would also have to cross soon. As we came to a junction in the track and followed it to the west rather than the east Bjorgolf spat in disgust. He claimed there was a ferry crossing further down the river to the east which would be quicker. He again spat in disgust and shook his head to emphasize his displeasure. We continued down the track for another hour until Sitric called a halt on the banks of another swollen river. This one seemed wider and the current stronger that the An Tulcha we had forded earlier. Moonlight glinted off the strong current of the river as it powered past, even in the dark it was clear a man would not be able to cross at this point. The ford we had been led to, if it was a bloody ford at all, had clearly been the wrong decision. We should have taken Bjorgolf's advice and gone to the ferry crossing.

"So, this must be the An Liffe," I thought aloud as I stared downstream to the east, where the town of Duibhlinn hugged the river's southern bank. The settlement emitted a bright glow in the gloom as fires burned on hearths and sentries patrolled the defences. We would have to wait until morning to see how formidable those defences were.

"Admiring the view are you?" Cerit asked as he joined me, gazing at our enemy's defences, which were a dark smudge in the distance. "It will be a brute and difficult to take, I am sure," Cerit continued, sounding rather cheerful despite what he had just said. "Our father requires our presence up ahead." I told the men to enjoy their rest whilst they could and followed Cerit into the darkness.

"This bloody ford is useless," Sitric was ranting as I joined him and Faelan in inspecting the ford. "Bloody useless," he repeated. "Ah, Gruffudd, good of you to join us. The river has swollen and made the ford impassable, if you hadn't noticed." Sitric's temper was close to boiling over, that much was clear. "Any suggestions?" He demanded of me, continuing before I could answer. "Faelan here thinks we should follow the river another few miles to the west." Sitric spoke acidly; it was clear he did not value the Irishman's opinion and seemed to be physically battling the urge to strike Faelan. "He thinks the river may be less

45

treacherous and a ford may be practicable." Sitric scowled and clenched his fists as Faelan repeated his faith in the idea.

"My man, Bjorgolf, claims there is a ferry crossing further down the river to the east, father," I opined quickly. Faelan shook his head with mock laughter, his moustache quivering in the dark.

"What? And go that close to Duibhlinn; have you no sense boy?" He looked appalled at the idea. It was easy to see why Sitric found the man frustrating; arrogance radiated off him and I wanted to strike him there and then as he continued to eye me mockingly. "We Irish know our own land well enough," he continued. "Better than a bloody Briton at any rate."

"Go boil your head, you pompous prick," I retorted, seething with anger. Cerit laughed at my remark as Faelan's small pig-like eyes widened in surprise. "The ferry will be the quickest route, even if it is close to Duibhlinn. Or do you not have the stomach to get close to the enemy?"

"Silence the both of you!" Sitric snapped, just before Faelan could respond. The short Irishman fixed me with a hate filled stare as Sitric rounded on us both. "We go to the ferry," he stated sharply before glancing angrily at Faelan. "Besides, if our army has done its job properly then the enemy should be bottled up behind their bloody walls. So there should be no danger, Lord Faelan." Sitric spoke with clear disdain and added the Irishman's title scornfully. With that he strode to his horse and snapped the orders. I winked at Faelan and smirked as I walked away, I could feel the Irishman's gaze on me as I laughed with Cerit.

"You told him, brother," Cerit chuckled. "My God, but that man is insufferable. Truly insufferable," Cerit shook his head in mock disgust. "Let us just hope this ferry crossing is still in operation or, I am afraid, our friend Faelan will enjoy your discomfort."

I chuckled at the truth of it and nodded my thanks to Cerit as he joined Wselfwulf and the rest of Sitric's warband. I carried on down the muddy track until I came to my wolves at the rear of the column. "Up you get you lazy whoresons!" I shouted, "We're turning around, so we will be leading the column. I want to set a good pace for these bastards; I want to make good time!" The men roused their tired muscles and got to their feet, a few muttering their agreement with Ruaidri's grumblings.

"To the ferry crossing then?" Bjorgolf enquired and grinned broadly at my nod. "Old Olaf will still have his ferry in operation, I am sure. The old bugger is a tight bastard, all about the money he is."

"I hope you're right Bjorgolf," I said. "Or Sitric will have my head, of that I am sure." We set off back down the track, as Sitric and Cerit rode to the head of the column and rode ten paces ahead of us, deep in conversation.

We continued east along the An Liffe's bank for what must have been two miles until we came across a small rectangular hut. Smoke escaped from a hole in the centre of the thatched roof and drifted over the track as Sitric called a halt. To the right a small wooden jetty jutted out into the river and a small timber ferry was securely anchored to it.

Sitric turned in the saddle and settled his eyes on me. "If you would care to do the honours, Gruffudd?" Sitric did not wait for me to acknowledge the commands before snapping more orders at me. "I want to get the men over this bloody river within an hour." He skilfully turned his mount and trotted back down the column to Faelan, whose men now made up the column's rear. Cerit fixed me with one of his customary smiles before dismounting.

"He is in a foul mood tonight, don't you think?" Cerit nodded at Sitric's back as he disappeared down the column's flank and into the darkness. "Come to think of it, he has been brooding all day. I think his age bothers him," Cerit shook his head sadly before gesturing at the small hut. "Shall we?"

I called for Bjorgolf to follow and the three of us made our way to the hut's door. The post-and-wattle walls smelt musty and damp in the cold night air as Bjorgolf hammered on the thick timbers of the door.

"What the fuck do you want at this bloody hour," a hoarse voice demanded from the other side of the door before opening it ajar. An old thickly bearded and weather battered face appeared through the gap, letting light from the fire escape at the same time. "Oh, Odin's hairy-arse!" The old man laughed as he recognized Bjorgolf, "it's been a long time you bloody rascal." He smiled broadly at Bjorgolf through his few remaining broken teeth before opening the door fully and ushering us in.

"It is good to see you too, uncle," Bjorgolf boomed through a broad grin and embraced the skinny old man. Bjorgolf laughed at my surprise as we took a seat on the old man's straw-filled bed. The hut was small, but clearly served the old man well. The gravel floor was dry and the fire warm. I was glad to be out of the rain and into the warmth of the old man's hut, even if just for a short while. "This is my mother's brother, Olaf Eiriksson," Bjorgolf declared. "He's the money grabbing bastard I told you about, who owns that ferry outside." The two laughed as

Bjorgolf clapped one of his bear like hands on the old man's shoulder.

"I am Gruffudd son of Cynan," I introduced myself and nodded at Cerit. "And this is my foster-brother, Cerit Sitricsson. We require the use of your ferry." I looked at the old man, who couldn't stop smiling and seemed overjoyed at Bjorgolf's arrival at his lonely home. "I will pay you generously Olaf Eiriksson, but we must use haste. The men outside must cross within an hour." I took three of Gunnald's silver arm rings from my pouch and tossed them one after the other to the old man, who grabbed them greedily.

Olaf examined the silver and licked his lips happily. His dark eyes looked up from his new silver and he smiled broadly. "Well then, there is no time to waste!" the old man declared and jumped enthusiastically to his feet, before draping himself in an ancient sealskin coat. We followed the old man outside and he showed no surprise at the number of men who had appeared on his doorstep in the early hours of the morning. He still chatted warmly with Bjorgolf as my wolves began to board his wooden craft with some of Sitric's men. "I am glad you are well, Bjorgolf." The old man said fondly, "I heard about the ugly business and the wrongs you were dealt," he added sorrowfully. "Still you are a true man at heart and you will serve Gruffudd well, I am sure of it." The old man shot me a sideways glance as the wooden craft reached the other bank of the An Liffe. "You treat him well Gruffudd son of Cynan, or you will have me to answer to, you hear?"

"I shall, don't you worry," I promised through a suppressed grin. Bjorgolf slapped the old man on his back and said his farewells before embracing the skinny figure as we disembarked. "He's fond of you, although I can't see why," I mocked. Bjorgolf took the jest as it was intended and simply laughed as did the men in earshot.

It took ten more trips for old Olaf to get the rest of the men across. Sitric followed last with Faelan and nodded his approval at me as he trotted past to the head of the column whilst the arrogant Irishman ignored me completely. Again, the men got their gear together and continued the march through the sticky mud to Muirchertach's camp.

We reached Muirchertach's camp shortly before sunrise and were guided to our position in the Irish lines as they camped outside Duibhlinn's walls on the boggy ground. Sitric and Faelan went to report their arrival to Muirchertach whilst the rest of us bedded down for what remained of the night. It was then that I decided to share my fears with Cerit and Bjorgolf. The three of us had walked away from where the men grumbled and slept.

I recounted the tale of what I had stumbled across in the woods and what the assassin had said at my new hall before he died. Cerit was alarmed at the tale and was even more shocked that Trahaearn had planned such an elaborate scheme. Bjorgolf simply listened and scratched his arse in the process.

"So, you are sure this other man went back to our camp?" Bjorgolf interrupted. He shook his head sadly as I nodded. "Trahaearn is a slimy bastard. So, you have no idea who this other man is?"

"No," I stated simply. "But he was talking in the tongue of the Britons and certainly went back to our camp. There is no doubt of that in my mind," I spat in disgust as I relived the scene in my mind.

"Shall I inform father?" Cerit asked. "I know there is not much we can do, but surely he will be able to find out who in our small force has a command of Briton?" Cerit knew it was a long shot but was still disappointed when Bjorgolf put him down.

"That would be foolish," Bjorgolf stated sharply. "No, our best chance of discovering the identity of this traitor is to do nothing."

I looked at Bjorgolf thoughtfully and saw the sense of it. "This traitor has no idea that we know he is in the camp," I thought aloud. "So, if we do nothing to scare him off or start a man-hunt, he will act again."

Cerit shot me a worried look. "You don't want him to act again, surely?" Cerit sounded appalled. "Are you mad brother?"

"This time, brother, we will be alert to the danger, but first, we need to wait for an opportunity that an enemy agent wouldn't dare to miss," Bjorgolf smiled in the gloom and Cerit simply shook his head in disbelief that I was prepared for the enemy agent to act again. "So, Bjorgolf do you fancy playing a dangerous game?"

"I love a bit of danger," he declared through a wicked grin and rubbed his hands at the prospect whilst Cerit just looked at us both in bewilderment.

"Mad, you're both mad." He repeated, as we returned to the camp and bedded down for the night. I would snare this agent of Trahaearn's and God help him when I did.

V

I did not sleep well and woke shortly before first light. The camp was slowly coming to life as men grumbled at the damp conditions and began to cook their breakfasts in pots over their camp fires. The morning was filled with a dense white mist as I stared towards Duibhlinn in the hope of catching a glimpse of the defences, but the mist was too thick. We were camped outside bow shot and on boggy ground which squelched under foot. The An Liffe's swollen state did little to avert the damp conditions as the water could not drain away. As men moved backwards and forward the ground churned under foot and as a result some areas had become nothing more than muddy quagmires.

Bjorgolf was already awake and boiling a pot of stew over the camp fire with Ronan. The stew hardly smelt tempting, but it would have to do. "Morning," Bjorgolf grumbled. "Weather is bloody miserable again. Never changes on this godforsaken island." Ronan let out a short bark of a laugh and rumbled his agreement.

I sat on a small boulder near the campfire and was lost in my own thoughts. My warband were woken when Bjorgolf had finished cooking the stew, aided by Ronan who kicked Ruaidri awake. "Watch what you're doing, you simple bastard," Ruaidri cursed at Ronan. "Another bloody day of boredom and damp awaits," he quipped to Oengus who was another of my rogues. Ruaidri had quickly gone from an entertaining character in my small warband to a moaning pain in the arse and Oengus was just the same. The two were becoming tiresome; I would need to knock their heads together sooner rather than later. Ronan must have read my thoughts as he met my hostile glance and rolled his eyes at their moaning.

As the sun rose and started to burn off the mist Duibhlinn's defences came into view. An earthen embankment had appeared beyond the mist, with a wooden palisade perched at its top. The defences were eerily shrouded in mist as I stared at them. Every ten paces a sentry watched our lines; every movement they made seemed ghostly in that damn mist. The ground in front of our position was worryingly open and we would be extremely vulnerable to missiles should we attack from this position.

As the morning wore on and the mist dispersed the defences seemed even more imposing. At strategic points the palisade had been replaced by a stone wall. In places the stone wall was half built and, in those places, a make shift barricade had been erected over the stone foundations.

Bjorgolf's voice disturbed my thoughts and almost startled me as he approached from behind. "Remember what I told you. They look formidable from a distance, but up close the timber is rotten in many stretches of the defences." He was sharpening his dagger as he watched with me. "A few determined men with axes will get us in, no problem." He grinned and looked to the right where Sitric and Cerit approached, "I think you are wanted again." Bjorgolf walked back to the campfire, unsheathing his blade and drawing his whet stone across the already razor-sharp blade.

"Morning!" Cerit called cheerfully as they approached. I returned the greeting and nodded at Sitric who nodded back. Sitric's face was pale and the skin had started to darken under his eyes. His eyes were bloodshot and his expression weary, he clearly had not slept at all that night.

"Muirchertach is holding a council of war shortly and all captains, lords and men of import are to attend," Sitric said wearily. "And that means you are expected to attend, Gruffudd. Muirchertach is quite taken with your exploits and especially your fight with Gunnald." He paused to flex his arms and yawned loudly before he continued. "Muirchertach has also asked for your presence after the council."

Cerit raised an eyebrow at Sitric's words and grinned broadly. "My congratulations brother, it does seem your exploits have got you noticed."

"Indeed," Sitric cut across. "As you know, Muirchertach rewards bravery well. So don't be too modest when he asks you about your deeds." He let out a rare smile at that. "Who knows, he may have a further use for you!" Sitric said in a knowing voice.

"Thank you father," I managed and he turned, gesturing for me and Cerit to follow. Cerit clapped my back and repeated his congratulations in his usual high spirited manner.

We weaved our way through the Irish lines and came upon Muirchertach's tent in the centre. The tent was a grand thing, brightly coloured in cloths of blue and gold, the colours of Munster. Muirchertach's banner hung limply at the tent's peak, occasionally stirring dispiritedly, and heavily armoured guards ringed the vast structure The tent was almost as big as my grand new hall; this truly was fit for a king.

Two guards stiffened to attention as we entered the musty interior, the smell of unwashed men in close proximity was almost overpowering as we pushed our way through the waiting huddle of lords and notables. At the far end of the structure stood a raised dais, five foot high. Perched on its top and flanked on either side by five chairs was a majestic throne, carved out of strong oak and crafted beautifully. On it sat Muirchertach the King of Munster and hopefully, soon to be, King of Duibhlinn. He was a strongly built man, due to the hours of sword practice he put in daily. He had a neatly cropped beard and a golden crown sat atop his raven-black hair which fell neatly down to his shoulders. He wore a blue cloak, which was secured by an expertly crafted golden brooch, over his gleaming mail. His expensively wrought sword sat in its gaudy scabbard which hung at his side over black breeches and he wore shin guards which gleamed. He cut an intimidating figure which boasted his power and wealth.

I stood with Cerit facing Muirchertach. Sitric had ascended the steps at the platform's edge and took one of the seats at the king's right hand side. Faelan sat at the king's left and shot me a cruel stare. I winked back at him and he quickly looked away, returning to a conversation he was having with a stout elderly lord to his right.

"Made a friend for life there, I assure you." Cerit commented seriously before breaking into a laugh. "The most powerful men in Munster and some from Duibhlinn are here Gruffudd, a fine gathering!" he exclaimed enthusiastically. Cerit was enjoying himself. The chance to make powerful connections was the reason why, I am sure.

I was about to comment but just then a skinny old man, who looked in very poor health, rose from the chair immediately to the king's right and all present went silent. He wore the robes of a monk and carried a staff with a golden cross attached to its top. He thumped it on the dais' wooden boards to silence the murmuring audience. The little white haired man rasped confidently in a peculiar high pitched, almost feminine, voice. As the man droned through the pleasantries and formalities of why the council was being held, Muirchertach's gaze fell upon me. I am not ashamed to admit that his gaze unsettled me greatly. He had piercing eyes and it felt as though he could read my thoughts. He looked away just as the old man concluded the introduction. The old man turned and hobbled back to his seat as Muirchertach rose.

He walked to the platform's edge and spoke loudly so that his commanding voice would be heard by all those present. "My dear friends, we hold a council during these significant times to discuss how we are to liberate the people of Duibhlinn." Muirchertach emphasised the word 'liberate' as he continued his address. "For too long have the honest, God worshipping and hard working people of Duibhlinn suffered under the tyrannical heel of Gofraid the usurper. The man does not deserve the title king; he has exploited the good Christian people of this land. He has cheated, he has murdered, he has stolen and he has worshipped the Pagan gods!" All around men shouted their disgust at Gofraid's alleged crimes. "We have been joined in our just and noble crusade by the respectable nobility of this Christian land." He gestured with both arms at the men around him, some of whom nodded their respect to the words. "Let all Christian peoples of this land unite against this ungodly adversary!" Muirchertach had captivated his audience and they cheered his well chosen words, "God is on our side! We cannot fail!" He shouted the final words of his address above the cheers, which only served to raise the volume in the tent even further.

Cerit was seemingly captivated by Muirchertach's address and he nudged me in the ribs with his elbow before raising his voice, so that he could be heard above the din. "He spoke well don't you think brother?" I nodded my agreement. Muirchertach had certainly delivered a well worded and effective address. He had all those present in the palm of his hand and pressed home his advantage.

"It is for that reason," his commanding voice silenced the crowd. "That I propose we assault the palisades in two places at first light tomorrow. Remember, God is on our side but we must act quickly in this just cause. We must rid the world of the tyrant!" The tent erupted to the sound of applause and agreement.

I could not help but admire Muirchertach's carefully crafted words. He had to hold the council of war out of custom, but it was nothing more than a formality. He had known all along that his word would be final, but his skilful address had given the impression that he had asked the audience for their agreement. They cheered him and he basked in their praise.

Muirchertach retired to his throne and the old man stepped forward again. His peculiar voice carried across the audience. "Are there any counter-proposals to the suggested action?" A few men shifted uncomfortably close by but none dared step forward. The old man nodded to himself and declared. "As God is our witness, the motion is carried unanimously." A cheer rose from those present before the crowd began to disperse. *Jarls,* Lords and mercenaries streamed past me as they made for the exit and returned to their men.

Cerit clapped me on the shoulder as Sitric approached, "Best of luck, brother." He smiled and exited the tent into the daylight. The tent had emptied, surprisingly quickly, as Muirchertach and the old man with the feminine voice descended the steps of the platform and made towards me and Sitric.

The two men stopped just short of me and fixed me with their knowing stares. It had been months since I had last been in Muirchertach's presence, when he had promoted my pedigree to all those present at a feast. I had never met the old man and eyed him curiously. His skin seemed stretched over his long, bony and worryingly pale face and the gaunt features were marked with the tell-tale scars of childhood smallpox. His hair was perfectly white and only a few wisps of it remained on his scalp where dry skin flaked horribly. The man resembled a wretched creature, which sent a shiver down my spine. His face twitched slightly as his piercing eyes bored into me, making me shift uncomfortably before he spluttered loudly. I tried not to notice as spittle and phlegm flew out from between his few remaining rotten teeth.

Sitric bowed his head to Muirchertach, who nodded back, and then turned to the old man. "May I introduce my foster-son Gruffudd son of Cynan." Sitric spoke in a respectful tone to the old man.

The old man, without looking at Sitric, talked sharply in his peculiar voice and gestured vaguely with his bony hand towards the exit. "That is all Sitric Sitricsson, you may return to your duties." Sitric turned and marched from the tent into the fresh air.

Muirchertach smiled at me. "Forgive my manners, this is my advisor, Father Cathal." The old man's eyes seemed to penetrate deep into my soul as he stared at me, unblinking. The man may be a monk but there was nothing Godly in Father Cathal's eyes. His gaze was most unsettling and somewhat threatening. Muirchertach must have sensed my thoughts as he chuckled, "Father Cathal is, how should I say?" Muirchertach frowned and clicked his fingers as he searched for the word, before a triumphant grin spread across his face. "Ah, yes, he is my eyes and ears." The old man smiled mischievously at Muirchertach's words. "There is little that goes on in Ireland without Father Cathal knowing. He has a peculiar interest in you, Gruffudd son of Cynan."

I shot Father Cathal a worried look which was greeted with a dry rasp of a laugh. "Your actions do not go unnoticed young man," his face seemed almost evil in the musky tent. "The killing of Gunnald was most useful. Most useful indeed. The world is a much better place without his Pagan soul spoiling it."

Muirchertach nodded his agreement. "I must congratulate you on such a fine deed," Muirchertach boomed. "I have already rewarded you by granting Gunnald's lands but I have another task for you," Muirchertach clapped a heavily muscled arm round my shoulder and guided me to the face of the dais. There we stood directly in front of Muirchertach's beautifully crafted throne. "You aspire to one of these don't you?" Muirchertach gestured at the throne and continued, "I have a task for you. Complete it for me and I shall help you get one."

"Anything," I stammered. "Whatever the task is, I shall do it for you." Father Cathal chuckled maliciously behind me as Muirchertach slapped my back enthusiastically. I knew he was being too friendly and that he would demand more of me, but it still took me by surprise.

"You may not thank me once I tell you; it is a most dangerous task. But first I must teach you an important lesson in the game of kings." He stood face to face with me as he spoke. "I know that we shall win tomorrow, but, and I must stress this. I do not wish to slaughter the people whom I wish to rule. That is an important factor, Gruffudd, and one you would do well to remember."

I nodded nervously as he continued. "The freemen, merchants and traders of Duibhlinn will not thank me if I unleash my army on their property. What will the men do after the suffering that will undoubtedly be inflicted upon them when they assault the walls?" Muirchertach answered his rhetorical question, "They will rape and pillage and of that I am sure. I do not want the animosity of those who make the town wealthy. They know Gofraid's cause is lost, but some foolish *Jarls* support him and he has mercenaries in his pay. So how, Gruffudd, do I defeat Gofraid without assaulting the town?"

I looked at Muirchertach blankly as he let my thought-cage absorb his words. I was not concerned about the puzzle he had just set me. Rather, my mind was working on what task he was going to order me to do, as the task and the puzzle must surely be connected to one another.

"To kill the serpent, you must strike off the head." Father Cathal's voice sounded behind me, drawing a long bony finger across his throat. He let out another dry, evil laugh as he chuckled to himself, obviously relishing the prospect of what was to come.

"Exactly," Muirchertach confirmed. "I must find a way to remove Gofraid. I believe that, without his presence, his mercenaries won't fight. That way those *Jarls* still foolish enough to support him will be in a hopeless situation and sue for peace." Muirchertach smiled as the realisation dawned on my face. "I want you to return here shortly after dark, Gruffudd, with four men. A small number will be needed and Father Cathal will be waiting for you."

Muirchertach beckoned for me to leave. As I neared the entrance Muirchertach called, answering my unasked question. "Yes Gruffudd. To become a king a king must first die. Gofraid must be removed."

VI

"He wants you to do what?" Cerit sounded appalled at what I had just told him. "I thought he was going to reward you, not send you on a suicide mission!" He was truly astonished by the task Muirchertach had set me.

"It will be a dangerous errand. I am not disputing that," I replied patiently. That was true, it was dangerous, and what was worse I had no idea how it was to be done. "What I need you to do is take the nine men I leave behind under your protection." Cerit looked back at me with a concerned expression. "Don't worry; I will be taking Ruaidri with me. I will save you his constant griping," I quipped.

Cerit's expression momentarily switched to a smile as he laughed at my words but it soon switched back to the worried, almost disapproving, look he had fixed me with moments earlier. "Father won't allow it," Cerit stated, almost believing his own words.

"He doesn't have a choice," I retorted firmly. "Muirchertach's word is final. You, as well as everyone else in this camp know that." Cerit shrugged his shoulders at the futility of trying to talk me down. "Besides, if I do this then I am sure that by the summer months I will be on my way to Gwynedd."

Cerit smiled at that, "I hope you are correct." He turned to walk away but called over his shoulder. "Don't go getting yourself killed." He walked back to where Sitric's warband was camped, shaking his head as he went.

Cerit's words had done little to change my mind. I was determined to return to Gwynedd and claim my birthright, but I was realistic enough to know I couldn't do it without Muirchertach's backing. As I walked back to my men, Muirchertach's words played over in my mind; "To become a king, a king must first die." I nodded to myself; Gofraid must die for me to return to Gwynedd. I would have to do whatever it took. I knew it was a near impossible mission, fraught with danger, but I would not fail; had God not been on my side thus far? I crossed myself and muttered a silent prayer. Later that evening I would be embarking upon the most dangerous task I had yet faced and I still did not know how it was to be done.

My worried expression and the distance I kept from my men since returning from Muirchertach's council of war troubled Bjorgolf greatly. He had done his best to get the information out of me. All I had told him was that we were to assault the walls at first light tomorrow, but Bjorgolf knew that it was not the prospect of an assault that worried me. The men watched me from where they sat, muttering amongst themselves. They speculated as to what was troubling me and I ignored the fact that Ruaidri was taking wagers on what it was. So far the favourite was that we were to retreat. But the speculation did little to improve their mood. As I was worried, so they too were worried. The sun began to set when Bjorgolf tried again to discover what worried me. This time he got his wish.

"I had the honour of a personal audience with Muirchertach and his advisor, Father Cathal, earlier." Bjorgolf raised an eyebrow at that but said nothing as I continued. "Muirchertach promised to aid me in my quest to reclaim Gwynedd, but he wants something in return."

Bjorgolf chuckled. "But of course he does. I have heard of Father Cathal and I wager that if he is involved then it is nothing good."

"You have the right of it my friend," I looked at him seriously. "You, me and three others are to go to meet with Father Cathal shortly. From there, I assume, we somehow get ourselves into Duibhlinn undetected. Once in, we find our way to where Gofraid is most likely to be and kill him before Muirchertach attacks at first light." I had sounded confident but I certainly wasn't, it could not be that simple surely.

Bjorgolf grinned broadly in the fading light. "Well bugger me, he doesn't expect much does he?" Bjorgolf laughed loudly. "We will have to have all the luck in the world tonight but fortune favours you Gruffudd. So, I am thinking that tonight Gofraid dies."

The prospect seemed to reinvigorate Bjorgolf who rubbed his hands and smiled broadly as we both returned to where the men were beginning to get a fire going. The light was fading quickly and soon darkness would be upon us. It was time to get the men ready and make our way to Father Cathal. I glanced around the campfire and saw I had the men's interest as they looked up at me expectantly.

"Some of us are going for a stroll in the dark," I said cheerfully to the men who looked back at me confused. "Bjorgolf and Ronan grab your weapons, but make sure they won't reflect light. No mail or war helms, I don't want to be tickled by the enemy's arrows." Bjorgolf and Ronan, grinning, gathered their weapons. "Ruaidri and Oengus, aren't you two always bleating that you are bored?" Without waiting for them to respond I added sharply. "Well now is the chance for you to bloody do something, get your weapons together."

They quickly obliged. Oengus grinned at the chance of having something to do whilst Ruaidri scowled at his brother, who held out his hand. There were a few groans from the men left behind as they all handed hack silver over to Ronan who, it seemed, had guessed correctly as to what bothered me. Ruaidri was last to, reluctantly, hand his silver over. I chuckled to myself as Ronan shot me a triumphant look and shrugged his shoulders. "Lucky guess, so it was. I always like a flutter on the most unlikely outcome." The huge Irishman chuckled softly to himself as he strolled over to where Bjorgolf and Oengus were waiting. Ruaidri was the last to follow and I turned to face my remaining wolves.

"Bjarni, you and the others look after our wargear and take yourselves over to Sitric's warband. You are to be under Cerit's protection, so follow his orders and behave yourselves." Bjarni was the most senior of the nine that were to be left behind. He was an ex-trader in his middle years and would be capable of making sure the others didn't step out of line.

In moments I was ready and trudged through the mud to where Bjorgolf, Oengus, Ronan and Ruaidri waited. None wore any wargear. We could not afford to take the chance of giving ourselves away. All wore their dirty, mud covered breeches and grubby tunics. In the dim light they did not look like warriors. They stood with their weapons in filthy clothes, grinning like madmen. They looked like murderous brigands or thieves, but that was what we were to be that night. It took me moments to strip off my mail and wrap a dark green cloak around myself, smothering the iron pin in mud so that it would not glint in the moonlight. We were ready and made our way through the Irish army until we came to Muirchertach's tent in its centre.

As we approached the entrance to Muirchertach's tent the two guards stiffened to attention and a man stepped out. He was of average height and of a slight build, he was clearly no warrior. He was dressed in dark coloured breeches of a chequered design and wore a dark tunic which was draped in a black cloak. He had lank black hair and a forked beard, through which he smiled a greeting.

"Gruffudd son of Cynan, I presume?" The man asked in a polite manner. I nodded and he beckoned us into the tent. He introduced himself in a smooth voice; I was right this man was no warrior; he spoke like a diplomat but his eyes were cold, never still and dangerous; this man was a killer but not one that killed honourably. "My name is Fergus; I am in the employ of Father Cathal." That did not surprise me as this man would not be out of place hiding in the shadows, waiting to slip a silent blade into a target's back. "You shall wait here. If you will excuse me, I shall fetch my master."

The tent had been partitioned by canvas sheets, to make living quarters for Muirchertach and his immediate retinue. Fergus slipped into one of the compartments. Bjorgolf winked at me. "We play a dangerous game, Gruffudd." Oengus and Ronan grinned mischievously at the prospect of causing some trouble. Ruaidri, on the other hand, looked as though he wished he was anywhere but in this situation. "What's the matter Ruaidri?" Bjorgolf chuckled. "Thought you were yearning to get at the enemy?" Ruaidri spat at Bjorgolf's jest as the others laughed mockingly.

Fergus re-emerged from the compartment, followed closely by Father Cathal. Father Cathal grinned as he inspected me and my waiting band of cutthroats. "You look the part men," he said wickedly in his odd voice. "Don't take any chances and be ruthless," he rasped sharply as a coughing fit took hold. It passed in seconds and he gave me a calculated stare. "You know what is expected of you. Fergus will go with you. This is his field of expertise." Fergus chuckled softly at Father Cathal's words. "The deed must be done before the army attacks, do not fail me Gruffudd. If you fail your dreams will die with you." Father Cathal's eyes glittered menacingly at the thinly veiled threat. "Now go. And may God be with you all." Without waiting for a response he turned on his heel and stalked back to his compartment in Muirchertach's great tent.

Fergus showed us all a friendly smile as he gestured for us to follow him outside. Two of Muirchertach's royal bodyguard had appeared and escorted us towards the front lines. None questioned our passage and the sentries ignored us as we reached their positions. The meeting with Father Cathal had all been too brief, was there no plan in place? No contact on the inside that would help us? I had asked Fergus those same questions and he had just tapped his nose with his index finger. I tried not to show it but I could feel the fear rising from my stomach, Father Cathal just expected us to get in and kill Gofraid. I shook my head at the thought; the old monk was mad, but I had been set the task and must see it through. The royal guardsmen wished us luck and returned to the safety of the camp.

Fergus surveyed us in the gloom; he nodded as though impressed by what he saw. They all, bar Ruaidri, smiled as Fergus and I faced them. They looked fearsome in the dark. Bjorgolf rubbed some of the dark mud onto his face and the others followed suit, as did I. Ronan looked like a creature from the underworld as his deformed face twitched into a blackened smile, his double handed axe added to the appearance. Bjorgolf and Ruaidri carried blades, as did I and Oengus concealed a short axe. Fergus looked pleased at the preparations and then turned to face me. "Follow me. We best be going," he whispered.

We followed him quickly as he skirted to the left and trotted forward twenty paces before he dropped into a crouch. I followed suit as did those behind me. I twisted round to check that everyone was still with us. Ronan was behind me with Oengus and Ruaidri behind him, Bjorgolf made up the rear. We stayed still for several minutes to become familiar with our surroundings.

We were a hundred paces from the palisade which loomed atop the earthen embankment to our front. The night was silent as we crouched on the boggy ground. My God, but it was cold, the freezing water leeched into my woollen breeches around the knees as I crouched unmoving. Fergus beckoned me to follow and we moved forward at an excruciatingly slow pace. My men followed as the walls of Duibhlinn began to loom larger and larger in front of us. A loud squelch and a muffled curse sounded sharply behind me. Fergus stopped dead and lowered himself slowly down until he lay flat on the ground, I followed suit and glanced behind me. Ruaidri shifted uncomfortably as he rubbed his ankle. Stupid idiot I thought. The man had been a pain for days and if the enemy did not kill us there and then, I was in the mind to throttle the bastard. But no enemy responded.

We lay still for what seemed ages on the freezing cold, boggy ground. A palisade section of the wall loomed above us, thirty paces to our front and a sentry stood atop. We stayed very still as he slowly paced fifteen paces down the wall and stopped. He turned his back to us and shouted a comment at a sentry thirty paces or so to our left. What it was I could not tell. The sentry to our left laughed at the man's words and he barked another comment that provoked further laughter.

A few moments afterwards the sentry to our left disappeared behind the wall. I hoped he had not noticed us and had discreetly gone to raise the alarm. Fergus began to slither forward on his belly, taking great care not to make a sound. The rest of us followed his example and neared the foot of the earthen embankment. It rose ten foot above us on a sharp contour. Fergus silently drew a wicked looking dagger from his clothing and slid it quietly into the embankment. He used it to aid his progress until he came to the foot of the wooden palisade. I could see the sentry's breath steaming in the cold night air as he stood staring at Muirchertach's army. Fergus crouched very still at the foot of the palisade for a minute and gestured for me to follow. This we did one by one until we were all up. I crouched behind Fergus, leaning into the rotten timber of the palisade. The palisade stood six foot high and must have a fighting platform a foot off the ground the other side. As Bjorgolf finally crawled up the embankment and took his position, the sentry moved.

My heart beat fiercely as I heard the thumping of the sentry slow. He halted right above me and I heard the scrape of his boots on the timber platform as he turned on his heel to look over our heads at Muirchertach's positions. The sentry's boots scraped again on the wood as he turned to face the settlement beyond the wall. Fergus rose slowly, keeping his back on the damp timber of the palisade. He stood still as the sentry made the unmistakable noise of voiding his bladder.

Fergus turned so that his belly was flat against the wooden wall taking a firm grip with one hand on the top of the palisade and then the other. Slowly he dragged himself up and edged above my head, so that he was directly behind the sentry. Fergus swung a leg onto the top of the wooden palisade with a cat-like stealth. The unfortunate sentry heard nothing as Fergus clamped a hand over the man's mouth and sank his wicked blade into the base of the sentry's skull. I heard the faint scuffle of the man's death but Fergus had killed him quickly and efficiently. There was a brief pause and then a drip of hot liquid fell on my forehead, then another and another. I wiped the warm substance with my arm as Fergus' voice whispered sharply over the palisade.

"Quickly, grab the bastard's arms and lower him down the other side, don't want his mates coming across him now do we!" I grabbed the man's arms and began to drag him over the wall as Ronan grabbed the man's legs when Fergus lifted them into view. I realised then that it was the sentry's blood that had dripped on my head and shuddered as we laid him carefully on the ground.

I followed Fergus' method of getting over the wall and my heart raced as I slowly rose and peered into the town of Duibhlinn. The sentry to our left had vanished whilst a sentry thirty paces to the right was completely oblivious as six killers dropped over the palisade to enter his town. The defences fell away onto a road immediately behind the wall. We descended the embankment quietly. To our front lay a large building of wattle-and-post with a dark window just below the thatched roof. The building was flanked on either side by much smaller huts, which must have been homes.

There we waited, at the base of the defences, staring into the town. Nothing moved as we crouched still for several minutes, which dragged slowly by. It did not feel right, it was somehow too quiet and I felt certain we were being watched. I was about to raise my concerns but just then Fergus turned and grinned happily at me. "We're in, follow me." Fergus rose and began to trot towards the street which led up the road to the left of the large building.

Fergus turned and paused to make sure everyone was there. Shit but that was my job I thought.

He started again just behind my shoulder and grinned as I glanced back at him; we were all there. Just as we neared the street a strange buzzing noise whipped past me with a rush of air. I froze as the arrow thumped into Fergus' heart and drew my blade quickly as men streamed out of the large building and surrounded us. I looked quickly from Fergus' motionless corpse to a man in full war gear striding towards me. I almost gawped at the man's horrendous appearance. He stared at me with vicious ice blue eyes as torch light reflected off a piece of metal that was strapped to his nose. Horrific scars dominated his cheeks as he stared coldly at me.

He spoke in accented Irish. "Do you yield?" he demanded through a scornful gaze. I looked about me as his men eyed us threateningly. It had all happened so quickly. Moments earlier Fergus had allayed my fears and seemed confident all had gone well, now he was dead. I glanced about me and knew that to fight back would be foolish. My mission was over. I let my blade drop to the ground and heard my men follow suit. The man turned sharply on his heel and strode back to the large building. Strong hands gripped me tightly as my legs were kicked from under me and I was manhandled towards the same building. I almost wept for the shame of defeat, I had failed utterly.

VII

My head spun as another fist smashed into my skull. My whole body ached; blood oozed from my broken nose and split lips. Bright flashing lights clouded my vision as the fist again connected with my cheek. I was on my knees, with my hands tied securely behind my back. I was defenceless as my tormentor aimed a kick which drove the wind from my body. As I fell the man laughed and kicked me again in the side. My mind was awash with the thought of failure and tears formed in my eyes as the man kicked me again and again. My God, but I was taking a rare beating. The man stopped briefly as I regained my breath. My ribs ached badly with every breath I managed to take. I grimaced as he kicked again and I felt a rib crunch under the impact.

All I could hear above the ringing of my ears was the laughter and cheers of the men who had captured us. I did not know how my men fared as I struggled for breath. The man forced me back onto my knees and took a fistful of my hair as he tormented me. I sensed him clenching his fist but before it could connect a voice cut sharply through the crowd. The man let go of my hair and I sagged forward, but still made an effort to stay on my knees and salvage a morsel of dignity.

I spat a sickening combination of phlegm, spittle and blood as my senses began to return. I shook my head violently to clear my vision, but my ears still rang sonorously. The man with the piece of metal strapped over his nose stared coldly at me. He crouched on one knee in front of me and cocked his head curiously as I looked either side of me to see if my men still lived.

The metal nosed man, as though reading my thoughts, laughed bitterly. "Your men are alive, for now. They are under guard in a different building." His oddly accented Irish unsettled me further. "If indeed they are your men. You are the leader, are you not?" I spat at his answer and he laughed mockingly as he wiped the bloody spittle from his mail. My whole head rocked with the impact as he stood and drove his fist into my jaw. His men laughed as I shook my head in an attempt to kill the pain. "Have you no manners? You stupid little shit." He eyed me threateningly as he continued. "Give me your name and the purpose of your mission." He pulled a sharp knife from his boot and ran his finger along the length of the wicked steel threateningly. "For if you do not give me any answers then I shall have to let my blade pull the answers from you. I shall start with your fingers; I shall take them one by one. If you can withstand that I will do the same to your toes. Then your ears, then your eyelids and then," his voice trailed off as he drew a finger across his throat.

I resisted the urge to vomit as I eyed him defiantly. Metal-Nose was a killer, there was no mistaking that. If I did not speak then he would almost certainly carry out his threat. He fixed me with a calculated stare and then nodded to himself and smirked, "Perhaps that is the wrong route to go down with you." His men looked at him curiously as he toyed with me. He turned round and snapped an order I didn't understand, as my ears still buzzed with the pain.

A commotion followed minutes later as another bound man was dragged into the room and pushed unceremoniously to the floor. There was no mistaking who it was. Bjorgolf spat curses as he rose unaided to his knees. His eyes widened in surprise as he recognised who the battered prisoner was in front of him. The man with the metal nose laughed again, he was clearly enjoying himself. He clicked his fingers and one of his men smashed his fist into Bjorgolf's face. Bjorgolf recovered well and spat in his opponents face. Growling like a cornered animal Bjorgolf eyed his opponent defiantly. The man punched Bjorgolf again and took a fistful of his hair; he turned for his master's order and that was his mistake. Bjorgolf butted the man squarely in the stomach, which brought a gasp from the watching men and a few jeers. The man doubled as Bjorgolf, roaring like a bear, launched himself forwards. Bjorgolf's hands were bound behind his back, but he was still a formidable opponent. He kneed the man in his face and stamped again and again on the man's ribcage before several men managed to wrestle the big Dane to the ground.

Metal-Nose laughed coldly and spat in disgust at his man, curled up like a ball on the floor moaning in pain, who had been beaten by a bound prisoner. He walked to where Bjorgolf was restrained and made a gesture to his men. One of the men took Bjorgolf by the hair and thrust his head backwards so that his neck was exposed. Metal-Nose still held his dagger and I gasped as I realised he meant to cut Bjorgolf's throat. Just before his knife connected I shouted across the room. "Spare him! And I shall tell you all you wish to know."

Metal-Nose stopped his knife dead and slowly rose and turned to face me. He smiled coldly, as his men grinned at their master's triumph. Bjorgolf roared at the man to fight him fairly, but he was silenced by a fist to the jaw.

Metal-Nose clapped a hand on my shoulder and knelt in front of me. His face was inches away from mine as his cold blue eyes stared at me with nothing but contempt. He spoke calmly in his odd accent. "My name is Maelgwn, son of Rhiwallon in the employ of King Gofraid of Duibhlinn." The man clearly expected me to recognise his name and cleared his throat when I showed no sign of recognition. "Now you will remember your manners and give me your name."

I croaked an unrecognisable word through my dry throat before coughing and spitting a mixture of spittle and blood out of my mouth. Maelgwn gestured for one of his men to bring a skin of ale forward which he poured into my mouth. I swallowed some of the stale liquid and spat the rest of the foul stuff out. I fixed Maelgwn with a stare full of hatred. "My name is Gruffudd, son of Cynan. Perhaps you have heard of me?"

Maelgwn smiled quickly before responding. Some of his men within earshot now looked at me curiously. "I have indeed heard the name," he spoke mockingly. "But I do not believe a warrior of such bravery or pedigree would let himself be caught like a common criminal."

Bjorgolf cursed him from behind. "He is who he says, you ugly bastard. My word is iron and if you do not believe me then kill me you fucking whoreson." Bjorgolf stared defiantly at Maelgwn who chuckled softly before turning back to me. This time he spoke in a strange dialect of Briton.

"So then, do you speak the truth?" He demanded and seemed worried when I nodded. "What the bloody hell were you doing sneaking into Duibhlinn in the dead of night like a common thief?" Maelgwn's voice was full of curiosity.

"Forgive me, but your accent is strange to me," I managed. "But I understand you well enough. I shall not lie to you. I am here to kill Gofraid so that unnecessary death and destruction can be avoided tomorrow."

Maelgwn looked at me shocked. "Tomorrow, why tomorrow?" He asked urgently then eyed me knowingly as the realisation dawned on him. I knew my life was in this man's hands and I did not much like the prospect. "You should know that your men sounded like a herd of cattle to my sentry's ears when you crossed the land between our forces." He smiled slyly as he continued. "The men of Powys are skilled archers and have good eyes in the dark. That is a lesson you should do well to remember, if you live beyond this night."

I eyed him bitterly. "Your sentry died easily enough though." I spoke defiantly as I continued. "You stand no chance when Muirchertach attacks tomorrow and I wager Gofraid's coin is not worth dying for."

Maelgwn laughed. "The man you killed was not one of mine. Rest assured you would already be dead if he were. No, my man left the palisade to alert me. You were so slow to come over the wall that I had enough time to trap you perfectly."

Maelgwn's men grinned triumphantly behind him at their master's cunning. "Whether Gofraid's coin is worth dying for? Of that I am not entirely sure, he pays me well." Maelgwn shrugged his shoulders as if he did not much care. "I have already sent for the captain of Gofraid's bodyguard and he will be here shortly with an escort to take you to the royal hall." Maelgwn fixed me with a cold stare as he added matter-of-factly. "There Gofraid will do with you as he sees fit."

Maelgwn turned to walk away as I called desperately at his back. "Whatever Gofraid is paying you, I can match it if you let me and my men go." Maelgwn paused and eyed me blankly.

"You truly do not recognise my name?" he enquired and nodded to himself when I shook my head. "It would surprise you then to learn that my brother is Cynwrig, son of Rhiwallon. You may know of him as Cynwrig of Powys. He is Trahaearn of Arwystli's ally and rules some of the land which you lay claim to." With that he turned his back on me and walked over to a squat man with a gap toothed grin who eyed me suspiciously.

I stared at Maelgwn's back in horror. My heart sank. The brother of one of the usurpers of my birthright held me captive in an enemy town. My heart sank further as the realisation dawned upon me, I was a dead man. The squat man who Maelgwn had just talked to eyed me curiously and snapped orders in the strange Powysian dialect before disappearing out of the door and into the night. Maelgwn's men talked animatedly amongst themselves, and eyed me with a mixture of excitement and suspicion. I glanced at Bjorgolf who looked at me expectantly. "We're buggered." That was all I could manage as Bjorgolf nodded to himself, as if in acceptance. Just then there was a hard hammering on the door to the building and a group of heavily mailed men filed into the light.

A short man in full wargear strutted cockily towards me, raising a hand to silence Maelgwn. The man stopped in front of me and Bjorgolf and removed his shining war helm, which was plumed with white horse hair. He had a long drooping moustache, similar to Faelan's. His blonde hair was slicked neatly back and fell to his shoulders. A flowery scent drifted off the man as he eyed me triumphantly. Arrogance radiated off the man and I hated him instantly as he reminded me of that bastard, Faelan.

Maelgwn again tried to talk to the man who raised a hand and ordered Maelgwn to remain silent. "So these are the spies that came over the wall?" The man asked the rhetorical question to himself and did not expect an answer but still raised a hand as if to silence Maelgwn yet again and hissed sharply. "Not bad work for some dung stinking Britons." His ten men laughed dutifully at his jest whilst Maelgwn and his men eyed the royal guardsmen with nothing but hostility.

Maelgwn's voice cut coldly across the guard captain's evident enjoyment. "You will show me respect, captain." Maelgwn added the man's title acidly eyeing the guard captain with evident dislike.

"When I want the opinion of a cheap Briton mercenary I shall ask for it. But then again, I do not rate the opinion of people who sell themselves for money. You are like a cheap whore Maelgwn." The guard captain clearly meant this as a jest for his men to laugh at and was disappointed when none did. His men eyed Maelgwn's overwhelming numbers warily whilst Maelgwn's men stared back with hatred. I knew the guard captain was stepping dangerously, you could feel the tension rising with every passing moment.

The Britons had a reputation for their prickly pride and blood feuding, something the guard captain had clearly forgotten. I could sense the tension in the room was close to boiling over and glanced at Bjorgolf who grinned at the prospect of seeing what would happen. Maelgwn grabbed the captain's arm and pulled him close. "I do not appreciate those words, you perfume doused woman."

The guardsman dragged his arm free and backhanded Maelgwn across the face, rubbing his knuckles after colliding with Maelgwn's metal nosepiece. "Do not lay a filthy hand on me, you vile shit of a Briton." Bjorgolf laughed at the scene as Maelgwn adjusted his nose piece and the guard captain rounded on the source of laughter threateningly.

Just then Maelgwn barked in Briton. "Now!" His men drew their weapons and descended on the royal guardsmen in fury. Maelgwn grabbed the guard captain who froze at the horror which unfolded before his eyes. Maelgwn butted him in the face, the metal nose drawing blood, but he did not let the guard captain drop. Maelgwn drew the knife from his boot and forced the guard captain to his knees before gripping the man's head in a firm lock.

The captain bleated pitifully as Maelgwn traced his blade gently down the man's cheeks, toying with him. In a move which shocked even Bjorgolf, Maelgwn quickly drew his blade across the guard captain's face. Blood sprayed over me and Bjorgolf as the man screamed hopelessly. Maelgwn held up a lump of gristle and blood which he threw to the floor. He pulled the guardsmen's head back up by grabbing a fistful of the man's neatly combed hair. I stared in disbelief at the bloody mess which had replaced the guardsman's handsome features. Maelgwn had cut off the man's nose and then sawed his knife very slowly across the man's throat. Blood sprayed over me like a waterfall as the man slowly died and Maelgwn let his body fall to the floor.

Maelgwn spat at the corpse and stared at me. I do not claim that I was anything other than terrified. Maelgwn calmly rounded on me and forced me upright. I felt the cold sharpness of his blade near my wrists and braced myself for the cut that was to come. I could not believe it when my hands were cut free from the bonds and simply stared in disbelief at the cold-blooded slaughter I had just witnessed. Maelgwn crossed to Bjorgolf and cut his bonds also. Bjorgolf met my eye and grinned broadly at being set free, seemingly unfazed by what had just happened.

Maelgwn again faced me as I stood motionless, still expecting to be cut down. But instead the Powysian smiled at me and spoke calmly. "It was pleasing to kill that jumped up prick. Gofraid's guardsmen have been terrifying the townspeople for weeks. Treat everyone else like shit they do and strut round like the privileged fuckers Gofraid has turned them into."

I did not know what to say as Maelgwn knelt and cleaned the blood off his knife in the dead guardsman's cloak. "What will you do with us?" I demanded as calmly as I could, trying not to betray my nervousness.

Maelgwn fixed me with a knowing stare, "I have decided Gofraid's coin is not worth dying for."

I could not hide my relief and smiled broadly at Maelgwn. "But why help the enemy of your brother?" I asked in Irish so Bjorgolf could understand. I sensed Bjorgolf's surprise as he eyed Maelgwn suspiciously.

Maelgwn looked at me sadly and turned his back to me and Bjorgolf. His hands reached to the back of his head and untied the leather thong which secured the metal nose fitting to his horrifically scarred face. He removed the nose piece and turned slowly to face me and Bjorgolf. I was taken aback by the brute violence which had shaped the man's features. I sensed even Bjorgolf was shocked by the brutality Maelgwn had clearly suffered.

Maelgwn's face was dominated by the lump of bone and gristle where his nose had once been; it was now a mess of flesh and chipped bone. He looked like a creature from hell, the horrific scars on his cheeks further added to the devilish appearance. He reattached the metal nose piece quickly and for once, looked as though he was capable of feeling sorrow.

His voice briefly betrayed his emotions, but he soon corrected them and spoke calmly. "I said he was my brother, but what I did not say is that I have no love for him." He looked away thoughtfully and nodded to himself as if he had made up his mind to justify his decision. "As you should know, Gruffudd, our people will not accept a ruler who is either disfigured or simple." I swear a tear appeared briefly in the corner of his eye but it was gone just as quickly as it appeared. "I was a handsome youth in my day," he smiled wistfully at the memory. "Cynwrig is a year younger than I and in my seventeenth summer our father, the brother of the King of Powys died. As is the custom of our people my father's lands and wealth would be split equally between his sons. It was then that Cynwrig stopped being my brother and became my bitter enemy."

The whole room had fallen silent. "Cynwrig invited me for a feast at his hall and there he killed my friends and laughed as his companions held me to his feasting table. There he took a knife to my face and did what you see before you." He gestured at his horrifically scarred face. "His men threw me into the woods and left me for dead. It was then that I swore vengeance and joined a band of Powysian mercenaries who were leaving to fight against the Frenchmen who now dominate *Lloegr*." Maelgwn had used the Briton term for the land which the Saxons called England. "From then, Gruffudd, I was ruthless and men thought I had no soul, that I was the creation of the devil. I now command this band of mercenaries and you have offered me a chance at what I have so long craved." He paused as he fixed me with a cold grin. "If I help you achieve your goals, I will sail with you to Gwynedd when you are ready. There I shall kill Cynwrig and spit in his dead face."

I grinned as Maelgwn finished his story. I had a new ally and I followed Maelgwn and his men out of the barrack building which had become a charnel house. We walked out into the dark streets of Duibhlinn where the squat, gap toothed, man Maelgwn had sent on an errand, before the massacre of the guardsmen, waited with several mercenaries and my remaining men.

My men grinned at our unexpected survival but grimaced at the sight of my battered face. My whole face throbbed and every breath was a struggle, but that did not concern me. I had escaped death and had found a new ally. I marched next to Maelgwn as his men escorted us deeper into Duibhlinn. Tonight, I thought, Gofraid dies.

VIII

The people and soldiers of Duibhlinn slept as we strode closer and closer to our goal. Only once did a dog bark as our column marched up a long street. My body still ached horribly from the beating I had taken but I was determined to reach our target and see the task through. Maelgwn had sent an advance party comprising of six of his best archers to make sure the royal hall had not been alerted to our approach.

It sounded to me as though we made enough noise to raise the dead, but nothing moved as we turned left onto another street. The street began to rise on a steady incline and we followed it to the top of the small hillock where Maelgwn called a halt just before the road forked to the right. We were deep within the walled town now and the men were nervous. The smell of open sewerage and rotting vegetation hung heavily in the air as we knelt close to the edge of the street.

Maelgwn was being cautious. "We shall wait here until my *helwyr* return." He clearly rated his archers who he had nicknamed his *helwyr*. The archers were proud of their nickname, which meant hunters in Briton. Maelgwn had assured me they were the best bowmen in Ireland and I did not doubt it.

Suddenly my heart skipped a beat as a dog, its rest disturbed by our presence, began to bark repeatedly from behind a house to the left, earning a mocking chuckle from Bjorgolf who knelt just behind me. I cursed under my breath at the noise the bloody animal was creating; it was making me nervous, and soon someone would be bound to investigate the animal's constant barking. I glanced over my shoulder and saw Oengus. "Oengus go and put an end to that bastard animal's noise." The dog was making too much noise for my liking and I was amazed nobody had emerged onto the street to find out what the hell was going on.

Oengus rose to his full height and beamed a wicked smile at me as he removed the short axe from the concealment of his cloak. "With pleasure, bloody thing is giving me a headache, so it is." A couple of the men in earshot laughed nervously as Oengus trotted across the street and disappeared over a wattle fence.

Bjorgolf edged up to my side and nodded at Maelgwn's back. "I hope his lads come back soon. I do not like this waiting around one bloody bit."

I grumbled my agreement. I felt horribly exposed and was sure we would soon be discovered if we remained still. The lack of action by the enemy unsettled me further; so far we had encountered no one and no challenge had been shouted during our advance through Duibhlinn's maze of streets and alleyways. A deep feeling of suspicion was rising in my gut. It felt as though it was almost too quiet, I still did not know where Maelgwn's loyalties truly lay. The slaughter of the guard captain and his men had been as loud as it was chilling; surely the bodies must have been discovered by now? The noise suddenly became louder as the dog barked a challenge; Oengus wasn't half taking his bloody time.

Just then a sharp yelp signified the end of the beast's life and I breathed a sigh of relief as Bjorgolf muttered good riddance to the troublesome animal. Still our column waited, kneeling in the street's filth, as I clumsily moved forward to ask Maelgwn why he showed no signs of movement. The mercenary raised a fist to silence me before turning round, holding a finger to his lips. Suddenly his head jerked around and his hand went for the hilt of his blade. Then I could hear it, the unmistakable sound of soft footsteps came from the right. Whoever it was was trying to approach our position stealthily. Maelgwn tensed as the set of footsteps drew closer and closer. The Powysian slid his blade silently from its scabbard, moonlight glinting off the cold steel. Maelgwn was ready to strike as a voice, betraying its fear, whispered nervously round the corner of the building. "Maelgwn?"

"Show yourself," Maelgwn whispered sharply back. Maelgwn braced himself, ready to thrust his blade at the newcomer, as a head peered around the corner. Suddenly Maelgwn's wide shoulders relaxed and he let out a soft chuckle. The newcomer moved into view and knelt next to Maelgwn, keeping his voice low. It was the gap toothed man whom Maelgwn had sent ahead with the advance party.

The man spoke excitedly. "They haven't got a bloody clue, not a bloody clue!" The man's pleasure radiated through his gap-toothed grin as he continued. "I've left the lads watching 'em and they'll put the bastards down if they so much as make a move at our approach."

Maelgwn did not betray any emotion as he spoke. "How many of the whoresons are there?"

"Only the usual two guarding the gate, we will be able to get in soon enough." The gap-toothed archer was clearly confident. Only I and Maelgwn could hear the man's words and, as I glanced over my shoulder, I smiled at Bjorgolf, reassuring the big Dane that all was well.

Maelgwn, evidently satisfied, clapped the gap-toothed archer on his back before sending him back to his forward position. Maelgwn's scarred features turned to face me and a wicked grin beamed across his face in the moonlight, giving him a ghoulish appearance. He licked his lips and rubbed his hands in anticipation of the killing he knew was about to come. "My *helwyr* will drop the bastards as soon as we begin our approach. Once the guards on the gate are down and my lads have cleared the courtyard I'll send them over to open the gate."

He waited for me to nod my head in acknowledgement before he ploughed on with his plan. "As soon as the gate is open we'll rush in and storm the bastard's lair. Once we're in the hall it will be up to you and your cutthroats to get Gofraid, I'll watch the rear and keep the escape route open."

Maelgwn paused for a moment to see my reaction and I nodded my acceptance. It was a good plan and Maelgwn clearly had a good grasp of how to carry out a raid. I opened my mouth to speak but flinched at the pain in my jaw. I rubbed my tender jaw and Maelgwn chuckled at the sight; bastard, I thought, but I needed him. The Powysian rose to his full height. "I suggest you hack off Gofraid's rotten head to prove you've carried out the deed. Once it is done we shall retreat to the harbour and on to my ships. There we shall wait until sunrise and see what happens. Agreed?"

"Agreed," I repeated firmly. Gofraid's hall was a mere hundred paces away and I knew my future would be made or broken in the coming minutes. I drew my blade and checked its edge with my thumb as the familiar sound of men drawing their weapons rippled down the line. I glanced over to where Bjorgolf, Ronan, Ruaidri and Oengus waited at the head of the column and their presence made me smile with confidence. Maelgwn signaled for the column to move forward and we began to move towards Gofraid's lair.

Maelgwn broke into a trot as we followed the street round to our right and my heart began to quicken as the dark smudge of Gofraid's hall loomed ahead of us in the darkness. A fire burned in a brazier as two guards, barely conscious, slouched around it, more interested in keeping themselves warm than watching for threats. I smiled to myself; we had the element of surprise, the guards had no suspicion of any danger and that would make my task easier.

Bjorgolf fell-in alongside me. "What is the plan then?" His voice betrayed a hint of disappointment at having been left out of the decision making.

"We burst in and kill everyone, quite simple really." I panted back at him. I felt guilty at not having consulted Bjorgolf but I knew he would like the plan's simplicity. Bjorgolf looked set to speak but I pre-empted his question. "Don't worry, Maelgwn and his lads will watch our backs to make sure we don't get trapped in the bloody place if anyone tries to stop us."

He grunted at my answer. "Can we trust him? The bastard meant to kill us not too long ago." The doubt was clear in Bjorgolf's voice; he did not like the Powysian and did not feel comfortable trusting someone who had almost killed us.

"Yes, we can trust him." The truth was that I agreed with Bjorgolf and I did not feel comfortable putting my life, not for the first time, in the Powysian's hands. Bjorgolf grunted in acceptance, evidently not satisfied, but he chose not to push the matter further.

We were almost there now. My bruised and cracked ribs ached with every breath and my jaw throbbed as we trotted forwards. Even blinking hurt as my swollen left eye protested at the simple action, but I had to ignore the pain. The familiar pre-battle feelings began to take hold as we moved closer and closer to the drowsy guards. My knees began to weaken and my stomach sank as we bore down on the guardsmen, who still hadn't noticed our advance. I could not believe how easy this was proving; we were almost upon them now. Thirty paces, twenty!

Moonlight glinted off drawn weapons and a glint must have caught one of the guardsmen's attention. He rose sharply, knocking over his stool, and went for his blade, but it was all too little too late. The first guardsman called out in alarm, the fear evident in his shrill cry, as eighty killers charged towards him. The second guard had recovered his wits as arrows zipped overhead and screams of pain sounded from within the courtyard.

We were almost upon them when three arrows, almost at the same time, thumped into the first guardsman's chest. The man grunted as he dropped to his knees, his blade clattering on the street as it fell from his grip. The second guard, armed with a spear, fled towards the gate and hammered on it helplessly. He screamed for his life as we drew closer and closer. As the frightened guard turned to glance over his shoulder an arrow punched through the side of his neck and thumped into the hard timber of the gates. The spear clattered to the ground as the man made hopeless gurgling noises as he tried to keep his footing, clutching the arrow which had punched through his neck and pinned him to the timbers of the gate.

Bjorgolf swung his blade in a wide arc at the first guardsman, who still knelt in the street staring dumbfounded at the three arrows protruding from his chest.

The powerful blow took the man under the chin and cut clean through as Bjorgolf's momentum carried him forwards. I did not see the man fall and turned my attention back to the gate. The second guard's knees at last buckled as I drew within five paces of him. The arrow snapped under his weight as he collapsed to the floor. Then I was at the gateway.

Maelgwn's Powysians pressed all around me and hammered on the gate. I glanced around and saw Bjorgolf, as ever at my side. The Dane thumped the hilt of his blade on the timber. The guard still lived and gurgled pitifully as men, unable to move due to the press, were forced to stand on him. A Powysian looked down and stamped viciously on the guard's head, silencing him completely. Movement above caught my eye and I glanced up to see one of Maelgwn's *helwyr* scaling the courtyard's walls.

Moans of pain sounded from the courtyard as the gates screeched open on their ageing hinges. I glanced about me as the heavy timber gates inched further and further apart. Bjorgolf shouted his impatience as Ronan shouldered his way to my left side, gritting his teeth for the fight to come. I glanced over my shoulder to see Ruaidri and Oengus at my back, growling their frustration. Then suddenly the gates sprang open.

A cry of triumph erupted from the Powysians as we streamed through into the courtyard. Three dead guardsmen lay sprawled around the royal hall's barred door, several arrows sticking out of the motionless corpses. I bundled over the dead men and threw all my weight against the hall's doors, a decision I instantly regretted. I recoiled violently from the pain in my ribs; damn, but with the blood lust of battle flowing through me, I had forgotten the beating I had taken earlier. Maelgwn and his Powysians surged past me and began thumping on the strong doors.

The sound was intense as men screamed their frustration and hammered on the hall's door. Only moments had passed but I knew we could not dally.

I glanced around and caught Ronan dragging a male thrall free of some barrels. The thrall, a scrawny middle aged man with red hair, launched himself at Ronan screaming in hatred and fear, whirling his fists like a windmill. It was an uneven contest and Ronan smacked the thrall in the jaw with the long wooden staff of his double-handed axe.

I glanced at the heavy weapon and knew what had to be done. Time was short and I screamed at the broad Irishman. "For God's sake Ronan, stop pissing about and get over here. I need your axe!"

The great bushy head nodded in agreement as he hefted the huge axe above his head and brought it down in a vicious arcing blow that would have decapitated an ox. The floored thrall raised an arm in a futile attempt to protect his head but Ronan's axe cut clean through the thrall's arm, just short of the elbow, and punched through his face splitting his head in two. The Irishman lumbered towards me and I pointed towards the door.

Ronan surveyed the scene for a short moment and nodded his head. The Irishman shouldered his way through the crowd of Powysians and screamed at men to move out of his way. The giant slammed his axe into the timber and wrenched it free as the wood began to splinter.

Maelgwn had noticed what the big Irishman was doing and screamed an order in his strange Briton for his own axemen to join the effort. Still only moments had passed since we had burst through the courtyard gates and I knew we would have to hurry as calls of alarm began to sound nearby.

The axes rose and fell in the dim light as they bit deeper and deeper into the royal hall's doors. The sound of splintering timber was met with a cheer from Maelgwn's Powysians but I cursed, for this was taking too long.

A call of alarm sounded from the gateway and the gap-toothed *helwyr* sprinted towards the press of Powysians. I intercepted the man and grabbed hold of his tunic as he called Maelgwn's name desperately.

"There's no bloody time for him, what the hell is going on?" I screamed in the man's face and was rewarded with the answer as an arrow clattered to the ground near my feet.

The arrow brought the *helwyr* to his senses. "Those bastards have got help on the way!" I thrust the man clear and cursed under my breath. I could see through the courtyard gateway and it was clear an assault was being prepared by somebody coming to Gofraid's aid.

"Shit!" I screamed aloud as the gap-toothed *helwyr* sprinted back to his position and skillfully darted round the gate to fire an arrow before darting back behind cover. I glanced behind me at the crowd of Powysians and shouldered my way into them. "Get yourselves over to the gate now, you good for nothing bastards!" The ferocity in my voice prompted a handful of men in earshot to run towards the gate. Some looked at me stunned.

I grabbed the nearest man by the collar of his tunic. "You want to die?" I screamed in his face. "No? Then bloody move you whoreson!" I shoved the man towards the gate as others followed suit. The axemen needed a few more moments and I would have to buy it for them as a challenge was shouted from the gloom beyond the courtyard gates.

I cursed and trotted towards the gate as men came to save their king.

I glanced around; I had around twenty men which would have to do. Eight men could stand abreast in the gateway and I took up position in the front rank as I shouted at the men in Briton. "Form up! Form up on me, you bastards!"

Arrows zipped over our heads from behind as the *helwyr* fired into the dark press of screaming men who surged up the street towards us. I knew these Powysians were good but they would really have to prove it now. I took a deep breath. "Shieldwall! Shieldwall!"

Most Britons, to my amazement, rejected the shieldwall as a tactic and did not like to fight in disciplined ranks, but I judged Maelgwn to be a talented commander and guessed he would have taught his men the defensive tactic. It amazed me how the Britons had not adopted the stratagem as it created a formidable wall of shields and a guaranteed stubborn resistance. I breathed out a sigh of relief as the shields smacked together and I knew that we could hold them.

The attackers came into view as they neared us. A well armed youth with a dashingly plumed helmet screamed for his men to follow him. The youth wanted to make a name for himself and rushed his men so that they attacked in a disorganised manner. They would suffer I thought and smiled to myself, recognising that this youth was not too dissimilar to myself. Only I knew my business.

The youth remained remarkably unscathed as the *helwyr's* arrows thumped into the men around him, further disorganising the enemy attack. I judged the youth's party numbered double my scratch force that defended the gate and knew instantly that the enemy was faltering. The *helwyr* found their targets with ruthless efficiency. More men fell in the youth's front rank, but their momentum carried them on.

The confident youth screamed in Irish as he hurled himself at me. His attack had begun to falter, which he realized and, doing exactly what I had done against Gunnald, he led by example. He threw himself at my shieldwall and his shield smashed into mine as his men followed him. I could hear the youth grunting as he tried to force my shield loose, but I was too strong for him. All around him his men screamed in anger and pain as they began to take casualties in the uneven fight.

This was when a shieldwall came into its own. The front rank would absorb the momentum of the enemy charge and hold the line as the men in the second and third ranks struck with their axes or spears at the undefended heads of the attackers. The tactic was working well as a spear glanced over my shoulder to take one of the youth's men in the eye. The youth grunted and screamed in alarm as the same spear zipped again over my shoulder and glanced off his plumed helmet.

His men were losing the fight and were taking heavy casualties as my disciplined ranks cut the youth's men down with a frightening efficiency. The rear ranks of the youth's force were beginning to edge back and some turned their backs to flee as their ranks began to break. I smiled as the pressure on my front rank evaporated; the bastards were fleeing. The youth withdrew and backed cautiously away as four of his men formed a protective ring about him. The retreating men began to scream in pain as the *helwyr's* arrows punched through their backs and dealt them dishonourable wounds.

The youth was calling over his shoulder for his men to reform and to hold until help arrived and they were beginning to do so. I glanced over my shoulder and saw that the doors were beginning to yield to the axe strokes and I suddenly knew what would have to be done to allow me the time to get to Gofraid.

I stepped clear of my front rank stepping over the bodies of the repulsed attackers. The youth saw me and pushed his way clear of his protective bodyguards. I raised my sword in front of my face in challenge and called for the *helwyr* to cease fire. I had challenged the youth to single combat and honour dictated he would have to accept the challenge or be seen as a coward. I judged that I had a better than evens chance of winning and knew that, if I took away their leader, then it would buy me enough time. The youth almost reluctantly stepped forwards until he was within ten paces and he spat defiantly at my feet.

He eyed me with nothing but loathing and I could see that he was scarce over fourteen. He was a tall lad for his age, but not well developed; his frame showed no signs of strength that would challenge me. I did not want to have to kill a youth in an unfair fight, for there was little honour in it, but it had to be done.

The youth spat his disgust and tried to sound as fearsome as he could in his unbroken voice. "You traitor, I will gut you. You will scream for mercy."

I ignored the jibe. "Who do I face?" I demanded in a cold voice. I was young myself, still in my nineteenth year, but I knew I would win and that confidence came through.

"I am Prince of Duibhlinn." The defiance in the youth's voice was clear as he announced his title. "My mother's sister is Gofraid's wife and Queen. I may still spare you if you surrender now." I detected a trace of nervousness in the youth's voice as he delivered the threat.

I laughed. "You are not Prince of this land. Your baseborn family usurped it from my foster-father, Sitric Sitricsson." I spat my disgust and grinned at the youth's surprise. "Tonight Gofraid dies and so do you."

I darted forward quickly and struck like a hammer blow. The youth was much weaker than I and had not been expecting such a vicious opening blow. He raised his shield just in time as my strike, aimed at his neck, bit deeply into the wood of the small round-shield. I used all my strength to retrieve the blade, splintering the youth's shield and making it useless. My strength had knocked him off balance and I brought my blade down again in a powerful blow, aimed at his shoulder. The youth ducked and dodged the strike as my blade glanced off his helmet, severing the dashing plume of white horse hair. Horsehair showered down as I attacked again. The youth had been so taken aback by my speed and ferocity that he had not yet been able to launch an attack of his own. He brought his blade across in an attempt to deflect mine. His eyes widened in fear as my blade hammered into his and shattered it. I quickly reversed the swing and sunk my blade deep into the youth's neck and forced it down, deeper, into his chest. Blood spurted into the air as I withdrew the blade. The youth crumpled instantly to the floor and his four men screamed their outrage and charged towards me. They made it five paces before they were all expertly brought down into a twitching heap by Maelgwn's *helwyr*.

I took one last look at the dead youth and shook my head sadly. There was no honour in it but it had been necessary I told myself. My thoughts returned to the task in hand as a loud cheer rang out from the royal hall's door where the axes had almost found their way in. Still only moments had passed since we had killed the guards on the gate and my fight with the youth. I ordered my scratch force to remain in position and hold the gateway as I made towards the press of men around the hall's doors. A loud splintering noise sounded from the doorway as I shouldered my way towards the front rank where my men waited. The great doors would soon be open and I knew I had bought the time I needed. I smiled triumphantly to myself; soon the wolf would be amongst the shepherd's flock and the wolf was hungry for blood.

I made sure that Bjorgolf, Ruaidri and Oengus were with me as we braced ourselves to charge the splintered doors when the time came. Still the axes bit continuously into the splintering timber and holes were beginning to emerge in the oaken doors. Maelgwn shoved his way through the tight press until the devilish face, with its metal nosepiece, faced me. I took one look at the Powysian and was glad that, for the moment at least, he was on my side. His blood splattered features surveyed the splintered timber coolly. "They're nearly in; God knows how many of the scum are inside. But, it's your job to kill them." His cold blue eyes fixed on mine. "Make sure you're bloody quick about it. This racket is bound to be noticed."

"It's already has been noticed," I stated calmly and immediately put Maelgwn's thoughts to rest. "I've seen the bastards off for now, at least. I've left some of your rogues there and they're enough to keep our escape route open.

Your *helwyr* are keeping them behind cover sure enough. They aren't too bad for Powysians."

Maelgwn chuckled at the compliment and took it as it was intended. "I'll make sure we keep the road open and no bastard cocks this mission up for you." Maelgwn shouted orders for his men to reinforce the gateway, calling over his shoulder. "Just make sure you get to Gofraid quickly. Most of Duibhlinn will be awake by now and on their way here!"

I ignored the Powysian's words. I knew he was right but did not want to be reminded of it. Ronan shouted in triumph as a section of the door to his front collapsed under his axe strokes. The big Irishman backed up and then thundered forwards at full pace, dropping his shoulder at the last minute and splintering through the remains of the door. A roar went up from the Powysian axemen who, caught up in the blood lust of battle, charged in after the ugly Irishman.

I screamed my own war cry through my split lips, ignoring the pain, and followed the axemen inside. Bjorgolf, Ruaidri and Oengus bellowed their own challenges and followed me into the King of Duibhlinn's hall.

Inside there was chaos. My foot caught on a thick piece of splintered timber and I stumbled forwards, almost losing my footing, as Bjorgolf and the others thundered past. Torches glowed brightly on the walls of the building as I surveyed the scene. A disemboweled foeman lay sprawled on the shattered wood at my feet, still mouthing words that would not come. Gofraid's remaining bodyguards were bolstered by his thralls, who fought for their lives with assorted weaponry. The hall was equally as grand as mine and at the far end a group of six mailed guardsmen protected an ageing man who, still in his bedclothes, carried a small Irish round-shield and a shining blade. Gofraid! I cursed the man's name and charged into the mêlée.

I slipped on a thrall's gut-rope and skidded into an enemy shield, cursing as a spear thrust narrowly missed my head and thumped into Ronan's shoulder. I hacked blindly with my blade and felt it cut through the spear shaft as I recovered my footing. My assailant's eyes widened with horror as a battle maddened Ronan, oblivious to the pain in his wounded shoulder, swung his two handed axe clumsily with his good arm. The man howled in agony as the axe head shattered his sword-arm. His pain did not last for long as I thrust my blade into his unprotected throat. I stepped over the dying man and faced my next opponent who was a young thrall, scarcely over sixteen. His eyes were wide with fear and he drooled from the mouth as he swung a wooden cudgel clumsily towards me. I went to parry the blow and my blade bit into the thrall's wrist, severing the hand. He screamed in pain as the cudgel fell harmlessly to the floor. Oengus' short-axe whirled quickly from the right and thumped into the thrall's temple, killing him instantly. Then there was breathing space.

I glanced quickly about me as Bjorgolf beat a mailed man to death with his bare fists as he straddled the prostrate man on the floor. The Powysian axemen cornered the remaining thralls and one of Gofraid's bodyguards before butchering them mercilessly. The Powysian axes rose and fell on the cornered defenders as blood and gore splashed up the walls and seeped into the rush matting on the floor of the great hall.

"Form up! On me!" I made sure Bjorgolf, Ronan, Ruaidri and Oengus were at my side. The Powysians, ignoring my call, stooped to plunder the corpses of the defenders they had butchered, but I did not care. A big mailed warrior, in his middle years, argued with Gofraid and gestured forcefully at a wooden door at the back of the hall. One of the King's bodyguards noticed my small party cautiously advancing and gained the burly warrior's attention, pointing frantically towards us. The warrior shouldered to the front of his five remaining men and bellowed for them to form on him. Time was against us. I cursed for this was taking too long. Gofraid screamed for his men to charge us and they obliged. "For Gofraid!"

I bellowed my own challenge and powered forwards, not caring to see who followed me. The gap closed quickly and I narrowly dodged a spear thrust, which would have skewered me, ramming my blade into the man's face. The man screamed as he dropped his spear and clutched his ruined face, dropping to the floor. I glanced to the left and saw Ronan, one handed, decapitating a guardsman with a powerful swing. The severed head arched into the air, gushing blood as it went, before it slammed into a wall and sickeningly smacked to the floor.

Bjorgolf was locked in a fierce struggle with the burly warrior who called loudly. "Protect the King! Get him into the bedchamber!"

Gofraid, realising the fight was lost, moved quickly to the door and hammered on it with the hilt of his sword. Before I or any of my men could react the three remaining guards broke away from their fights with Ruaidri and Oengus and made for Gofraid. I charged forwards just as Gofraid disappeared through the bedchamber's door.

I had Ruaidri and Oengus at my side and the three bodyguards did well to parry our initial blows. A battle maddened scream sounded behind me as Ronan, biting his bottom lip against the pain in his shoulder, lifted his great axe with both arms and swung it down in a frighteningly powerful arc. The axe missed my head by inches as it smashed into my opponent's shoulder. Broken rings of mail and blood cascaded against my face as the axe punched down through the man's chest and exited through his splintered ribs. Ronan fell with the effort and I pushed on over the ruined corpse to aid Ruaidri.

I thrust forward with my blade, hoping the man would be too distracted by Ruaidri, but the man caught my blow on his shield before parrying one of Ruaidri's hacks expertly. I was vaguely aware of Oengus striking home against his opponent and this distracted the stubborn guardsman for a split second, enough for a gap to appear. I thrust my blade through the opening and felt it cut through the man's thigh and glance off the bone. The man groaned at the pain and fell to one knee as Ruaidri tried to finish him off, but he parried again. God he was a stubborn bastard.

He parried another of Ruaidri's thrusts and forced me backwards with his shield before a dull metallic clunk sounded and the man crumpled. Oengus had split the man's helmet and skull with his short axe and stooped to drag the weapon free.

"Get that bloody door open!" I screamed at Ruaidri and Oengus, for there was no time to waste. Bjorgolf trotted up to me and swore loudly, the tip of his blade had shattered during his fight with the big warrior. I glanced over to where the big warrior lay motionless; his head a bloody mess of shattered bone and brain matter.

Bjorgolf followed my gaze and shrugged. "Bastard shattered my blade so I had to beat him to death with it instead. Stubborn bugger wouldn't die so I had to cave his stupid bloody skull in."

Ronan, spent from the fight, had propped himself against the wall and nursed his wounded shoulder. Bjorgolf grunted that I would be bloody well lost without his common sense and I watched as the big Dane scooped up Ronan's axe. Bjorgolf shouted for Ruaidri and Oengus to move and swung the fearsome weapon at the bedchamber's door, which rocked in its hinges and began to splinter easily. We only had moments left and I muttered a prayer for Bjorgolf's axe to serve its purpose quickly. And I had my wish.

A lucky strike smashed through a gap in the door's timber and shattered the bar that locked the door. A loud female scream sounded from behind the door as Bjorgolf booted it open. The Dane thundered into the bedchamber and I followed with Ruaidri and Oengus.

A middle aged woman, still in her bed gown, cowered behind Gofraid. The King of Duibhlinn muttered incoherently as he shielded his Queen. Gofraid was an ageing man of average height with greying black hair. He sweated profusely from the brow as he braced himself for our attack. He held his small round-shield strongly but his blade shook uncontrollably in his hand, betraying his fear.

He eyed my beaten, blood-encrusted and unforgiving face and shuddered. I stepped forward and raised my blade and snarled at the frightened monarch. "This is for Sitric, you bastard."

I struck with all the speed I could muster and the King clumsily raised his shield just in time, glancing my strike wide, but the force knocked him off balance. I shouldered into him as he struggled to keep his balance and he sprawled onto the large bed of furs in the centre of the room. Gofraid yelped in fear as he narrowly avoided another blow, discarding his shield as he rolled free. I bounded to the front of the bed and then he came at me. He struck like a cornered, desperate and frightened animal and I parried his blade well before swinging my sword upwards. Gofraid screamed in agony as my blade severed his sword arm half way between his elbow and hand. His wife screamed in horror as her husband's severed limb slapped to the ground. Gofraid fell to the floor staring at the bloody stump in horror as blood sprayed horrifically from the wound.

I towered over him and spat. "This is for all the wrongs you have ever dealt." I gripped my blade in both hands and held it over his breast. He shook his head and whimpered as the blade rose. "For Sitric," I said loud enough for him to hear and thrust the blade down.

Gofraid's wife screamed uncontrollably as I withdrew my blade from the dead King. Ruaidri thumped her in the jaw to silence her, but she would not be quiet. He threatened her with his blade until I cut across. "Leave her; I'm sure Muirchertach will find a use for the stupid bitch."

Her wailing would not stop and it only got worse as I took Oengus' short axe and knelt near the King's corpse. My foster-father's nemesis was dead and I had struck off the serpent's head.

IX

Maelgwn grinned wickedly at my gruesome appearance. I was drenched in Gofraid's blood and the warm sticky liquid felt revolting on my skin. My stomach churned and it took a huge effort of will power not to show my weakness by retching or vomiting. Gofraid's head was surprisingly heavy as it pulled on my belt. I had wrapped the dead king's head in his own bedclothes and had secured the grotesque package to my belt. An arrow zipped over the courtyard wall and clattered on the ground and another one followed suit, almost hitting Bjorgolf in the shoulder.

"That was too bloody close," Bjorgolf grumbled. "We need to get the hell out of here or we'll be dead men soon enough." Oengus and Ruaidri muttered their agreement as they supported Ronan's weight between them.

Maelgwn nodded his agreement. "You lot have the right of it, we need to leave. Now." Maelgwn's men had stripped all the corpses of worth and seemed more than pleased with their plunder. A few sported new weapons or mail but were more than happy to leave when Maelgwn gave the order.

My pouch weighed heavily, almost full to overflowing with the wealth I had plundered from Gofraid's bedchamber. Bjorgolf had discovered a strongbox, which he had prized open, containing a hoard of silver coins and I had allowed the men to take as much as they could carry in their pouches; naturally after I had helped myself to the largest share. Gofraid's fine sword also hung from my belt. The expertly crafted steel would serve a useful purpose.

Maelgwn barked more orders and the helwyr fired a volley down the street, which was rewarded with several screams of pain. The men I had left to guard the courtyard gate were still in position as Maelgwn barked orders at them in the strange Powysian dialect of Briton and the rest of his men began to form a marching column. The men smartly started forward and then began to trot down a narrow street which ran down the right side of the hillock on which Gofraid's hall stood.

As we joined the column and followed the rest of Maelgwn's men down the street the sound of a hastily organised pursuit quickened our pace. The gap-toothed *helwyr* put two of his fingers to his mouth and whistled sharply as a roar sounded from behind us. The *helwyr* nimbly filtered out of the column and formed up behind us before loosing a volley at the men leading the enemy pursuit. I did not need to see if they found their targets; the screams and yelps of pain said it all. I risked a glance over my shoulder and saw the enemy diving for cover as another volley of well aimed arrows hit home. I muttered a silent prayer of thanks as our column, with the *helwyr* in close pursuit, reached the bottom of the hillock and turned left further into the dark rabbit warren of Duibhlinn's streets.

The gap-toothed *helwyr* called his men to a halt again and they unleashed another frightening volley up the street which dropped five pursuers and caused a few to jump for cover. Again I risked a glance over my shoulder to see the archers loose more of their deadly shafts, plucking a finely dressed man from a horse. Cries of outrage and despair sounded behind us as the enemy pursuit shuddered to a halt and the men gathered around their fallen *Jarl*. The gap-toothed *helwyr* whistled for his men to follow and sprinted down the street after our column.

The column turned sharply to the left down an alleyway. Gofraid's severed head thumped repeatedly against my thigh with every stride, making me wish I had left the bastard's head attached to his shoulders. We darted down another alley and then another before coming out onto a dark street. My ribs ached from the exertion; all I wanted to do was rest, but there was no time. The column came to the end of the street and turned left on to a track which ran parallel to the An Liffe's bank and the harbour.

The sound of pursuit had long since been lost and Maelgwn ordered the column to march calmly to his ships. A dark row of ships' hulls loomed imperiously along the An Liffe's bank. We passed ship after ship until we came to what seemed like the centre of the beached vessels. Maelgwn halted the column and whispered orders sharply at the man stationed at the ship's bow. The man, suddenly disturbed from his tired thoughts muttered a curse and a threat until he realised he spoke to his master. A few of Maelgwn's men chuckled at the hapless sentry, who now scuttled off to do his master's bidding.

The scarred face turned to me, fixed with a triumphant grin. "We seem to have done it." As his eyes dropped to the blood encrusted rags at my waist, which contained Gofraid's head, the Powysian's expression became serious. "How does it feel to kill a king I wonder?" The rhetorical question did not need an answer as the triumphant grin suddenly returned. "Now we wait a couple of hours for first light and then see what the day brings."

I nodded as enthusiastically as I could at the plan. There was not much else we could do, but wait. There was still no sign of the sunrise. But, soon I knew we would discover whether Muirchertach's gamble had been successful. Those thoughts plagued my mind with doubt as I regained my breath.

Bjorgolf clapped me on the shoulder. "Well done, lad." That was all he needed to say, his evident pride said everything. The sentry had returned to the ship's bow and held out an arm for Maelgwn to haul himself up. The sentry on the ship opposite did likewise and it was not long before the Powysians were scrambling up the sides of their ships and Maelgwn beckoned for me to follow. I gripped his forearm as he helped to haul me up the side of the closest boat. I cursed as I lost my footing on the vessel's deck and bumped down on to a hard rowing bench below, earning a chuckle from a few or Maelgwn's men.

Bjorgolf and the rest of my men aided Ronan, who cursed loudly at the pain in his shoulder, up the side of the ship. The big Irishman sighed with relief as his arse hit the wooden deck. He was pleased to finally get some attention to his wound. Bjorgolf knelt by the ugly Irishman and examined the sticky mess of his shoulder. Ruaidri grinned at his brother happily, proud of how well his kinsman had fought, before shaking his head in mock disapproval. "That's what you get you clumsy oaf. Too slow you are."

That was the best Ruaidri would offer his brother in the way of praise and I knew it. Ronan eyed his brother seriously, wondering whether his brother truly mocked him or not. After a few moments Ronan shrugged his shoulders as he came to a conclusion and offered his best in terms of thanks to his brother. "Piss off you bloody rascal before my clumsy fist improves your features."

We all laughed. We had done it. We had achieved our goal and, for now, we were safe. Relief washed over me as I stared at the cloudy night sky, wondering what the next day would bring. I subconsciously made sure Gofraid's head was still at my side and that my pouch, full of silver coins, had not disappeared. In the next few hours we would know whether or not Muirchertach's plan had worked. Then sleep took me.

I cursed as Bjorgolf nudged me awake. "Shit, how long have I been asleep?" I stared at the distant skyline and knew it could not have been for long. But the first signs of light were beginning to show in the east.

"Not long," Bjorgolf replied. "You looked buggered so I thought I'd let you get a few moments sleep. You are my lord after all; don't want you getting me killed just because you're bloody tired." He chuckled softly at his own jest.

"Thank you," I replied, for I did not know what else to say. Ronan snored loudly next to me; there was no sign of Maelgwn. Most of his men slept but a few kept watch. Oengus stirred beside Ronan and swore as he cleared his throat. Ruaidri was drinking heavily with one of Maelgwn's men and bartering a deal over an item of jewellery he had forced from Gofraid's Queen. The men deserved some rest and I was happy to let them have it.

Bjorgolf's elbow nudged my tender ribs and I cursed loudly in his direction. "Sorry," he said dismissively. "But something is happening over there." He pointed down the An Liffe's bank where torch light illuminated a column of men marching along the same track which we had used earlier. Seagulls, disturbed from their rest, screeched their displeasure loudly as they circled in the air before floating back down to rest on roof tops and shipping. My hand instinctively went for my sword hilt as I began to fear the worst. Had we been discovered?

Footsteps sounded on the timber behind me as Maelgwn worked his way to our position from the end of the ship. He did not say a word as he stared at the approaching column. Before they drew level with our ship a voice barked orders in Danish. My heart seemed to stop beating as I waited anxiously to see what they would do. The column, double the size ours had been, shuddered to a halt and the Danish mercenaries stepped forward. I let out a sigh of relief as they made for the four longships to our left and began to scramble aboard.

Bjorgolf called down to them in Danish. "Hey there!" He waved to get a man's attention on the opposite ship. "What are you lot doing?"

"Have you not heard?" The man called back. "Gofraid is dead. His *Jarls* are refusing to pay for our sword arms until we have fought. But we took what was owed from them." The man sounded delighted to be leaving. "Gofraid promised to pay us to serve him. Now he is dead, why should we risk our lives in this futile war?"

I could not help but grin and my spirits soared. The mercenaries were leaving and Gofraid's *Jarls* were struggling to exert their authority over these men whom they so desperately needed. It appeared Muirchertach's risky and elaborate gamble might well be paying off.

Bjorgolf was equally pleased. "I wish you luck, brother," he shouted across at the man. Maelgwn did not have a good grasp of the Danish tongue and demanded to know what had been said. Bjorgolf translated the man's words to Maelgwn, who made a rumbling noise which I guessed passed for approval.

More men appeared on the banks of the An Liffe and boarded their ships. We watched for the next hour as men boarded their longships, abandoning Duibhlinn to its fate. The river was still swollen from the persistent rainfall we had endured for the last several weeks, so I watched in high spirits as mercenaries backed their oars and sailed their ships down river towards the sea. The sun was beginning to rise in the distance as night turned to day and I knew Muirchertach's assault could not be far away. I crossed myself and hoped his scouts had spotted the Danish ships cutting their way through the An Liffe's powerful current, towards the sea which lay a short distance to the east.

Maelgwn strolled across the deck, glancing towards a departing warship which had just finished backing oars and was preparing to head down river. A heavy hand clapped my shoulder. "It seems your King Muirchertach was right. Gofraid's *Jarls* are buggered." He laughed admiringly at the grand scheme Muirchertach had plotted. "We can make our way to the walls, I think. There we can see what happens. And, perhaps, you can reap the rewards."

Bjorgolf clapped my back fondly and my men grinned happily at the thought of what rewards were to come. Maelgwn snapped orders at his men and they began to gather their wargear before jumping down from the ships onto the soggy mud of the An Liffe's bank.

As the sun rose above the horizon light began to sweep over the land. Duibhlinn, shocked by the news of their king's death, waited anxiously for what fate had in store for them this day. Maelgwn ordered his banner unfurled as we approached the main gate. The yellow cloth snapped in the wind and the rampant red lion, with its blue claws and tongue, seemed menacing. Maelgwn's banner was that of his family, the rulers of Powys, the banner of the house of Mathrafal. His men quickened their step and puffed out their chests with pride under the bright banner.

Again I felt my hands subconsciously checking that Gofraid's head was still secure to my belt along with all my plunder. Something I instantly regretted as my fingers probed the crusted blood on the tatty cloth, sending a shudder down my spine. My whole body still ached from the night's events and my eyes weighed heavily. I could not help but look at Maelgwn's banner and his men with envy. This is what I wanted, my men to march under my banner, a banner as grand as that of Mathrafal.

Bjorgolf noticed my gaze and chuckled softly. "You need to get yourself one of them." He nodded at the banner and pushed the point further. "All great lords have one and you should be no different. You come from a royal house like him," he nodded at Maelgwn. "So, don't you have one?"

The question stirred the hatred in my heart and for a moment I wanted to lash out at something. I shook my head at the shame of it, for I did not know. Maelgwn had told me that his banner was that of the royal house of Powys. He had told me with such evident pride but I felt nothing but jealousy. My father had died in exile and the only banner I had ever truly known was Sitric's black raven on its white

109

field. Bjorgolf looked at me expectantly and I met his gaze.

"I do not know, I truly don't." Bjorgolf looked surprised but the tone of my voice betrayed my feelings. "Both my mother and father died when I was young. No one has ever told me and I never asked." My embarrassment was evident and Bjorgolf clapped my shoulder in apology. I would find out, I promised myself. My thoughts had been so preoccupied with the hope of returning to the lands of Gwynedd that I had not even devised my own banner, something most lords took great pride in doing. Most inherited their banners from their fathers, but not me. The shame of my father's exile burned deeply within my heart, I had taken an oath before almighty God that I would not suffer a similar fate; and I knew that I would reclaim my family's honour.

The streets were thronged with nervous townsfolk and equally nervous warriors who awaited news of their fate. The sun had risen; it would be a bright autumn's day I thought. The ever-present smell of sewerage dominated the senses as we approached the street on which the main gate lay. The nervous crowd parted to let our disciplined column of men pass, but we still made slow progress.

As we approached, the gate opened and a group of horsemen under a white banner clattered through. We halted as the crowd pressed forwards and surrounded the horsemen. It was difficult to hear oneself think as the crowd chattered expectantly amongst themselves. Maelgwn's men pushed members of the crowd with their shields and cuffed a few round the ears to make sure we did not become pressed by the throng.

A well dressed warrior in a fine coat of mail, which dropped to his knees, addressed the crowd as I looked on. He spoke in Danish and his voice was full of nothing but despair. "We have surrendered the town to the Irish." A collective groan went through the waiting crowd. The man continued in his monotonous tone, dejected by defeat and shame. "None of you loyal men shall be harmed, by promise of the Lord Muirchertach. All *Jarls* are to pay homage to Muirchertach or face the consequences." With that the man dug his heels into his mount and pushed his way through the mob as the other horsemen followed. He glanced curiously at me as he rode past and soon disappeared into the town. The nervous crowd began to disperse and the gates remained open as triumphant war horns blew from Muirchertach's camp. Individuals and groups scattered from the crowd and into town, undoubtedly to hide their valuables from Muirchertach's victorious forces, for although he had promised not to harm any of the townsfolk, few were foolish enough to believe some of his victorious army would not go in search of plunder.

As our column reached the open gates Maelgwn clasped my forearm in friendship. "You must go to Muirchertach's camp alone. I shall return to my ships and there, I shall await word." His grip was very tight on my forearm as he continued. "You and your small band fought well. You fought like true Britons." His face contorted into another wicked grin, which was clearly meant for friendship but resembled nothing more than a snarl on such a horrifically formed face.

"Thank you, I shall not forget this." I released the grip and turned to walk away. I smiled at the triumph and called over my shoulder. "Just don't ever let me catch you sneaking over a wall. For I may have to improve your looks." My small band of battered, bloody and tired men laughed as did Maelgwn.

I trudged through the open gate and followed the road from Duibhlinn conscious of the blood crusted package tied to my belt. Muirchertach's army had begun to descend upon Duibhlinn, cheering victoriously, but I did not see Muirchertach himself. Faelan had passed my small band, under his green and orange striped banner, and did not even acknowledge our presence as he trotted his fine mount past. Perhaps the pompous bastard simply did not notice a small band of five dirty, weary, men who more resembled vagabonds than warriors.

We made for the grand tent in the centre of Muirchertach's camp, which still stood majestically. The commander of the guard demanded to know who we were and what our business was. He didn't seem to trust anything I said, but a croaky old voice sounded from behind the entrance to the tent. "I recognise that voice, Captain," Father Cathal hobbled out of the tent, using a staff for support. "That is all," he ordered the commander of the guard who, eyeing us suspiciously reluctantly moved aside. Father Cathal signalled for me to follow him into the musky interior of the tent.

Sections of the tent had been stripped bare and only Father Cathal's compartment remained. "Follow me, Gruffudd, but your men must stay here." His voice betrayed no emotion and so I ordered Bjorgolf and the rest to wait outside. I followed Father Cathal into his compartment and was amazed by its simplicity. It was very plain and contained only a small cot and a writing desk with a simple wooden stool.

Father Cathal sat on the stool and eyed me curiously. "I take it that Fergus is dead, seeing as he is not in attendance?" The question wasn't really a question at all, but a statement. He tutted softly as I shook my head. "His death is regrettable, but he was expendable." Father Cathal's voice was cold, "So then, as I can see, you succeeded. Tell me how."

So I recounted the tale of Fergus' death and our capture. I informed him of Maelgwn's decision to switch sides and his reasons for it. I told him of our advance to Gofraid's hall and the assault which followed. I told of Gofraid's death and our retreat to Maelgwn's ships. "And here I am," I ended the tale.

Father Cathal had listened patiently and seemed completely unfazed by the trials and tribulations I had endured during that night. He pointed his walking staff at the bloody package still tied to my waist. He stared at it curiously as flies buzzed around the dry blood. "I take it that is the proof of your success?"

"Indeed," was all I could manage as I loosened the ties which fastened the proof to my belt. I strode forward a couple of paces and untied the filthy cloth. I watched Father Cathal slowly as I unwrapped the contents and let Gofraid's severed head drop on to the table. Father Cathal betrayed no emotion as he inspected the gruesome trophy, prodding it several times with his walking staff.

Again he moved the head with his staff, before commenting dryly. "That is Gofraid, sure enough. Well done." That was all Father Cathal said as I stood still for a long while as he sat there in deep thought.

I began to grow impatient as the waiting stretched on and the old monk just sat there, seemingly forgetting my existence. I fidgeted slightly and that seemed to bring Father Cathal's thoughts back to me.

"I suggest you go and get some sleep. For this afternoon Muirchertach will be crowned King of Duibhlinn and rule these lands in his father's name." Father Cathal paused, seemingly examining my reaction. I tried my best not to show any emotion. All I felt was tiredness. "This evening a great feast will be held in the royal hall, all notables are invited. Which includes you." He seemed to add the last words begrudgingly. "Muirchertach will be overjoyed by the day's events and will reward you greatly I am sure."

I looked at Father Cathal, as he seemed ready to say more. But the wicked old monk descended into a coughing fit and swung his walking stick towards the door. I turned to go, but his harsh voice called behind me.

113

"Take that bloody thing with you!" He swiped his walking staff across the table and knocked Gofraid's head towards me. It made a sickening thump as it hit the floor and rolled grotesquely to stop at my feet. "Now be gone, get some rest." I wrapped Gofraid's head in the disgusting rags which had once been his bedclothes and turned to leave. Father Cathal's voice called behind me. "Be at the royal hall at dusk."

I stepped out of the musky compartment and into the sunlight where Bjorgolf and the rest of my men waited. From there we headed to where Sitric's men had been camped.

Some of Sitric's men were still there under Cerit's command and he looked aghast at my appearance. "My God, you look like you've been dragged face down across the whole of Ireland!" Cerit shook his head in genuine concern.

"I am well enough brother; does it not improve my looks?" The men laughed at the jest. The camp was in high spirits after the bloodless victory and congratulations were in quick supply for myself and my tired men.

Cerit eyed the bloody package warily. "What the hell is in that?" He pointed at the blood-soaked rags and tried not to grimace as Gofraid's head tumbled out and onto the muddy floor. "Jesus Christ!" Cerit blasphemed before crossing himself.

"Where are father and Wselfwulf?" I demanded. Cerit gestured vaguely towards Duibhlinn as he curiously inspected the head.

"This is Gofraid's head?" He enquired and seemed pleased when I confirmed that it was. "I shall send it to father, he shall be most pleased." Cerit enthusiastically put an arm round my shoulders and ordered one of his men to take the hideous trophy to Sitric in the town. "You must rest brother. I wager you shall sleep for a week!"

"I cannot afford to sleep for a week," I replied, perhaps too harshly. "Tonight I attend Muirchertach's feast after his crowning." I did not much look forward to the prospect of feasting, drinking and making polite conversation. I knew my tone of voice had betrayed as much, not that it deterred Cerit.

He beamed a delighted smile at me. "Excellent, I shall be there too. I will wake you shortly before I leave." He looked me up and down and laughed. "On second thoughts, I shall have to wake you well before we leave; you look like hell. There will be ale to drink and women to chase! You must look acceptable, brother!"

I could not help but laugh and then strode over to where Bjorgolf and my men rested. Ronan and Oengus were already asleep and Ruaidri regaled the others with his tale of the night's events.

Bjorgolf eyed me wearily. "You did well, lad. Very well." He seemed genuinely proud and that brought a smile to my face. "Just a bloody shame my blade is buggered after that fight in the hall." He drew his blade and, true enough, the tip of it was bent slightly and nicks had been taken out of the sharp edge. It was in a sorry state and I smiled broadly at him. "What the hell are you smiling at? It's not bloody funny, that blade has served me well for years."

I laughed and remembered why I had taken Gofraid's expertly wrought sword. I untied it from my belt. Bjorgolf recognised the worth of such a blade and broke into the broadest grin I have ever seen. "This is for you, my friend." I said, trying to keep my emotions in check. "You served me well today, just don't bloody break this one as well."

The men laughed as Bjorgolf inspected his new blade with evident pride. None could deny that the big Dane deserved such a reward. I opened my pouch and passed some of the silver coins to Ruaidri and he nodded his appreciation. "I'll give the other two their share when they are awake." That was all I could say as I lowered myself to the ground. I longed for the overdue rest which was to come and ordered Bjorgolf to send word to Maelgwn to meet me at the royal hall at dusk. The prospect of the celebrations and feast to come did not put a smile on my face as I lay wrapped in my cloak. No, my mind was fixed solely on Gwynedd. This summer, I told myself again and again. This summer I shall set sail for Gwynedd. I allowed my thoughts to wander but sleep took me quickly.

X

Cerit looked me up and down before smiling to himself. He let out a small chuckle and eyed me mockingly. "You don't look too bad, brother. I shall make a fine example of you yet."

I guffawed sarcastically back at Cerit, who laughed even more at the scowl I shot in his direction. He had persuaded me to borrow some of his spare clothes, which were a perfect fit. I wore a dark red tunic, which was gaudily decorated with golden braid around the collar and the cuffs. The darkly chequered breeches went well with the tunic and I borrowed Cerit's spare cloak, which was dark green and expertly made.

Cerit seemed very pleased with my appearance and beamed another smile at me. "Just a shame I can't do anything about your looks, eh?"

I chuckled at the jest and nodded my agreement. "Well, I cannot disagree with you there." The beating I had taken from Maelgwn and his men still ached like hell. My cracked lips had swollen and throbbed continuously. I had thought my nose broken but Bjorgolf had declared it wasn't, but that did not stop it hurting like a bastard. My left eye had swollen shut and was so tender I did not dare touch it. My right eye had a nasty gash along the eyebrow and a nasty looking cut was beginning to heal under it. I must have looked terrible, I felt it too. But I was pleased I had lost no teeth and hadn't had many bones broken although my ribs ached with every breath and I was sure several must be cracked.

The sun was setting as I worked my way through the celebrations in Duibhlinn's streets. I walked with Cerit and he took great pleasure in recounting Muirchertach's crowning ceremony which had taken place hours earlier during the early-afternoon. The streets were thronged with townsfolk and soldiers alike, some drinking themselves insensible. Others seeking more pleasurable activities in the town's taverns and whorehouses.

It seemed that few mourned Gofraid's passing. Many sang Muirchertach's praises and drank their ale to his name. Night was beginning to set on Duibhlinn's new era and the people celebrated what was to come, or perhaps they celebrated the fact they had not seen their property pillaged by a rampaging victorious army.

I walked alongside Cerit as we strode up the street which, only hours earlier, had been littered with dead and dying men as Maelgwn's helwyr loosed volley after volley at the men attempting to come to Gofraid's aid. The street had been cleaned up well; there was no evidence of spent arrows or dried blood. Cerit listened with interest as I recounted the scenes this street had witnessed during my desperate attempt to get to Gofraid. As we neared the gateway of the royal hall Cerit announced our identities to the guardsmen, who allowed us to pass with hardly a second glance. I felt a pang of regret as I stepped quickly over the spot where I had killed the youth who had so bravely tried to make a name for himself. I was thankful Cerit had not noticed me quicken my pace as I did not want to have to recount that part of the tale.

As I walked under the arch of the courtyard entrance I looked back again to where the youth had died and told myself again that the lad's death was necessary. The courtyard was full of well dressed men and women, some drinking and others socialising. Cerit halted and crossed himself as a strongly built man in his middle years approached. The face was horrifically scarred and the man wore a metal nosepiece, further adding to the devilish appearance.

His face twitched into a smile, causing Cerit to cross himself again. I chuckled at Cerit's reaction as Maelgwn approached. He, too, found Cerit's reaction amusing and nodded his head respectfully in greeting as he tried to suppress laughter.

We clasped forearms and I turned to Cerit. "I have the honour to introduce Maelgwn, son of Rhiwallon, of the royal house of Mathrafal of Powys. I owe my life to this man." Maelgwn bowed his head respectfully at my acknowledgement of the fact I was heavily in his debt.

Cerit quickly wiped the bemused expression from his face and beamed one of his customary smiles at the Powysian. "Honoured to meet you, my lord." Cerit's tone was nothing other than flattering and respectful. "If you saved my brother's life, then I too am in your debt."

Maelgwn raised an eyebrow in amusement. "I could have killed your over-confident brother instead, easily enough. In fact I still may." Cerit eyed Maelgwn warily as the Powysian let the awkward silence stretch for a few heartbeats. Maelgwn had spoken so seriously that Cerit was unsure how to take the words. "I jest of course," Maelgwn barked through a laugh. Cerit nervously joined in as I laughed at his discomfort. Maelgwn clapped an arm round my shoulder as he steered me towards the hall's entrance. "Lets find some ale then, I'm bloody well parched."

Cerit followed at my side and looked in awe as we entered the hall through the doorway. The doors had not yet been replaced and the timber was horribly splintered from where the axes had done their work hours earlier.

The hall, like the street outside, had been cleansed remarkably well. There was very little sign that a bitter and desperate battle had been fought under the great oaken roof beams. The feasting table had been cleaned and expertly repaired and was thronged with notable men and women of Muirchertach's lands. Thrall girls served ale and wine to the king's guests and tried their best not to flinch as drunken men groped their bodies. Maelgwn grabbed a jug of ale from a thrall girl, who surrendered the ale without protest and shrunk away from the Powysian's scarred features.

Several discarded drinking horns and tankards littered a bench at the hall's edge as we made our way over. Maelgwn picked up a tankard before gesturing for me and Cerit to follow suit. The mercenary poured himself a generous amount of ale and passed me the jug, I filled my tankard and Cerit did the same. Maelgwn raised his ale in a toast and boomed out his customary words. "For God and Powys!"

Cerit and I raised our ale respectfully at Maelgwn's toast and the three of us drank deeply; the cool liquid was refreshing and I instantly wanted more. Maelgwn had downed his ale and finished off the jug greedily, Jesus, but the man could drink. He sat on the bench and hammered the jug several times on the timber to gain a thrall's attention.

A young thrall girl heeded Maelgwn's call and approached us happily, swaying her hips for attention. A look of shock passed over her pretty face as she took in Maelgwn's features. The devilish face blew her a kiss and she almost shied away from us, earning a harsh bout of laughter from the mercenary. But Cerit quickly intercepted her and took the jug of ale from her hands, flirting merrily. The girl blushed at Cerit's words and giggled as he slapped her rump as she turned to walk away.

Cerit admired her as she strolled away, swaying her hips again. She glanced back over her shoulder at Cerit and smiled. I clapped him fondly on the shoulder. "Chasing the women already are you, brother?"

Cerit blushed as Maelgwn barked a laugh and poured himself more ale. "What a fine looking thing she is." Cerit looked longingly at her retreating figure again, before turning his friendly smile back to me. "I think I stand a good chance, perhaps the company I keep makes my looks more attractive to the ladies."

I could not help but laugh and Maelgwn

sarcastically joined in. "Why? Are you saying I am ugly?" The mercenary shot Cerit a threatening glance, causing him to apologise immediately. The mercenary continued to stare menacingly at Cerit and let the awkward silence continue as Cerit shifted uncomfortably on his feet. The mercenary slammed his fist on the bench, making Cerit jump, and barked laughter. "You are more nervous than a virgin on her wedding night!"

I laughed as Cerit's face flushed with embarrassment. "I meant no offence," he stammered as Maelgwn downed another generous amount of ale.

"I jest, you fool," the Powysian mocked. "Between my scars and Gruffudd's purple swollen eye, you must look like an angel." Cerit chuckled dutifully and eyed the mercenary warily. Cerit so clearly did not know how to take Maelgwn and that amused me, although I too was still getting used to the man's blunt character and odd sense of humour.

I cursed as I looked over Cerit's shoulder, causing Cerit to turn and stare. He too cursed as he turned back. Maelgwn eyed the approaching figure, before greedily gulping down another large amount of ale. "You two look like you've seen the devil."

I turned and fixed Maelgwn with a worried expression. "The devil may just be right." The Powysian chuckled at my words, but I did not jest, for Father Cathal approached.

The old monk's walking staff clunked on the stone floor as he approached with a short, overweight man at his side. Father Cathal paused and eyed the three of us before shooting Cerit a cold stare. "Go away young man," he said coldly. "Go chase that thrall if that is what takes your fancy." Cerit shot me a look of pity and he needed no encouragement to escape Father Cathal's presence. Maelgwn chuckled at Cerit's flight, which brought a flash of anger across the old monk's face.

Maelgwn casually glanced at Father Cathal, before looking away and spitting a mouthful of phlegm at the stone floor. Father Cathal eyed the mercenary threateningly. "Tell me, whom do I have the displeasure of meeting?" The old monk's voice was cold and threatening as I stood awkwardly between the two. Maelgwn did not respond and I could feel the hatred radiating off the old monk. I silently cursed Maelgwn, for Father Cathal was a very dangerous man and one you would do well not to offend.

Maelgwn rose slowly and downed the remaining contents of his tankard before fixing Father Cathal with a stare of pure malice that threatened imminent violence. The old monk did not flinch but met the stare and replied in-kind. I looked at the overweight man to Father Cathal's side who stared at the ground. That was the best strategy I thought, try and remain anonymous as Father Cathal still stared at Maelgwn. It was like two of the devil's henchmen squaring up to each other.

Father Cathal raised his walking staff and went to strike Maelgwn on the arm, but the mercenary reacted with frightening speed and gripped the walking staff firmly. Father Cathal eyed the Powysian with pure hatred as he feebly tried to release his staff from Maelgwn's vice like grip. Maelgwn pulled sharply on the staff, forcing Father Cathal to release the cane and fight for his balance. I held out an arm, which the old monk grabbed to steady himself.

Father Cathal continued to grip my arm for support and spat at Maelgwn. "Give me back my staff, you heathen scum." I shot Maelgwn a worried expression as he raised the walking staff. He looked as though he would snap the wooden prop over his knee. I shook my head desperately. Maelgwn noticed my warning and simply shrugged his shoulders, letting the staff clatter to the floor. The Powysian nodded at me and turned on his heel. Maelgwn grabbed another jug of ale and drank the contents as he strolled out of the hall and into the courtyard.

I stooped to retrieve Father Cathal's staff and the old monk snatched it from me. "You keep unsavoury company, Gruffudd son of Cynan. Tell me, who was that man. I shall break him." The old monk spoke menacingly and I could not help but feel uncomfortable under the man's gaze.

"His name is Maelgwn, son of Rhiwallon. He is of the royal house of Mathrafal, the family that rules the Briton Kingdom of Powys. He is most useful, I assure you, for, were it not for him, I would be dead and Gofraid might still rule here." I had done my best to spare Maelgwn from Father Cathal's wrath, but I still cursed the Powysian for making an enemy out of the dangerous old cleric.

The monk eyed me knowingly and nodded. "I shall spare him any misfortune then." I did not trust Father Cathal's word and doubted the wicked old man would let this incident go unpunished. The monk spluttered horribly, wiping his sleeve across his wrinkled face.

The old monk gestured at the man to his side. "This is Finan, a lord of Leinster. He is married to the sister of Gofraid's recently deceased queen." Father Cathal crossed himself at the mention of the queen's death. I had ordered her unharmed and assumed Father Cathal was probably responsible for the woman's passing. "He is a loyal ally of King Muirchertach and seeks to repent for his family's sins."

I fixed Finan with a blank expression as I assessed the man before me. He was at least a head shorter than I and his face was dominated by thick jowls and he was cleanly shaven. His short cropped black hair was balding and had receded badly. I judged him to be well past his fortieth year and glanced at his rotund physique. The man's green eyes were puffy and watery, he had clearly been weeping and his face was full of sorrow.

Father Cathal's face broke into a malicious grin as he went on. "He seeks to repent as his son fought for Gofraid, you see." Finan nodded at Father Cathal's words and the old monk was clearly enjoying recounting the tale. "His son was a favourite of Gofraid's, seeing as the heathen bastard had sired no sons of his own, legitimate ones at any rate. He looked upon Finan's son as one of his own and treated him fondly."

Finan's eyes began to water again as Father Cathal shot him a glance full of distaste. "It was the folly of youth. Gofraid promised him he could be a prince if he fought well against Muirchertach. He was so young, but did not act with my permission." Finan blurted the statement out and quickly fell silent as Father Cathal raised one of his calloused hands to silence the man's blabbing.

"As I was saying," the old monk cleared his throat. "Gofraid promised the little brat that he would be his successor." Father Cathal raised his hand again to silence Finan's protest at his words. "The impudent child only went and took his father's warband and answered Gofraid's call to arms." Father Cathal shot Finan a look of disgust at the man's weakness. Indeed the incident did not say much for Finan's authority and ability as a lord.

It was clear that Finan was no warrior or leader of men. His jowls wobbled as he sobbed silently and Father Cathal, insensitively, continued to recount the tale of the shame his son had brought on his family.

Father Cathal grinned spitefully as he continued. "So, you see, last night when an unknown assailant descended on Gofraid's hall, this hall here in fact," Father Cathal gestured vaguely about him. "Finan's son, the aspiring princeling, tried to come to Gofraid's aid. My informants tell me he was cut down mercilessly in single-combat. They tell me he had been challenged by a fearsome warrior, who perhaps should have let the young lad live." Father Cathal seemed amused by the tale. "The lad was only fifteen you see. Such a shame, Muirchertach would have reconciled him, so he would. What kind of a cutthroat would cut down such a young lad, eh?"

I silently cursed the old monk, who looked innocently back at me. The youth's bravery flashed back at me; the stupid bastard should have retreated. I felt another pang of regret as I remembered my blade biting into his neck and his eyes widening in horror, his blood spraying from the wound and onto my face. My heart filled with sorrow for the young lad. But it was necessary, I told myself. It was necessary.

Father Cathal coughed silently to tell me he still expected an answer. I cursed the old bastard again in my head, as I stammered an answer. "It sounds as though he died bravely and with dignity." That was all I managed and Finan bowed his head in respect at my words. Shit, but all I felt was guilt. Should I have spared the young lad? No. His death was necessary to get to Gofraid. His death was but a steppingstone on my quest to Gwynedd.

Father Cathal's bony ribcage shuddered as another coughing fit took hold. The bastard deserved it and I smiled as he struggled to halt the spluttering and did my best to ignore the disgusting concoction of phlegm and spittle that dribbled from the corner of his mouth. He turned to face Finan. "Leave us," the old monk ordered as he waved his walking staff to emphasise the command. Finan bowed his head and walked away. I felt the anger rise in my chest as Father Cathal wrapped his free right arm around mine and began to guide me towards the top table at the back of the hall.

The walking staff clunked on the stone. "Did you kill the lad then?" He did not wait for an answer. "Of course you did. Not much happens without my knowing." The old monk coughed again and paused, waiting for another coughing fit to take hold. He muttered his thanks to God when one did not. "Finan is a fat, slimy, bastard so he is. But a wealthy one, very wealthy in fact." Father Cathal paused in front of the top table and turned to face me. "Beware of wealthy enemies Gruffudd. If you ever give me cause to doubt you, or your intentions, just remember I could make your life very difficult."

I wanted to strike the old bastard but just nodded my acknowledgment of his threat. I silently cursed Maelgwn again. Why did he have to goad Father Cathal in such a way? Bloody hell, I hoped another coughing fit would take the old monk and send him to hell. A familiar voice boomed across the hall as Father Cathal hobbled away. "Ah! There you are, Gruffudd come here!"

Muirchertach looked resplendent in his royal clothes. He was expensively clad and looked majestic as he enjoyed his ale and the finest feast that could be assembled. The King of Munster and, now, of Duibhlinn, beamed a broad smile at me. He was five years my senior and was strongly built from the hours of sword practice he insisted upon taking daily. Sitric sat to his left and raised a tankard of ale in salute, I nodded back and Sitric beamed a proud smile at me. Faelan sat to the king's right and shot me a sour glance before looking away to talk to an elderly man at his side.

"You shall be rewarded greatly Gruffudd! Greatly indeed!" Muirchertach was merry from the ale he had consumed and the joy of victory added to his good mood. "Your foster-father is most proud, most proud, are you not?" He nudged Sitric heartily and Sitric nodded his agreement. "I have acquired you a small hall in Duibhlinn. It seems its owner was killed last night whilst perusing a band of killers. Most distressing. Anyway his family has disappeared so it is yours. It shall serve you well when you wish to stay in this fine town!"

"Thank you, my King." I smiled happily and ignored the pain in my bruised face, for I was wealthier yet again. My thoughts wondered at the wealth I could now amass and what kind of a force I could take with me to Gwynedd.

Muirchertach's voice rumbled again from the high seat where he was slumped casually. "Father Cathal shall give you the details. Now enjoy yourself tonight, for you shall hear from me again soon." I bowed respectfully and turned to leave the king's presence. My spirits rose, my heart skipped a beat and I felt invincible for all was going well.

Father Cathal had described the hall's location and I had repeated it to Cerit, so that he too could remember it if I forgot. Maelgwn had disappeared but Cerit was enjoying the celebrations and was by now very drunk. The celebrations had raged for a few hours and musicians played a quick tune, as I admired the skills of an elderly crwth player, and those still capable danced. Many of the guests had passed out or retired to their homes. But not me, I was merry from the ale and could think of nothing but preparing to set sail for Gwynedd.

Cerit sat on the bench where we had earlier sat with Maelgwn and the thrall girl he had flirted with straddled him with her arms wrapped round his neck. The two began to kiss and so I left them to it. I walked unsteadily towards the high table and found a forgotten jug of ale which I added to my tankard. The musicians began to play a slower tune as men danced with thrall girls, mistresses or wives. I made to leave but an arm grabbed me and dragged me into the mêlée of dancers.

I was about to protest until I was struck dumb by the woman's beauty. She must have been the same age as me and stood slightly shorter than I. Her long auburn hair flowed over her shoulders and down her back. She had a beautiful, freckly, face which betrayed a carefree nature and her green eyes made me freeze.

She laughed at my dumbstruck expression and took

127

my hand in hers. "Not much of a dancer are you!" She laughed mischievously as she guided me to a bench where we sat. She surveyed my bruised features and asked with genuine concern. "My God, but you have taken a rare beating. Who did this to you?"

"I got it last night," I stammered and reddened as she giggled at my awkwardness. I had bedded many thrall girls but I had never felt my heart quicken such and my knees weaken at the sight of a woman.

"Tell me how." She demanded and listened excitedly to my tale. I told her the whole tale, my tongue loosened by the ale, from start to finish of my mission to kill Gofraid and my escape from the hall, not a day ago. She placed her hand on my thigh and looked into my eyes. "You must be Gruffudd then. I thought you must be I saw you with that horrible monk earlier." She smiled shyly, "I have heard of you. My brother regards you fondly, not that he confides much in me though."

I could not help but smile. "You have heard of me?" I laughed as she nodded, "good things I hope. Tell me, who is your brother?" I was too bashful to ask her name and judged that I might know who she was from her brother's name.

"You have probably heard of him," she said mischievously. "He is Muirchertach, King of Munster and now King of Duibhlinn." She laughed as I gawped at her. She cuffed me playfully round my ear as I stammered apologies. "What have you to be sorry for? All we have done is talk; there is no scandal in that."

Her carefree attitude made me even more uncomfortable. "Your brother is one of the most powerful men in Ireland and a man I respect. I should not be talking to you, especially as I do not know your name." I apologised immediately as she looked as though she had taken offence.

She quickly laughed, making her even more

attractive. "Oh, don't be such a bore!" She mockingly slapped my shoulder, "I thought you were a brave warrior, full of adventure and confidence. Yet you seem dumbstruck by a woman talking to you."

"Not just any woman," I blurted out and reddened immediately. She laughed and looked at me mischievously.

"Do not be embarrassed. I only wish to have a conversation with you, not elope with you!" She giggled at her own jest and my evident embarrassment. "My name is Orlaith and I think you are a very interesting person, Gruffudd, although my husband to be would not agree."

My heart sank for she was betrothed. "May I ask to whom you are promised?" I asked the question awkwardly and I could not hide the jealousy from my voice.

"His name is Faelan." My spirits fell even further; the bastard did not deserve such a woman. She looked at me, shaking her head sadly. "It is not true love. In fact I do not like him much, but I must keep my brother happy. He has promised me to him, you see." She could not hide the displeasure in her voice as she continued. "My brother says he needs him and I have to marry him to keep him loyal. I don't want to but what can I do?"

I looked at her pretty face and I wanted to put my arm round her as her eyes filled with sorrow. She rose; perhaps it was for the better, before I could make any clumsy effort to comfort her. She looked down at me fondly. "You would be very handsome I think, were it not for all the bruises."

I laughed at the truth of it and was instantly silenced as she kissed my cheek softly and went. Nobody seemed to have noticed as she disappeared back into the crowd. I rose and left the hall, the cold night air refreshed my senses as I passed through the streets, stepping over more than one drunkard. My thoughts swam with Orlaith's image and I smiled all the way back to the camp, for I think I was in love.

XI

Autumn soon turned to winter as I waited for
Muirchertach's summons. The king had sent a messenger
to my small hall in Duibhlinn several weeks after the
celebrations I had attended in his honour. The messenger
had passed on Muirchertach's usual pleasantries and
informed me that he still supported my claim to Gwynedd's
throne. The messenger had also promised me that
Muirchertach would soon send for me to discuss the
proposed expedition. That was six long weeks ago. Now
the wind was strong and the air cold. I had retreated to my
vast estate of Sord Cholmcille which I had been granted
following the defeat of Gunnald months earlier. The estate
generated a handsome profit from the tenanted farmsteads
and their produce which was enough to offset the hindrance
of having to entertain a monastery full of tiresome monks
and an abbot I truly had no respect for. Ljot had proved
useful; he had maintained the hall well and had even
rounded up most of Gunnald's escaped thralls, as well as
discovering Gunnald's hidden hoard of silver.

I had granted Maelgwn permission to use my small
hall in Duibhlinn and that he was welcome to use any of the
stores he wished. The Powysian mercenary had appreciated
the offer and had soon moved in to the hall with the
majority of his men. He and his men lived there at my
expense, but that did not worry me. The Powysians had
proved their worth to me and, in part, I owed my success to
them. When I had last visited, a week earlier, Maelgwn had
turned the small courtyard into a training zone. He made
his men practice with their weapons and drilled tactics into
them. They were a fine group of warriors and I was pleased
to have them.

My men, on the other hand, had grown soft as we
wintered in Sord Cholmcille. Ljot and Ronan, who had
received flesh wounds, were fully recovered and they

regained their strength daily, which was more than can be said for the others. Oengus and Ruaidri spent their days gambling or pursuing the women of the local village. Twice Bjorgolf had had to smack their skulls together and teach them their manners.

Bjorgolf was growing frustrated at my lack of action, but that did not bother me much. I knew I would have to start getting the men battle ready and soon. But I was in no mood. The dark grey clouds and the persistent howling of the wind perfectly reflected my mood. Orlaith's image dominated my thoughts and I longed to see her again. I had become a recluse and had refused several invitations to Duibhlinn from Cerit and Sitric, on the off chance that I would have to be polite to Faelan. I was callow in those days, but soon I snapped to my senses.

One night I had a troubled dream. I dreamed of failure and slaughter. I dreamt of a windswept battlefield, littered with the dead and I woke abruptly, feeling hot and sticky. The wind howled outside and the room was cool but I sweated profusely, my hands felt clammy and my head throbbed. I drifted back in and out of consciousness all night. I could picture an unfamiliar face calling my name repeatedly, telling me I must not fail. Then my mother's voice recounted Myrddin's prophecy, loud and clear, as though she still lived.

That morning I woke feeling reinvigorated. I took a cold breakfast with my sword-brothers and then ordered them to don their wargear. Bjorgolf grinned at my renewed energy and vigour. We sweated all morning in the cold air as we practiced working as a unit and in individual combat. My muscles ached as I panted for breath, but I felt good. The sweat steamed from our warm bodies as it met the cold winter air.

Soon before midday it began to snow and the wind howled, but I made the men practice well into the afternoon until the light began to fade. This was the first time in weeks that I felt like my old self, my muscles ached from the day's exertions but I felt better for it. To my surprise none of my men grumbled, not even Oengus or Ruaidri. My small warband mirrored my feelings, they were simply glad to be active and doing something useful with their time.

The next morning I took a walk with Bjorgolf, who rubbed his hands together for warmth. The snow had blanketed the area and gleamed a perfect white as we crunched through it. The wind had vanished but dense and heavy cloud still dominated the skyline. The heavy clouds threatened more snow and Bjorgolf commented as much before deciding to bring up what had been troubling me all these weeks.

"I am glad you have stopped brooding over that woman." Bjorgolf's breath steamed as it met the cold winter air. He shook his head when I did not respond, "I was like you once you know. Head over heels in love I was." He shook his head at the memory. "She was a fine thing, a bit plump mind. But good fun."

I laughed at his words as I caught their meaning. "I am sure that she was not a king's sister though." The jealousy again burned in my heart. Faelan was a pompous bastard with a cruel heart. He could not be less suited to Orlaith if he tried. Yet she was promised to him and, for that, I cursed Muirchertach.

Bjorgolf, oblivious to my thoughts, continued. "My advice is live life. Can't harm to carry on chasing her if that's what you want." I shot Bjorgolf a surprised look; it certainly would harm my prospects if anyone found out about my feelings. "I know she is Muirchertach's sister and promised to that lump of pig shit Faelan. But just be bloody careful."

"I don't know," that was all I could manage as I let the sentence trail off. Bjorgolf took the hint and dropped the issue as we entered the woodland to the hall's west. Leaves crunched under foot as we walked through the virgin snow. The woodland floor was frozen and sticks snapped as we trekked deeper into the trees.

I stopped to admire the peacefulness of the woodland. The quiet, disturbed occasionally by a cawing crow, settled my mind and I often sought such remoteness when my mind was troubled. My thick woollen clothes and winter cloak kept my body warm but my leather boots did little to stop my toes getting cold. I wriggled them as I rubbed my hands for warmth. Bjorgolf belched, disturbing my peace but it served to bring my thoughts back to the present.

The big Dane laughed and apologised. "So do you mind telling me why you have dragged me out to this bloody place? Why couldn't we have talked by a fire with a nice draught of ale, eh?"

I ignored the jest, "I plan on setting sail for Gwynedd once winter lifts." I let the words sink in for a moment. I surprised even myself with what I said next. "We go, with or without Muirchertach's help. I cannot wait forever." I had toyed with the idea for the past weeks and the lack of word from Muirchertach had done little to ease my frustration. I knew I could not wait forever and the time felt right. If I had to do it without the Irish then so be it.

Bjorgolf seemed unfazed by my words. "Well you need more bloody men. What have you got, eh?" Bjorgolf let the question hang in the air before answering it. "You've got fourteen rogues, who are good I grant you. And you've got that bloody mercenary and his lads. His lads are good but I still don't trust that ugly whoreson."

"I know, I know." I said dismissively. "But I know where I can get more." Bjorgolf raised an inquisitive eyebrow. "That hoard Ljot found. It is enough to buy ten ships and the men to crew them. I cannot believe my luck, but I am one wealthy bastard now." Bjorgolf joined in my laughter at the words, but it was true. I was now very wealthy and knew how I would spend that wealth. "Duibhlinn's slave trade is still strong. I wager there will be plenty of captured warriors and useful men in those slave pens."

Bjorgolf took a deep breath, which failed to hide his surprise. "What are you saying? That you want an army of thralls and disgraced warriors?" Bjorgolf evidently thought my idea foolish. "Half those bastards will have failed their previous oaths if they were daft enough to be enslaved and the other half will be starved, almost to death! By Odin's beard, who knows what kind of trouble you will unleash!"

"I know, but I have thought it through." In truth I had not given the idea the thought it deserved, but it seemed the quickest option to bolster my forces. Bjorgolf shook his head, still not comfortable with the idea but I continued anyway. "I will bring them here to train them, far enough away from Duibhlinn for them not to cause any trouble."

Bjorgolf still looked sceptical at the idea. "Perhaps, but who knows what they will do if they get the chance to go back to Duibhlinn?" Bjorgolf did not like the idea but he shrugged his shoulders as if to concede the argument. In truth I knew he was right; I could create a host of trouble for myself and the traders of Duibhlinn, for which of them would not wish for the chance to kill a person who had done nothing but treat them as animals. "Besides, your friend Faelan now controls much of the slave trade. I doubt he would take kindly to your custom, especially seeing as you wish to bed his future bride."

I shook my head at Bjorgolf's argument. "Faelan is a bastard sure enough. But silver will make that kind of man blind." I knew Faelan for what he was, the man would take a purse of silver from the devil were it offered. And besides, I had made up my mind and there was no changing it. I knew former warriors from distant and perhaps not too distant lands would be rotting in those pens. I just hoped that those men would not be broken and that I could give them back their dignity and freedom. So long as they fought in my shieldwall, and fought well, I did not care from what background they had come.

"So be it." Bjorgolf declared. "I just hope you bloody well know what you are doing."

By then it was mid-day and we had began to head back to the hall when Bjorgolf froze. He dropped immediately into a fighting crouch and held a finger to his lips. My heart began to race as I listened and my sword hand went for the hilt of my blade. My ears strained but I could not hear anything and did not know what Bjorgolf was playing at. I was about to say as much when I heard it.

I drew my blade instantly as a twig snapped and a pheasant squawked off to our right. I glanced at Bjorgolf who shrugged his shoulders; it was difficult to tell how far off the sounds had come. The trees and undergrowth were still as snow began to drift to earth from the sky. My legs were firmly planted to the ground as I stared intensely into the thick woodland; still nothing moved. The dull thump of a bowstring sounded and I instantly dived for cover. I had dived into a holly bush and swore under my breath as the barbed leaves scratched my cheeks. Curse my luck. I glanced to where Bjorgolf hid behind a fallen tree and swore as I saw how close the arrow had been to taking his life. The wooden shaft still shuddered as another zipped through my holly bush, inches from me. I cursed and rolled to my side hitting my elbow against a boulder, sending a jarring pain through my sword arm. The boulder was big enough for me to hide behind as I rubbed my throbbing arm.

I glanced back across at Bjorgolf who gestured in the direction from which our assailant had loosed his arrows. I risked a glance over the boulder but could see nothing other than trees, undergrowth and drifting snow flakes. Just then a bush rustled fifty paces to my front and I glimpsed a hooded figure shoot another shaft in our direction. The arrow clattered into the top of the boulder and spun harmlessly over my head, showering me with shards of rock. I ducked back down behind the boulder's shadow, damn but that had been too close.

We were trapped. I knew the hidden bowman's location but I was helpless. I knew if I made a move there was a good chance one of his arrows would bury itself into my flesh. I risked another glance over the boulder, but the woodland was still. Bjorgolf shifted uncomfortably behind the rotten trunk of the fallen tree. I caught the Dane's eye and he shrugged his shoulders at the hopelessness of the situation. I looked about me and noticed a tree with a thick trunk five paces ahead and I swallowed hard as my mind raced. To this day I do not know why I did it, but before I could think I acted; I sprang up from my hiding place and darted towards the cover of the tree ahead. A rush of air slapped past my left shoulder as an arrow shot inches over my body. Before I knew it my back was against the trunk and I breathed a sigh of relief.

I glanced back to where Bjorgolf peered from his hiding place and shook his head at my rashness. The bowman had my position locked in his vision. As I moved slightly a wickedly barbed arrow ripped bark from the tree's trunk and smacked into the boulder I had concealed myself behind moments earlier. As the bowman's attention was fixed solely on me, Bjorgolf made his move and dashed for a thicket of undergrowth, skidding into the limited safety. The bowman missed the Dane by a good few feet this time; he was rattled and so I took another chance. I darted from cover and hurled myself behind a sturdy oak.

My heart was beating so quickly that I could feel its vibrations in my ears. Bjorgolf did not risk another move as our assailant loosed another missile towards his hiding place. The thump of the bowstring as our attacker loosed another arrow indicated he was much closer than I thought. I tensed myself for a foolhardy charge in the man's general direction and, just before I broke cover, I heard a stick snap and bushes rustle. I peered round the ancient oak to see a cloaked figure, bow in hand, sprinting away deeper into the woodland and out of sight. I stayed very still for a few minutes. I could not risk movement again. Perhaps there was more than one attacker. I thought about it. No, if there were more than one bowman it was likely I or Bjorgolf, or both, would be dead.

Bjorgolf shouted for me to stay still, but I did not listen. I stepped out and sprinted towards the bush the bowman had used for cover. No arrow flew at me and nothing moved. I thundered through the bush and rose ready to strike, but no one was there. I peered deep into the gloom of the trees but all was still.

Bjorgolf cursed as he came to my side. "What the hell were you playing at? You could have been bloody killed." He shook his head. "Bloody coward has fled. Sprinted like a spooked deer he did. Straight into the trees. Bastard." Bjorgolf spat in the direction the bowman had fled.

"Trahaearn's other man?" I wondered aloud and the thought unsettled me deeply. Bjorgolf grunted that it was a possibility and I cursed. I had let my guard drop but it would not happen again.

Anger burned in my chest as we neared the hall. Neither I nor Bjorgolf had spoken a word as we cautiously escaped the woodland and trudged towards the great hall. I was in a dangerous mood and the Dane knew it, so he kept his thoughts to himself. I cursed aloud as we neared the outbuildings for there were a dozen horses being tended to by the thralls. I thrust open the doors and marched into the hall. I was in no mood for visitors and my scowl spoke for me as a mailed man tried to greet me. I stormed past him without offering acknowledgement and froze.

"Are you not pleased to see me, Gruffudd?" Orlaith's voice stopped me in my tracks. She wore a thick cloak trimmed with fur to protect her from the cold. The thick material was wrapped about her slim figure, her auburn hair looked perfectly straight and she smiled at me happily.

My foul mood seemed to evaporate at the sight of her smile. "Always pleased to see you, my lady." I could not help but grin broadly. "What brings you to my home?"

She returned my grin, dazzling me with her beauty. "My brother has sent me to summon you to Duibhlinn. For he wishes to meet with you. Why? I could not tell you." Her smile faltered slightly as she continued. "That is not the only reason I am here. I am to marry Faelan in a week's time in Duibhlinn." Her voice betrayed her displeasure and she frowned slightly at my expression. "Perhaps you did not know? You do not have to attend, but my brother believes that you should." Her voice trailed away.

I had been so overjoyed at her arrival that the news did not register straight away, but her words soon sunk in and my heart sank. I had heard the news weeks previously when I had visited Maelgwn in Duibhlinn; it was the very news which had turned me into such a recluse those last few weeks.

"I shall think on it." I managed as I did not want her to think of me as a jealous fool so turned to leave, before I added any further comments. "I have much to tend to. I would be honoured if you would stay the night and dine with me later. Your bodyguard will also be most welcome; I shall have my thralls prepare the bedchamber for you. Now if you would excuse me, I have to train my men." She politely curtseyed and nodded her thanks as I turned and left.

Bjorgolf fell-in beside me and chuckled at my flushed cheeks. I shot him a scowl for I was still in a foul mood and now I was flustered and cross with myself for being so impertinent. The thought that one of Trahaearn's agents was close at hand did little to soothe my troubled thoughts. Bjorgolf nudged me in the ribs. "You did not lie. She is a fine woman; just don't do anything I wouldn't do." Bjorgolf winked at me and laughed.

The truth was that I had few duties that needed my immediate attention, but I could not bear to show Orlaith what a foul mood I was in. I kept myself busy and tried not to think of Trahaearn's agents and my mood had improved by the time the light faded, especially seeing as the monks from Sord Cholmcille monastery had not bothered me in a whole week.

As I enjoyed a cut of mutton I glanced across to where Bjorgolf entertained Orlaith's bodyguard. They all drank merrily with my warband as they boasted of past exploits. Ruaidri treated us all to a repeat of his saga tale of my fight with Gunnald and Orlaith seemed entranced by Ruaidri's tale, nodding approvingly in the appropriate places and smiling happily as he mentioned my heroics.

I could not help but admire her; she looked beautiful in the firelight. She wore a dark green dress with a finely crafted necklace made of gold and silver about her neck and a strange, but beautiful, ring crowned by a mysterious purple stone. We had feasted politely and I had enjoyed the encounter, except for the disapproving scowls Orlaith's maid had shot me.

As the night wore on the men became very drunk and laughter filled the hall as few of the less able drinkers passed out or vomited. Orlaith did her best to ignore the sight of drunken men making fools of themselves and spoke to me quietly, so only I would hear. "Oh, Gruffudd. Why couldn't you be a wealthy land owner that my brother needs to keep loyal?" she asked in a light-hearted manner. "For then I wouldn't have to marry such a pompous oaf and his hideous moustache." I laughed dutifully at her jest but could not help but think she spoke the truth. Did she have feelings for me also? My heart leapt with joy and I smiled happily. "Perhaps, I should not bore you with my troubles of the heart. I think it is time that I retire for the night," she spoke almost reluctantly.

Her maid eyed me cautiously; damn but what a miserable cow that maid was. If she did not scowl so much, perhaps she would be pretty despite her middle-age. "Please don't," I stammered. "I enjoy our conversations. And I am a wealthy land owner. A royal one at that." She cocked an amused eyebrow. I was not trying to be arrogant and impress her, but I guessed she knew as much. "Perhaps," I continued very awkwardly and paused.

"Perhaps what?" She asked mischievously. Her maid leaned closer, the pretence of pretending not to eavesdrop gone.

I swallowed and felt so nervous that my hand shook uncontrollably. I prayed she would not notice for we sat next to one another at the head of the table. Bjorgolf caught my eye and winked. I smiled at the gesture and it gave me the confidence to speak. "Perhaps your brother would find me a more suitable candidate for you?"

I could not believe what I had just said and her maid looked outraged, as though she would slap me for my forwardness at any moment. Orlaith laid a hand on her maid's arm to calm her and shot me a serious look. "You should not jest such."

I swallowed hard again; my mouth had gone completely dry. "I do not jest." I detected a glint of pleasure in her green eyes and a smile quickly flashed across her face. The smile vanished before her maid noticed. She spoke formally but her eyes showed she did not mean what she said. "Gruffudd, I cannot go against my brother's wishes. Faelan is to be my husband, for better or worse." Her maid gave an approving nod, and shot me a triumphant smirk, as Orlaith continued. "Now if you will excuse me, I must retire for the night. Thank you for your hospitality."

I did not judge her words to be from the heart, at least I hoped not. Her eyes had betrayed her feelings when I had clumsily all but declared my love for her. I felt my heart skip a beat and my groin harden slightly as she took my hand in hers and squeezed it gently before releasing her grip and curtseying formally before retiring to her bedchamber.

Her maid shot me another disapproving scowl and followed Orlaith into the bedchamber. I relived the moments in my mind over and over as I sat still on the bench. I judged that she had feelings for me too. I thought of the feel of her skin on mine as she took my hand in hers and squeezed it, she must love me too, I thought. But then doubts crept into my mind, perhaps it was her way of rejecting me gently. Orlaith's bodyguard were all passed out or bedding down for the night whilst only Bjorgolf and Ruaidri still drank.

I went over to them and grabbed a jug of ale, gulping the contents down. "Easy lad," Bjorgolf laughed. "Summoning the courage, eh?" He shot me a knowing glance. "Smitten on you she is, isn't that so Ruaidri?" Bjorgolf nudged the rogue heartily who grinned his agreement. Bjorgolf rose as a plump thrall woman cleared the remains of the feast and began to clean the hall.

"I'm not the only one who is in love then?" I questioned truthfully. Bjorgolf shot me a surprised look and tapped a finger to his nose.

"She's a fine woman she is. Reminds me of the one I told you about. Knows how to cook too, always a good skill for a woman to have." Ruaidri laughed and I joined in, Bjorgolf shook his head in mock disgust and went to bed down for the night.

Just then the maid came out of Orlaith's bedchamber and sat on a wooden stool, shooting me a glance of disapproval. I nudged Ruaidri, "I will pay you well to take that miserable cow out of here and give her a good time. She bloody well needs a smile putting on her face."

Ruaidri laughed and held out his hand. He grinned as I dropped some of Gofraid's silver coins into his palm. He shot me a mischievous glance and grabbed a jug of ale and an extra tankard. I made as if I would bed down for the night and Ruaidri approached the maid and began to charm her with the help of the ale.

It must have taken over an hour for Ruaidri to charm the miserable cow. But they eventually scurried out of the hall and into one of the outbuildings. I waited a few moments before I approached Orlaith's bedchamber. I steadied myself as I summoned the courage. I had fought fearsome warriors, thrown myself at enemy shieldwalls and completed daring missions worthy of a saga tale yet I could not bring myself to knock the door. I steeled my resolve and took a deep breath before knocking delicately.

"Who is it?" Orlaith's voice sounded from inside. "If it's you Hild then I don't want anything." Hild must be the maid's name. I laughed softly at her tone and edged the door open. "Is that you, Gruffudd?" She asked quietly.

I stuck my head round the door. A torch still burned on the wall giving off enough light. She shook her head at the sight of me. "You should not be here." Her voice betrayed her excitement as much as the fear of discovery. "How did you get past Hild?"

Orlaith looked beautiful as ever as she bit her bottom lip. She knew I should not be there, yet she did not tell me to leave.

I edged into the room and closed the door softly

143

behind me. "Hild has taken quite an interest in one of my men. She is a little busy at the moment, if you follow my meaning." My confidence was growing and I knew I should not be there but I could not bring myself to leave.

She giggled and put her hand over her mouth. "Truly? Hild has left me all alone and at the mercy of a fearsome warrior?" She laughed as I nodded. "Well that is a surprise."

I stood at the foot of her bedding and she pulled the furs back and stood. She wore a simple bed gown which dropped to her ankles, it clung to her slim figure and my groin stiffened as she rose. She padded quietly towards me and took both my hands in hers. "We should not be doing this." She knew she was right but she still kissed me softly on my cheek.

I could not believe what was happening and felt overwhelmed by the moment as she drew back. I bent forwards and kissed her passionately on the lips. She recoiled slightly and I apologised immediately. She released her hands from mine and held up a finger to silence me. She stood on her tiptoes and returned my kiss fiercely.

I embraced her, running my hand over her body. She giggled in excitement as she took my hand and guided me to the bed. I let myself be pushed down. She kissed me again and drew the furs over us. She pressed her body onto mine as we kissed passionately. She stripped me of my tunic and ran her finger over a scar on my shoulder before kissing me again. I could hold back no longer as I felt her breasts press against my skin through her bed gown. I kissed her on her neck and my heart felt as though it would burst with joy, for tonight Orlaith was my lover.

XII

It had been three days since we had left Sord Cholmcille
for Duibhlinn and I had been in very high spirits ever since.
Bjorgolf had guessed why and I was pleased that he no
longer felt the need to give me any lectures on love. The
night when Orlaith and I had been lovers played over and
over in my mind. I loved her and that night had felt so
right, yet I was soon to attend her wedding to one of the
men I detested most in this world. Faelan was a pompous
bastard whose company I found intolerable and we shared a
mutual dislike for each other. He was nearing his thirtieth
year and I found it strange that he had not been married
previously. The bastard was rich and was head of one of
Munster's oldest families. Muirchertach needed to keep the
little Irishman happy and so he had promised him Orlaith's
hand in marriage. And for that I cursed him again.

The small garrison of thralls I had left at my hall in
Duibhlinn had struggled to play host to Maelgwn and his
fierce warriors. But I did not care. The Powysian was a
bloodthirsty cut-throat and, for that reason, I was very
pleased he was my ally and not my enemy. He had grinned
broadly when I had told him why I wished to buy thralls to
bolster my forces, yet Bjorgolf still disapproved. The Dane
had tried to persuade me against the idea again as we
approached the slave market on the banks of the An Liffe.

"For the last time, I know what I am doing." I told
Bjorgolf firmly. "Now, that is the end of it." Bjorgolf
nodded his head to finally concede the argument yet,
clearly, he was still not happy with the idea. Ljot and
Oengus did not seem to share Bjorgolf's reservations as
they followed us into the slave market.

The market was unusually quiet. Likely it was due
to the weather. The wind was biting as it blew in off the
Irish Sea and up the An Liffe into Duibhlinn. The snow had
ceased the day we had left Sord Cholmcille yet snow still

blanketed the roof tops of Duibhlinn. The street was slushy as the snow melted underfoot and mingled with the mud and sewerage, forming something which resembled the broth I had been served for breakfast and I shuddered at the thought. The stench was the first thing to hit me and I almost recoiled at the intense smell of people packed closely together in such a small place. The smell of the slaves' waste further added to the sickly air.

Bjorgolf cursed as the stench hit him. "Fuck me, smells worse than when your mother spreads her legs, Ljot." Ljot cursed Bjorgolf as he and Oengus mocked him.

A slave trader moved to intercept me as we moved past a pen of some miserable looking female captives. The man bowed deeply as he introduced himself as Olaf Bjarnisson. He was flanked by two huge guards who eyed my small party warily. The two were armed with cudgels and had clearly been employed from one of the local taverns. One stared at me through an ugly pock-marked face before rubbing his bloated belly.

The trader steered me towards a pen full of half-starved women and children who looked at me blankly before looking away. "They are freshly imported from northern England, Cumbraland to be exact." The trader seemed disappointed when I told him I was not interested in the poor looking creatures. "They are a defeated people, my lord." The trader pleaded, "So, they will be docile enough for you. Perfect for kitchen work, or other uses. We bought them off those Frenchmen who are still trying to pacify the north of the country; they strike a hard bargain I may add." I had no interest in the poor specimens and the trader finally gave up trying to persuade me. "I have other, more expensive, stock if you need. My lord."

The trader steered me round the pen I had just inspected and into a rotten warehouse, where the stink of damp and shit were almost intolerable. Two guards looked up from their gambling and grunted at their master as he guided me further into the gloom. Ljot held his hand over his mouth and nose in an effort to save himself from the stench, whilst Oengus grinned broadly as we came level to a cage which contained five beautiful women.

"These are my finest, lord." The trader was clearly proud of his collection of beauties. "They are expensive, but worth it." He eyed me greedily as he pointed at a blonde haired girl who fearfully looked up at me. "That one is a virgin and half Dane half Saxon. For you, I will give a good price."

I doubted the man spoke truthfully and he seemed flustered when I told him as much. "I have no interest in female thralls; I have enough as it is." I sensed Bjorgolf stiffen slightly as the trader shot me a look of disgust.

"I have some fresh stock of men, or boys, if you prefer." The man looked at me distastefully. "We cater for all demands." The man's words were thinly disguised and anger rose in me.

I grabbed the trader by his thick winter coat. "You mistake my meaning," I growled threateningly. I heard Bjorgolf and my two men draw their weapons as the trader's guards started to come towards me with their cudgels. His guards had stopped short as they eyed my party warily. They knew they were likely to suffer if they attacked my men and their sharp steel and thought better of it.

The trader eyed me fearfully as he swallowed hard. "I meant no offence, my lord. Please, please I shall show you what else I have to offer." I heard laughter from the end of the warehouse and turned to look.

A large cage full of male thralls dominated the warehouse's rear and a giant of a man barked another laugh. He was powerfully built and gripped the iron bars with his giant hands. I released the trader and he beckoned hurriedly for me to follow. He called for his guards to lower their cudgels and they reluctantly agreed as Bjorgolf and my men continued to watch them threateningly.

As we came level with the cage I eyed the big man. I was taller than most men, yet he was at least two heads taller then I. He wore only a filthy rag around his manhood and seemed immune to the cold winter air. He was thickly muscled and had a round head, which was perfectly bald but his face was dominated by a wild red beard. He had some peculiar blue tattoos which curled up his powerfully muscled arms and on to his torso. He spat a curse at the trader in a strange tongue and butted the bars, making the cage shudder.

The trader recoiled and seemed bemused when I spoke. "How much for the big man?" The trader's eyes widened and he blinked repeatedly before asking me to repeat. "I said how much for the big man?" I replied patiently.

The trader looked at me in disbelief as the giant spat another torrent of what I assumed to be threats, and shook the cage violently. "I have not yet broken him, my lord. Is that wise?" The scowl I fixed on the trader made him shrug his shoulders in hopelessness and shake his head slightly. "For you, lord, I shall give a good price. Say, that pouch of silver?" He gestured at the bulging pouch fastened to my belt and smiled greedily.

I laughed at the price. "I shall give you my full pouch of silver for the giant and eight others." The trader scoffed and was about to reject my offer until I patted the blade at my waist and he shook his head sadly.

"He is of the painted people of the north. They are rare and therefore expensive." I patted my blade again and the trader nervously gave in. "Very well. We have a deal, lord?"

"My name is Gruffudd son of Cynan." I spat on my palm and held out my hand to seal the deal; the trader took it reluctantly. I smiled as Bjorgolf looked at the giant in awe. I had struck a bargain and the trader knew it. I turned

148

back to Bjorgolf. "Inspect the others and pick eight of the best."

Bjorgolf nodded his head before muttering to himself. The trader beckoned for his guards to open the cage. The two guards approached the cage, eyeing the giant fearfully. As the cage creaked open the giant let out an almighty roar and ran at the two guards. The first fled and the one with the ugly pock-marked face swung his cudgel clumsily. The cudgel glanced off the giant's shoulder as he wrapped his giant arms around the ugly bastard. The huge muscles forced the air from the guard as he lifted him off the ground before slamming him back down. The giant wrapped a massive forearm around the pock-marked head and twisted sharply. There was a dull crack as the man's neck broke and he went limp. The giant spat at the motionless corpse and its bloated belly before kicking the head, which rested at an unnatural angle. He was panting and drooling as his eyes scanned the room. The eyes settled on the trader at my side and the giant let out a wicked smile as the trader shuffled to hide behind me. Before the huge man could move he crumpled to the ground as a trickle of blood began to emerge from the blow which had taken his consciousness.

Bjorgolf stood above the fallen giant with the guard's cudgel in one hand. He shot me a worried look. "By Thor's hammer what have you let yourself in for?"

Maelgwn grinned in pleasure at the thirty men that stood before him in the small courtyard. The slave pens had been less fruitful than I had expected, but we had returned with a good number which swelled my warband to a full ship's crew. I suspected around two dozen of the slaves had previously been warriors and I hoped they still had fight left in their bellies.

The Powysian took a particular interest in the giant blue painted man who was on his knees under guard at the courtyard's edge. The heavily muscled hulk of a man looked resentfully around him and tried to shake his hands loose. Bjorgolf had securely bound the big man's arms and legs so that he could not try to free himself again.

"I like the look of him," Maelgwn said to me as he walked over to inspect the tattooed giant. We stopped just short and Maelgwn leant down slightly so that his metallic nosepiece was almost touching the giant's flat nose. Maelgwn grinned happily before rising back to his full height. "A formidable warrior that one. I bet he cost a fair bit. It would be a shame if he doesn't respect authority, eh?" The mercenary carried on before I could answer his question. "I've never seen the like before, where is he from?"

"He's a Pict," I replied confidently. Maelgwn shot me an inquisitive look as we walked back to the doors of the hall and turned to look back at the men gathered in the courtyard. "They used to rule the lands the Scots now hold. They were once a powerful people and the Romans built a huge wall across northern Lloegr to keep them out."

The Powysian looked at me dubiously. "Where the hell did you learn that?" He glanced at the tattooed giant again before looking back. "How the hell do you know he is one of them Picts?"

"I read about them when I was younger." I smiled to myself at Maelgwn's evident surprise. "Priests taught me all about the Romans, you know. I used to love the history but hated the letters and words being beaten into me."

Bjorgolf had heard my words and laughed at Maelgwn's surprise. He shot the Powysian a knowing look. "Full of surprises is Gruffudd!" Maelgwn looked away quickly and surveyed the thralls. It was clear that Bjorgolf still did not trust the scarred Powysian, not that Maelgwn seemed to care. I suspected it was down to a clash of wills; both were formidable warriors and hated being outdone by anybody.

I had made several more deals with other traders in the slave market the day before and the men I had purchased now stood before me in the courtyard of my modest Duibhlinn hall. I had purchased exactly thirty thralls, including the Pict. That put a smile on my face as I stood before them. Some were half starved and others resentful as they stared at their new master. I, or Bjorgolf, had inspected every one of them and knew which of them had been warriors. Including my rogues I now had a little over forty of my own men. I just hoped they would prove useful.

Twenty of Maelgwn's Powysians lined the courtyard and they and my men looked on with interest at the thralls who were soon to be their comrades. I cleared my throat and spoke loudly in Irish, in the hope that all of them would understand my words. "My name is Gruffudd, son of Cynan. I am of the royal house of Aberffraw and the true King of Gwynedd." I paused to survey the men coolly. They all looked up at me with a mixture of interest and resentment and I noticed a couple of men whispering a translation of my words for those who could not understand Irish. The big Pict just stared blankly at me as I cleared my throat.

"As you are aware, I bought you from the slave market yesterday. You are mine to do with as I wish." Some of them began to look at me with pure hatred and others in expectation, a faint hope growing in their hearts, as I continued. "I wish to sail to Gwynedd when winter ends and reclaim what is my birthright. I need good men to do this." A couple of them grinned as they began to comprehend what I was doing, whilst the majority just stared at me with resentment at the shame of being a thrall. "This morning you are all thralls. This afternoon I give you the opportunity to become warriors again." All looks of resentment were gone, replaced by confused and surprised expressions before they looked at me in pure disbelief as I let the words sink in. "I wish you all to swear yourselves to me and become part of my personal warband. I can promise you adventure, ale, women and most importantly of all. Respect." Most grinned broadly as they understood what was being offered whilst a few looked suspiciously on. "Remember this. I am Gruffudd son of Cynan and if you choose to follow me, then this afternoon you shall be free. Think upon that!"

I finished my address and began to retreat to the hall as they cheered my name. I grinned broadly as Bjorgolf clapped me on my shoulder and nodded approvingly at me. Maelgwn shot me a conspiratorial grin. "Fine words," the Powysian said happily. "Many would not agree with your methods. But, I think you've just won yourself a ship's crew." I smiled at the knowledge and hoped he was right.

That afternoon all but one had sworn their loyalty to me and was welcomed by my warband with a clap on the back and a draught of ale. I had sent Ruaidri into Duibhlinn with a pocket full of silver to ferret out some of the town's whores for my new men. Ruaidri had returned with ten whores and even returned some silver. I assumed the rogue had taken a bit for himself, but that did not bother me much. The giggles of the whores and the roars of laughter from the recently freed thralls were proof enough that they were enjoying their new found and unexpected freedom.

But I was not in such a jubilant mood. I stared at the one man who had not sworn an oath of loyalty. The giant Pict stared emotionlessly at me as I faced his round head and flat nose. Bjorgolf had checked that the man's bonds were secure and had insisted he be kept under guard in the outbuilding at the far end of the courtyard. I had tried to talk to the giant warrior in Irish, Danish, Briton and had even tried Latin as a final resort but the tattooed man just stared blankly back at me.

"I don't think the stupid bastard understands a

152

bloody word. You reckon the bugger is simple?" Bjorgolf ranted behind the Pict who turned to glance at Bjorgolf. The Dane shook his head again before screaming in the Pict's ear. "Surely you can understand what's going on, you thick sheep humping numbskull!"

I raised a palm to quiet Bjorgolf, who spread his arms with an exasperated expression. The Dane had many qualities which made him indispensable, but diplomacy certainly wasn't one of them. I tried a simpler approach; I pointed a finger at my chest, "Gruffudd. I am Gruffudd." The giant looked at me suspiciously and I repeated the action and my name before pointing at him.

The man's small blue eyes stared intensely at me over his flat nose and he pointed a finger at his chest and smiled as I nodded. "Gwcharki." The Pict stated firmly in his deep voice. He pointed at his chest again, "Gwcharki, Gwcharki." He repeated the word again and again until I silenced him with a raised palm.

I looked up at Bjorgolf. "Release him." Bjorgolf looked as though he would protest at the order but I shot him a threatening look. The Dane reluctantly drew his dagger and cut the bonds at the giant's feet and then cut the bonds which secured his huge arms.

The Pict rubbed his chaffed wrists and flexed his powerful arms. The blue tattoos twitched as he flexed his muscles again. The giant rose to his full height and had to cock his head slightly so that he did not hit the roof beam. He dominated the building and grinned broadly at me. Bjorgolf tensed as I stayed still for several heart beats. The big man made no effort to attack or make a run for it so I turned and exited the outbuilding, Bjorgolf needed no invitation and he followed me out quickly.

I beckoned for the giant to follow and he trudged out after us. Maelgwn's gap-toothed *helwyr* notched an arrow on his bowstring and eyed the huge Pict warily as our movements distracted him from keeping watch. We entered the hall where my new men were enjoying themselves and as one they all went quiet as they stared at the huge Pict. He grinned broadly at his new comrades and stooped to pick up a pitcher of ale, which he downed within seconds. The men cheered as he picked up another and then joined the celebrations.

I smiled to myself at the small victory; I had got the giant Pict on my side. He would be formidable on any battlefield and I was amazed he had ever been captured in the first place. My thoughts wandered momentarily to the prospect of seeing Orlaith wedded to Faelan in the morning. I quickly shook my head to rid the thought from my mind. For tonight was a night of celebration but I knew thoughts of losing the woman I loved would blacken the evening for me. My warband drank and feasted well in to the night and I allowed myself to smile at the sight. They looked a formidable group of warriors and I knew at that moment that one day, one day soon, Gwynedd would be mine.

XIII

The feeling of jealousy burned intensely in my chest as the bishop droned on and on. I stood at the back of Duibhlinn's Christ Church cathedral with Bjorgolf, both of us in our finest clothing which, as Bjorgolf admitted himself, was not much. The bishop, Patrick, was of the Benedictine order of monks and that did not surprise me. The Benedictines did not approve of social conversation and that suited a man like Patrick well. The middle aged wisp of a man had a monotonous voice which droned through the Latin words. The bishop's address had dragged for at least half an hour and Bjorgolf fidgeted at my side. I rewarded him with a nudge in the ribs and the Dane rolled his eyes at the boredom. Bjorgolf, if pressed, regarded himself as a Christian but I was not entirely convinced of the Dane's religion, not that it bothered me.

He leant towards me and whispered. "I don't know why you dragged me to this bloody ceremony. I'm a Christian man, but this is pure bloody torture." I chuckled at Bjorgolf's words and shot an old woman an apologetic look as she shook her head disapprovingly at us. She turned quickly round as Bjorgolf blew her a kiss and winked.

I could understand Bjorgolf's restlessness for I too did not wish to be there. I had attended out of politeness and because Muirchertach expected me to. Faelan was gaudily dressed in a burgundy coloured tunic, elaborately trimmed with golden lace. The bastard had clearly spent hours on his appearance and his shoulder length black hair was sleeked back immaculately. His extravagant drooping moustache had clearly been combed to perfection and oiled into place. God, but I hated him.

My heart felt nothing but loathing towards the arrogant cur and when I glanced at Orlaith that feeling intensified. I looked up at the rafters and uttered a silent prayer that the ceremony would soon be over or, better still, that Faelan would drop dead.

Bjorgolf noticed my action and muttered his agreement. "Amen to that." He shifted slightly and nudged me. "For what we are about to receive, I am truly sorry."

I fixed him with a puzzled look and recoiled at the smell. Bjorgolf chuckled as others in the congregation caught wind of the smell he had unleashed. The old woman turned back to stare at Bjorgolf and muttered her disgust. Bjorgolf muttered back at her quietly. "It's what I think of grand old Faelan. It's my wedding present to the animal bothering pile of shit."

The ceremony dragged on and on as I stared longingly at Orlaith's slim figure. I could not help but marvel at her beauty. I cursed Muirchertach again for promising her to Faelan. The more I thought about it the worse my mood became and the more my hatred of Faelan grew.

My thoughts wandered and I contemplated how satisfying it would be to spit Faelan on the end of a spear. Bjorgolf brought my mind back to the present. He nudged me in the ribs and muttered, with a degree of satisfaction. "Thank fuck that's over. I am looking forward to the celebrations." I shot him a scathing glance and he shrugged his shoulders in apology. "Plenty of ale to drink and food to plunder. If it's at Faelan's expense, I will make sure I get my fill."

I chuckled at Bjorgolf's words as the bishop ended the ceremony. I had deliberately looked away when Faelan kissed Orlaith to seal the marriage and I looked back as the newly wedded couple made their way towards the cathedral's exit. I stood close to the doorway with Bjorgolf as they approached and did my best to remain anonymous.

Faelan strutted proudly past but my heart wept as I caught Orlaith's eye. She shot me a fearful glance before Faelan steered her out of the cathedral after the bishop and into the sunlight. Muirchertach sent me a respectful nod as he walked past and Father Cathal hobbled after him. The evil old bastard shot me a cruel glance and smiled menacingly.

We waited until all the notable guests had left the cathedral. Bjorgolf cursed as the heavens opened and rain began to drizzle down on us. The weather wept with my heart, for Orlaith was now beyond my reach.

Nobody wished to talk to me as I sat on a bench in Muirchertach's great hall. The celebrations were in full swing and guests indulged themselves on the feast, drinking the ale and wine greedily. Bjorgolf had become bored of my brooding and boasted of past exploits with a thickly bearded barrel of a man.

I had spurned the advances of several young women and had told one of Father Cathal's thralls to piss off or face the consequences as he disturbed my thoughts. The slave passed on Father Cathal's summons but I did not care about the old bastard today. I was in no mood for his mind games. I told the thrall as much and threatened to cut his throat as he repeated Father Cathal's orders, evidently expecting me to jump and do the old monk's bidding.

I downed another draught of ale and spun round as something tapped me on my shoulder. I rolled my eyes and cursed as I turned to see Father Cathal standing behind me. The old monk scowled at me as he withdrew his walking staff from my shoulder and he coughed to clear his throat. "I see you are yet to offer your congratulations to the happy couple. Faelan has married a fine woman, wouldn't't you agree?"

The old monk had spoken innocently but I knew he expected a reaction and I was in no mood to tolerate his games this day. "Piss off, monk. I have no patience for your poison."

The monk's scowl deepened as he stared intensely at me and I instantly knew I had been foolish to provoke

157

the devil-spawned bastard. He spoke slowly and threateningly. "Your King, Muirchertach, wishes to discuss your proposed expedition to Gwynedd with you. He has asked me to bring you to him."

I looked curiously at the old monk; I could not help but think he was playing another trick on me. "Why didn't't you just bloody say so then." I spoke acidly at the hunched figure. I rose and gestured for him to lead the way.

Father Cathal did not move but spoke quietly so that only I would hear. "Talk to me like that again, upstart, and I shall make your life very uncomfortable." I knew I had pushed the boundaries with the old monk and that he would be a dangerous enemy but I hated him. I shot him a sly grin and nodded acceptance. He clearly did not like my tone and raised his walking staff to block my escape. "I know of you and the good lady Orlaith. You stay clear of her, or I will finish you."

Father Cathal let the threat sink in before gesturing for me to follow. The old bastard hobbled along with the aid of his walking staff and he did not utter another word as we approached the top table.

Before Father Cathal could gain Muirchertach's attention, my heart sank. Faelan, clearly emboldened by the wine he had consumed, strutted down from his place at the top table. He stopped short of me and thrust his handsome face and its immaculate features towards me. Those small, pig-like eyes locked with mine. The smell of stale wine carried on his foul breath. "Who invited you?" The Irishman slurred his words.

I glanced up at Orlaith who sent me an apologetic look and I glanced back at Faelan. "I am not here out of choice. I am here to talk with Muirchertach. Now, if you would be so kind as to remove yourself from my presence." I looked Faelan up and down with evident scorn. "You offend my eyes. Now move."

Faelan looked taken aback as Muirchertach rumbled

laughter and Orlaith shook her head for me to stop goading her new husband. Muirchertach spoke before Faelan's wine sodden mind could think of a retort to my insult. "Enough Gruffudd." The king rose and walked casually down from the dais so that he now stood beside us. He turned to look at Faelan, "Gruffudd tells the truth, he is here at my request." Muirchertach silenced Faelan with a raised palm before the Irishman could protest. "If you would care to come with me?"

The king put a strong arm round my shoulders and guided me away from my enemy. I shot Faelan a look filled with hate and the little Irishman spat in my direction before returning to his place at the top table. Orlaith tried her best to look cheerful as her new husband returned but he plainly ignored her conversation. Father Cathal hobbled behind as we went through a door into a chamber at the back of the hall. The chamber was warmed by a fire, which burned intensely in the hearth, and several well-crafted chairs were the only furniture in the small room.

Muirchertach sat first, on the grandest of the chairs, and then beckoned for me to sit. Father Cathal perched like a bird of prey on another of the chairs and then Muirchertach cleared his throat. My heart skipped a beat, for I was to learn how Muirchertach was to aid me in my quest to reclaim my birthright.

I listened intently as Muirchertach spoke. "As you know, Gruffudd, I have promised to support your claim. I have never been a man to go back on my word. So, I believe the time is right for you to make a bid for Gwynedd's throne. Once the winter lifts I expect you to sail. I have debated this with Father Cathal and we both believe this to be the best course of action." My heart swelled with pride in my chest, it was really happening. Soon I would set foot on the lands that were my birthright; I was going to go home. Muirchertach smiled happily at my evident pleasure. "Now,

Father Cathal shall tell you why we believe this is the right time for you to make your move."

I glanced at the old monk whose face twitched and contorted as he suffered another bout of the coughing illness that ailed him. The coughing fit was over before it really started and he drew an arm across his mouth to halt the spluttering and wipe the spittle from his chin. He cleared his throat. "Gwynedd is in a sorry state. By King Muirchertach's order, I have had agents working across the sea for the last two years. They report that the country is deeply divided following King Bleddyn's death at the turn of the year. The nobility of the land fear the expanding power of the Frenchmen who have taken England from the Saxons." I nodded at the statement, I had heard as much.

The old monk, not waiting for a reaction, ploughed on with his information. "Trahaearn, despite his usurpation of the throne, enjoys considerable support in the southern provinces of the country. His powerbase centres around his ancestor's lands of Arwystli and the men of Meirionydd will support him against you. However, the men of Ynys Môn and Arfon do not have much love for Trahaearn and are open to the return of the house of Aberffraw. The loyalty of the nobility of the other provinces is questionable at best."

I nodded at the information. If the lords of Arfon and Ynys Môn flocked to my banner I would stand a good chance. Father Cathal nodded as if reading my thoughts. "Your campaign will rest upon the support of those lords. I have received assurances from the lord Gwyncu, who holds the port of Abermenai on Ynys Môn, that he will support you and that your coming will be most welcome. The province of Arllechwedd to the east of Arfon is under pressure from Robert the Frenchman, who has a significant powerbase east of the Conwy River. We have not yet approached him, but you will surely have to contend with him sooner or later." The old cleric's face twitched again as

160

another fit of coughs rasped from his skinny ribcage.

As his spluttering ended the old monk continued. "Be wary of the Frenchman, Gruffudd that is my advice to you. As you well know, Cynwrig rules the province of Lleyn and is a firm ally of Trahaearn. However, my agents report that the nobles of Lleyn are ripe for revolt against their Powysian overlord. Of these nobles the three sons of Merwydd have the most influence and it is my belief that they will support you, for the right price. The late Merwydd was a proud man and his sons are reportedly of a similar ilk, so you will do well to keep them on side."

Muirchertach nodded his thanks to Father Cathal. The king shot me an amused smile. "A lot to take in, eh?" He laughed when I nodded. "Welcome to the world of kings, Gruffudd son of Cynan."

I grinned broadly at Muirchertach. "I thank you, Father Cathal, for your information." The old monk nodded respectfully. "My King," I fixed Muirchertach with a friendly smile, "You promised to support my claim. May I be bold and ask, how you will do this?"

Muirchertach grinned broadly, "of course you may! Of course you may!" He shrugged his shoulders, as if in apology. "There will be some good news in what I say. But some news, I think, you shall not much like." My thoughts twisted at the words, what was there not to like? The king continued. "I shall present you with a fine ship from my fleet; it shall be yours and will be adequate to carry your warband. You shall have the ship's master and several crew as well. It is also my belief that a king must ride at the head of his men, so one of my finest stallions you shall have!"

They were generous gifts and I gave Muirchertach my thanks, who waived his hand dismissively. "I shall also provide you with your foster-father and his men." I grinned happily at the news; it would be good to have a man as capable as Sitric at my side. "I thought you might be pleased with that. Sitric has agreed to be under your command as part of your personal force. He is a talented man in war, but please look after him." Muirchertach chuckled to himself. "He's getting old, you know. But he will still be of use."

I laughed dutifully at the jest but my heart sank when Muirchertach broke the bad news. "I shall also provide you with two hundred fine Irish warriors. But, and this is the bit you will not like, they will be under the command of my brother-by-marriage. Faelan needs a good victory to win a reputation and he will command my Irishmen in this noble quest."

Muirchertach silenced my protest with a raised palm and chuckled at my scowl. "I know you do not like him, but the campaign will do him good. I shall give him Mac Ruaidri the Lord of Cruach Brendain. He is an old head that I trust and he should keep Faelan in check. Remember, Faelan is in command of my Irish as I want him to make a name for himself, but he is under strict orders to follow your command. I hope this is to your satisfaction?" I nodded, albeit reluctantly. If Faelan was the price I had to pay in order to reclaim my birthright, then so be it. "Good, then you sail in two months time and I wish you good fortune."

The king indicated for me to leave and I nodded my head respectfully and repeated my thanks. I pulled Bjorgolf away from the ale and retreated to my Duibhlinn hall looking forward to the future and dreaming of what it would bring. Death or glory awaited and I thought of my plans. Soon I would sail for Gwynedd.

XIV

The weeks quickly vanished as I drilled my warband and pushed them to the limit. Shortly after Faelan's wedding celebrations we had retreated to my estate of Sord Cholmcille and there my men had developed into a formidable band of brothers. Gwcharki, the giant Pict, had proved an invaluable addition to my force. He was incredibly talented with practically every weapon imaginable. The giant had adopted a huge double-headed axe as his primary weapon. He was like a force of nature and had quickly learnt a spattering of basic Irish, as well as earning Bjorgolf's respect, which was no small feat.

I had spent a small fortune on equipping my men with strong Danish shields, clothing and a vast array of weaponry. My warband consisted of Danes, Irishmen, Saxons, men of the Isles, the giant Pict and even a Briton from the southern Kingdom of Deheubarth. All had been warriors in their previous lives and they regained their strength quickly. They were in high spirits as we reached my hall in Duibhlinn where we met to join forces with Maelgwn and his Powysians.

Our combined force made an awesome impression on the locals, who stopped to watch as we marched through Duibhlinn's streets and down to the harbour. Sitric and his warband were waiting on the quay and my foster-father strode forwards to greet me with a broad grin.

We embraced and I nodded my greetings to Cerit and Wselfwulf who flanked Sitric, their faces full of pride at what we were about to set out to achieve. I inspected Sitric's eighty men and smiled with genuine pleasure at the force I had under my command. I commented as much to Sitric. "They are a fine body of men, father. I am honoured you will be joining me on my quest."

Sitric had aged over of the winter and he grimaced as a strong gust of wind blew in off the An Liffe. "I've been with you from the start. I thought it best that I see you claim what is yours." Sitric gestured at a fine warship which loomed majestically in the harbour. "Muirchertach clearly rates you. What a beauty that ship is. *God's Wrath* I believe he named her."

I surveyed the beautifully crafted ship in awe and I could not believe she was mine. Bjorgolf whistled in appreciation and Cerit shot me a delighted smile. A chorus of cheers sounded up the street behind me and I turned to see a column of men approaching the quay. I noticed a man riding a fine Irish stallion at the head of the column and, as well as recognising the green and orange striped banner, I instantly identified the extravagant moustache.

I met Cerit's gaze and he rolled his eyes at Faelan's dramatic approach. War horns blew and his men sang a jaunty tune as the crowd cheered them on their approach along the harbour front. I turned to Sitric who had been exchanging pleasantries with Maelgwn. "I think it's time the men embark. I don't want Faelan thinking we're dawdling."

They grinned as they paced back to their men and called the orders for them to embark. The men began to clamber up the sides of the ships as Faelan's force took their places on the quay. I surveyed the scene as Maelgwn's men climbed aboard their two ships and Sitric's men did likewise. I watched with pure joy as Bjorgolf and my warband clambered aboard *God's Wrath* and began loading supplies. I turned as I heard the clip-clop of two horses approaching and groaned.

Faelan approached with an elderly man and halted just before me. The old man dismounted and nodded respectfully whilst Faelan stayed mounted and looked down on me. "My men will embark shortly." He said formally as he stared down at me. "We shall leave at midday tomorrow I think." He had said it so matter-of-factly as though he was in command and his attitude irritated me.

"No." I said flatly, "We leave with the morning tide. May I remind you who commands here?" I stared at the arrogant cur for a few moments before he stiffly nodded his acceptance and turned his mount back towards his waiting men. I watched Faelan's retreating figure and used all my self control to try and hide my feelings as I noticed the huddle, which I had assumed was part of the crowd, behind his men. A number, larger in size than Faelan's fighting force, of children, wives and peddlers accompanied the Irish force. I shook my head at the inconvenience. I wanted a fighting force that could move quickly not a bloody social gathering.

The old man smiled apologetically through a near toothless smile and then bowed his head respectfully before introducing himself. "My name is Mac Ruaidri, the Lord of Cruach Brendain. I am honoured to meet you."

"And I am honoured to meet you, my lord. It would be a pleasure if you would attend a feast at my hall this evening." Mac Ruaidri smiled at the polite formalities and nodded his head in acceptance of my invitation. He had perfectly white hair, which resembled the snowfall of winter, and sported a moustache in the fashion the Irish favoured although I was grateful it was not as extravagant as Faelan's. He seemed affable enough and struck me as a more competent commander than Faelan.

As if reading my thoughts he jerked his head in the direction of Faelan, who was ordering his men and their entourage to board their ships. "I'll keep him in check, don't you worry. He thinks he's going to conquer the world." Mac Ruaidri swung his foot into a stirrup and hauled himself into the saddle. "I shall look forward to this evening. Good day." The old warrior turned his mount and fell-in beside Faelan.

I watched the Irish clamber aboard their ships and nodded approvingly. Despite Faelan's leadership the men were in high spirits and well equipped, although I did not approve of their small shields or the fact that their families were accompanying them.

I marched down the quay to where Bjorgolf supervised the loading of supplies onto *God's Wrath* and the small merchant knarrs that would accompany us. Bjorgolf grinned at my approach. "She's a fine ship. You're a lucky lad." I agreed and marvelled at the warship's beauty.

A short stocky man cleared his throat at Bjorgolf's side and introduced himself. "I am Briain O'Briain and am honoured to serve you, my lord. I am the ship's master." I coolly surveyed him; he had a deeply lined, wind-battered, face and lank dark hair which was tied behind his head. He seemed a hardy sailor although I was slightly unsettled by his lazy eye, as I was not too sure which eye to look at. I nodded politely at the man before continuing to survey the scene.

I was in high spirits as my men completed the final preparations and looked forward to what the next few days would bring. As the afternoon wore on and the light began to fade I beckoned for Bjorgolf and Briain to follow me and return to my small Duibhlinn hall. I was to throw a final feast for my commanders and their guests and I was strangely pleased with the prospect of playing host. I hoped Orlaith would attend, so that I could say my farewells and gaze into her beautiful eyes once more.

It was a small affair but my thralls had prepared a fine feast. Orlaith was the only woman in attendance and most of the men tried their best to impress her, but I was furious. There was a dark bruise on her left cheek, which she had done her best to cover up. It did little to mar her beauty, but that fact did not concern me. I stared hatefully at Faelan, who sat at her side. The bastard's moustache wobbled every time he moved his mouth and I just wanted to rip the bloody thing off his face.

I talked when spoken to and I knew I was being a poor host. But I did well to check my temper; the bastard must be beating her, for why else would she have a bruise on her face? Faelan drank my ale and greedily gulped down my food. He talked animatedly with Mac Ruaidri who, clearly tolerating his commander, laughed half-heartedly in the appropriate places and nodded his head. Sitric and Wselfwulf had long since retired to their ships and Maelgwn rose to follow suit. The Powysian nodded his thanks for the feast and exited the hall.

Faelan rose to his feet and belched loudly. He laughed at my scowl, "I bid most of you a good night." Orlaith rose next to him and he turned quickly to face her. "You can do what you wish, woman. I do not desire your company tonight. You can wait for this poor excuse of a feast to finish, or you can go back to my hall. Do what you wish, I couldn't care less. Tonight I sleep on my ship"

Orlaith, evidently embarrassed at having been so publically humiliated, flushed and sat back down as her husband left the hall. Mac Ruaidri sent me an apologetic smile and was about to give his thanks when Faelan screamed at him to follow.

Cerit sent me a surprised look. "What a miserable bastard. You are going to need to keep an eye on him, Gruffudd." Orlaith suppressed a sob, which sounded more like a gasp. Cerit, clearly having forgotten her presence apologised immediately. "I meant no offence, my lady. I am sure your husband is a fine man."

Orlaith said nothing and Cerit shot me a worried glance as she held her head in her hands. Hild, her dour maid, came forward to comfort her lady. Cerit rose awkwardly, "I'd best be going, brother. I shall see you in the morning." With that Cerit escaped the sour mood of my hall and disappeared into Duibhlinn's streets to seek further entertainment.

I rose from my seat and walked over to where Orlaith sobbed. Hild shot me a scowl of disapproval and I shot her a threatening gaze in return which made her look away quickly. She took my meaning and retreated a respectable distance. I sat next to Orlaith and put a consolatory arm round her shoulder.

I half expected her to protest and push my arm away as formality expected, but instead she let her head rest on my shoulder as she cried. I did not know what to do but let her cry; I felt the sobs pull at the strings of my heart.

She glanced up at me, her green eyes were red from weeping and tears streamed down her cheeks. The bruise looked more prominent up close and I felt the anger rise in my chest. I swore then to myself that Faelan would get his comeuppance. She controlled her breathing. "Oh, Gruffudd. What am I to do?" I could not answer and so she continued. "I hate him, he is a bastard. He doesn't treat me well."

I struggled to control my temper, I wanted nothing more than to track Faelan down and gut him. But I tried to sound comforting. "How does he treat you?"

She looked down suddenly and wept again. She seemed ashamed. "He does not love me as a man should love a wife." She would not say more and wept into my chest as we sat there for a long time. I pressed her to explain, but she would not.

She called for Hild to leave us. The maid reluctantly left and waited in the thrall's quarters as I comforted Orlaith. She wept until she could not weep anymore and I still had my arm around her. I thought it best that she have these moments to let all her emotions out. She took my hand in hers and squeezed it gently.

She looked up into my eyes and spoke sadly. "Why couldn't I have married you?" She let the question trail off as I bent down and kissed her forehead. I loved her and she loved me, God but I cursed Muirchertach for promising her to that bastard Faelan. "I love you," she blurted it out and smiled when I repeated the feelings.

I rose and lifted her in my arms; she flung her arms round my neck and kissed me on the lips. I did not care of the scandal or Father Cathal's threat. I loved Orlaith and she loved me too, so we retreated to the bedchamber and made love.

Duibhlinn was shrouded in a thick mist as I worked my way through the port's streets. Ronan and Ruaidri had been sent to the hall by Bjorgolf to escort me back to the ships. The two had shown no surprise when Orlaith had left my bedchamber to return to her husband's hall. The two brothers grinned knowingly at me and seemed happy that I was in good spirits.

As we approached the ships, Sitric emerged from the mist with Wselfwulf close behind him. I halted and greeted the two as they marched towards me. I noticed the old Saxon carried a wooden box and he beamed a massive smile as he caught my gaze. Sitric spoke awkwardly. "Gruffudd, I have a gift for you. I feel now is the appropriate time and Cynan, your father, would have wanted you to have it."

He gestured at the box as Wselfwulf stepped forwards. The old Saxon winked at me as I opened the box. Inside was a folded length of cloth and as I pulled it free from the box I realised what it was. A banner! As I spread the dusty cloth the true splendour of the banner was revealed. The cloth was quartered in red and yellow and had a red or yellow lion with blue tongues and claws rampant in each quarter.

Tears pricked my eyes as I realised what it must be. Sitric's proud voice disturbed my thoughts. "It is your father's banner. The banner of Aberffraw. He wanted me to give it to you when the moment was right. I could not think of a better moment than now. Your mother, God rest her soul, would be so proud."

Wselfwulf smiled broadly and clapped my shoulder. "I always knew you would make a fine warrior lad. A bloody trouble maker too though mind. Now let's go and cause some trouble in Gwynedd, eh?"

I laughed at the old Saxons words. I was touched by the moment and struggled not to weep for joy. I scrambled up the side of the ship, draped in the banner. Bjorgolf grinned proudly as I handed him the banner, ordering him to fly it from the ship's mast. I nodded at Briain to get us under way and he shouted the orders for the men to get to their positions. I heard the masters of the other ships calling the same orders. My men cheered as my banner flew from the ship's mast; the cloth caught in the wind and flew majestically as the drum beat the rhythm of the oars.

One by one the ships followed *God's Wrath* down the An Liffe and out into the open sea. It was a proud moment, an emotional moment. Pride swelled in my chest as I looked about the ship's deck and Myrddin's prophecy played over and over in my mind. As my twenty ships snaked out of the An Liffe and into the Irish Sea I muttered a prayer to God and my heart leapt for joy. I was Gruffudd son of Cynan and I was going home, to claim what was mine, my birthright. I was going to Gwynedd.

Part Two

XV

The rain lashed against my face as I peered at the flat land ahead of *God's Wrath*. The dark smudge of windswept land spread along the horizon to my front, no more than ten miles away. So this was home I thought. A strange feeling of familiarity coursed through my veins, bringing a triumphant grin to my face. I gazed to my right and vaguely made out a giant jagged mountain through the thick cloud cover. The crossing had so far taken two days. The sea was rough and the wind vengeful.

Most of the men had joined me to catch their first glimpses of Ynys Môn. I knew the island was the breadbasket of Gwynedd, take that I thought, and the rest of Gwynedd would follow soon enough. I looked up at the ship's sail and felt my heart quicken as my banner snapped in the strong wind. I made my way back down the deck, ignoring the salty sea water which sprayed over the gunwale, to where Bjorgolf and Briain sat hunched in thick cloaks around the steering rudder.

I acknowledged the two men who grumbled a greeting back. Bjorgolf was not infected with the excitement most of my eager warband felt as they jostled each other to get a view of the outstretched land ahead of us. The Dane wiped a mixture of rain and sea water from his face, cursing in the process. "Don't know what the fuss is about. If it's anything like Ireland, they'll be sick of the place in a day."

Briain laughed at Bjorgolf's side. The Irishman knew these waters like the back of his hand and stood to get a better view of the land ahead, squinting with an expert's eye. "Not too long now. We shall be upon Abermenai before midday. I'm going to start the approach to the straits soon enough, my lord."

I muttered an acknowledgment at the Irishman's words. I counted all the other ships of my fleet to make

172

sure they were all there. I took it as a good omen for my coming campaign that I had lost none of my fleet to the vengeful sea during our crossing. I raised my voice over the wind as I turned back to face Briain's gaze. I glanced at the bridge of his nose to avoid the awkwardness of looking into his lazy eye. "Take us alongside Maelgwn. I cannot trust Cathal's words that we will be welcome in Abermenai." Bjorgolf raised a surprised eyebrow and I quickly dispelled his doubts. "Don't worry, Cathal's probably right. He usually is but I cannot be too careful."

Bjorgolf nodded his agreement as he rose and made his way down the deck. "Alright you bunch of whoresons. This isn't a bloody pleasure trip!" Some of the men grumbled and others talked excitedly amongst themselves as they began to make their way back to their positions, where Bjorgolf continued to hassle them. "Check that your blades are sharp, you may need them before the day is out. Get a bloody move one you bastards!"

The men began their pre-battle rituals as Briain brought us within hailing distance of Maelgwn's ship. I cupped my hands and hollered Maelgwn's name. I could make out the Powysian's figure and he waved an arm to acknowledge me. I cupped my hands again, "I want you to take your two ships to that beach there!" I pointed ahead of us at the land a few miles ahead. "Head straight on and you will come to Abermenai!" He shouted an acknowledgment and barked orders at his ship master.

Briain steered us away from Maelgwn's ships and back to the head of my small flotilla. The rest of my fleet followed *God's Wrath* on its course as we headed for the narrow entrance which would take us into the straits. A headland of dunes jutted out from Ynys Môn to our left and the men looked in awe at the huge mountain tops that had pierced through the cloud cover to our right.

I could make out Maelgwn's ships landing at the beach and the dark shapes of men began hopping over the ships' sides as the Powysian formed them up. Then they were lost from view. Soon after we rounded the headland I could not help but marvel at the landscape as the rain clouds began to dissipate. The vast mountain range of Eryri dominated the skyline to our right and the piercing mountain tops seemed to reach all the way to the heavens. I, like a good number of my men, stood open-mouthed in awe of the formidable peaks which resembled the jagged edge of a woodman's saw. My heart swelled with pride as I admired the harsh beauty of the lands of my birthright, my kingdom.

The grey sea calmed as we headed into the straits and I muttered a prayer of thanks to the Lord as the persistent rain, for the first time in days, stopped. Small fishing skiffs hurried away from our approach and I noticed the tiny shapes of peasants on the shore of Arfon looking on in awe as my fleet majestically slid along the straits. I guessed they watched with a mixture of fear and wonder as my fleet cut through the waters of the straits, for little did they know that their rightful ruler had come to claim what was his. The ship banked to the left as Briain aimed for a dark smear amongst the sand dunes which marked the port of Abermenai a couple of miles ahead.

Briain called for the sail to be lowered and screamed at my sword-brothers to pull the oars. Several of Briain's crewmen brought the sail down efficiently and stowed it away before taking up their oars and pulling in time to the beat Bjorgolf set on the ship's drum. I glanced behind to check that the other ships of the flotilla had followed suit.

My fleet must have made a fearsome sight as we approached the small port of Abermenai. I could make out the settlement clearly as we aimed for the small sandy beach. A dirty cloud of hearth smoke lingered above the port's skyline as I scanned the settlement, my eyes fixing on the church's belfry as the bell began to chime frantically

174

in alarm. Small round huts some of stone, but most of wattle and daub, clustered around the church and the lord's hall made up the bulk of the settlement. Cries of panic carried across the water as the fishermen, beside a rickety looking wooden quay, dragged their skiffs ashore and ran for their homes to safeguard their possessions and make sure their womenfolk and children ran for safety. A feeling of apprehension fell over me as the frightened cries of women and children sounded as they fled for the cover of the sand dunes which surrounded the settlement, with all the possessions they could carry.

As the beat of the ship's drum pulled us closer and closer to Abermenai my heart raced despite the apprehension I still felt. I was moments away from my first step on the soil of my kingdom. The church bell still tolled its warning as, what I guessed must be the last of the port's townsfolk either made for the safety of the sand dunes or barricaded their homes. My sword hand went for the hilt of my blade and I crossed myself, in the hope that no blood would be shed, as the man, whom I assumed to be the lord of Abermenai, cantered a sturdy looking pony onto the sandy beach. The man drew his sword and waved it above his head, gesturing for his hearth troops to form their ponies on him. I counted twenty horsemen below the man's banner, which was a yellow cross upon a red field, and prayed silently that it would not come to a fight.

We were but a hundred paces from the beach now. The wind made me squint as my men picked up the speed for the final approach, and I cursed as more men filtered onto the sandy expanse to our front. A man, whom I guessed to be the town's priest, rode a grey donkey at the head of a mob of armed townsfolk. The priest shouted instructions at the ragged mob who clumsily formed up into three ranks. I counted twenty men in the first rank, which meant there must be sixty of them, but I did not fear them, as, in my experience, pressed townsfolk and labourers

175

made unwilling warriors, but I wished to God that I would not have to fight these people.

We were moments from the beach now; I glanced behind me and swallowed hard. "To arms men! Prepare to beach!" All around the sound of clattering oars sounded as my men dragged them aboard before taking up their weapons. My warband began to form up in the ship's centre as *God's Wrath* ghosted towards the sandy beach.

Bjorgolf's voice sounded behind me. "We will cut them apart, I pity the fools." I nodded the truth of it. It was strange, I don't know what I had really expected as I prepared to set foot on the lands of my birthright for the first time, but I certainly had no wish for it to be remembered as the slaughter of Abermenai. Commands rang out from the men on the beach as they braced for the assault they thought was to come. I hoped they would recognise the banner of Aberffraw which flew proudly from the mast and realise that we were not a band of pirates intent on blood and plunder.

I drew my blade as *God's Wrath* ploughed into the sand, pitching me forwards. My men let out their battle cry as *God's Wrath* shuddered to an abrupt halt. "For God! For King Gruffudd!" My heart almost burst with pride as I heard the cry and followed my sword-brothers over the side. I landed heavily upon the sandy beach and glanced quickly over my shoulder. We had landed ahead of the rest of my fleet and had but a few moments until the next of my ships landed on Abermenai's beach.

I did not want my men to charge at the port's defenders and begin a slaughter so I screamed for my men to form-up. "Shieldwall! On me! Shieldwall!" It took moments for my men, Bjorgolf and Ronan beside me, to stand shoulder to shoulder and slap our shields together. Shouts of confusion rang out from the defenders and they made no move towards us as I gazed over the rim of my shield, prepared to give battle if it came to it.

The man whom I had assumed was their leader trotted his mount forwards and called over his shoulder at his men to dismount. As if in reassurance he pointed at my banner which flew proudly atop the ship's mast. The man skillfully hopped down from his mount and his hearth troops did likewise. The man drew his sword and raised it in salute. "The King has returned! All hail King Gruffudd!" His men, half-heartedly at first, repeated the cry again and again until it boomed out enthusiastically. The priest had dismounted from his donkey and was praying to the heavens as a sense of relief flowed through my body and a broad grin spread across my face for I was amongst my people, I was home.

I called for my men to stand down and I sheathed my blade before stepping forwards. Bjorgolf tried to grab my arm to stop me and cursed as I shook his arm free. The lord and his men still cheered my name as the priest sent some of the armed townsfolk to spread the word that their rightful king had arrived upon the shores of Ynys Môn.

Bjorgolf put one of his bear like hands on my shoulder to gain my attention as I stood still in-between the two forces, a feeling of intense pride strong within my chest. "What the hell is going on?" The Dane was confused, as were most of my men.

Bjorgolf did not have to wait long for the answer. Their lord sheathed his blade and marched forwards until he stood before me. The man wore an old mail hauberk and, from the hilt of his blade, I could see that he had some wealth although his helmet, complete with cheek guards that hid his features, was plainly designed. He removed his helmet to reveal a middle-aged and heavily lined dark face with a receding hairline of greying black neatly cropped hair and was clean-shaven except for a neatly trimmed moustache. He met my eyes briefly and dropped to one knee before speaking respectfully in the language of the

Britons. "My King, I am Gwyncu son of Owain, Lord of Rhosyr and the port of Abermenai. I pledge my sword and those of my men to your service."

I grinned happily. I was home; this was it. The moment for which I had been longing all these years. These were my people and they wanted me as their king. Soon I would reclaim all my rightful lands from the usurpers. I put my hands on Gwyncu's shoulders and told him to rise. He stood a head shorter than I and turned to face the crowd which was beginning to swell as the townsfolk heard word that their rightful king had returned. Gwyncu thumped the air and roared to the crowd. "The king has returned! Rejoice at his coming, for we are free! All hail King Gruffudd!"

Bjorgolf winked at me and chuckled at my embarrassment as the crowd shouted my name enthusiastically. Gwyncu gestured for me to follow him and so I called for my warband to form up before following the Lord of Rhosyr deeper into Abermenai. I placed a hand on Ronan's shoulder. "My compliments to Sitric, but the army is under his command as I discuss things with my people. He is to remain close to the ships until I send word and make sure he keeps Faelan under control." Ronan nodded that he understood the message and ran across to where Sitric's men were formed up under his raven banner.

The men of my warband grinned excitedly as women gave them drink and food, a few even kissed some of my men on the cheeks. The priest, who was a small, rotund and ageing man, had joined the grand procession which followed Gwyncu up the main street from the beach into the town. I tried to ignore Bjorgolf's mocking gaze as the priest acclaimed my coming to God's grace and sang my praises to the heavens.

Gwyncu's hearth troops, or *teulu* as he called them, had formed a guard of honour around me, Bjorgolf, Gwyncu and the priest as my warband followed closely behind. Gwyncu's features radiated with joy and he sang the praises of his soldiers, whom he described as the finest the province of Rhosyr could muster. Bjorgolf nudged me and muttered in Danish so that Gwyncu could not take offence. "If they are his finest, God help us."

I looked closely at Gwyncu's finest warriors and felt a pang of doubt. They wore an assortment of hardened leather and hides and only three possessed coats of ring-mail. Half possessed helms, from varying centuries by the look of things, and the other half were bareheaded. Although they seemed stout men Bjorgolf was right to doubt Gwyncu's word. As far as I was concerned they were untested in battle and would have to prove themselves to me. If I was to rely on these men I would have to see for myself what they could do, and quickly.

The procession led to Gwyncu's hall in the centre of the port, and he beckoned me inside. Gwyncu clapped his hands and some servants scuttled about to find their master's finest ale and food. My heart was filled with joy and almost burst with happiness for I could not have wished for a more successful homecoming. I liked to think that my mother's spirit was watching over me and had heeded my prayers that no blood would be shed this day. A day of happiness and merriment, the day of my homecoming.

It took almost two hours to disembark all the men and supplies from the fleet. Gwyncu and Abermenai's priest, along with most of the townspeople, stared in awe at the hardened warriors of Sitric's warband as they marched through the town's main street and out onto the grassy pastureland beyond the dunes which marked the boundary of the town. I had sent Sitric, whom I knew I could rely upon, and his warband to set up camp in the pastureland that led to Abermenai and to watch for any possible movement of Trahaearn's forces, which I guessed must soon hear news of my arrival. My warband joined Sitric's and my foster-father set about his task with total efficiency which seemed to impress Gwyncu greatly.

Faelan, on the other hand, was clearly disappointed with the enthusiastic welcome I had received and seemed intent on ruining my homecoming. He had allowed his men to roam the streets of Abermenai. The townsfolk were wary of the Irish but I doubt their small town had ever been so busy. Faelan's men bartered for, or bought, pretty much the whole of Abermenai's ale and they did the same with the fishermen's supply of smoked mackerel. His men would now be useless for the whole day as they succumbed to drunkenness and gluttony. Faelan and his rabble would be more of a hindrance than anything else, of that I was certain. The man's nature reminded me of a petulant child on whom you could rely to throw a tantrum if a sibling's accomplishment outshone theirs.

Faelan had commandeered the town's only tavern for his own personal quarters and use. At least the bastard was out of my sight. He had sent Mac Ruaidri, who acted as a peacemaker between the both of us, to explain his decision. Faelan claimed his men deserved the rest and whatever the town could offer, as they had suffered at sea greatly on the two day crossing to liberate these people. My blood boiled. Not for the first time, I cursed Muirchertach. Why had he sent the arrogant fool with me? Mac Ruaidri had shrugged his shoulders in apology and he, at least, had managed to keep his eighty men from joining Faelan's in running riot round Abermenai.

Gwyncu had insisted on sending his best horsemen out as messengers to the local nobility. I accepted Gwyncu's offer gladly as his men knew this land and would deliver my message with haste. They carried my compliments and a summons to a council to be held at Aberffraw in two days' time. Gwyncu had sent out a call to arms to all his tenants and vassal Lords of Rhosyr; he had also ensured me the lords of the province of Aberffraw would support me as would the men of Cemais.

I had also insisted that my summons be sent to the men of Arfon, Arllechwedd and Dunoding as well as to the three sons of Merwydd of Lleyn. From what Father Cathal had informed me and, from the information I had learnt myself over the last few months, I knew my coming would split Gwynedd. The thought troubled me, but it was necessary. The Lord of Arllechwedd was currently occupied with attempting to halt French encroachment into his territories from across the River Conwy and would hardly be likely to spare any of his forces, but I would need him on my side. Dunoding, stuck between Lleyn and Trahaearn's heartlands, was unlikely to support me and I judged the Lord of Dunoding would not join Trahaearn either but would rather wait until he could see a clear winner. It was the sons of Merwydd whom I needed, upon them my fate would rest.

As the afternoon wore on Maelgwn and his men finally appeared. The mercenary was fuming and I dared not jest with him, as he would more than likely cut my throat than laugh. He had got lost amongst the sand dunes between the beach where he had landed and Abermenai. The Powysian prided himself on his efficiency and the blunder had hurt his pride. I ordered Maelgwn to remain in Abermenai until I sent further word and instructed him to keep Faelan on a short leash. Maelgwn was in a dangerous mood and I judged that in itself would be enough to deter Faelan from further mischief. A small glimmer of hope crossed my mind that the Powysian would kill Faelan if he caused him any trouble and that brought a wry smile to my face.

I had sent Ruaidri, who had a natural ease with horses, to fetch my fine Irish mount which I had received as a gift from Muirchertach along with *God's Wrath*. I would ride for Aberffraw that afternoon and there I would wait in the home of my ancestors for the loyal men of Gwynedd to come and swear their oaths to their rightful king.

I rode at the head of the column with Sitric, Cerit, Gwyncu, and Mac Ruaidri as we plodded along the road which led to my family's ancient seat of power, Aberffraw. I had split my small force; Maelgwn held Abermenai along with Faelan and his Irish, whilst I marched my men, Sitric's warband and Gwyncu's *teulu* along the dirt track. Gwyncu had sent one of his men ahead to announce my coming to the town's headman, so that we would not scare the townsfolk. Gwyncu assured me that there was no garrison of any kind in Aberffraw since Trahaearn had usurped the throne.

My column entered the town during the mid-afternoon, to the cheers of the townspeople, under my proud banner which flew above those of the other lords. The sky was beginning to darken as I called a halt outside a large, but badly dilapidated, hall. The nervous town headman explained that this was the hall from which my family had ruled and that none, for thirty-six long years, had held this lordship.

I dismounted and inspected the rotten timber, shaking my head in disappointment as I surveyed the old palisade which encircled the hall. It was useless. In places the timber had become so rotten with damp that it had collapsed. If I were attacked here then the palisade would serve as nothing other than a slight hindrance to the enemy. It was in such poor condition I was sure a flock of sheep would have no problem breaching the defences.

Cerit disturbed my thoughts as we entered the old hall; the smell of damp was overpowering. The great hall, which had once been the court of kings, had clearly been home to livestock. The stench of animals and their waste assaulted the senses as I surveyed the hall. "A grand hall in its day, brother." Cerit shot me a friendly smile. "It will be a fine palace again one day soon I wager!"

A slight smile split my face at the words. Cerit somehow always managed to lift my spirits. But the smile was gone as I turned to face the headman. "I want here cleaned up today for in two days, I shall be entertaining some of the most powerful lords of Gwynedd." The headman nodded his head quickly and scurried out of the once beautiful building.

Sitric clapped a consolatory arm around my shoulders. "Don't worry. It will be as beautiful as it once was, I assure you. Your father spoke of this hall's majesty. Remember; from small beginnings grow powerful things."

I grinned ruefully at Sitric's words. We left the rotting old building as the rain started again and some townspeople hurried into the hall to begin the clean-up. I stared to the north of the hall and surveyed the flat, bleak landscape as the rain rolled in from the sea. Then I turned south and looked in awe at the harsh beauty of the mountains rising dominantly in the distance. I thought of what tomorrow would bring and looked again, thoughtfully, at the formidable mountain range. Across them lay my enemy.

XVI

I looked up at the morning sky and was relieved to see a
clear, almost perfectly blue, skyline. The townsfolk had
done a good job of cleaning out the old hall throughout the
whole of yesterday, so that it was fit enough for myself and
the other lords to sleep in. But the townspeople continued
to scrub at the fouled flagstones and replace the ancient
thatch on the roof as I tasked some of my men with
replacing the pitiful excuse of a palisade.

My thoughts were brought back to the present by
the entertaining spectacle which unfolded before my eyes.
Bjorgolf chuckled to himself as we watched Gwyncu's men
demonstrate their ability. Gwyncu had pressed all the men
of fighting age of Aberffraw, and a good number from
Abermenai, into a levy. The disorganised rabble brought
the number of men under Gwyncu's banner to around one
hundred and fifty. His levy, on the most part, was eager to
learn and enthusiastically took instruction from the men of
Gwyncu's teulu who supervised their training.

The ill-disciplined mob stumbled through their
manoeuvers and demonstrated a complete lack of skill at
arms. I sighed as I looked on; if this was the calibre of men
who would make up the bulk of my army, then I had a job
on my hands to build an army and get it battle ready within
a week. I did not relish the prospect.

Bjorgolf watched with his expert eye and chuckled
to himself every time one of Gwyncu's men stumbled or
made a fool of themselves, which was worryingly often.
Half his men were not even equipped with proper weapons,
but carried an assortment of tools and knives instead.

Cerit nudged me in the ribs. "They're keen, I'll give
them that, but you are going to have your work cut out,
brother." He gestured towards Wselfwulf, who now stood
beside Bjorgolf and joined the Dane in surveying
Gwyncu's levy. "Let Wselfwulf loose on them. He will put

the fear of God into the buggers and have them battle ready in no time, I promise you."

I remembered the old Saxon's strict training methods, which I had endured as a boy, and grinned knowingly. Cerit was right, but I had a better idea. I shot Cerit a mischievous grin. "Care to show them how it's done, brother?"

Cerit sent me an amused glance. "Why, it would be an honour dear brother. Not that it will be difficult to do better." With that he laughed and turned back towards Sitric's warband who had joined the growing audience who mocked Gwyncu's men.

Sitric strode up to me and nodded respectfully. "Want to show them how it's done, eh?" He laughed as I nodded back. "At least they're enthusiastic; we'll give them a professional demonstration." Sitric had gone to look even older over the winter and his hair was turning from grey to white, but the orders seemed to reinvigorate him as he barked commands to his warband to form up.

Bjorgolf trotted over to me as Wselfwulf rejoined Sitric's men. "I won't have that lot thinking they're better than us." He gestured at Sitric's men who were forming into four ranks of twenty, quickly and efficiently. "Can I let the lads show 'em how it's done?"

I shook my head and Bjorgolf shot me a disappointed look but did not argue. My men looked on as Sitric divided his force so that two ranks of twenty now faced each other across the trampled grass. Sitric shouted his commands to one of the sides and Cerit at the other. The two formations slapped their shields together smartly. Gwyncu and has men had stopped their exertions and watched with a mixture of awe and respect. The two formations closed on each other and the men pushed and shoved at the opposing shield wall, trying to make ground.

Sitric's men demonstrated their ruthless efficiency for the next hour. Gwyncu had joined me and shook his head in admiration. "Trahaearn stands no chance." Gwyncu spoke with a flat certainty and repeated his words again, almost to himself, as I looked at him.

"Have you any idea of the number or quality of the men Trahaearn and Cynwrig can command?" Since I had landed at Abermenai that thought had troubled me and I knew Gwyncu was not sure, but that did not stop me asking the question.

He shrugged his shoulders to confirm what I already knew and then turned back and applauded Sitric's men as they finished the demonstration before retreating back to their positions around the great hall.

I clapped Gwyncu on the shoulder. "Get your men together; I'm going to teach them a thing or two." The Briton grinned happily and shouted for his men to form up. The enthusiastic group of men, not deterred by Sitric's show of ruthless efficiency, rose to their feet and organised themselves into three disorganised ranks.

I turned to Bjorgolf and smiled at him. "You're going to enjoy this. Select twenty of our men and stagger them amongst Gwyncu's lads." Bjorgolf grinned broadly and nodded his acknowledgment before trotting over to where my warband waited.

I watched with a feeling of intense pride at how professional my sword-brothers were. They set a fine example for Gwyncu's men to follow. The enthusiastic group of Britons were eager to learn and made remarkable progress in tactics and skill at arms. Bjorgolf pushed them to the limit and beyond. Gwyncu and his teulu followed Bjorgolf's commands eagerly, along with the levy, and I smiled to myself as Gwyncu and his men absorbed everything they were shown.

As the day wore on to mid afternoon, the lords of northern Gwynedd began to arrive. Bands of men trotted their hardy mountain ponies to Aberffraw to meet their rightful king. I knew that soon I would be tested in the game of kings; I would have to strike a hard bargain with some of these men and I would have to ensure I had their full support. I rubbed my hands in anticipation as I marched back towards the great hall of Aberffraw where, tonight, my hopes would be dashed or made.

Three of northern Gwynedd's most powerful lords sat in front of me in a room at the back of the royal hall. I stared coldly at them as they shifted uncomfortably in their seats. My eyes rested on a strongly built man in his middle-years. His raven-black hair was neatly cropped and his moustache was perfectly maintained, he was well dressed and wore a fine coat of mail. He was Asser, Lord of Nevyn, the eldest of the late Merwydd's sons, and the right-hand of the man who dared to call himself King of Lleyn, Cynwrig son of Rhiwallon. He spoke for his brothers also and I knew this man could make my campaign very difficult if he so wished. He met my steely gaze and returned it in kind. I judged the man to be calculating and ruthless and hoped he thought the same of me.

Then my eyes fell on the youngest of the three. He seemed to be exactly the same age as myself. His lank blonde hair fell to his shoulders and he sported a stubbly beard. His blue eyes glanced nervously around the room as I let the silence stretch. I thought he looked more Dane or Norse than Briton and wondered whether that was the case. I did not think much of the young man and from what I had previously heard, I was correct in that judgement. He was Tudur, Lord of Cemais, the most northerly province of Ynys Môn and Gwynedd, and the small port by the same name. He was also the richest nobleman of Ynys Môn. From what I had gleaned, he was a fool and had grand aspirations to call himself King of Ynys Môn. I would have to watch the bastard closely.

Finally my eyes rested on an overweight, ageing, man. His breath wheezed from his lungs as he spluttered a cough loudly. His dark hair had greyed and he sported a thick moustache, which hid the whole of his upper lip. He wore a grubby padded tunic, which still held some of the remnants of his last meal. The man's name was Seisyll and he was the Lord of Dinorwic, a small village and slate quarry which lay between the Bishopric of Bangor and the old Roman fort of Segontium. The man may be well past his prime but nevertheless he commanded the respect of Arfon's nobility and was in attendance with the Bishop of Bangor's blessing.

The townspeople of Aberffraw had worked wonders on the old royal hall. The timber was still damp and, to an experienced eye, the dilapidation was evident, but I was pleased with their efforts. The thatched roof had been completely replaced and the hearth cleared where a warm fire now burned. Welcome to the world of kings I thought. Here were three men whom I needed but could not trust one bit. I had to win all three over or my campaign might well be over before it had even begun. Seisyll and Tudur eyed my guards warily. Bjorgolf and Gwcharki loomed behind me; they were both big men and were there to intimidate. Only Asser looked unperturbed. Tudur could not take his eyes from the giant Pict, who stared impassively past him. The blue tattoos unnerved the young man and I tried to suppress a smile of satisfaction.

I let the silence stretch a few moments more and cleared my throat. I had thrown a feast in honour of my guests and they greedily enjoyed my hospitality as they waited for their overlords to come to an agreement with their future king. I raised my voice slightly so that I could clearly be heard above the celebrations that went on the other side of the door. "My lords, first of all I would like to thank you for answering my summons. It has pleased me that such distinguished and notable men, as yourselves, have heeded my call."

I chose my words carefully and was rewarded with

a nod of approval from Seisyll and a sly grin from Tudur. Asser continued to eye me blankly. "You know why I am here. I am here to reclaim my birthright. I wish to see the house of Aberffraw restored to its rightful position. For too long Trahaearn, the usurper, and his ally Cynwrig have raped this land and despoiled it by their un-Godly actions." Asser's eyes flickered at my words, but he made no protest. Seisyll nodded enthusiastically whilst Tudur looked at me thoughtfully. I glanced at each in turn and grinned. "I believe we have to reach an agreement, my lords. A means to an end, I believe you say."

Asser nodded his head respectfully at my words, showing that we understood each other perfectly. He would be the hardest to win over, of that I was sure. Seisyll chuckled at the truth of my words and grinned broadly at me whilst Tudur's eyes glittered greedily. I judged that Seisyll would support me no matter what and Tudur would follow anyone for a handful of gold, that much was clear. Asser was the prize. I needed him most of all.

Seisyll and Tudur glanced at Asser, who sat between the two lords. He ignored their glances and spoke clearly, in a voice that was used to giving commands. "It is fair to say that we are open to your coming, my lord." He added 'my lord' respectfully and continued in his commanding voice. "Cynwrig is nothing but a petty tyrant, but one that I benefit from for keeping him on his precious throne. I care neither here nor there for Trahaearn. But tell me, if you will, what incentive is there for me, my brothers and these noble lords?" He held out his arms to gesture at the two lords who flanked him.

I smiled inwardly, the game was afoot and it was time to play. I spoke to Asser first. "Should you and your brothers join in my rightful campaign than you shall be rewarded greatly. You shall rule Lleyn in my name, paying me homage as your rightful king. You, Lord Asser, shall be the Lord of Lleyn and you may give your brothers and vassals which ever lordships you desire within the province of Lleyn." Asser nodded his head thoughtfully, I offered him much and he knew it. By supporting me he would become arguably the most powerful lord, besides myself, in Gwynedd.

I turned to Seisyll as Asser considered my offer. "Lord Seisyll, I shall reward the men of Arfon equally. Each lord will receive a handsome profit should they support me. I shall reward you with a sum that will double your annual income this year." I did not offer Seisyll a grand title, like I had Asser, as I knew he did not carry much influence outside of Arfon. The province of Arfon was under the thumb of the Bishop of Bangor and what I offered Seisyll had been fair in regards to his standing. Besides if I offered to install him as Lord of Arfon the Bishop would likely throw in his lot against me or, worse still, threaten excommunication. Seisyll's round face grinned broadly at my offer.

Finally I turned my gaze to Tudur, who eyed me greedily through his dark blue eyes. I instantly disliked him, but I needed his support as I could not afford to leave a potential enemy at my rear as I advanced further into Gwynedd. "Lord Tudur, I offer you a generous reward. I shall double the income that you make from the province of Cemais and then add half of that sum on again." His eyes glittered and he licked his lips at the thought. He would become wealthy indeed. I had no idea how I would be able to pay such a sum, but that did not matter. I needed him to believe that I would pay it. If I could not and had already been victorious over Trahaearn, then it would be unwise for Tudur to make the slightest complaint.

I let the silence stretch as the lords mulled over my offers. I cleared my throat and raised an eyebrow inquisitively to show that I expected an answer. Seisyll wheezed his reply. "The men of Arfon, with Bishop Dyfan's blessing, shall follow you into battle, my King." I nodded respectfully at the round face with its jowls as he nodded firmly, as if to seal the agreement.

Asser shifted uncomfortably in his seat; he held his right hand on his chin, deep in thought. He glanced up and met my gaze. "I, my brothers and my vassals will support you, my King. It will be a noble cause and one I know you shall win." I sighed inwardly with relief, the man was key to my hopes and he had supported me.

Tudur was the only one not to speak as he still thought on my proposal. The other two lords began to grow impatient and stared at the youth, whose greedy eyes betrayed his thoughts. "I believe I am owed a better price, lord." Seisyll took a sharp intake of breath as he stared, disbelieving, at the greed of the young man. I stared coldly at the youth. If he did not support me I no longer cared, now that I had the support of Asser and Seisyll; which I judged to be more than adequate. If Tudur refused my offer, which was more than generous, then I swore to myself that he would not reach Cemais alive.

Asser chuckled at the youth and fixed him with a knowing grin. "You really think you can command such a vast sum? What have you to offer, really?" The youth shot Asser a hateful stare and turned his greedy eyes back to me.

I spoke firmly, with a hint of a threat in my cold tone. "My offer stands. You will decide your fate now." He stared resentfully at me and glanced nervously at Bjorgolf and Gwcharki as my words struck home.

The youth nodded to himself. "It seems we have an accord, my King." He shifted uncomfortably in his seat as my eyes forced him to drop his glare, which betrayed his dark soul. I could not trust the little upstart and judged that one day I might well have to deal with him once and for all.

I rose from my ancient carved chair and nodded my thanks to the three lords. "My lords, I am grateful for your sound judgement. Now, it is time for us to discuss the campaign which is to come." I turned and beckoned

Bjorgolf forwards, "I wish all my commanders to attend a council of war immediately."

Bjorgolf grinned and spoke quietly so only I would hear. "At bloody last, my blade hasn't tasted blood for months. I hope it shall not have to wait much longer." I watched the Dane as he strode out of the room and into the feasting hall to summon my commanders. I knew he was right; our blades would taste blood very soon. I just hoped my new allies were up to it.

I glanced around the room at the expectant expressions of my notable lords and commanders. I faced them all from beside the fire hearth; the warmth seeped into my bones and I had never felt so alive. Bjorgolf and Gwcharki still flanked me as I eyed my audience; I caught Bjorgolf's eye and smiled as he winked at me. I had done well, I knew. But it was now time to plot the downfall of my enemies.

All my commanders were present except Faelan; I cursed the open disrespect the arrogant bastard displayed at every opportunity. Mac Ruaidri had offered his apologies and shrugged his shoulders at his commander's actions. I pitied the old Irishman, he had done his best to advise Faelan but the bonehead thought he knew better. Again I cursed Muirchertach and thought of Orlaith. I longed for her naked body and the love we shared for one another. I felt a surge of anger begin to rise in my chest and dismissed the thoughts immediately. I was here to fight for my birthright and, I swore to myself, if that bastard got in the way then I would break him.

I glanced around the room once again. How could I fail? I took heart from the battle hardened faces of Sitric, Asser, Maelgwn, Cerit and Mac Ruaidri. I knew I could win any campaign with such men, but I doubted the capability of most of my countrymen. It was clear that Gwyncu's warband had never had to fight a major battle in their lives and Seisyll hardly cut an inspiring military figure. I did not trust Tudur either; the bastard was out for himself.

I swallowed hard and cleared my throat. "My lords, I aim to march on our enemies within the next five days." I let my words sink in before I continued. "I shall leave a small garrison to guard our land from attack and defend our people. I plan that the majority of my army will gather at the old Roman fort of Segontium beside the river Seiont." I was not the only one to see Gwyncu cross himself at the old fort's name. I ignored him as I continued. "From there we shall march towards the peninsula of Lleyn and join with Lord Asser's forces. Speed is key, my lords. I envisage that Cynwrig and Trahaearn will take five days to muster their men and then another five days for them to join forces. I expect to defeat Cynwrig first and then turn on Trahaearn." I glanced around the room. "Any questions?"

Gwyncu stepped forward. "My King, I beg you to reconsider. The old Roman fort is cursed. The spirits of the old pagan gods roam the broken ruins. It is not the place for a Christian army to muster, it is cursed." Gwyncu crossed himself at the mention of the old Roman fort and again at the mention of the old pagan gods.

Sitric's voice boomed across the small room at the superstitious Briton. My foster-father had learnt the language from my mother and his mastery of the tongue surprised me. "Don't be a bloody fool. It is the logical point to muster an army; the Romans chose the ground well. I have been there in my youth and know it to be a sound choice." He gave me a reassuring nod before he continued. "Segontium lies at the top of a small hill, the land can be seen for miles around. It is easily defended and has enough open ground for the army to muster. Anyone who thinks otherwise is a muttonheaded fool." He shot Gwyncu a disapproving look and the Briton looked down at the floor rather than meet Sitric's unforgiving grey eyes.

Asser spoke next. "A fine plan, my King. Although

I fear you leave us open to an attack from the rear."
Everyone in the room fixed their attention on the powerfully built man as he continued. "The Lord of Arllechwedd has not honoured your summons. Robert the Frenchman covets all the land west of the Conwy River and he will likely seize the opportunity to attack deep into Arllechwedd, Arfon and Ynys Môn whilst they are weakly defended."

I cursed myself inwardly. I had forgotten Father Cathal's warning. Beware of the Frenchman he had said. "How can you be sure this Robert will try to take our land if we march to meet the usurpers?" I was wary of the Frenchman's reputation and it was plain that my countrymen feared him.

Asser spoke calmly. "For the past twenty or so years Robert has slowly expanded his control from the borderlands of *Lloegr*. He has all the lands east of the Conwy under an iron grip and he builds impregnable strongholds in the French fashion. They are like nothing you have ever seen before." I felt the doubt creep into my mind at Asser's words. "He fights differently, his horsemen ride down all who oppose him and his archers use the crossbow. Trahaearn, despite all his faults, has halted the Frenchman's advance. The Frenchman stares longingly from his castle at Degannwy at the lands on the western banks of the Conwy." Asser paused for a moment, as though gathering his thoughts. "Believe me, you must ensure the Lord of Arllechwedd's stronghold at Aber is loyal to you. They will be able to hold out against Robert for a short time, should he attack whilst our backs are turned."

All my commanders eyed me expectantly as I wondered what the hell a crossbow was. Before I could speak, Sitric turned to face me. "It is clear, Gruffudd, that we must march on this stronghold at Aber with haste. If the Lord of Arllechwedd does not wish to become Robert's puppet, or worse, then he will support you. Lord Asser's advice is sound; my men will be enough to scare the Lord of Arllechwedd." He spoke confidently and I did not doubt him. My foster-father had provided Muirchertach with sound advice on his rise to prominence, so my decision was made.

I spoke confidently and with authority as I gave the men their orders. "I shall cross the straits at first light tomorrow with my warband and Sitric's. From there we shall march on Aber and ensure that the Lord of Arllechwedd will support us." Sitric nodded approvingly as I met his eye, I was pleased to have his approval and continued confidently. "Maelgwn will cross the straits with me and establish himself in Segontium. I feel his looks will be enough to deter any pagan spirits." The men laughed at the jest, a couple did so nervously I noted. "Mac Ruaidri, you shall give my compliments to Faelan and advise him that he is to hold the port of Abermenai as we meet the enemy." The old Irishman was clearly despondent that he and his men would miss out on the inevitable fighting that was to come. But I did not wish to have Faelan thinking he knew best and undermining my authority at the slightest opportunity.

I turned my gaze on my countrymen. "Lord Asser, you will withdraw your forces to a convenient location, I shall leave that to your discretion. There you shall wait for my advance and we will join forces once my army has mustered. You shall send word as soon as you are in position." He nodded at my words, I did not doubt the man would be pivotal to the coming campaign and was relieved that he clearly had confidence in my plans.

I glanced at the nervous Gwyncu and smiled to reassure him. "Lord Gwyncu, you shall wait for Lord Tudur's arrival at Abermenai and from there you shall cross the straits and join Maelgwn's force at Segontium."

I turned a cold stare on Tudur. "I expect your forces

to have joined up with Gwyncu's in two days time. You shall cross the straits as soon as you arrive. Speed is key." The two lords nervously nodded their heads at my words.

"Lord Seisyll, the men of Arfon shall join Maelgwn at Segontium with all haste. There you shall all wait for my return." The jowls wobbled as Seisyll nodded his acknowledgment. I felt the energy course through my veins as I rattled out my orders.

Once I had ensured everyone knew what was expected of them and how many vassal lords were to protect our lands I concluded the council. "I bid you all a good night, my lords. For tomorrow our campaign begins in earnest."

As the commanders began to file out of the room I caught Maelgwn by the sleeve and called for Sitric to remain, the rest exited the hall. I heard cheers as the minor vassal lords, who still enjoyed the feast, heard that we would soon march on the enemy. I beckoned Bjorgolf and Gwcharki.

I spoke firmly as I met their eyes in turn. "Sitric get your lads ready now. Bjorgolf, I want you to get my men ready as well. I want to make the short march to Abermenai tonight; we shall cross the straits at first light. I want to deal with the Lord of Arllechwedd by midday and from there I wish to meet with Robert the Frenchman." I glanced at Maelgwn. "Can you spare a ship and its crew?" The Powysian nodded and I smiled back. "Good, have them sail down the straits to Aber after we have marched. Once the Lord of Arllechwedd is dealt with, I shall sail to meet with this Frenchman."

They all looked at me with worried expressions and I knew what they feared. I had to take this gamble; if I could get the Frenchman on-side then I would be all but guaranteed victory. It was a gamble, but one worth taking. "Oh, and Maelgwn? I want my enthusiastic countrymen as battle ready as you can get them. I know you like a

196

challenge." The Powysian laughed as we left the hall.

There would be little rest for me tonight. Tomorrow I headed into the unknown and possible battle. One way or another, the stronghold at Aber would be taken and I would meet the Frenchman.

XVII

I knelt on the cold, damp, shingle and grinned triumphantly despite the rain. I was the first of my men to land on the soil of Arfon. I glanced up at the old Roman ruins that crowned the small hill ahead and knew my choice had been correct. The old stonework dominated the hill and would command a good view of the land surrounding it. The sun had not long begun to rise and the grey morning light flooded the landscape from the east. I bent forward and kissed the ground symbolically; today my campaign got underway. My men cheered heartily at the act. They cheered me and I indulged them until Bjorgolf snapped at them to keep quiet and form up.

I raised my hand in thanks to Maelgwn as his ships ferried the last of Sitric's men across the straits. He waved his farewells as his ships backed oars and began their return to journey to Abermenai. The Powysian would occupy the Roman fort once we had got underway and then send one of his ships down the straits to Aber.

It was a crisp spring morning and the land was beautifully covered in a thin mist as the grey skies threatened rain. The mist shrouded our journey as we began the march which would take us along the old Roman road near Seisyll's lordship of Dinorwic and then on to Aber and whatever awaited us there. I rode at the head of the column with Sitric, Cerit and Seisyll. The overweight lord sat precariously on his mountain pony as it bent under the weight of the man, and struggled to keep pace with our fine Irish mounts. I tried not to chuckle at the man. Poor pony I thought, having to carry his bulk, but the hardy beast seemed to be coping.

Cerit did not speak, but his expression said it all. He stared away to the left as we continued along the dirt track which led from Segontium and along the foot of the vast mountain range which dominated the landscape to our right. He wore an amused smile and I knew he was struggling not to openly mock Seisyll as he merrily chatted away about nothing. Cerit was a total contrast to our father.

Sitric rode in stony silence behind me and Seisyll. He wore a blank expression and it was plain that he was tolerating Seisyll. He had argued against the fat Briton's presence as we marched to Aber, but I thought it best to let the man come. I needed the men of Arfon and so I needed Seisyll too. I began to regret the decision as his jowls wobbled and his voice droned on monotonously. I thought back to Orlaith's wedding ceremony and wondered why Seisyll had not become a priest, he was certainly suited. No wonder he was a good friend of the right honourable Dyfan, Bishop of Bangor.

A dark smear appeared ahead of us through the mist and the smell of fires burning in hearths carried over to me. Seisyll's voice exclaimed happily. "Welcome to Dinorwic, my King. The finest township in the whole of Gwynedd." He gestured with evident pride at the earth embankment and crude palisade which surrounded the settlement.

I nodded at his words, but Dinorwic did not impress me. The earthen defences had clearly been erected centuries ago. I would not have been surprised if the Romans thought exactly the same as I when they had marched past the same settlement hundreds of years before. I thought Seisyll's usage of the word 'town' was generous too as it clearly wasn't densely populated.

As we marched on a small crowd cheered our passing and, for the most part, my men ignored the cheers. But Seisyll's twenty men called greetings and ran over to their relatives and talked excitedly of where they were going. The rotund figure turned in his saddle to face me. I was still amazed the pony supported his weight. "A fine place, my King. The finest of all, eh?" He smiled approvingly when I nodded my head in agreement. "A shame all of Gwynedd is not so."

I did not respond to his comment and let the conversation trail off. As I glanced back at the small column of hardened warriors I caught Ronan's eye and the ugly bushy beard contorted into a smile as he nodded a greeting. The huge Irishman proudly carried my banner and I smiled inwardly as the banner stirred in the wind. I tried not to listen as I heard Bjorgolf, Ljot and Ruaidri mocking the portly lord on the hardy little pony. Thankfully Seisyll did not understand their words and no harm was done to the man's pride. I still could not understand why the lords of the land insisted on using ponies rather than a full sized mount such as my Irish stallion, whom I had named Iago. The mount was majestic and worth a fortune, so the name of my grandfather was fitting.

Seisyll had sent five riders ahead on their ponies to act as our eyes and ears. The mist wore off as we marched on for a few more hours and I edged Iago to the side of the track as Sitric doggedly pushed on at the head of the column as we crested a hill. Cerit and Seisyll joined me as I marvelled at the harsh beauty of the landscape. To my left Ynys Môn came to a halt in the distance, where a windswept island absorbed the crashing waves. The mountain range of Eryri still dominated the landscape to my right whilst I stared in awe to my front. Out of the mist jutted a huge bulk of a mountain which overshadowed everything around it. In its shadow, a couple of miles ahead, lay a settlement which clung to the timber palisade of a fort at the head of a heavily wooded valley.

Seisyll followed my gaze. "The fort of Aber, my King. Lord Einion rules here like his own kingdom. He keeps Robert happy and is wary of Trahaearn, he pays homage to both." I nodded at the man's information and asked what the huge mountain was called. Seisyll grinned broadly, clearly enjoying being the centre of attention as Cerit and I listened with interest. "That is the ancient mountain of Braich-y-Dinas, my King. A sacred place, an old place. They say some who live in the mountain's shadow still follow the old ways." He crossed himself before continuing. "The ancients crowned the summit with a fortification. An un-Godly circle of stones lies beyond the abandoned hilltop. There the sorceress, Tangwystl, sometimes goes." He crossed himself and muttered a prayer to the heavens before clicking his tongue and urging his pony onwards.

I glanced at Cerit who, evidently amused by Seisyll's superstition, laughed. "Intriguing, eh brother?" I nodded; it certainly was. "Ancient fortresses, pagan rituals and a sorceress! What have you dragged us all into?"

I laughed as we trotted our mounts forwards after the column of men, who churned the dirt path into a quagmire of sticky mud which sucked at our horses' hooves. In the distance a church bell sounded the alarm as my armed column marched towards Aber under the proud banner of Aberffraw.

The church bell still chimed repeatedly as the last villager rushed through the gates. The gates thumped shut as my force deployed along the track which led through the handful of roundhouses towards the gates of the fort. I eyed the fort warily; it was the best maintained I had seen so far in Gwynedd. The timber was scarce a year old and men lined the fighting platforms and peered over the palisade towards me as I trotted within hailing distance on Iago.

Sitric and Cerit trotted alongside me. Cerit held a white cloth on a tree branch to show we came to talk. Seisyll's pony shuffled after us and the large man struggled to stay on its back. His jowls wobbled comically and his rotund frame heaved at the exertion of trying to remain in the saddle. We came to a halt level with the first roundhouse and stared at the wooden gates which barred our path. A banner caught briefly in the wind, four yellow crosses on a green field, which I did not recognise.

I sensed Sitric and Cerit stiffen as a handful of bowmen appeared on the fighting platforms next to the gates. Seisyll eyed me fearfully and for a moment I thought the man would turn his pony and scurry back to the safety of my men, but he held his ground.

The gates creaked open a fraction as four men marched out and down the short track towards us. They all wore full wargear and were led by a short man in a plumed helmet. The leader stepped over a discarded wicker basket of leeks and came to a halt. I looked him up and down from the saddle as he removed his helmet to reveal a head of snowy white hair and a forehead dominated by a long scar. He stared back at me over a bent nose and announced himself. "I am Einion the Lord of Arllechwedd and I have the privilege of commanding this fine fort before you." He gestured at a young man, who I guessed to be in his early twenties, beside him. "This is my son, Rhys. I assume from the banner that you are Gruffudd son of Cynan?"

I nodded to confirm my identity. "I am Gruffudd son of Cynan. I have come to this place to enquire as to why you did not obey my summons?" I stared coldly at him and his eyes flickered towards my men and then he glanced at Sitric and shook his head.

He held out a hand to silence his son and considered his answer briefly. "My King, this is frontier land. I cannot afford to attend feasts whilst Robert the Frenchman threatens my boundaries."

I held up a hand to silence him. "A messenger or your son would have sufficed, don't you think?" I asked the question to no one in particular but Seisyll grumbled his approval at my side and fixed a hate filled stare on Einion. The Lord of Arllechwedd shifted uncomfortably under the stare and shuddered as I spoke. "One way or another, Lord Einion, I shall be sure of your loyalty before the day is out. I cannot afford to leave this area undefended if the Frenchman decides to attack. I know that I shall be successful before the sun rises in the morning." I spoke threateningly to ensure my next words hit home. "But, it is for you to decide whether you live to see it."

Einion looked at me dumbfounded and struggled to hide his shock at my words. He had clearly not expected such an ultimatum and he raised his hand again to stop his son saying something that could get them killed. He struggled to hide his fear, "Y-y-you would not attack your own people?"

I showed him an emotionless expression as I let the silence stretch. "Are you my people, Lord Einion?" I raised a hand to silence him. "You did not swear loyalty to me like the men of Arfon, Lleyn and Ynys Môn." Seisyll glowed with pride at my side at the mention of his province. "I have an army of hardened warriors; you see some of them before you now." I smiled coldly as he glanced again at my waiting warband. "They are the men that stormed Duibhlinn in the night and killed King Gofraid. Learn from his mistakes, Lord Einion." It was clear that Einion had no idea of what had transpired in Duibhlinn but he did not utter as much.

He glanced again at my small force. "Not so much of a host, my King," he said. I wanted to laugh; I thought this man to be a shrewd leader to keep his people safe from the encroaching Frenchmen yet he was proving to be a fool. "I think I shall take my chances."

I barked a short, sharp laugh full of menace. "You fool. This is but a small portion of my army and I have more on their way, should you prove to take the wrong course of action." As if on cue, Einion's eyes widened in surprise as he glanced towards the sea. I turned round to see Maelgwn's promised ship cutting through the waves as it headed towards Aber. "You shall promise me your son and a quarter of your garrison to join my army, so that I know I can rely on your loyalty. Refuse and before the sun rises in the morning, you will be dead. As will every last man, woman and child that shelters behind your walls."

Seisyll glanced at me nervously, obviously not comfortable with my words. But I did not care. I had no desire to slaughter innocent women and children but Einion did not know that. He glanced behind him at the fort and shook his head at the hopelessness of the situation.

He glanced back at me nervously and swallowed hard as he bent down on one knee. "You are welcome at Aber, my King. I extend to you our warmest hospitality and the forces you require." He bowed his head respectfully and his son followed suit as did the two warriors behind him.

I nodded at Einion. "A wise choice, lord." I turned Iago and trotted back to my men, with the others close behind. Seisyll spurred his shuffling pony alongside me and sported a broad grin and Sitric clapped me on the shoulder proudly. His smile betrayed his pride and I felt my heart swell with satisfaction. I was pleased to have the approval of my foster-father who was such a hard, but fair, man.

I raised my voice so that it would carry to all of the warriors present. "The Lord of Arllechwedd has chosen to side with us in our campaign to reclaim my kingdom from the usurpers." I raised a hand to quieten the men as a cheer broke out. "We shall feast in Aber this evening and you shall wait here for my return. Any man who molests the townspeople or betrays Lord Einion's trust will be hung from the nearest tree." I let the words sink in. "Do not fear, men, for your blades will taste blood soon! We shall carry this war to our enemies and destroy them utterly!"

The men cheered enthusiastically as I nodded to Sitric. My foster-father grinned approvingly before shouting commands at his warband to enter Aber. Cerit shot me a triumphant grin as he trotted his mount after Sitric. I dismounted and Seisyll's jowls wobbled as he babbled his praises.

I ignored the rotund lord and walked to Bjorgolf, who clapped me on the shoulder before meeting my gaze with a deep scowl. "What the hell are you playing at? Is there to be no fighting in this war!" Some of my men laughed at the jest and some others grumbled at the truth of it.

"Don't worry, my friend. There will be plenty of killing to come, of that I am sure." I put an arm round Bjorgolf's shoulder and steered him out of earshot. "I want ten men, who I will take with me to see this bloody Frenchman that they're all so scared of."

I do not know why but my mind wandered to the thoughts of the meeting I had disturbed in the forest, following Gunnald's defeat, all those months ago. Narrowly avoiding the assassin's knife at Sord Cholmcille and of the hooded bowman in the woods; there were too many unanswered questions. Then an idea dawned upon me, it must be one of my men, but which one? I met Bjorgolf's eye, "Just make sure that Ljot, Oengus, Ronan and Ruaidri are amongst them."

Bjorgolf seemed as though he would question the demand and then realisation dawned on him. "You don't think, I mean can you be sure that its one of them?" He shook his head. "I do not believe it could."

I spoke truthfully and I knew he would understand my point of view, indeed he must have been thinking the same if he had understood the meaning of my order. "Who else could it be, eh?" He shrugged his shoulders and tutted to himself. "All four have been there from the beginning, they have all grumbled at one point or another over the months. No I cannot be certain, but I hope to find out."

I mounted Iago and trotted after Sitric and Seisyll's men as they entered the fort of Aber. Bjorgolf clearly did not think any of my men could be working for Trahaearn, but who else could it be? I raised a hand to acknowledge the halfhearted cheers of the townspeople as their would-be king rode past. I would make a quick inspection of Einion's fort and then I would sail to the castle at Degannwy and see if a deal could be reached with Robert, a prospect I did not look forward to.

It was midday as I clambered aboard Maelgwn's ship and I recognised the gap-toothed *helwyr* whom I clapped fondly on the back. Maelgwn had already ensured the ship's master knew the destination and we were soon underway. I glanced at the huge mountain of Braich-y-Dinas as the ship ploughed through the grey waves. Rain began to roll in again from the sea and I thought I made out a figure on the mountain top, watching my ship labour through the rising waves, but I could not be sure.

I glanced around and was satisfied with the men Bjorgolf had selected. I smiled reassuringly at them. Gwcharki, Ljot, Oengus, Ronan, Ruaidri and five others grinned back. I could not help but feel a rising sense of fear as we cut through the waves towards the mouth of the river Conwy which was, I had been told, where I could find Robert's castle at Degannwy on the east bank.

A lump of rock jutted out into the sea ahead of us as the ship began to bank to the right. As the longship straightened up and aimed for the river mouth I thought of what was to come. Was it possible Robert would even negotiate with me? I shook my head at the thought as Bjorgolf approached and rested beside me.

He glanced at me thoughtfully before glancing back at the four men I suspected. "How do you plan to discover if any of them are disloyal?" I could not help but notice the scepticism in his voice. He shook his head ruefully as I tapped my nose with my right-index finger to indicate that I had devised a scheme.

But that would have to wait as Maelgwn's ship master shouted and pointed ahead. An oddly shaped hill dominated the eastern bank of the river and perched on top stood a strong wooden tower, surrounded by a palisade. I studied Degannwy through fascinated eyes, this was the first time I had seen a French fortification and I prayed it would be the last. A strong wooden keep was ringed by a well-made palisade on the steep hillside; it would be a costly affair to attack I thought. I straightened my belt and made sure my blade was securely fastened at my hip. I brushed a speck of mud from my gleaming mail hauberk and glanced ahead. A busy port, dominated by Degannwy castle above, stretched along the riverbank. An audience was beginning to gather at the quayside and watched as my ship approached. I glanced towards a dozen trading vessels which rested on the mud-banks in the river's mouth as they waited to be re-floated by the tide.

I swallowed nervously as we prepared to beach and a group of ten heavily mailed men on powerfully built horses pushed their way through the crowd. I stared nervously at the strangely clad soldiers and kept my emotions under control. I touched my sword's hilt for reassurance and uttered a prayer to my mother's spirit to watch over me. I was about to step into the dangerous unknown, I was going to meet the Frenchman.

XVIII

The horsemen reined in their powerful beasts, and eyed me confidently. They were strange men, different to any I had seen before. They wore long coats of mail, which covered them from their necks to their knees. Their heads were crowned with an oddly styled helm which sat snugly on their heads. I noticed the mail split at the crotch and flowed down to the horsemen's knees; a clever design I thought, which would give the horsemen added protection in a fight. Oddly they wore a red tunic over their mail with a golden cross embroidered upon their chests. Each sported a strange kite shaped shield which was strapped across their backs. The long shield, which came to a point at the bottom, would be cumbersome and impede its user I thought, although it would prove useful in defence. All but one carried long spears, which they held comfortably. The remaining rider carried a standard, which I guessed to be Robert's, the very same the men wore on their tunics, a gold cross upon a red field.

The lead rider called out in strangely accented Briton. "Who are you? If you wish to secure your boat here at Degannwy, you must pay the harbour fee."

The crowd muttered nervously amongst themselves as I let the silence stretch. The strange horsemen shifted uncomfortably as I composed my reply. "I am Gruffudd son of Cynan, the true king of Gwynedd. I have come to seek an audience with Lord Robert." I glanced back at my men, who were battle ready and tensing themselves to strike.

The rider turned in his saddle and snapped an order in a strange language. A horseman from the rear of the small group turned his huge mount and thundered back down the quayside and up towards the castle. The lead rider smiled, "I have sent news of your arrival to my lord. I shall wait for word. But you are not to set foot upon the soil of

Degannwy without permission, lord."

I nodded at the man and glanced up at the castle where helmeted heads looked down at my ship. Some of the crowd had become bored and returned to their duties, whilst others milled about as we waited for word. The French horsemen watched my ship in a well disciplined formation, impervious to the rain which still lashed in from the grey sea.

My nerves began to grow as the minutes stretched and there was still no sign from the castle. I clenched and unclenched my hand around my sword hilt as we waited. I received a reassuring nod from Bjorgolf as he came to my side. "They look like hard bastards, sure enough. We'll have them though if it comes to it." He smiled confidently at me as he surveyed the French horsemen.

"I hope it doesn't come to it." I glanced at the shingle where our ship was perched and sent a silent prayer to the heavens. We were vulnerable to attack and if the Frenchmen had any skilled bowmen in the castle we would be bled horribly. I wondered again what a crossbow was and hoped it was not as lethal as the longbow the Britons favoured. "Robert may not even acknowledge my right to Gwynedd's crown," I muttered to Bjorgolf. "He could easily try and kill us all now."

Bjorgolf chuckled, "I doubt it. Besides, we would take a good number of them with us. They won't risk it." The certainty in Bjorgolf's voice settled me, but my nerves soon rose again as Bjorgolf pointed down the quayside. "You may get your answer soon enough."

Another troop of French horsemen trotted down the quayside and came to a well drilled halt besides the first group. A rider nudged his mount forward and spoke calmly in their strange language to the horseman who had previously questioned me. The two glanced at me before the new rider let his mount walk a few paces forward. He was dressed exactly the same as the other horsemen but seemed to have a greater air of authority.

He brought his mount to a halt and removed his helm. I heard the faint jingling of his mail as he raised a mailed arm and pushed his mail hood back. He seemed of average height and his light-brown hair was oddly cropped, almost looking as though a bowl had been placed on his head and cut around. He was clean shaven and, I guessed, in his late thirties. His blue eyes fixed with mine as he let the silence stretch a few moments.

He called up to me in faultless Latin. "You are Gruffudd, son of Cynan? The son of an exiled prince who has returned to claim his birthright. Am I correct?" His tone was full of arrogance and he plainly did not expect me to respond. He had spoken in the language of diplomacy, which only educated men would understand. He had expected to embarrass me in front of my men and ridicule my royal claim.

"You are correct." I spoke confidently and the man hid his surprise well, although I caught a faint glimmer of shock in his eyes. "Tell me, do I have the honour of addressing the Lord Robert?"

The man let out an amused laugh. "Alas, no. I am Baldwin de Dissard and am merely the castellan of the fortification you see above." He gestured up at the formidable symbol of power that dominated the local landscape. "Lord Robert will grant you an audience in good time, although he has matters of more urgency to deal with presently."

The man turned his mount and snapped orders in what I assumed to be the French tongue at his troop of horsemen. As the horsemen turned their mounts in perfect unison and waited for their leader, he turned in the saddle and glanced back up at me. "Follow me, lord. You may bring two of your followers, should you feel it necessary." He did not wait for a response but spurred his mount to the head of the well disciplined column of horsemen.

I turned my gaze to Bjorgolf's reassuring face. "You and Ronan are to come with me to meet the Frenchman." Bjorgolf nodded his head firmly and called for Ronan to make his way to my side. I turned to Ljot. He had proved both capable and loyal when I had trusted him with the responsibility of safeguarding Sord Cholmcille whilst the rest of us campaigned in Duibhlinn. "Ljot, you are in command of the ship. Should we not return before mid afternoon, you are to fight your way clear of Degannwy and return to Sitric at Aber. Tell him, he is to bring the army to Degannwy and butcher the Frenchmen. Now repeat what I have just told you." Ljot repeated my orders word for word and I nodded my head in satisfaction. "Good, I hope it does not come to that. But that is what you must do should we be deceived by Robert's hospitality."

I nodded at Bjorgolf and Ronan; the two nodded stoically back and followed me over the side of the ship. I felt a rising feeling of doubt in my gut as I hopped down from the ship and onto the shingle of the beach. I glanced around me and sensed that Bjorgolf and Ronan were wary of the French horsemen as we approached the rear of their column. As soon as we drew level with the rear of the column, Baldwin de Dissard called out an order in French and the whole troop of horsemen pressed their knees into their mounts to coax the beasts into a walk. We walked quickly, almost trotted, after the powerful warhorses down the quayside and up a steep muddy road which led to the castle.

The mounts were taller and much broader than Iago and the other Irish mounts I had seen. Most were black and all were strong beasts and they ascended the steep incline easily enough. My legs ached with the exertion as we approached the castle. I clasped my sword hilt again for reassurance and glanced at the heavens; watch over me I mouthed silently. I swallowed hard and felt the usual pre-battle feelings, for I was about to enter the Frenchman's lair.

The castle walls were very well maintained and manned by surprisingly few French soldiers. Most sported the oddly shaped shields which were almost as tall as the men themselves and all wore the same design of mail as the horsemen. I glanced up at the watchtower above the gates and stared in fascination at the two men who occupied it. They were dressed in a similar way to the foot soldiers that patrolled the timber walls. Both carried odd wooden contraptions instead of the usual spears and long shields which the Frenchmen seemed to favour. I noticed that the contraptions had a bow-like design at the end with a short-stubby arrow lodged in it. It must be a crossbow I thought.

Bjorgolf nudged me in the ribs to bring my thoughts back to the task at hand. Baldwin had halted his column ten paces before another palisade, calling an order in French, and his horsemen began to dismount and lead their horses to a stable building. I glanced at the inner palisade and admired the design of the castle. The usual outer palisade ringed the castle's boundaries and protected the outbuildings and training ground. However, perched atop a huge mound of earth stood a sturdy wooden tower which stood four floors high. A ditch ringed the mound and contained pointed stakes that would impede any attacker who was lucky enough to pierce the second palisade which protected the ditch. A strong set of wooden gates swung open to allow us through and we followed Baldwin up a series of wooden steps that led from the base of the mound to the strong oak doors which guarded the wooden tower.

Baldwin sensed our admiration for such a fine set of defences and gestured up at the wooden tower. "Welcome to the keep, lord." A large ring of iron, almost the size of a man's head, hung at chest height from the door. Baldwin took the iron ring in his hand and hammered it twice on the oak doors. A wooden peep-hole was shoved open and within seconds the strong doors were being dragged open.

We followed Baldwin into the dry interior of the keep and were thankful to be out of the rain. The first floor was almost completely bare, except for a wooden staircase which, attached to the rear wall, led up to the next level. We followed Baldwin up the staircase onto the second level and there he turned to us. "You will wait here, lord. I shall announce your presence to Lord Robert and he will call for you when he is ready."

Baldwin gestured at a row of wooden chairs to our left and we took his invitation. I sat on a chair in the centre of the row between Bjorgolf and Ronan. Bjorgolf muttered to nobody in particular. "By Freya's tits, what a place. Makes Duibhlinn look like child's play. We'd lose a lot of good men attacking this bloody thing."

Ronan muttered his agreement and I nodded at the truth of it. It was a fine defensive structure and one which would bleed any opposing force. A cunning commander would need a considerable amount of luck and daring to even stand half a chance of taking Degannwy castle. Robert commanded a fine fortification and I dreaded to think what his other castles were like. I just hoped Trahaearn or Cynwrig did not possess anything similar.

I glanced around the second floor and admired its construction. High windows allowed sunlight to light the room and a series of blocked slits ran the length of the room. Each slit was spaced four paces from the next and I guessed that during an assault, if the defenders had been forced back to the keep, the slits could be unblocked and provide the crossbowmen with a commanding line of fire and almost impenetrable defence. Another embroidered cloth sporting Robert's colours hung from the wall ahead of us.

I glanced down at the timber floorboards and clenched my clammy fists. None of us spoke as we awaited Robert's summons. A guard stood rigidly to attention at the foot of the staircase Baldwin had ascended earlier. Bjorgolf had tried to hail the guard and provoke a conversation, but the guard had ignored Bjorgolf and continued to eye us suspiciously. Bjorgolf had spat a curse at the guard but, luckily I thought, the man did not understand Danish and had not taken offence.

After what had seemed an age I heard footsteps and Baldwin descended the staircase, before striding into the centre of the room. "Lord Robert will see you now, lord." He eyed Bjorgolf and Ronan and spoke in a commanding voice. "Alone."

I glanced at Bjorgolf and Ronan as I rose from the wooden chair. "Wait here," I spoke in Irish, in the hope that the Frenchmen could not understand, and raised a palm to silence any protest. "If you hear a call of alarm, kill the guard and barricade yourselves here. You two could keep that staircase defended until Judgement Day." Ronan nodded his shaggy-bush of a head in acknowledgment and Bjorgolf fixed me with a grim expression. "Do not worry Bjorgolf. I can look after myself."

I turned and strode over to Baldwin. The Frenchman shot me a knowing glance. "Do not worry, lord. Robert is an honourable man, which is why I have not demanded your blade." Baldwin nodded at the guard as he began to ascend the staircase. The guard shot me a sour look which turned into a snarl as I winked back at him before following Baldwin up the staircase to the third level. There I hoped I could persuade the dangerous Frenchman to support my claim to the throne.

Baldwin bowed his head respectfully and cleared his throat. "Gruffudd son of Cynan, my lord." Baldwin bowed his head respectfully again as a heavy set man stopped dictating to a monk, who scratched at a piece of parchment with a quill. Robert eyed me with disinterest before dropping his gaze to continue dictating to the monk.

The monk sat at a desk in the middle of the room and Robert loomed over him. The design was similar to that of the floor below, only this one had a partition which led to the rear third of the room where I assumed lay the castellan's bedchamber. Two guards eyed me warily to my right and another guard blocked any retreat down the staircase. Despite the sunlight which penetrated through the high windows, a candle burned on the desk. The monk seemed to be in his middle years and his tongue protruded from his narrow lips as he concentrated on etching the correct words onto the parchment. Ink stained his bony hands and his oddly cut hair strangely added to his intelligent appearance. I decided that he reminded me of a young Father Cathal.

Robert's voice disturbed my thoughts. The cleric's quill had stopped and now he and Robert starred at me patiently. "Welcome to Degannwy, Gruffudd son of Cynan. I trust that you are impressed by my motte and bailey?"

I did not understand Robert's phrase but guessed he meant the castle. "Indeed, lord. It is a well chosen position." Robert nodded and strode round the desk before perching himself upon its corner to my right. The desk creaked under the weight. I judged Robert to be around his fortieth year and his closely cropped black hair had greyed at the temples. He was cleanly shaven and had a hardened round face, lined and weather beaten. His brown eyes did not hide the malice behind them and I resisted the urge to shudder. He was a strongly built barrel of a man and had been thickly muscled in his youth, but now the muscle had begun to turn to fat, but he was still physically strong.

He wore full mail like his foot soldiers, including a tunic which sported his banner. His mail hood was down and hung at the back of his neck. He spoke in almost perfect Briton. "Tell me, why do you come here?"

I suppressed my fears and spoke calmly in a clear tone. "I have come to negotiate, Lord Robert." He nodded his head for me to continue. "I plan to reclaim what is mine from the usurpers Cynwrig of Powys and Trahaearn of Arwystli. The two have despoiled Gwynedd for too long and I aim to send them screaming from this world." Robert's eyes glittered menacingly and a satisfied smile crossed his face as I ploughed on. "I shall be victorious and, Lord Robert, I believe we should be friends."

Robert clapped his hands together loudly, causing the monk to jump in his seat. He glanced at Baldwin and grinned happily. "Anyone who wishes to rid the world of Trahaearn and his un-Godly soul is a friend of mine, young Gruffudd. It is my belief that a friend should help another friend in return for a small favour."

I nodded at Robert's words; I knew he would want something from me, but I was certain I could not trust this man. "Indeed, Lord Robert. That is my belief also. Tell me what it is that you propose."

"I shall provide you with eighty good men from my lands. They will be Britons of course; I will not risk any of my countrymen in your venture." He paused a moment as I nodded at his words. "In return I ask that you pay me tribute to the sum of one hundred cattle per anum for the next five years. I also request that you acknowledge my conquest of the province of Rhos and also grant me the lands of Rhufoniog and the lands that stretch to the mountain of Braich-y-Dinas."

I stared at Robert blankly for a moment as I considered his proposal. He stood to gain a considerable amount if I agreed. He was not offering me much in return, although I judged my acceptance would ensure he would not attack my rear whilst I marched on Trahaearn. "I am most grateful for the promised support, Lord Robert. Although I offer you a counter-proposal." The monk's eyes flickered between myself and Robert, full of interest. Robert nodded his head, so I continued. "I will not pay you the tribute you desire but will acknowledge your claims to the said lands, for as long as you can hold them."

Although I had refused to pay the tribute I still offered Robert a generous reward, which he too recognised. He knew I would never capitulate to his first offer, indeed I would have been judged a fool to have done so. He nodded his head and strode over to me. He held out his hand, which I clasped in mine. "We have an accord, Lord Gruffudd." Robert shook my hand firmly and then released the grip before returning to the monk. The monk grabbed a fresh piece of parchment and Robert began to dictate another letter in French.

Baldwin caught my eye and beckoned for me to follow him. We began to descend the staircase and I could not help but smile. Things could not have gone better, I had been promised Robert's support and, with it, the knowledge that he would not attack my rear whilst I marched to confront Trahaearn and Cynwrig. I could not have envisaged such a successful conclusion. I had played the game of diplomacy well and I sensed Muirchertach would have been proud of my actions in the world of kings. Even Father Cathal would have approved as I had gained everything I had wanted and given nothing away. For, what Robert did not know, was that I had no intention of honouring our agreement. I had played the game and played it well.

XIX

We reached the safety of Segontium shortly after nightfall. My whole army was encamped around the perimeter of the old Roman fortification and Maelgwn had erected a large tent, for my own personal use, in the centre of the old ruins. Only Sitric, Maelgwn and their men felt comfortable in the old stone foundations. My countrymen had, on the most part, insisted on camping beyond Segontium's boundaries as they believed pagan spirits haunted the ancient stones.

That night I believed their fears were well founded. I had returned wanting to do nothing other than rest but, instead, I was confronted by a demented old hag. Maelgwn had shrugged his shoulders apologetically and had claimed he was powerless to do anything other than let her wait for me. I had laughed at the scarred Powysian's rare fear, but now I could see why he had not ejected the old woman.

She sat, cross-legged, in the centre of my tent in a trance. Her eyes were closed and she muttered incoherently to herself. She wore filthy rags and her wrinkles were deeply encrusted with filth that much was clear in the dim candle light. The stench was her worst characteristic; the smell of a human body that had not been washed in years assaulted the senses.

I glanced about me and was relieved that I was not the only one to feel uneasy. Bjorgolf, as ever, stood at my side and he gazed at the old hag with an interested eye. Sitric stood with his arms crossed at my left side and fixed the scene with an emotionless expression. Maelgwn, who the old hag had threatened to turn into a toad, lurked behind me and crossed himself occasionally. It was rare for the Powysian to display any feelings of fear and that added to my unease. Cerit held his left hand over his mouth and nostrils in an attempt to save himself from the woman's stench.

Seisyll had refused to enter the tent when he had

discovered the woman's identity and, to Bjorgolf's amusement, the rotund Briton had crossed himself several times to ward off evil and scuttled away from the Roman ruins, he claimed, for his own safety. I am not ashamed to admit that I wished I had followed the man.

Gwcharki and Ronan had come with me and my retinue to the tent in Segontium's centre; the two seemed remarkably unmoved by the woman's presence. The giant Pict had flexed his huge arm muscles and watched the scene with an air of amusement. Ronan, I noticed, gripped a small necklace of a wooden cross in the palm of his left hand and he watched on with a grim expression.

Just then the old woman's eyes shot open and scanned the faces of the men before her. She cackled, a dry and malicious noise, to herself before rising to her full height. She had once been tall for a woman but now was bent with age. Her bare feet were black with filth and her long, sinister, finger nails almost curled at the tips. I noticed she wore a necklace of small bones, with a raven's severed head at its centre.

I gripped my sword hilt to steady my nerves and, as she noticed the gesture, she let out another cackle. A small bundled package lay behind her on the tent's floor and she glanced at it before glancing back at me. She licked her dry lips with a dark, serpent-like, tongue and cackled again.

Gwcharki chuckled to himself, earning reproving glances from Sitric and Bjorgolf. The Pict shrugged his shoulders with an amused smile and watched on. The old woman pointed at me and launched into an incoherent rant which lasted several minutes. Nobody moved, we were all seemingly transfixed by the odd scene which played out in front of us. I could not understand the language in which she spoke and, so it seemed, nor could anyone else.

The old hag finished her rant and ran her long, bony, fingers through her filth encrusted wild grey hair which fell to her waist. "Gruffudd son of Cynan!" Her voice screeched at an unnaturally high pitch. All eyes turned to me as she went on. "I am Tangwystl, wife of the late Llywarch Olbwch who was Lord of Rhos. The Gods of old speak through me."

All but Sitric and Gwcharki crossed themselves, even Bjorgolf. The old hag shuddered uncontrollably and dropped to her knees, shrieking like a wounded animal. She began to foam at the mouth and dropped to her back, writhing on the grassy floor. We all stood still with fear and looked on until the old woman stopped writhing. She lay on her back and the only sign she lived was the unnaturally quick rising of her chest as she took in breath.

Suddenly she sat bolt upright and her large eyes were almost wholly black. Her pupils had expanded a frightening amount and she scanned the watching faces. She rose to her full height, the bent spine straightened, so that she seemed to dominate the room. She spread her arms and fixed her un-Godly eyes on me.

I felt my skin creep with fear and my throat go dry, I crossed myself to ward off evil but it did nothing. Her eyes seemed to penetrate my soul and I felt my heart quicken as sweat trickled down my spine.

Her voice had changed; she spoke clearly and in a dominating voice. "Gruffudd son of Cynan, I am honoured to be in your presence." I swallowed hard and all present looked from the old hag to me. "I am Andraste, the Warrior Goddess of the Celtic peoples, and I speak through the mortal body of Tangwystl." She laughed as most of the men crossed themselves. "Christ has no power over me. The faith of the white Christ may have swept the land, but there are some who still follow the old ways. Their faith keeps me strong and I have the gift of foresight."

Even Sitric and Gwcharki looked on in amazement as she moved forward and took both my hands in hers. The dark pools of her eyes seemed to search my mind and she smiled to herself. "Gruffudd, you shall be king. Let all those who follow you know that, one day, you shall rule Gwynedd in its entirety and beyond." She shook her head and continued to stare at me with those unblinking eyes for a few heartbeats. "Know this; there lies betrayal and struggle ahead. Your path will not be easy, but persevere you must. I give you but one warning; a power rises in the east and threatens the very existence of our people, they aim to sweep this land clean and take its riches for themselves. Should they remain unchallenged they will hunt our people to extinction." She let my hands go and scanned the faces of the others.

She moved silently and passed between myself and Sitric. I swear a cold air breezed over us as she passed. She stood in front of Gwcharki and looked the huge warrior up and down. She took one of his broad hands in hers and looked up into his eyes. She spoke in a strange language and then let the Pict's hand drop. He nodded at her and shifted uncomfortably on his feet as men stared at him.

The old woman returned to the centre of the tent and glanced back at me one more time and smiled before her body began to shudder again and dropped to the floor. The body writhed uncontrollably until the old hag sat upright and struggled to her feet, her back bent again. She glanced at the bemused faces that stared at her and she chuckled to herself. She moved over to the bundle and unwrapped it. It revealed a scarlet cloth which was expensive and finely made that much was clear.

She hobbled towards me and placed the cloth in my hands. I glanced down at the cloth and could not believe its beauty. It was old but in brilliant condition; small grey lions were embroidered into the scarlet cloth and she smiled as I studied it.

She looked up into my eyes and spoke in a croaky voice. "This fine tunic is made from the cloak of the late king, Gruffudd son of Llywelyn, who ruled Gwynedd before the time of King Bleddyn." She mumbled again to herself and her eyes glanced down at the floor and then back up to mine. "You must wear this tunic over your mail when you meet the enemy, so they know the rightful king has returned."

She began to mumble incoherently again and pushed past Sitric and exited the tent into the cold night air. Her voice called from outside. "Farewell Gruffudd, should you need to consult the Gods, look for me at the stone circle beyond Braich-y-Dinas."

I heard her cackle one last time as I left the tent to find her, but she had vanished into the night. I still could not believe what had transpired in the tent and looked, dumbfounded, from Sitric to Bjorgolf and shook my head. I glanced again at the symbolic tunic she had presented me with and marvelled at its beauty. All true men of Gwynedd would follow me after this; of that I was sure.

I returned to the tent and sat on a stool at the rear as Sitric cleared his throat. "What a load of bollocks!" All eyes turned to him as he chuckled to himself. "The demented old bat claiming to be a Goddess. I do not believe it. There has to be a reasonable explanation for her behaviour and apparent powers am I not right?" I shrugged my shoulders and Sitric shot me a look full of scorn.

Nobody could explain the events we had just witnessed and most shifted uncomfortably under my gaze. "Well, my lords," I began as a commotion sounded outside. Bjorgolf gestured for Gwcharki and Ronan to follow him. I watched as the three men exited the tent and then sighed as I recognised the voice of the new arrival.

I sensed that there was almost a collective groan as Faelan stormed into the tent. Cerit rolled his eyes and looked at me sympathetically. Ronan tried to halt the man, but Faelan turned on him. "Lay a hand on me, you ugly goat humping bastard, and I'll fillet you. So help me God!" Ronan looked towards me and relented as I nodded my head.

Faelan stormed past Maelgwn and shouldered Cerit as he advanced on me. The arrogant bastard was red in the face and, from the look of his eyes, had clearly been drinking. He halted in front of me as Mac Ruaidri rushed into the tent and groaned as he witnessed the scene. He sent me an apologetic look and glanced down at his feet as Sitric shot him a loathing stare.

Faelan puffed out his cheeks and stared at me resentfully. His drooping moustache quivered as he ranted. "Just what the hell do you think you're playing at?" Spittle landed on my cheek as he fumed. "Muirchertach will be furious that you are leaving a commander of my talent to guard some shit hole!" He shook his head in exasperation, "I lead the best fighting men in Ireland who are certainly the best in your whole goddamned excuse of an army!"

Bjorgolf started forward but I raised a hand to stop him. I would let Faelan vent his frustration and make a fool of himself I decided. The small, pig-like, eyes watered as he continued to fume. "The conduct of this campaign has been flawed from the bloody start. What the hell Muirchertach was thinking of supporting you, you upstart bastard, I shall never know!"

There was a sharp intake of breath at the insult and I felt the anger begin to burn in my chest. I began to rise to face the pompous fool but, before I could, Sitric strode the five paces towards him and rammed his fist into the Irishman's face. Faelan fell to the floor and clutched his nose as Sitric towered over him. My foster-father spoke threateningly. "Just what Muirchertach was thinking by sending you, I shall never know!" There were a few chuckles as Sitric turned the tables on Faelan. "Apologise to Gruffudd, or I shall make sure that you fall from Muirchertach's favour. I know your dirty little secret and I can ensure you that your name will be worthless!"

I placed a calming hand on Sitric's shoulder and almost shuddered as his grey eyes locked with mine. He nodded at me respectfully and retreated to his original position. Faelan still lay on the floor and looked up at me with hate filled eyes. I smiled as I noticed the blood trickling through his fingers. I glanced round at the on-looking men. "Leave us. Mac Ruaidri and my guard, you stay. The rest of you leave." The tone of my voice made it clear I would tolerate no protests and so Sitric, Maelgwn and Cerit strode out of the tent and back to their men.

Bjorgolf, Ronan and Gwcharki blocked the exit and Mac Ruaidri shifted uncomfortably, unable to meet my gaze. I turned back to Faelan. "Get up. Unless you are planning on spending the night there."

Faelan stood and eyed me uneasily, still clutching his nose as the blood began to dry on his fingers. I decided that I would have to flatter the arrogant fool to try and stop the bastard from disobeying any more of my orders. "Lord Faelan I am in command of this campaign, not you." I held up a hand as he began to open his mouth. "King Muirchertach had the foresight to offer me his finest commanders and warriors and I understand your frustration." I smiled, as if in apology, at Faelan and the Irishman nodded his head warily at my words.

I glanced at Bjorgolf, whose expression said it all; he did not approve of what I was doing. It was plain he thought I should kill Faelan there and then. The thought had crossed my mind, but I did not want to lose Muirchertach's support. "I have need to place some of my most capable men at Abermenai to ensure we have a means of escape, should we need it. I need one of my most talented commanders there, do you understand? Could you imagine if I left that honour to anyone else?"

Faelan nodded his head warily. "It was my understanding, Gruffudd, that I and my men would see action. Is that not so?" The Irishman still demanded an answer to his thoughts in a surly manner.

"Indeed, indeed, Lord Faelan." I shook my head, as

if I had made a great error and had realised it for the first time. "Once Cynwrig is dealt with, I shall need a capable commander to garrison his lands. I cannot entrust that to my new allies and I was assured you would be the most capable of Muirchertach's commanders for the role. You shall have to keep order and rule Lleyn in my name until the campaign is over. That, Lord Faelan, is why you were included in this expedition. You will see action, I am sure." I knew Asser and the sons of Merwydd would not thank me, but I wanted the intolerable Irishman out of the way. What harm could he do there? The sons of Merwydd had supported me, which meant the people would support their decision, and they were certainly capable of ruling Lleyn in my name until I head dealt with Trahaearn. But I needed Faelan out of harm's way and could think of no alternative.

The mention of ruling lands, even if for a short while, had gained Faelan's attention and he nodded at my words. "Ah, I see." Faelan sounded pleased with the outcome. "Indeed, I am certainly the most capable for that task. Now, I shall return to that shit-hole of a town and continue to excel in my duties." He nodded at me to signify that he had deigned to end the conversation and began to leave the tent. "Come Mac Ruaidri, we have work to do."

Before the elderly warrior could follow Faelan I called out. "I wish to talk with Mac Ruaidri. I need to ensure he understands what role you are to play, Lord Faelan." Mac Ruaidri glanced at me warily and nodded his head as Faelan shrugged his shoulders and disappeared into the night.

Bjorgolf eyed the old warrior sympathetically as I waited for Faelan to be well out of earshot and then turned my anger on him. "What the hell do you think you are doing?" Mac Ruaidri was clearly taken aback by my change in character, but the old man had failed in his duty so I did not care for his feelings. "You are supposed to be babysitting that bastard of an idiot!" I shook my head violently as I continued to shout at the diminutive figure. "You have failed so far, Mac Ruaidri, bloody failed. One thing I cannot abide is men who fail in their duties. And you, sir, have bloody well failed!"

Mac Ruaidri did not dare to meet my gaze and mumbled an apology as he shifted uncomfortably from foot to foot and fidgeted with his thumbs. I jabbed a finger at his chest. "You will not fail me again. You are to watch that sheep's arsehole like a bloody hawk. He steps out of line one more time and I shall have your head, understand?" The Irishman nodded, trying to hide the shame of the rebuke I had just given him, but his flushed cheeks betrayed his feelings. "Now get out of my sight."

The Irishman left and Bjorgolf whistled softly. "Jesus bloody Christ, but you didn't half lay into him." Bjorgolf shook his head in mock sadness. "Quite pitied him. I am thinking Faelan was more deserving of your anger though."

I nodded at the truth of Bjorgolf's words. I had barely slept since setting foot on Gwynedd's soil and I badly needed some rest. "I have to tolerate Faelan for Muirchertach's sake. Christ, I cannot see why he sent the bloody fool with me. I curse him for that!" I turned and sat on the cot that had been prepared for me and chose to ignore Bjorgolf's next remark.

"Not the first thing you have cursed him for, I am sure. A fine young lady comes to mind. Faelan leads a charmed life, that's for sure." He shot me a knowing look. "Get some rest, lad. You need it."

I nodded my thanks and settled down on the furs. I was still in my full war gear, but I did not care for I was too tired. Just as I closed my eyes I groaned audibly and spat a curse as another commotion sounded outside the tent. I glanced at Bjorgolf. "What now!" I sat upright and sent a mud-splattered man a foul stare as he was escorted into my presence by Ronan.

226

The man was sweating and covered in mud, he stank of horse sweat and I guessed he had rushed here with all haste. "Well man, what is it?" I demanded.

The man swallowed nervously and spoke urgently. "Lord Asser sends his compliments, my King. He requests that you march to him at Clynnog Fawr, with all haste. He and his brothers have withdrawn their forces to the church of St. Beuno at Clynnog Fawr, as agreed." He glanced from me to Bjorgolf nervously as I raised an inquisitive eyebrow. "The usurper Cynwrig of Powys has descended upon my master, my King. His forces are beyond a stream and there they are camped not far from my master's position. Cynwrig plans to attack in the morning, my King, should Lord Asser and his brothers not agree to join his supporters and march against you."

Despite my tiredness I felt renewed energy flow through my veins. "Thank you, you may take whatever vitals you need and return to your master with all speed. Tell him that I shall honour his request for aid and that I shall be there, in person, with reinforcements before sunrise." The messenger nodded and before he turned to leave I demanded more of him. "Tell me, how many men does Cynwrig have?"

The messenger crossed himself. "He outnumbers my master two to one, my King. His forces number three hundred." The messenger nodded respectfully and hurriedly exited the tent.

Bjorgolf met my eye and grinned excitedly. "Bjorgolf, summon all my commanders here with haste. If my countrymen insist that the place is haunted then bloody well force them here. For we shall meet our enemy at sunrise."

Bjorgolf nodded and trotted out of the tent. I smiled to myself and remembered the tunic Tangwystl had presented me with. I unbuckled my belt and propped my sheathed blade, which was attached to the belt, against a support pole in the tent's corner. I put the tunic on and admired its beauty, it was a perfect fit but sleeveless. It reminded me of Robert's French soldiers and the tunics they wore with his banner. I buckled the belt back over the tunic and touched my sword hilt for luck.

I turned as Sitric and some of the other commanders began to filter into the tent. I would march a third of my army to Clynnog Fawr during the night and surprise Cynwrig at sunrise. We would have no rest, but there was a battle to be fought and won and I knew we would win. I felt my heart quicken as I thought ahead, for tomorrow I would meet one of the usurpers in the field and destroy him utterly.

XX

Asser gripped my forearm in friendship as my force swelled his warband which had sought sanctuary at the church of Clynnog Fawr. Asser's younger brothers glanced nervously at me and almost recoiled as they caught sight of Maelgwn's devilish features in the dim light. Our night march from Segontium to Clynnog Fawr had gone remarkably well and we had arrived during the early hours of the morning. I had left the main portion of my army under Sitric's capable command and marched my warband with Maelgwn and his men along with Gwyncu's teulu and levy to face the enemy.

Asser had already met Maelgwn, but his brothers had not. He clapped a stocky man on the shoulder. "This is my youngest brother, Gwgon." The man nodded at me respectfully. He was almost identical to Asser in appearance, only he had a ruddier complexion and I judged him to be around ten years Asser's junior. Asser gestured vaguely towards the other man, who was as thin as a stick with a shock of red hair and seemed sickly. "And this is the middle brother, Meirion. Do not expect too much from him on the battlefield, my King. For he is better suited to diplomacy and the games of power." Meirion inclined his head at his brother's words and smiled at me broadly.

I gestured towards Gwyncu and Maelgwn. "You are all well known to Lord Gwyncu. But I have the pleasure of introducing you to Maelgwn son of Rhiwallon, a fearsome warrior indeed." Asser recognised Maelgwn from my council of war and nodded respectfully at him as Gwgon followed suit.

Meirion cocked his head to the side, almost like a bird. "Ah, so it is true. The brother of Cynwrig, our enemy, is amongst us." Asser glanced from his brother to Maelgwn and eyed the Powysian with renewed interest.

Maelgwn grinned wickedly. "Our father is the only thing we have in common. I have come here to kill my brother, he has it coming. The bastard did all this to my face and I shall kill him, you leave him to me. Understand?"

The three sons of Merwydd nodded their acceptance warily and had the sense not to question the Powysian's loyalty any further. I glanced at the sons of Merwydd and yawned audibly. "I do apologise, my lords. We have a few hours yet, if you would excuse me I have other duties to perform."

The three men nodded and I moved out of earshot with Maelgwn and Gwyncu. "I shall rest for a while and shall wake well before sunrise. You are both to move your forces towards Cynwrig's position on my order. There we shall wait for the first glimmer of the sun and launch our attack. Asser and his brothers shall move their forces around the rear of the battle and so we shall encircle Cynwrig. Today he will die."

A triumphant grin spread across Maelgwn's face and Gwyncu nodded nervously before both turned and returned to their men. I listened to the sounds of the night and glanced up at the church tower, which loomed above me. I turned at the sound of footsteps and smiled as Bjorgolf approached out of the darkness with a young monk, who I guessed to be of a similar age to myself.

Bjorgolf clapped a hand on my shoulder and gestured at the monk. "This is Tyrnog, he says you can have the grand honour of sleeping in the church building tonight - at least that is what I think the bugger was trying to tell me." Bjorgolf gestured at the monk, who glowed with pleasure. "I shall stand guard, don't worry and I will make sure you are awake in good time."

I muttered my thanks and nodded at the monk as he led me and Bjorgolf towards a dark door.

Tyrnog had a round, friendly face and he was strongly built. His dark hair was cut in the usual fashion for a monk and he was clean shaven. "You are welcome in the church of Saint Beuno, my King." The doors squeaked on their hinges as Tyrnog pushed them open. He carried a lit candle in one hand, which did little to illuminate the interior of the church. "You will marvel at the church's beauty tomorrow, my King. Once the usurper is defeated and you are victorious."

I clapped a hand on Tyrnog's shoulder. "I'm sure I shall. Saint Beuno is fortunate to have such a grand church dedicated to him." Tyrnog beamed at the praise and babbled that he believed Saint Beuno, whoever he was, would indeed be proud.

Tyrnog had prepared a small spot for me to rest, near the door. As I slumped to the ground and rested my head a sharp voice sounded from the church's interior. "Who are you to enter the church of Saint Beuno uninvited?" The candle light revealed a large, hooked nose as the man came into view.

"Tyrnog, how dare you bring these armed men into the sanctuary of our church. Do you forget that Cynwrig the usurper lays siege!" The candle light further revealed a wrinkled, pock-marked, face which sported a huge mole on the man's shrunken cheeks.

I raised a hand to stop Tyrnog's apology and fixed the elderly priest with a tired expression. "Forgive me, Father?"

"Trillo, Abbot Trillo." The elderly abbot snapped impatiently, adding his title acidly. "Young Tyrnog has overstepped his authority. You are not one of the sons of Merwydd. Who are you, eh?"

"I am Gruffudd son of Cynan." Abbot Trillo's eyes widened a little in surprise at my name. "Tyrnog was only following my request. I wished to offer prayers to Saint Beuno and have a moment to rest."

The abbot shot Tyrnog a suspicious look before he turned his bird-like gaze back on me. His eyes loomed over his hooked nose. "That is commendable of you, my King. Saint Beuno shall bless you with fortune, I am certain. But, the decision lay with me, not young Tyrnog. He shall have to answer for this." Abbot Trillo spun on his heel and shuffled back into the darkness of the church and I shot Tyrnog a conspiratorial smile.

"Don't worry Tyrnog. I am in need of a household monk, if you can read and write." The young monk nodded enthusiastically. "I shall have words with your abbot tomorrow then. Look after him Bjorgolf."

Bjorgolf grinned broadly and slapped the young Tyrnog on the back. "That I shall, if he finds me some food. I'm bloody starving." Bjorgolf had only picked up a few words of Briton and so patted his stomach so that Tyrnog would understand. He chuckled as Tyrnog scuttled off to find some food to satisfy his appetite. Bjorgolf grinned mockingly at me before he laughed. "Did you say you wanted to offer prayers to Saint Beuno? Never heard such bollocks in my life!"

I chuckled, "I don't know what you're laughing at, Bjorgolf. Come, we have prayers to offer the good Saint Beuno." I burst into laughter at Bjorgolf's expression and gestured him forward. We knelt at the altar and I offered prayers to the good saint to bless us with fortune.

I returned to the small bed of hay Tyrnog had prepared for me and let my thoughts wander. Soon I would face Cynwrig and, if God willed it, I would be victorious. As soon as my head rested upon my rolled up cloak I knew it would not be long until I caught up on some much needed sleep. In a few hours Bjorgolf would wake me and we would snare Cynwrig in a trap and kill the bastard.

***

Ljot cursed as a branch snapped back and slapped him in the face and I muttered under my breath at the noise, behind me Bjorgolf cuffed him around the head telling him to be quiet. I could hear a few twigs snap underfoot and a few muttered curses here and there. Silence was key yet I was certain a deaf man could have sensed our approach. I cringed as Oengus' foot crunched a small branch. Christ, but we made more than enough noise to announce our presence to the enemy yet there was no call of alarm.

I held up my fist and my warband came to a halt. Maelgwn's men soon followed suit and the Powysian groped his way through the dim morning light to my side. There were a few more muffled curses from the rear as Gwyncu's men caught up with our position. They were to be the reserve.

Maelgwn had blackened his nosepiece, giving him a more threatening look. The mercenary grinned wickedly as he tested the edge of his dagger. "Soon the bastard dies. He shall not die well." The statement was said with such

233

conviction that I believed Maelgwn would fight his way through the bowels of hell and the devil himself to get his vengeance on Cynwrig.

We clasped forearms as I nodded at his words. "Move on my command; when the sun begins to rise we attack." The Powysian nodded and threaded his way back towards his waiting men.

Bjorgolf crouched next to me in the eerie half-light and accepted a piece of bread from Tyrnog. The young monk had tracked down a basketful of yesterday's bread and distributed it amongst my men as we waited at the woodland's edge in silence. I had insisted Tyrnog remain in Clynnog Fawr but the monk had disobeyed me and followed us forward. There was no sending him back now, yet I feared for the thrashing he would surely suffer at Abbot Trillo's vengeful hands.

I listened to the sounds of the approaching morning as wood pigeons cooed and crows squawked in their nests. Somewhere in the distance an owl hooted and some of the men close by crossed themselves at the haunting sound. I could hear the faint ripple of a stream twenty paces to our front and the sounds of Cynwrig's camp beyond that. A camp fire still smouldered faintly and I could make out the shapes of the men who slept around it, despite the thin mist that lingered above the stream. Cynwrig's sentries had failed to spot our advance and, seemingly, Asser's advance round their rear.

Forty paces ahead the woods gave way to the stream and its banks. Beyond the stream, where Cynwrig's warband camped, lay flat grassland which extended a hundred or so paces to another set of trees where the sons of Merwydd blocked any retreat. To the right the stream flowed gently through the grassland and down to the sea, whilst to the left the shadow of a steep mountain loomed.

I glanced at the horizon and felt the familiar pre-battle nerves as the first signs of the day's sunrise began to show. I clenched and unclenched my sword hilt and felt for my dagger as I waited. Light began to seep onto the land and Cynwrig's camp began to stir. I noticed a banner hanging limply in the still air but could not make out what it was. I whispered to Bjorgolf. "Unsheathe the banner. Let's make sure Cynwrig knows who comes to kill him." I smiled with satisfaction as Bjorgolf passed on the command and Ronan took the protective leather cover off my family's banner.

A slight breeze stirred through the trees and caught the red and yellow cloth, making the rampant lions stir as if they clawed the air, impatient to get at my enemy. I sensed that was an omen to begin my attack. I rose from the crouch and drew my blade, I heard the stirring of bushes and the snap of sticks as my whole warband rose and made ready with their weapons. I glanced either side of me and saw my men go through their own pre-battle rituals. Maelgwn caught my eye, grinning broadly at the prospect of the slaughter he would bring to his brother and his men.

I thumped my blade into the air and brought it down in a great arc. "Forward!" I pushed my way through the tree branches to my front and pounded through the undergrowth. My men began to scream their challenges as we broke clear of the cover and I heard the first cries of alarm and the dull thump of bowstrings. And then the first screams of pain began as Maelgwn's *helwyr* found their targets.

Cynwrig's men stirred and gaped in shock at the overwhelming number of men that emerged from the shadowy woodland and sprinted towards their positions. Some turned their backs and began to flee as I splashed into the stream and vaulted up onto the bank, but most of Cynwrig's men drew their weapons as we closed on them.

An arrow thudded into the side of a man's head to my front and he crumpled to the turf. I jumped the fallen man, slashing my blade at another of Cynwrig's men. We were amongst them, the scene was chaotic; Cynwrig's men were cut down mercilessly as the momentum of my assault carried us forward. I parried a desperate lunge which was aimed at my chest and took my attacker in his throat. My blade cut through the skin and into his gullet, like a knife through cloth. I did not wait to see him fall but brought my blade down on a man who knelt before me, pleading for his life. The blade split his skull and stuck fast.

I fumbled for the blade but it was lost as my momentum carried me on. I was not aware of who was around me, only what lay ahead. I drew my knife as one of Cynwrig's men screamed a challenge and came at me with a short-axe. I dodged his hack and rammed the wicked dagger through his right eye, grimacing as the slimy mess of the burst eyeball spoilt my grip on the weapon as I tugged it free. The dagger slipped from my grasp and I cursed as a big man thundered towards me with a short spear. I managed to twist away from the point but the man shouldered into me and sent me sprawling onto the turf. I swallowed hard as he loomed above me, ready to thrust his spear down. I closed my eyes and waited for the death blow to arrive, but it didn't. Nervously I opened my eyes to see the big man on his knees mouthing words that would not come, a spear point sticking through his chest. The big man took one last look at me and fell forward; Tyrnog stood above him and placed a sandaled foot on the man's back before wrenching his short spear free.

Bjorgolf clapped him on the shoulder and dragged me upright. "Little bugger was a heartbeat quicker than me!" The Dane exclaimed fondly before ruffling Tyrnog's hair. The young monk beamed with pleasure as he held his short spear with a surprising familiarity.

As I looked around it was all but over. My men chased the survivors of Cynwrig's warband towards the woods at the far end of the clearing, where Asser and his men lay in wait. I retrieved my dagger and my blade and surveyed the carnage that lay before me. Maelgwn's men fought like lions against the remnants of Cynwrig's forces, who protected their lord stoutly. Cynwrig's banner was at the centre of a group who were forced to retreat into the water of the stream and now they panted as Maelgwn's men encircled the doomed formation.

I trotted over to the bank and watched Cynwrig's last stand. He propped himself up against his own banner, which he held in his left arm. His sword arm dripped blood into the small stream but he still had his blade. Only five of his men were still alive and they formed a protective shield in front of their lord. The stream flowed over their ankles, in a grotesque mixture of mud and crimson. Men had died in the stream and their blood flowed with the water to where Cynwrig waited for death. I could not help but feel what an idyllic scene the stream must have looked as it flowed through the grassy meadow and into the sea, until men destroyed its beauty with anger and hate.

I stared at Cynwrig. He was a few years younger than Maelgwn, but the two looked nothing alike. Cynwrig's brown hair fell roughly down to his shoulders and he sported a full beard. He had had no time to don his wargear and stood in his breeches and a simple un-dyed woollen tunic. A broken arrow shaft jutted out of his left shoulder and a sword stroke had sliced open his right cheek. Blood seeped freely from the wounds as he tried to keep himself upright. His right leg was bent oddly from the knee and I grimaced as I saw a sharp shard of bone sticking through the dark cloth of his breeches where his leg had broken. He spat at Maelgwn's men and called at them. "What are you waiting for? Bastards!"

Maelgwn's men jeered at Cynwrig and some even bared their arses as a final insult to their master's nemesis. Maelgwn stepped forward from the formation and turned to the gap-toothed *helwyr*, uttering something I could not hear. The gap-toothed *helwyr* smiled and signalled at the six other bowmen around him. They drew back their bow strings and loosed their arrows at Cynwrig's five men. Cynwrig's bodyguard barely had time to shout a warning as the arrow shafts punched into their bodies. The five warriors fell and splashed into the stream's waters where they lay, dead or dying. Cynwrig looked appalled and spat his disgust at the *helwyr*. "Fight me fairly!" He screamed, raising his blade in a defiant final challenge.

Maelgwn sheathed his blade and stepped forward until he stood on the bank of the stream. The two men eyed each other and Cynwrig swallowed hard as he recognised his brother, whom he had wronged so many years ago. Maelgwn grinned triumphantly and unfastened his metal nosepiece, so that Cynwrig could see the horror he had caused. Cynwrig shuddered and stared at his brother in disbelief.

Maelgwn clutched the nosepiece in one hand and threw it at his brother. The nosepiece glanced off Cynwrig's forehead and I saw the lump in his throat move as he swallowed nervously. Maelgwn chuckled sadistically at his brother's hopelessness. "Fight you fairly? Fight you fairly!" He thundered at Cynwrig. "Like you fought me fairly, all those years ago?"

Tears began to form in Cynwrig's eyes as he eyed Maelgwn. "I ask for forgiveness, brother. I wish to meet God with a clear conscience." Cynwrig spoke passionately and made an attempt to cross himself. His sword arm shook uncontrollably as he awaited his fate.

Maelgwn laughed. "You shall never have my forgiveness and it is not God that you shall meet, but the devil." With frightening speed Maelgwn splashed through the stream and hurled himself at his brother.

Cynwrig swung his blade desperately at his attacker, but Maelgwn was too quick. He tackled Cynwrig and the two splashed into the red water of the stream. Maelgwn pinned Cynwrig's arms to the stream's stony floor with his knees as he sat on his brother's chest. The trapped Cynwrig thrashed wildly in the frothy water in an effort to release himself from his brother's vengeful grip. Maelgwn picked up Cynwrig's blade and hurled it downstream, so that his brother would not die holding his blade like a warrior.

Maelgwn's men cheered as he drew his wickedly sharp dagger and held it up to the rising sun like a trophy. He kissed the cold steel of the blade and grinned as he toyed with Cynwrig. Maelgwn ran the cold steel slowly over his brother's cheeks and grinned with pleasure as he began to carve wicked slashes into his brother's face.

Cynwrig screamed frantically in pain and called for mercy, but Maelgwn ignored his brother. A piercing scream sounded as Maelgwn, with a ruthless efficiency, sliced off his victim's ears and flung them over his shoulder. Cynwrig was pleading for death and screaming uncontrollably as Maelgwn enjoyed his revenge. His men watched on with grim expressions as Maelgwn's blood soaked face grinned sadistically at his brother's helpless screams.

Maelgwn spoke so that all could hear. "Cynwrig, you shall wander through hell. And you shall do so deaf and mute!" Maelgwn's men cheered their approval as their master forced his blade into Cynwrig's mouth and cut out his tongue. Cynwrig screamed an inhuman sound as he stared up at Maelgwn who, beaming with joy held the severed tongue before letting it fall into the river.

I was struck dumb by the display of savagery and I shook my head in pity for Cynwrig. The man was a usurper and had wronged his brother, but no one deserved a death like this. The guttural screams still escaped Cynwrig's blood-filled mouth as Maelgwn gained his final revenge. The Powysian seemed as though he was bending down to kiss his brother on the forehead, but I shuddered when I realised what he was doing. Cynwrig's screams grew in intensity as Maelgwn's teeth bit into his nose, through bone and cartilage. Maelgwn looked like a creature from the depths as hell as he stood upright and spat out the lump of offal, which had been Cynwrig's nose.

Cynwrig was unrecognisable, his face a ghastly display of butchery and ruthlessness, but he still breathed. Maelgwn looked down one last time at his brother and spat at his ruined face before standing on his head, forcing it below the water line. Everyone watched on in silence as Cynwrig drowned under his brother's foot. I glanced at Bjorgolf, who shook his head in disbelief at the cruelty he had witnessed.

When Maelgwn was certain Cynwrig had died he held out a hand. One of his men strode forward and offered Maelgwn his axe. The Powysian took the long-handled weapon in both hands and thrust it down with all his force. He severed Cynwrig's head in one clean stroke. He passed the axe back to the man and stooped to reclaim the gruesome trophy. He took a fistful of the wet hair and held the mutilated head for all to see. In a final act of revenge he spat in his dead brother's face before picking up a discarded spear and lodging the head onto it. The Powysian's men cheered as he held it above them like a trophy.

I glanced either side of me and Bjorgolf spat in disgust at the display of savagery whilst Tyrnog had fallen to his knees in the shallow water and prayed; the lad had seen horrors this day which were probably beyond his wildest dreams. I tapped Bjorgolf on the shoulder as I turned to leave Maelgwn's men and their gruesome trophy. "Come, Bjorgolf. There is nothing left to see here. We shall pull back to Clynnog Fawr and then back on to Segontium."

Bjorgolf shook his head again and turned away from the savage Powysians. Like me, the Dane was deeply shocked by the barbarity of Maelgwn and his men. "I hope to God we never have to face an army of his countrymen, if they are all like him." I mumbled my agreement to the statement as Bjorgolf grumbled again. "Evil bastard, I shall not be making an enemy of him in a hurry."

As my men looted the dead I shook my head again at the brutality of the Powysians. I was no stranger to death, blood or cruelty yet I had been shocked to the core. I wager even Father Cathal would have been shocked by the act. Yet the day had gone well, Cynwrig lay dead and his small army routed. Trahaearn had been deprived of his ally and I had the advantage.

XXI

Tyrnog and his fellow monks, under Abbot Trillo's watchful eye, sang praises to the heavens for my victory. The church of Saint Beuno was indeed a magnificent structure and I marvelled at its beauty as I knelt at the foot of the altar. I offered prayers of thanks to God and the good Saint Beuno. I was the first to receive mass from the Abbot and I crossed myself as the transubstantiation took place in my mouth.

All present received the mass and gave thanks for the decisive victory we had won. Asser had butchered Cynwrig's fleeing supporters and had performed well in the field. I could not fault the decisiveness of the victory, none of Cynwrig's supporters had survived, yet Maelgwn's barbarity troubled me. The man was a powerful force of nature and I was relieved I did not have to fight against him. I hoped Bjorgolf's doubts of the Powysian's loyalty were poorly founded.

As the congregation began to flood out of the church, I waited to talk with Abbot Trillo. The elderly abbot had lectured Tyrnog for following my men into battle and, as far as I could see, he still owed the young monk a beating for forgetting his place within the hierarchy of the small monastery. Bjorgolf stood at my side and fidgeted awkwardly as we waited for Abbot Trillo.

The old abbot came into view and hobbled towards us, he dragged a clubbed foot I noticed and used a staff for support. "You wish to talk with me, my King?"

"Indeed I do, Abbot Trillo." I spoke respectfully to the man. "I am in need of a good monk to act as a scribe and confidant, as well as keeping my men on the path of righteousness, of course." I had taken a liking to Tyrnog for his enthusiasm and conduct during the battle, as had Bjorgolf. Besides the young monk had saved my life and I believed I owed him, in return, a future which involved no beatings from his abbot.

Abbot Trillo sighed and eyed me keenly. "I cannot suggest anyone that is worthy, my King. You must ask his holiness the Bishop of Bangor for his recommendation or the Abbot of Ynys Enlli." A sly smile split the old priest's face. "However, I do not believe the Bishop will look fondly upon you. Trahaearn is a generous parishioner, you see."

Bjorgolf had understood none of the conversation, but he knew it was not going well. The Dane fixed the old abbot with a belligerent stare which made him drop his gaze from me. I continued in a respectful tone. "I care little for what the Bishop of Bangor thinks. Forgive me, but I know my cause to be just in the eyes of God." Abbot Trillo inclined his head to acknowledge the truth of what I had said.

"That's as may be." He croaked and looked from me to Bjorgolf awkwardly. "Alas, I still cannot help you. We are but a poor parish, my King."

I sighed and reached for my pouch. I dropped the remainder of Gofraid's silver coins into my palm. "If I were to make a donation to the upkeep of your fine monastery, Abbot. I would require a hardworking and honest monk to serve the kingdom." Trillo eyed the silver greedily. Like most clerics I had met he was out to make himself a profit, I doubted half of what I gave him would have gone to those of his parishioners who needed it most.

"Of course, my King. The monastery and parish will be a better place due to your generosity." Abbot Trillo took the silver greedily and weighed it in his bony hands. "Young Tyrnog is an enthusiastic character; I trust he shall serve you well. Now, if you will excuse me, I have many duties to perform this day." The old abbot turned and shuffled back from the direction he had come.

Bjorgolf stared hatefully at the man's back. "Bastard, typical bloody priest. All out for themselves they are." I clapped Bjorgolf on the back and led him out of the church of Saint Beuno and into the sunlight.

The sun had burned away the early morning mist and it promised the beginnings of summer. I glanced towards the mountains and noticed a grey cloud float over them, but the sun shone as my victorious men formed up into a column. I took that as a good omen that God approved of my cause.

Tyrnog was hopping about outside the church's entrance and looked at me hopefully. I smiled at him happily. "We march soon, make sure you are ready." The monk grinned enthusiastically and scuttled off to an outbuilding as quick as he could.

Bjorgolf chuckled at his enthusiasm and laughed as Tyrnog emerged moments later with all his possessions bundled into a small pack fastened to his back. He trotted over to us and Bjorgolf clapped him fondly on the head before leading him over to my warband who, having suffered no casualties during the morning's fight, were in high spirits.

Maelgwn and Gwyncu approached me and nodded their greetings. I nodded back to them, I felt awkward around Maelgwn following the butchery he had orchestrated hours earlier. "My lords, we shall march shortly. We head to Segontium, where we will organise ourselves over the next two days. And then we shall march on Trahaearn."

Gwyncu nodded enthusiastically and headed back to his men. The Lord of Rhosyr and his men had tasted victory in their first battle and were in high spirits. Little did they know what a pitched battle against an organised enemy would be like. Maelgwn nodded stiffly and marched back to his waiting Powysians, who flew the banner of Mathrafal with pride.

I strode over to Asser, whose men were also preparing to march and he greeted me happily. "A fine victory. My warmest congratulations again, my King. Rest assured that I and my men are capable of uniting Lleyn against the usurper Trahaearn."

I smiled my thanks. "I know you are more than capable, Lord Asser. I plan to organise my army and we shall march on Trahaearn in the coming days." Asser nodded his head in approval. "Once you are satisfied of the loyalty of the men of Lleyn I require you to march on the fort at Deudraeth and take Dunoding. I believe that those men loyal to Trahaearn will have answered his call to arms and joined him in Meirionydd, so you should face little opposition."

Asser smiled confidently. "It shall be done, my King." I placed a hand on his shoulder and he raised an inquisitive eyebrow.

"I shall be sending you reinforcements, under the command of Lord Faelan." I noticed the suspicion in Asser's eyes and spoke quickly to show I did not doubt his loyalty. "I do not doubt your loyalty, only I wish for the Irishman to gain vital experience under a watchful gaze."

Asser looked sceptically at me. "Then why do you need to send him to me?" He guessed the answer to his own question and laughed. "You want him out of the way, eh?"

He laughed again as I nodded. "If he oversteps himself at any point, you have my permission to do what you will with him." Asser laughed and turned to return to his men. I began the short walk to the head if the column and smiled. I could not fail.

The whole army cheered our arrival when we arrived back at Segontium. I could not have wished for the march to Clynnog Fawr and the defeat of Cynwrig to have gone smoother. None of my sword-brothers had been killed, although a few sported new wounds. Maelgwn had lost only two men and Gwyncu's teulu had returned completely unscathed, although a dozen of his levy had met their ends. Men cheered as Maelgwn carried the spear with Cynwrig's head still attached and the men chanted my name as I rode Iago into the encampment.

That was two days ago. The weather had changed yet again and Bjorgolf cursed as we waited for all my commanders to answer my summons to a council. "I never thought the weather would be as bad anywhere else as it is in Duibhlinn. But I was mistaken, here it is bloody worse!"

I laughed at Bjorgolf's grumblings; the weather changed several times a day and was completely unpredictable. The roads made the situation worse. What was a passable mountain road one hour could be turned to a treacherous quagmire the next. The walls of my tent flapped so hard in the strong winds, I thought the tent may be blown away. I had led my army into the mountains of Eryri and there we waited as the storm raged outside.

Faelan, thank God, had marched a day earlier to the port of Nevyn. There he would remain for the rest of the campaign. I was pleased to be rid of him. The landscape was bleak, vast peaks dominated the scenery all around and my army had struggled along the barely passable roads. The Romans had built a road through these mountains, but we were yet to find it. We needed to find it, or the advantage of speed would be lost. Trahaearn's army was still reported to be camped in Meirionydd, where he hoped Iorwerth the King of Powys would join him. Speed was key; I had to draw Trahaearn into battle before the King of Powys, if indeed he intended to support the usurper, marched to his aid.

The tent flaps opened as Sitric along with Cerit and Wselfwulf emerged from the gloom. Ronan and Ruaidri stood guard outside the tent whilst Bjorgolf and Ljot flanked me on either side. Sitric shook his hair like a soaked dog and splattered the canvas walls with the moisture. "This weather is foul, worse than bloody Ireland." I sensed Bjorgolf smile as Sitric's words repeated our earlier discussion.

Cerit shook his head. "Truly woeful, why anyone would want to call this land their own I shall never know." He sent me a friendly smile and stood aside as Maelgwn emerged from the darkness accompanied by another man.

The other man was Owain, son of Edwin, Lord of Tegeingl. He commanded the eighty men I had been promised by Robert. They were all Britons from Owain's lands and they were dressed in a similar manner to my other countrymen. The wealthier warriors wore mail coats, some rusted with age and others plundered during raids,

247

whilst the rest wore an assortment of padded tunics or, if they were lucky, hardened leather. They all carried the small shields which were favoured by the Britons. I still could not understand their obsession with the small shield as the large round shields my men carried were well balanced and offered the owner strong defence and an alternative means of attack, whilst the small shield left its owner perilously open to attack. They carried an assortment of weaponry but the majority sported the traditional short spears.

Owain, despite being only ten summers my senior, was balding and had a battle scarred face. He had fought against the Frenchmen's incursions into his home province of Tegeingl until they had erected their castles. Robert's castle at Rhuddlan dominated the provinces of Tegeingl, Rhos and Dyffryn Clwyd and so Owain had been forced to sue for peace, or lose all that he loved. It had left a bitter taste in his mouth which was made worse by having to do his new master's bidding. But Owain seemed more than happy to be part of my army. He claimed it was like old times.

Tudur and his vassal lords from the province Cemais were next to arrive, shortly followed by the men of Arfon and Rhys son of Einion, who commanded the few soldiers that had been provided by the Lord of Arllechwedd. Tyrnog sat happily at a desk in the corner of the tent, where he watched the lords and allies of Gwynedd with interest. Tyrnog had proved to be a remarkably good judge of character and had a sharpness that was unnatural for his age.

I rose to my full height and cleared my throat. "My lords, the weather is against us and the roads are made more treacherous by the day. We must find the Roman road that leads through the mountains, or we shall lose more precious time." I glanced at the faces of those present and noticed Tudur grumbling to a small group of his vassal lords.

"Lord Seisyll," the rotund man almost jumped at the mention of his name. "You will send out your finest scouts at first light to find this road, understood?" Seisyll's jowls wobbled as he nodded his head in acknowledgment. "The army will continue along our present course until the Roman road is discovered. All clear?"

There were a few grumbles from the minor lords and they found a voice for their complaints in the Lord of Cemais. Tudur stepped forward and ignored Sitric's cold stare as he eyed me. "My King, I do not see the advantage we gain in struggling through the mountains of Eryri. It is folly; we must select a defensive position and let Trahaearn attack us." His allies mumbled their agreement, whilst the other lords eyed Tudur with a mixture of interest and disapproval.

I chuckled to myself. "If that is your belief then I thank God you do not lead this army." Tudur's eyes widened and his cheeks reddened. "We must persevere. If we withdraw and go on the defensive then we hand all the advantage to Trahaearn." Sitric and my other loyal commanders rumbled their approval.

But Tudur was not so easily swayed. "My King, we hand him the advantage by advancing through this bleak landscape!" He gestured at his few supporters, some of whom shifted uncomfortably as my gaze passed over them. "I and some sensible men believe we should return to Segontium and wait for Trahaearn's army there."

I shook my head firmly. "No. If we do as you plan then Iorwerth, the King of Powys, may well join Trahaearn.

If that happens, my lords, then we shall be outnumbered and the advantage shall lie with Trahaearn." I held up a hand to silence Tudur. "Those who wish to defend everything, defend nothing." A chorus of agreement broke out and some of Tudur's supporters now distanced themselves from the young lord. "No, my lords. We shall not defend. We attack, attack we must. Speed is key; we must bring Trahaearn to battle. And soon."

Sitric and Maelgwn shouted their approval and Tudur reluctantly became silent, knowing his cause to have been lost. "Now, my lords, you must return to your men, for tomorrow, God willing, we shall advance into Meirionydd and draw Trahaearn into battle."

As my commanders began to exit the tent I caught Sitric's words to Tudur. "Why the haste to withdraw, eh?" He did not wait for an answer. "Only cowards fear to meet their enemy." Tudur simply smirked at Sitric and strode away from the battle scarred warrior.

I yawned my farewells to Sitric and Cerit, who were last to leave. Bjorgolf wearily nodded at me. "I guess the little brat doesn't want to fight?" I nodded my head in reply and Bjorgolf chuckled. "Always knew he was a coward, watch him."

The words were spoken truthfully and I knew it. I unbuckled my belt and pulled the mail hauberk over my head. I was tired but could not relax as I bedded down for the night. I needed to bring Trahaearn to battle and soon, or all would be lost. Those were my last thoughts as I finally surrendered to sleep.

I was relieved the rain had stopped as I walked Iago down the muddy track. Seisyll's riders had fortunately found the

Roman road and the track we were following led directly to it. I had sent the riders further ahead, in case Trahaearn had any forces in the area. This was the main route into Meirionydd and I doubted he would leave it undefended. I glanced up at the grey sky and prayed that it would not rain again today.

A hill crest lay two hundred paces ahead and a rider appeared over it. His mountain pony trotted as fast as it could down the road. I recognised the man as one of Seisyll's scouts. Bjorgolf and the others may well have mocked the hardy beasts but they had come into their own on the high mountain passes. It was now easy to see why my countrymen favoured the beasts in such a harsh and mountainous country.

The man edged his pony round the marching column of Sitric's warband, which was my vanguard. My warband followed close behind and I glanced over the heads of the assorted Britons to where the baggage train, Maelgwn's men and the camp followers made up the rear. Bjorgolf, Gwcharki, Ronan, Ruaidri, Ljot and Oengus acted as my bodyguard and the rider came to a halt ahead of my small group.

Ronan took the man's short spear and dagger whilst Bjorgolf put an arm round his shoulders and steered him towards me. The man walked awkwardly, from spending the last couple of days in the saddle. He bowed his head respectfully. "My King, there is an old fort a short way ahead. It is garrisoned by the enemy."

The man spoke excitedly and I saw Oengus raise his head with interest; I did not know he could understand Briton but chose not to question the fact. "Very good, we shall meet the enemy soon then. How many do they number?"

"Just a small garrison, my King. No more than sixty men I think." I clapped the man on his shoulder and he retrieved his weapons from Ronan before trotting back to his pony and throwing himself into the saddle. He coaxed the little beast forward and the pony trotted past the marching men and into the distance.

I turned to Bjorgolf. "So, we shall see what Trahaearn's forces are up to before the day is out." Bjorgolf and the rest of my bodyguard grinned triumphantly, for there would soon be killing to be done.

As we crested the hill I saw the dark smudge on the landscape. I guessed it to be a Roman fort, for the site was chosen well and commanded the old road. It lay on a natural hill which was flanked to the left by a vast mountain range. Otherwise the fort commanded an unhindered view of the old Roman road which drove, like a spear, relentlessly over the landscape. We would reach the fort soon and I knew it must be taken. Trahaearn had clearly left these men in this strategic position in a gamble to delay my advance. One way or another, the fort would fall this day and I would march into Meirionydd before sunrise. I could smell my prey and felt my heart quicken beneath my mail. The garrison must be slaughtered; I could taste victory as I walked Iago on to meet the enemy.

XXII

"Castell Tomen, eh?" I said the name aloud again as I watched my army came to a halt before the fort. I turned to where a prisoner was held between Ljot and Oengus. The man had been captured by Seisyll's scouts as he tried to flee into Meirionydd. He had planned to carry news of our arrival to Trahaearn who, the man claimed, was camped a day's march away in a wooded valley. The prisoner had claimed King Iorwerth of Powys was marching to Trahaearn's aid and would arrive any day. Speed was key.

The man's head sagged and his eyes rolled as Bjorgolf punched him again. He had taken a spear thrust through the armpit which had punctured his lung and every breath was a struggle for him. Pinkish blood bubbled and frothed in the corner of the man's mouth. He knew he was dying, but he also knew it would be a slow death. I could end his suffering, or prolong it, he knew that too as I stared into his dark eyes.

"How many men garrison the fort?" He made no effort to answer so Bjorgolf backhanded him again. Each breath was agony for the man and he winced again as the movement of his rib cage pulled at his wound. "Tell me what I want to know and I will end your suffering. Understand?" Bjorgolf threatened to strike the man again but he shook his head.

"I understand." He wheezed and more blood bubbled in the corner of his mouth. "There are enough men to keep you here for days." He spluttered and grimaced at the pain of taking another breath. "T-T-Trahaearn will march," he spluttered again. "When the K-K-King of P-Powys comes to his aid."

I nodded to myself. So that was his plan. The garrison of Castell Tomen was to be sacrificed to buy Trahaearn time. I nodded to Ljot who drew his dagger and cut the prisoner's throat. The man gargled his last sound as Ljot cleaned his blade in the man's woollen cloak.

I turned to Bjorgolf and spoke quietly enough for only him to hear. "The bastard is sacrificing his garrison in the hope that they can delay us sufficiently." I shook my head. "Well the usurper won't have his wish. Tonight we will take that fort and we shall march on Trahaearn with haste. The bastard will have a surprise in the morning."

Bjorgolf chuckled to himself. "Trahaearn is a cunning whorseon, for sure. But I am thinking he has met his match." The Dane glanced at Castell Mur and shook his head, it would not be easy.

"Oengus, you understand Briton?" The Irishman glanced at me with a surprised expression before nodding warily. "Good, then send my compliments to my countrymen and tell them they are to surround the fort. We are to lay siege." Oengus nodded and trotted off to relay my commands.

The men watched him go as Ruaidri uttered his surprise that his friend had a command of the Briton tongue. I beckoned Ljot towards me. I glanced at the sky; the light was beginning to fade quickly. "My compliments to Sitric and Maelgwn, inform them they are to come to my tent at once." Ljot nodded and scurried off in the direction of Sitric's warband.

I turned and stared at Castell Tomen with the remainder of my bodyguard. I heard my banner snapping in the wind as Ronan proudly held it aloft; I hoped the garrison could see it too and know they were doomed. I had previously tried to send a deputation, headed by Seisyll, to demand the garrison's surrender but they had been met by a flurry of arrows and Seisyll had taken an arrow in his thigh. But the rotund lord would live. There would be no mercy; I would have to destroy Castell Tomen's garrison, for the fort was too strategic to be left to the enemy.

I surveyed the old Roman fort again. The old stone walls had crumbled to their foundations, but Trahaearn's men had erected a new palisade atop the Roman stonework. An earthen mound dominated the fort's corner to my left, where an old wooden watchtower perched precariously. The fort was rectangular in shape and the remains of Roman outbuildings beyond the walls stubbornly refused to yield to the coarse vegetation of the mountainous landscape. It was a fine defensive structure in a very strategic location. It must fall and quickly, but how?

Bjorgolf cleared his throat thoughtfully and gestured vaguely towards the old fort. "Any ideas?" He grinned as I tapped my nose in a knowing manner. In my mind I plotted Castell Tomen's fall.

"Are you mad?" Cerit shook his head, not for the first time, at my plan. "I am sorry, brother. But what you propose is sheer madness. What will the army do if you are killed?"

I knew Cerit's concerns were well founded but I did not much care. I had to show this army I could deliver victory from any predicament and this was how I would do it. "My mind is set, brother. This is the only way Castell Tomen can be taken in the time we have."

Maelgwn grinned at me knowingly. "I like it." He said simply. "Daring and perilous; you are full of surprises

Gruffudd." The Powysian nodded his head again at my plan and chuckled.

Sitric, so far had said nothing, he stood with his arms crossed and deep in thought. He scratched his beard before speaking. "Very well, I can see the logic. But I shall send Wselfwulf with you." Cerit shot him a concerned look, which he ignored. "I think your lads will be enough but let me send Wselfwulf and twenty of my men with you."

Sitric had a knack of making things sound like a request when in reality they were an order. I indulged him and conceded to his 'request.' "I shall be honoured to have Wselfwulf under my command. My duties of late have kept me away from the old whoreson; it will be good to fight at his side again."

Sitric nodded his head. "It is settled then?" He smiled as I nodded and repeated my orders. "If you are taken, killed or incapacitated I am to withdraw the army to Segontium." I nodded that he was correct. "Then, God willing, it will not come to that. For if it does your campaign will be over. May God be with you."

My foster-father was not prone to such statements and I inclined my head respectfully at his kind words. He turned on his heel and marched out of the tent with Cerit at his side. Cerit shot me a worried look as he left, but I knew nothing was to be gained by playing it safe and starving the enemy out. Maelgwn chuckled to himself again and clasped my forearm before leaving the tent.

Only Bjorgolf, Gwcharki and Tyrnog remained. Bjorgolf grinned broadly and patted his blade. "About bloody time we had a proper fight." Gwcharki rumbled the harsh noise which passed for a laugh whilst Tyrnog crossed himself.

"Where you not at Clynnog Fawr?" I asked Bjorgolf mockingly. For I knew what the answer would be.

"You call that a fight? I only killed one of the curs, that's not a bloody fight." The Dane laughed as he caught my eye. "Well then, better get the lads together. They will be earning their keep tonight, sure enough."

I made sure my belt was securely buckled and I rubbed soil into my mail hauberk to ensure it did not reflect any light, before doing the same to my helm. I fastened the leather strap securely under my chin and Tyrnog grinned at my appearance. The young monk had somehow managed to get his hands on some hardened leather, which he had strapped around his torso, as well as a leather cap. There was no discouraging the monk and that amused me. Here stood a man of God and he was ready for war.

I exited the tent and strode into the night; Tyrnog and his short spear close behind. Bjorgolf and Wselfwulf were waiting outside, the two talking like old friends. I clasped the old Saxon's forearm in friendship. "It will be good to fight at your side again, old friend."

The scarred face contorted into a smile. "Aye, it will. Sitric wants me at your side, holding your hand like a bloody babysitter, so that is where I shall be."

I laughed at the old warrior's words. "I could think of no other place for you. Besides, we Britons always have to watch you Saxons." We both laughed as I nodded to Bjorgolf and surveyed my waiting sword-brothers.

I was proud of the men I had turned from thralls to warriors. They were fierce and loyal, they were mine. I raised my voice so that it would carry to them all. "Tonight men, we are going to go for a walk up that hill." I gestured towards the glow of Castell Tomen. "And we are going to teach those bastards a bloody lesson. No mercy, my wolves, no mercy!" They smiled to themselves, none thought of the risk they were about to take but of the plunder they could earn. They stifled their cheers for I did not want the enemy to know something was afoot in my camp.

I clapped Bjorgolf on the shoulder and turned to Wselfwulf. "Tonight, old friend, we shall fight our way into legend." The Saxon smiled and trotted after me into the darkness.

I could feel my blade thudding repeatedly against my thigh as we plodded into position. The weather had turned again and rain swirled over the boggy ground between my camp and Castell Tomen's walls. Good I thought, for that would hamper the enemy sentries' line of sight, God willed it.

I glanced about me as the men fanned out behind me. Wselfwulf was to my right and Bjorgolf to my left; both caught my eye and grinned menacingly. Were they not born so far apart I would have thought them brothers. I glanced behind me and Tyrnog smiled back as he gripped his short spear and Ronan's shaggy head nodded reassuringly. It was time.

"Forward." I whispered and men passed it down the line. I dropped to my knees and lay down flat onto my belly. I started to crawl forwards and heard a few muffled curses as my men followed suit. I led sixty men towards the enemy defences, which could hold more than double my number. Surprise and speed would be everything.

It reminded me of my desperate mission in the siege of Duibhlinn all those months ago and I thought back to how Maelgwn had caught me and so nearly buggered all my dreams. I could not consider failure, it was not an option. My heart began to race under my mail as I edged closer and closer to the watchtower mound on Castell Tomen's flank. There, where the fort would be least defended, we would scale the palisade and climb the mound. We would stream down the other side and into the fort. Speed and surprise were everything. I touched my sword hilt for luck and muttered a silent prayer. I headed for Castell Tomen through the dark night and I brought only death and despair to the defenders.

I could not believe it as my men bunched around the palisade at the foot of the watchtower's mound, no sentry had noticed us. I could hear the sounds of the fort beyond. Men snored whilst a few grumbled around their campfires. Wselfwulf put his back to the timber and cupped his hands as he bent a little. I put my right foot into his hands and he launched me upwards, my hands grabbed the top of the palisade and I dragged myself over. Bjorgolf followed and Wselfwulf soon after. The ground was saturated and our feet sank into the sodden earth, so that it seeped into my boots. I began to slither up the mound with Bjorgolf and Wselfwulf on either side. I glanced back and saw Ronan's bushy head peering over the palisade; I would clear the watchtower and signal the men forward.

We reached the base of the watchtower and still we had not been noticed. I quickly glanced into the fort's interior and guessed from the campfires that the prisoner had lied, there could be no more than fifty men. A wooden ladder led up to the watchtower's summit and I silently climbed the twelve feet. I muttered my thanks, for the good fortune that had brought me so close to the enemy undetected, and drew my dagger stealthily.

The sentry, curled up in a ball, snored at the watchtower's summit. He stirred slightly as I put an arm round his neck and he realised what was happening too late. Before he could utter any noise I had rammed my dagger into his throat and he was still. I withdrew the blade and wiped it on his sleeve.

I slid silently down the ladder and nodded to Bjorgolf. The Dane slithered back down the way we had come and soon I heard the muttered curses as my men began to scale the palisade. Still we had not been noticed, I could not help but marvel at the incompetence of Trahaearn's men.

I waited until the top of the mound was filled with my men. Only then did I draw my blade and slide down the mound's other side into the fort. I rose to my feet, with Wselfwulf beside me, and screamed a challenge as a man realised what was happening but my blade took him in the throat before he could react.

Calls of alarm sounded as my sword-brothers screamed their battle cries and launched themselves at the startled enemy. Within moments we had slaughtered the men around the campfires closest to the watchtower mound but I could hear their lord hastily organising a defence.

Men screamed with pain as they fell to the sodden ground. Tyrnog spitted a defender with his small spear before Ronan finished him off with an axe stroke to his scalp. I rushed forwards to where a group of panicked enemy desperately huddled together for defence. I hurtled into a man in the front rank who was shouting orders at the frightened press of men.

My blade sliced into his forearm as he tried to parry my strike. A startled scream escaped his lips and he dropped the blade before falling to the floor and out of the fight. It was a desperate struggle as Trahaearn's garrison fought for their lives, I could hear screams all around as I parried a spear thrust. Tyrnog's spear darted past my head and sank into an enemy's chest. The monk twisted his weapon and pulled it free before the man fell.

Wselfwulf was screaming in his harsh native tongue as his blade flashed around him. Bjorgolf's blade took a man in the base of his chin and I gasped as the point smashed through the man's mouth and sprayed shards of teeth over me. A shard went in my eye and I faltered. Before I knew what was happening the wind was driven from me and I gasped. My vision cleared just as Bjorgolf's blade took my attacker in his belly, splitting his stomach and the man screamed as his gut-rope spilled out. Bjorgolf parried another blow as he fought desperately to pull me away.

I still could not breathe and felt my chest where a few mail-rings had buckled, but still held. I breathed a sigh of relief as I realised the mail had saved my life. Wselfwulf turned to face me and I could not hear what he said over the din. I tried to scream a warning but it was too late.

An axe stroke split the skull of the man who acted as Wselfwulf's shield and a spear thrust came over the man's falling body. The spear pierced the Saxon's mail and punched into his shoulder blade. Wselfwulf's face contorted with agony as he screamed and threw himself at the attacker. I fought against Bjorgolf's grip but the Dane pulled me back.

Wselfwulf had disappeared amongst a desperate throng of defenders who fought grimly on. Bjorgolf had stopped dragging me and checked to see I was alright. I was in a daze I heard nothing clearly, only noise. My eyes scanned the scene, the dead lay all around and the sickly-sweet smell of burning flesh caught the air as a corpse smouldered in the nearest camp fire. I saw Wselfwulf fight clear of the desperate group of defenders and the Saxon butted one of the men before a finely dressed warrior swung his blade, the tip caught the old warrior in the throat and I screamed in despair as he fell.

Bjorgolf tried to hold me back but I clutched a broken spear shaft and rose to my full height. I pushed Bjorgolf away and sprinted towards the mailed warrior. The man saw me coming too late. He screamed as I rammed the splintered wood into his face. I did not realise it but the man had died instantly, I pounded his lifeless face with my fists and sobbed until Bjorgolf dragged me off the man.

The fight was over; my men cheered and stooped to loot the dead. We had butchered Trahaearn's garrison and Castell Tomen was mine, but I did not care. I scrambled over to where Wselfwulf lay. The old Saxon still clung to life as blood escaped the thin wound at the base of his throat. The blood bubbled at the wound and in the corners of his mouth.

He blinked at me and smiled as he recognised me before his face contorted in agony. I took my old tutor's hand in mine and wept. The Saxon tried to say something but could only splutter. He squeezed my hand with his last effort and his eyes glazed over. I wept for the old man, who had died protecting me. Tears ran down my cheeks as I looked into Wselfwulf's lifeless eyes, I thought back to the lessons I had shared with Cerit. To fond memories of the old warrior's approval, as he watched me and Cerit grow.

Bjorgolf rested his hand on my shoulder before leaving me to my grief. I glanced up as Tyrnog muttered the prayer for the dead and closed the old Saxon's eyes. He made the sign of the cross and uttered more words, but I did not listen. I still clutched Wselfwulf's hand in mine as my eyes searched for the old warrior's blade. Tyrnog noticed my glance and stooped to pick up the Saxon's blade with its curious hilt.

The monk laid the sword on Wselfwulf's chest and I placed the dead man's hands around it. I glanced around me again. I had not noticed my men encircling the scene. Some crossed themselves before returning to loot the dead. It was victory, Castell Tomen was mine and the majority of my men lived. But it was a hollow victory. The road to Meirionydd lay open and Trahaearn would pay.

XXIII

Sitric mumbled a few final words as he placed the last stone over his friend's final resting place. Cerit cuffed back a tear as he bowed his head and paid his final respects. He had taken Wselfwulf's death badly. Sitric had accepted the news with an emotionless expression, but I knew he was hurting inside. It had been barely an hour since Castell Tomen had been taken and I had ordered the shallow graves to be scraped into the boggy ground which lay below the old Roman fort.

Rough crosses had been made and I glanced to where Ruaidri and Oengus hammered the last marker into place. Ten crosses for ten good men who had died taking the fort from Trahaearn's men. I heard a scream as Maelgwn executed the survivors of the fort's garrison; there could be no mercy after what had happened.

I had ordered the foundations of an old outbuilding to be broken and the old Roman bricks and stones covered the graves of the dead, so no fox or animal could feast on the corpses. The graves cast a shadow in the torch light as I shivered. The wind howled and the rain continued, I had long been soaked through and I no longer attempted to keep dry.

Tyrnog prayed for the dead and those who had known the men bowed their heads in respect. I could not believe Wselfwulf had been killed, he had seemed indestructible to me somehow. The old Saxon had been there since the beginning. He had taught me to fight and in a way had made me the man I was. Tyrnog finished his prayers. "Amen," the monk finished and crossed himself before walking slowly away to leave the men to say their final farewells to their dead comrades.

I crossed myself and mumbled a prayer for Wselfwulf's soul. Sitric put a consolatory arm around Cerit as the two walked back to their men. I shook my head; could Wselfwulf's death have been avoided? I could not be certain.

Bjorgolf's voice disturbed my brooding. "He died well, lad. Do not blame yourself." I shook my head; why did the Dane have to have such a talent for reading my thoughts? "He died in battle; it is what the old bugger would have wanted. He wouldn't want you brooding over it, lad. Take my word on it."

I nodded at Bjorgolf's words, I knew he was right. The Saxon had always said he would die like a warrior and not in his sleep as a useless old man. But I could not help but think he would have rather died in a mighty battle worthy of a saga tale. Because of me, he had died in a bleak, windswept, decaying old fort in a skirmish. Trahaearn would pay for this.

The army had begun to move down the remains of the Roman road and headed towards Meirionydd under the cover of darkness. Seisyll and has teulu had been left to garrison Castell Tomen and deal with Trahaearn's dead. The Briton had taken an arrow to the thigh and would suffer huge discomfort if he travelled further with the army. He had been reliable so far, so I could think of nobody more suitable to hold the strategic fort. I think he had been relieved at the news. He commanded forty or so men on foot and I judged that to be sufficient for the moment. Seisyll's six scouts had proved useful and so I retained their services, the small mountain ponies had fanned out in to the distance and scouted our route into Meirionydd.

I marched at the head of the column with my bodyguard. Ruaidri led Iago and had formed a bond with the Irish stallion. Ruaidri, although he had his moments, was a useful man to have. Ronan, as always, proudly carried my banner despite the darkness. Ljot and Oengus talked quietly between themselves whilst Gwcharki tried out his Irish on Bjorgolf. The big Pict had learnt passable Irish and Bjorgolf clapped him on the shoulder at the achievement and Tyrnog tried to teach them both words in Briton. My mind raced ahead to what the day would bring, Trahaearn must be found and brought to battle before tomorrow's end. Or I was certain all would be lost.

The rain had stopped and the wind settled as the first light of the morning began to creep over the mountain peaks. The sky was clear and I hoped, the day would be dry. The Roman road was in poor condition but we had made decent enough time. We had descended into Meirionydd shortly before sunrise and now I called a halt.

The men were grateful for the respite. I had force marched them through the night from Castell Tomen and into the heartlands of Meirionydd. Mountains still dominated the skyline to my left but gentle hills rolled down the land to my right. The land was heavily wooded and it made me nervous. Trahaearn could easily hide his army in one of the numerous wooded glens and valleys and take me by surprise. None of the scouts had returned, or were even in sight and that troubled me as a knot of doubt formed in my gut.

Sitric strode down the column of resting men. "Any news?" I shook my head; the lack of word from the scouts was worrying. "May I suggest you send out more riders?" I shrugged my shoulders. The only horsemen I had left in the column were twenty of Tudur's men. Sitric knew that too. "You will have to send them. Damn, but we should have heard back from them by now."

I knew he was right; the lack of word troubled me deeply. I turned to Bjorgolf. "Send word to Lord Tudur, his horsemen are to scout the country ahead. Make it clear to him that they are to report back as soon as they set eyes upon the enemy or my lost scouts." Bjorgolf nodded and trotted over to where my bodyguard lounged. Oengus rose to his feet and quickly scampered down the column.

Bjorgolf looked grim as he stomped back. "Oengus has gone to tell the bugger now. I just hope Tudur's men aren't as cowardly as he is." I nodded my head in agreement as Sitric also mumbled his approval of Bjorgolf's words.

The land ahead looked so tranquil in the morning light; it was hard to imagine two armies were in close proximity and would soon tear this beautiful landscape to bloody ruin. A faint cloud of smoke rose above a small hill a few miles ahead, where I guessed villagers went about their daily lives blissfully unaware of the army which would soon march past them.

Sitric scratched his beard thoughtfully. "We will have to find the bastard today. If the Powysian King joins him, it will be a bloody business." I nodded at the truth of it. If Iorwerth joined Trahaearn's army then my ability as a commander would be pushed to the limit. "Besides, we owe the bastard."

I knew Sitric spoke of Wselfwulf's death. Without the old Saxon's company Sitric seemed colder. He wanted to ensure his friend had not died in vain. I wanted that too, Wselfwulf's death would be avenged upon Trahaearn and his men. The sound of hooves caught my attention and I glanced at Tudur's riders as they cantered their ponies down the broken Roman road.

The ponies flicked up tufts of earth as they went. The ground was still wet, as it always seemed to be in this land. A bird of prey circled high above us and I envied it. What I would not give for that bird's vision now. I cursed to myself. Where are you Trahaearn? It did not seem right; I could not quite explain the doubt that crept up my spine. But I knew something was wrong. Seisyll's scouts had been reliable thus far, yet they had vanished. Damn Trahaearn, damn him all the way to hell. I would find him and I would beat him.

The smoke intensified as we marched further down the road. The small drifting wisps of smoke I had noticed earlier had thickened into a great black column. Tudur's horsemen had also disappeared and I cursed as I coaxed Iago forward. Bjorgolf had protested against it but I had ignored him. The army marched five hundred paces behind me as I peered into the distance.

Cerit reined-in besides me and sat his mount quietly as I scanned the area. I still could not see the source of the smoke but I could smell it. A small track peeled away from the Roman road and disappeared into a thicket of trees. Beyond the trees I could see the great column of black smoke drifting up into the sky. It could be seen for miles and I wondered if Trahaearn stared at the same column of smoke. Hoof prints showed on the track in both directions. Whoever had descended upon the source of the fire had already fled.

There were no sign of my scouts in the distance as the Roman road led to the crest of a hill, three hundred paces ahead. I clicked my tongue and urged Iago forwards, I heard Cerit follow suit. I was wary, ashes drifted in the breeze as we trotted down the road. The track curled to the left and then back on itself to accommodate a mound of boulders, I could not help but think it might be a trap but I pushed Iago on regardless.

Cerit cursed as we reined-in. "Poor bastards." He crossed himself before retching and turning his head away. He ran his sleeve across his mouth. "This is not war, it is barbarism."

I could not answer, only felt anger rise in my chest. A small farmstead and its outbuildings burned violently to my front, I could feel the heat as the timber was engulfed in the fury of flames. Mountain ponies lay butchered on the muddy ground; joints of meat had been hacked off the hardy little beasts.

I spat in disgust though at what faced me, fifteen paces ahead. An elderly peasant hung from a tree, his blue face and open mouth staring absently at me. At his feet lay what must have been his wife, she lay dead her skirts ripped and blood spattered. I dismounted and knelt beside her. Her skull had been broken by a heavy blow and, for good measure, her throat had been slit. Whoever had done this had not let the peasants die well.

And I knew why. They had given their hospitality to Seisyll's scouts. To the right of the dead peasants lay six beheaded corpses in a mound. Blood had pooled amongst the corpses and the sight almost made me vomit. Ringed around the heap of headless bodies were six wooden stakes and upon each stake was a head. I recognised one of the faces and crossed myself echoing Cerit's words; poor bastards indeed. The lifeless faces were thick with flies and I struggled to contain the contents of my stomach as flies crawled on open eyes and in the mouths of the dead. Crows circled above and I knew it would not be long before they drifted to the ground to feast upon the dead.

I could not bear to look at the sight any longer. I mounted Iago and, in stony silence, kicked the Irish stallion into a canter and followed the track back to the Roman road. Cerit's complexion had paled and he shook his head again at the savagery my scouts had endured. Sitric led the column as it marched past the track that led to the charnel house. I aimed Iago towards him and joined him at the head of the column.

He took one glance at Cerit's pale face and raised an eyebrow. "That bad, eh?" I nodded and Sitric shook his head. "I assume you have discovered our missing riders then?" I nodded and Sitric shot me a worried look. "All of them?"

I shook my head. Tudur's horsemen had not been amongst the dead. But they had headed in this direction, I cursed as I suspected treachery. A rider appeared over the hill crest, closely followed by three others. The riders coaxed all the speed they could out of the ponies as they thrashed at them in desperation. So that is where Tudur's horsemen had gotten too. The riders glanced nervously over their shoulders and I noticed splatters of blood on themselves and the ponies. I had sent twenty yet only four returned.

I began to urge Iago towards them but halted quickly. A troop of horsemen appeared on the crest as the frightened scouts reached the safety of the column. The horsemen reined-in as their leader rose his fist in the air to stop their pursuit. They did not ride the small mountain ponies I had become accustomed to, but full sized warhorses similar to the French mounts I had seen in Degannwy. The enemy horsemen remained motionless and watched as my column shuddered to a halt.

Sitric screamed at my side. "Form up! Form up! Shieldwall!" Sitric's warband led the column with my men and they quickly formed into three ranks and slapped their shields together as I trotted Iago behind the safety of the formation. Sitric and Cerit had followed me and my foster-father cursed. "Bloody horsemen, hate the bastards."

I counted the horsemen who still did not move. They numbered thirty and sat in a loose formation as they gazed at my army. A banner caught in the breeze to reveal three golden crosses below a white dove on a blue field. The lead horseman sheathed his blade and turned his mount. He kicked it into a canter as his horsemen followed suit. I heard the thunder of the hooves as the troop of horsemen galloped away.

"Advance!" I called and my shieldwall marched slowly forward, keeping the formation tight in case the enemy horsemen reappeared and charged. We crested the hill and I swore as Sitric chuckled and Cerit crossed himself.

Sitric turned to face me and smiled. "Got the bastard."

A mile ahead of me the old Roman road stretched into a narrow wooded valley, but in front of it on the grassy plain camped an army. It was beginning to break camp and it looked as though Trahaearn was planning a withdrawal to the security of the narrow pass. I laughed; there was no way he could withdraw before I was upon him.

Trahaearn must been cursing for his plan had failed. Castell Tomen had failed to stall my advance and it was obvious the King of Powys had not, for the moment at least, joined him. I turned in the saddle and fixed my eyes on Bjorgolf. "All my commanders to me, now!"

Bjorgolf grinned and nodded his head before he turned and shouted orders at my bodyguard. Ljot, Oengus and Ruaidri sprinted back down the hill to where the bulk of my army waited to see what the commotion was. I turned to Cerit. "Remain here with the shieldwall, Trahaearn is buggered. Only call for me if he advances."

Cerit nodded to acknowledge the commands as he surveyed the panicked enemy. I turned to Sitric and shared a smile before we turned our mounts and headed towards the army. Cerit's force was enough to deter any advance.

I laughed at my enemy's folly. I had him. Castell Tomen had fallen quickly, with only a token resistance. Trahaearn had clearly gambled his hopes on Castell Tomen's garrison holding out until the King of Powys joined him. He had been so confident that he had not felt the urge to send patrols down the mountain road and that would be his undoing.

His horsemen had found my scouts and butchered them, but that was a small price to pay. The enemy had discovered my advance too late and I had caught Trahaearn with his breeches down. His army was vulnerable and outmanoeuvred. He was outnumbered and his panicked army was doomed.

I glanced from each excited face to the next as my optimism infected all present, even Tudur looked happy. "We've bloody well got him!" I announced. "Speed is key, my lords. Speed. You must follow my commands without hesitation or we may lose this chance!" I gestured behind me to where Cerit and the shieldwall still stood. "Beyond that crest you will see Trahaearn's outnumbered and panicked army. The fool is trying to withdraw but he is too late, too late!" I clapped my hands together in happiness.

I glanced at Sitric, who nodded encouragingly. "My lords, we shall fall upon him with speed. His men won't stand, they can't stand." I caught Maelgwn's eye and he grinned wickedly. "My men and Sitric's are already in place, my lords, so they shall be the centre of the line." There was no questioning the logic; they would be the battering ram of my formation. Trahaearn was finished I thought to myself.

"Maelgwn, your Powysians shall form to the right of my men and form a shieldwall." The mercenary nodded and licked his dry lips in anticipation. "Lord Owain, your men shall form up to the left of my position with the men of Arfon. Stay in line until we engage the enemy, do not charge. Understood?" The Lord of Tegeingl smiled through a broken toothed grin and nodded his head firmly.

"Lords Tudur, Rhys and Gwyncu, you are the reserve." Gwyncu and Rhys nodded their heads in acknowledgment but Tudur's expression turned sour. "Do not worry, for you shall enjoy the thrill of the chase before the day is out." The Lord of Cemais, appeased for the moment at least, nodded reluctantly.

"To your men, my lords. Victory awaits." I mounted Iago and trotted forwards with Sitric to join Cerit at the hill's summit. Trahaearn had realised the futility of his withdrawal and was hastily forming his army up to receive the attack he knew would come down the steep hill to his front. His army lay at the mouth of the valley I had learned was named Dyffryn Glyncul.

My heart raced as I surveyed the enemy. I had him. Trahaearn had been outmanoeuvred and was in a difficult position; my force march through the night had paid off. I unbuckled my belt and passed it to Bjorgolf as he passed up the tunic Tangwystl had presented me. I smiled as the scarlet cloth clung to my mail and I again marvelled at the beautiful embroidery of the grey lions. Bjorgolf passed me my belt and I buckled it over the tunic.

I turned to Ronan. "Unsheathe the banner!" The huge Irishman grinned through his bushy beard and withdrew the protective case. The yellow and red cloth caught in the wind and the rampant lions clawed threateningly in the direction of the enemy. Let the bastard see, I thought. Let him look up to the hill to where the true King of Gwynedd sits below the banner of Aberffraw. I grinned triumphantly as I glanced from Sitric and Cerit to my bodyguard and then to my army as it formed up. Trahaearn was trapped. I had brought the usurper to battle and he was doomed.

XXIV

War horns sounded as Trahaearn's army formed up to
receive my assault. The Lord of Tegeingl's men and the
men of Arfon, sounding their own war horns as if in answer
to Trahaearn's, completed their advance to my left flank
and began to form up as I surveyed the enemy. I marginally
outnumbered Trahaearn and I knew my men would be
better warriors than his if the assault on Castell Tomen was
anything to go by. The road shot like a spear down the
steep hill and into the heart of the wooded valley of
Dyffryn Glyncul beyond Trahaearn's army.

His forces were arrayed just under a mile away and
I grinned to myself. His foot soldiers were formed up in a
loose, ill-disciplined, formation under the various banners
of their lords. It was his horsemen that concerned me most.
I guessed that there were fifty horsemen in total and they
were formed up in two disciplined ranks on the enemy's
left flank facing Maelgwn and his Powysians. Trahaearn
seemed to have no reserve and that surprised me.

Everything I had heard of Trahaearn suggested he
was a capable military leader. Yet all I had witnessed from
his forces and those of his ally, Cynwrig, was ineptitude or
just sheer over confidence. I stared at my nemesis' position.
A group of horsemen sat behind the centre of the enemy's
battle line under a banner which snapped in the wind. All I
could make out from this distance were flashes of green.

I glanced around me and sensed my men were
impatient to advance. The banners of my army snapped in
the wind, Sitric's black raven on its white field stirred next
to the red and yellow of my banner. Maelgwn sported two

banners. The banner of Mathrafal caught in the wind whilst Cynwrig's crow-pecked rotting head served as the other.

I glanced at Sitric and Cerit beside me and then back at my bodyguard and grinned as Bjorgolf caught my eye. I drew my blade and waved it in the air. "Forward my wolves, forward. We march to victory. God wills it, God wills it!"

The men to my front cheered and the whole line took up the cheer. The line rippled forwards as the men in the front rank began their disciplined descent down the steep hill. Iago found his footing superbly and I felt the usual pre-battle feelings sweeping through my pumping body. The blood-lust flowed through my veins and I grinned as my men began to shout their own war-cries and jeer at Trahaearn's waiting force.

The gap between the two armies seemed to decrease rapidly once my men had reached the bottom of the hill. Still the enemy had not moved, their loose formation seemed to rustle like a tree in the wind as men jeered my advancing line. A few bared their arses as we approached and Sitric's men began to thump their shields repeatedly as the gap closed.

We were three hundred paces off and the noise was almost unbearable as the whole line joined Sitric's men and the battle thunder grew. I surveyed my advancing line; all were in place. I glanced behind me to the reserve who followed in our footsteps and smiled. My army marched steadily on, like an unstoppable wave from the sea.

Sitric raised his voice to be heard above the din. "I am proud of you Gruffudd; today we reclaim your birthright!" I grinned and nodded my thanks at the praise. Cerit beamed a smile at me and clapped me on my shoulder. Two hundred paces now and still the enemy let us come. I watched on approvingly as Maelgwn's *helwyr* halted and loosed a volley of arrows at the horsemen who seemed content to wait for them.

A horse reared and threw it's rider as the first arrow struck home. More horses shrieked and men screamed as the arrows punched into the horsemen or the horseflesh beneath them. I marvelled at the lethal accuracy of the longbow and the damage caused by Maelgwn's six *helwyr*, I promised myself then that I would raise a warband solely of bowmen. Another volley hit home and the horsemen decided they could take no more.

A horn blasted loudly and carried across the battlefield as Trahaearn's battle plan was undone. With only a hundred and fifty or so paces between the two forces Trahaearn's horsemen reformed and coaxed their mounts forward. They had taken casualties but they still looked formidable. The rear rank waited until the first had walked ten paces forwards and then they followed.

The horn blew again and the horsemen broke into a canter. "Halt!" I screamed and nodded in satisfaction at the discipline of my men as the order was carried down the line and my advance shuddered to a halt. The horsemen still cantered towards us, eighty paces now. The horn blew again and the horsemen lowered their long spears and charged. Trahaearn's foot soldiers, despite the desperate attempts from their lords to stop the disaster, screamed their war-cries and followed the horsemen into battle. I smiled triumphantly to myself, timing was key, Trahaearn's horsemen charged only towards death.

The blue banner with its three golden crosses and its white dove fluttered majestically in the breeze as the horsemen thundered towards Maelgwn's men on my right flank. The gap was closing quickly, sixty paces, fifty, forty. Turf flew into the air behind the horsemen as they screamed their challenges and selected their targets. Thirty paces now, I gripped my sword hilt with the tension. Maelgwn's voice carried clearly over the thunder the horsemen created. "Shieldwall! Shieldwall!" The shields slapped together. "Now! Now!"

Horses screamed as they ploughed into the ground and riders flailed as they were plucked out of their saddles. Maelgwn's *helwyr* could not miss. The charge faltered and the enemy banner fell with its rider from the saddle. The horsemen had been undone by six bowmen and the remainder were blocked by the sprawled corpses of their comrades and the thrashing hooves of injured mounts. Those that had survived, their momentum broken, turned their mounts and fled. I laughed with joy before I glanced from the right flank to my front and shuddered.

I could not help but admire the bravery but shook my head at the folly. Like their ancient ancestors against the Romans, Trahaearn's men surged forwards in an unorganised rabble, screaming their fury and brandishing their weapons. The gap began to close as they hurtled towards my line.

They screamed with renewed vigour as they laboured towards us and saw we waited for them. Twenty paces, there would be no stopping them if I did not act now. Timing was key as I felt Sitric stiffen at my side I took a deep breath. "Shieldwall, shieldwall!"

The call went down my line and the shields smacked together and linked with Maelgwn's. The Lord of

Tegeingl's men and the men of Arfon would cope, of that I was certain.

The enemy charge faltered a little as a formidable wall of round shields blocked their path. The round shields my men used, in the Danish fashion, were bigger and stronger than the small buckler shields the Britons and other Celtic peoples favoured. The lead men would never have come up against such a sight and they almost stopped in their tracks but the momentum from behind spurred them on.

It was clear from this distance that the men we faced were largely the levies of Arwystli and Meirionydd. The ancient tactic of the Britons was on full display this day. Trahaearn's rabble smashed into my well disciplined formation and recoiled. The wall of shields held firm as men grunted and fought against the press of Trahaearn's men. A short spear hurtled over my head and a rock glanced off my shoulder as the men at the rear of Trahaearn's position targeted me. Iago reared as a rock hit his flank and I dropped from the saddle.

I cursed as I splattered into the turf but Bjorgolf helped me up as Sitric and Cerit dismounted. The sound of battle raged as my shieldwall held firm. I could hear the ring of steel upon steel and the screams of pain as the men in my second rank struck home with their axes and spears. The injured began to fall out of my line, and the formation shuffled as men replaced their dead or injured comrades in the front rank as Trahaearn's men began to exploit any gap in the shields.

Sitric gestured towards my left flank were the Lord of Tegeingl's men struggled to hold back the onslaught. I turned to Bjorgolf. "Lord Tudur is to bolster the left flank

279

now, hurry!" Bjorgolf nodded and grabbed Oengus before sprinting towards Tudur's position in the reserve.

I glanced about me; my men were holding Trahaearn's force back. Men screamed in fury and pain all around and I guessed Trahaearn's supporters were taking horrible punishment. Then I saw him, Trahaearn and his commanders surged forwards on their fine mounts.

The group of horsemen and their green banner pushed through the rabble and into my shield wall. A heavily mailed man swung his blade savagely down and cut into the shoulder of a man in my front rank. The gap opened and the enemy surged into it.

I did not think, I acted. I sprinted forwards and threw myself into the gap. My bodyguard screamed their war-cries and followed me. I could hardly breathe. The press of men and the stink of horse sweat was almost overpowering.

A horse screamed as Ronan's big axe smashed into its jaw, cutting through bone and the shattering the beast's ugly yellow teeth. The terrified animal reared and the rider hung on desperately but Tyrnog's short spear darted up and punched deep into the horse's chest. The animal fell backwards and was lost from sight as another horseman took his fallen comrade's place.

He thrust his blade down towards me and I gaped in fear as I could not move. Ljot's shield shot forwards from behind me and deflected the blow. I breathed a sigh of relief and suddenly felt the pressure subside as my men cheered. The horseman screamed as he was dragged from the saddle and butchered as my men fell upon him. The horse bolted and broke clear of the throng before racing away towards my reserve.

The press subsided as my men surged forwards. Only seconds earlier I thought I would die and now I grinned with joy as Trahaearn's army broke. The mass charge had failed and his army disintegrated as the casualties became too great. Everywhere my men surged forwards in pursuit of the enemy, there would be no holding them back.

I nodded my thanks to Ljot and mounted Iago as Ruaidri brought the mount forwards. Sitric and Cerit had joined the pursuit and I shook my head at the chaos. In every direction Trahaearn's supporters fled with my men in close pursuit. I looked for the usurper and found him. He and the band of horsemen had spurred clear and raced down the mud track towards the wooded valley. Bastard, he would live to fight another day. I had not even stared into the face of my enemy. I spat, he was beaten and he had run, he was nothing.

A long line of dead marked the point where Trahaearn's charge had met my shield wall. The majority of the dead wore a mixture of woollen tunics, hides and leather, marking them as levy-men, whilst only a few were mine. Dying men called for their loved ones and the injured screamed for help. The battle was won, but now chaos reigned as my army ploughed into the enemy's camp and their followers.

Everywhere I looked; bands of Trahaearn's supporters were caught and butchered before my men stopped to loot their bodies. I sat Iago and surveyed the broken enemy and shook my head at the simplicity of the victory. Trahaearn's army had beaten itself.

Fugitives followed their leader down the road or streamed into the woodland whilst my victorious army looted the battlefield. But the fight was not completely over. I trotted Iago forty paces to my right where Maelgwn's men tried desperately to halt the escape of a well-disciplined warband.

The enemy warband fought a grim defensive withdrawal despite the casualties they were taking. A banner flew in the formation's centre; the cloth displayed dark green and red cheques and flapped in the wind. These men were better equipped than the rabble that had broken itself on my shieldwall. The men fought with large rectangular shields and, strangely, a long spear, not the short spear the Britons favoured.

Maelgwn called for his men to form up and called his *helwyr* forward. He nodded a greeting as I halted Iago. The Powysian spat. "Stubborn bastards, can't they see they have lost?" The enemy formation had stopped and the oddly shaped shields absorbed the volleys the *helwyr* spat at them.

I swallowed to clear my dry throat and called out at the enemy band, which now numbered less than fifty. "You have fought bravely men, surrender and you may keep your lives." I glanced at the enemy band who were now surrounded as Gwyncu's followers joined Maelgwn's Powysians and waited for the kill.

The *helwyr* stopped their futile fire and a heavily mailed man stepped out of the formation. He was a short barrel of a man with a full grey beard that stuck out of his dented helm. "We shall not surrender, lord. The men of Meirionydd have too much honour for that."

I spat in disgust. "Honour! What know you of honour?" The man bridled as I continued. "You take up arms against your lawful king, you have no honour."

The man shook his head. "Gruffudd is no king of ours. We only acknowledge Trahaearn as our rightful King, as does God." The man snorted in disgust and then spat phlegm at me.

I had wanted to spare the men for their valiant actions but I could not stop what happened next. The gap-toothed *helwyr* drew his bow and loosed, the arrow took the old warrior in the left eye and killed him instantly. The men of Meirionydd screamed their fury and broke formation as they rushed towards me. It was useless. Maelgwn's Powysians met the desperate charge as Gwyncu's followers swarmed upon the brave men. It was butchery.

I shook my head sadly at the man's stubbornness and turned to Sitric and Cerit as they trotted their mounts towards me. Sitric raised his hand in greeting. "Bastard got away. The whoreson ran." Sitric spat in disgust. "Coward."

I nodded. "I thought he would have had too much honour for that. His army is broken and the bastard has fled like a rabbit from a fox." I had won the battle but not the war it seemed, for Trahaearn would live to fight again.

I glanced again at the battlefield. The bodies of Trahaearn's supporters littered the field. I guessed he had lost over half his number and I had lost very few men, but the bastard had run. Cerit cleared his throat. "What now, brother?"

I clenched my fist and punched it into my palm. "We chase the usurper, all the way to bloody Arwystli and Powys, all the way to the end of the world if I have to." I spoke with such ferocity that I surprised even myself. Damn him, I wanted to finish Trahaearn today. But he lived and so I knew I must follow him for I could not rest easy upon Gwynedd's throne until Trahaearn was dead.

283

I turned to Bjorgolf who had appeared at my side with Tyrnog. The two men carried two enemy banners each and dropped them at Iago's feet. I glanced down and saw the mud splattered banner of the horsemen and the bloodstained banner of Meirionydd. The battle was won but not yet the war. "Bjorgolf, I want my commanders here with haste. I have not finished with Trahaearn yet."

All along the road lay discarded shields, weapons and even wounded men. Trahaearn's army had shed everything that could slow it down and I cursed him. My men had had no rest as we chased the remnants of Trahaearn's army through the mountains of Meirionydd throughout the day following the battle and the night and throughout the next day.

Now I sat atop Iago and stared down into the rolling hills of Arwystli and, beyond that, Powys. Trahaearn and the remnants of his army that still followed him were a black smudge on the landscape as the sun began to set, in the distance. The bastard had escaped me and back into his heartlands.

There had been no sign of the King of Powys' army and so I could not risk following Trahaearn into Iorwerth's lands. The Powysians had not marched to Trahaearn's aid and I did not plan on giving them justification to do just that by pursuing the fugitive through Powys.

Sitric's expression mirrored my mood. My foster-father looked on with a grim expression and scratched his grey beard. "The whoreson flees to the safety of Arwystli and the protection of the Powysians." Sitric shook his head in anger. "The bastard will be back, mark my words."

I nodded at the truth of it and turned my back on Trahaearn and his fleeing followers. I had, for now, won control of Gwynedd but could not rest easy. So long as Trahaearn lived I would not be able to sit comfortably on Gwynedd's throne. Any dissenters would rise in his name. No, I would have to kill the bastard to secure my throne.

My mood improved little over the next three days as my army retraced its steps through Meirionydd and up the Roman road into the mountains. It had begun to rain, again, as soon as we set foot in the mountains and I cursed the weather. I should be celebrating Trahaearn's downfall and setting about ruling my kingdom but I brooded. My army marched in high spirits after the victory and grinned as some peasants cheered our passing. But I was not alone, Sitric and Cerit had wanted to see Trahaearn dead to avenge Wselfwulf and they too cursed the man.

We reached Castell Tomen during the middle of the third day of our retreat from the borderlands of Powys. Scorched black earth and blackened bones showed where Seisyll's men had burned the bodies of Trahaearn's garrison. The army set up camp and settled down for the night as I brooded in my tent.

Bjorgolf and Tyrnog dared say nothing as I kept silent and relived the battle in my mind. I was certain I could have fought the battle against Trahaearn differently and I cursed out loud. Tyrnog jumped at the sudden curse whilst Bjorgolf ignored my gaze and Gwcharki, who silently stood guard at the tent's rear grinned at the monk's reaction.

Ruaidri and Oengus stood guard outside and I could hear the two call out a challenge and I cursed again. I was in no mood for any more troubles. Ruaidri ducked under the flap and entered the tent. "Messenger to see you from

Mac Ruaidri, Gruffudd. Urgent." Ruaidri had spoken hurriedly and his eyes betrayed its importance.

I groaned. "Very well, bring him in." A filthy mud splattered Irishman entered the tent and bowed formally. A feeling of dread crept up my spine as I looked at the messenger. He had ridden hard. A filthy, bloodstained, bandage was bound around his left arm. He stood awkwardly and I noticed a broken arrow shaft in his right thigh; the man looked set to drop but he held himself steady. A huge purple bruise showed on his forehead where a gash had just started to scab over. "Well?"

The man fought to keep his balance and cleared his throat. "I have ridden hard, lord, at Mac Ruaidri's request. He sends his regrets, lord, and wishes you to know he had done his utmost to prevent.."

I cut across the man. "Yes, get to the point."

The man swallowed hard. "It is with great regret, lord, that I must announce the sons of Merwydd have risen against you in rebellion."

I almost asked the man to repeat himself. I heard an intake of breath from all present and Bjorgolf shot me a worried glance. "You are sure?"

"Aye, lord, Lord Asser and his brothers, with all their men, descended upon Lord Faelan's forces and routed us." The man shifted uncomfortably under my shocked gaze.

Asser and his brothers had promised upon their honour to support me. There had to be a reason why they had turned on Faelan and risen in rebellion. I shook my head and glanced from Bjorgolf back to the Irishman.

"Why have they risen in un-Godly rebellion against their rightful ruler?"

The man glanced nervously around the tent, as though looking for an escape. "Lord Faelan ordered the sacking of Nevyn, lord."

I exploded. "He fucking what!" I rose quickly and grabbed the leg of the stool I sat on; I threw the stool with all my force at the floor, smashing it. "I will kill the bloody idiot, God help me. I will bloody break him." I turned to Bjorgolf. "We break camp immediately and march to Segontium. There we shall wait and see what damage that idiot has done. We march through the night."

Bjorgolf ran out of the tent to pass the orders on to my commanders. Damn Faelan and damn bloody Muirchertach too. I glanced again at the messenger. "Why the hell did 'Lord' Faelan order the sacking of Nevyn? What was he bloody thinking; no wonder the sons of Merwydd have rebelled."

The messenger looked down at the floor. "He said we deserved the freedom of the town and the headman refused, lord. So Lord Faelan killed the headman and set the lads loose." I shook my head in wonderment as the messenger continued. "Mac Ruaidri tried to stop him, lord, but he threatened to kill him too. When Lord Asser heard of the events he attacked during the night." The messenger babbled as he fought to hold back tears. "Most of the lads were drunk and were butchered. Mac Ruaidri kept his lads away from Lord Faelan's and was able to fight his way clear and return to Segontium. Lord Faelan escaped also, lord, and has proclaimed himself Prince of Abermenai."

I cursed Faelan. The bastard had not only disobeyed my orders but turned the sons of Merwydd against me and could well have ended my campaign. I cursed again. I would march to Segontium and there I would have to deal with Faelan and the rebels. Damn him.

XXV

I cursed loudly, again, as my army set up camp around
Segontium. My bodyguard waited patiently behind me as
we stood on the shingle beach and waited for the boat to
reach us. I had tasked Sitric with the responsibility of
keeping my army together whilst I crossed the straits to
Abermenai so that I could confront Faelan. Cerit had
insisted on coming with me and glanced nervously at me as
I picked up a small rock and launched it as far as I could
into the straits, cursing in the process. Faelan would pay;
the bastard could single-handedly have ended my
campaign.

Bjorgolf was sensible enough to keep the awkward
silence as the boat edged closer. The day was bright and I
could see my beached fleet at Abermenai. It seemed an age
since I had landed at the small port. The oarsmen raised
their oars and held them steady as the ship ploughed into
the shingle and juddered to a halt. Briain, the ship master,
shouted a greeting and soon wished he hadn't as he saw the
expression on my face.

I had left five ships on the banks below Segontium,
in case a speedy withdrawal was needed across the water.
But Faelan had seemingly ordered the five ships back to
Abermenai. I had been forced to send a nervous fisherman
across the straits in search of *God's Wrath* and carry my
orders to Briain. The Irish shipmaster looked nervously
from me to Bjorgolf and shrugged as he waited for my
bodyguard to board the fine vessel.

Ten men crewed the ship and were grateful as the
men of my bodyguard, including Bjorgolf, took their places
on the oar benches and began to row the ship back to

Abermenai. Cerit still did not try to break the silence, although he seemed about to on several occasions. The anger flowed through my veins as I stared at Abermenai, I would make the bastard pay.

I turned my eyes on Briain and the Irishman shifted uneasily. "Tell me, why did you take *God's Wrath* back to Abermenai when I had specifically told you to wait for my return at Segontium?"

The Irishman swallowed nervously. "Lord Faelan said that it was your wish for us to ferry him and his men back across the straits and stay with him at Abermenai." I knew it was not Briain's fault but I looked him up and down acidly, making him flinch. Damn Faelan and I cursed Mac Ruaidri too. I had made my instructions clear to the old warrior and yet again he had failed to keep Faelan in line.

Fishermen waved at me as we passed their small skiffs and cheered my name. At least the people in this part of Gwynedd were still behind me. I cursed the situation. The sons of Merwydd had, quite rightly, attacked Faelan and routed him. Mac Ruaidri had kept his warriors under control and they had been enough to guarantee a safe retreat to Segontium. I had sent Faelan with the two hundred Irishmen, Muirchertach had entrusted him with, to Nevyn where I thought he would be unable to cause any trouble. How wrong I was. Instead of quietly sitting out the rest of the campaign and helping Asser and his brothers to assert their authority over Lleyn and Dunoding, Faelan had sacked Asser's lordship and lost half his men. Idiot.

Cerit glanced at me nervously as the ship shuddered as it ploughed into the sandy beach of Abermenai and came to a halt. He cleared his throat and his voice betrayed his nervousness. "What do you plan to do, brother?"

"Whatever I damn well please. The bastard must pay for what he has done." I spoke menacingly and Cerit crossed himself as I jumped over the side of the ship and landed on the sandy ground.

Fishermen and townspeople flanked my progress up the main street, cheering me and my bodyguard. They were disappointed by my lack of pleasure or enthusiasm; little did they know of how badly my campaign had gone over the last few days.

As we came to the tavern that Faelan had commandeered, for his own personal use, Cerit nudged me in the ribs. "Do not do anything foolish, brother."

I shot him a threatening look and approached the doorway. Two of Faelan's men stood guard and moved to block my path. They brought their spears together to block the door and stared impassively past me.

I spoke viciously to both of them at once. "Who are you to deny me entry?" They glanced nervously at each other and did not move. "Lower your weapons or I shall lower them for you."

The guard to my left swallowed nervously. "Lord Faelan is not to be disturbed, my lord. He has ordered us to keep all persons away from him, including you."

I laughed in a short, threatening, manner and the guard eyed me nervously. "Lord Faelan has no authority in these lands, move aside."

The guards relented and moved reluctantly to one side as I barged past them and opened the door of the tavern. Nothing could have prepared me for what I saw and I reached for my sword.

Faelan stood, with his breeches down, in the centre of the room. A young male thrall knelt in front of him and pleasured the Irishman. Faelan cursed as I barged into the room, disturbing his afternoon's entertainment. The thrall turned and ran as he noticed the armed men pushing into the small tavern. Faelan hurriedly pulled up his breeches and fastened them over his erect penis.

Two guards stood at the far side of the room and Faelan turned to them. "Guards, eject these men!" The two guards glanced at each other and then at me and my bodyguard. They nodded at each other and remained perfectly still.

I drew my blade in rage and made for Faelan. The Irishman screamed in fear and retreated until his back hit the wall of the tavern. The Innkeeper looked on and eyed the Irishman with distaste, as did I.

I swung my blade and the Irishman ducked, the blade thumped into the wattle wall and debris cascaded on Faelan's body. He curled up in a protective ball on the floor as I reversed my blade. I went to thrust down and finish the bastard, but strong arms pulled me back. The blade stopped inches from the Irishman's shoulder and I cursed as I was restrained.

I knew it was Bjorgolf who held me back as Cerit gripped my sword arm. He fixed me with a nervous, but knowing, expression. "Brother, you must control yourself. If the campaign is lost do you really think Muirchertach would support you again if you killed his brother-by-marriage?"

I shook my head and struggled against Bjorgolf's iron grip. I spat at Faelan who looked at me through petrified eyes. Hate coursed through my veins as I struggled. I wanted to gut the bastard. He possessed the woman I loved, had turned my allies against me and disobeyed my orders at every opportunity. Cerit slapped me across the face "Gruffudd you must not kill him. You must not." Cerit shook his head sadly. "If your campaign fails, as it well may then you must not lose Muirchertach's favour. Understand?"

I nodded reluctantly and released my grip on my blade. The steel fell the floor and Bjorgolf's grip relented. Cerit looked at me nervously and held out a hand, I took the offered hand as he helped me to my feet. I glanced again at Faelan and spat at him. "Bastard." I muttered and turned my back on him.

I did not hear what Bjorgolf said to me for my thoughts were filled with Orlaith. Poor Orlaith, the woman I loved who had been forced to marry that monster. I had caught Faelan being pleasured by a male thrall and Orlaith's words flooded back to me; 'he does not love me as a man should love a wife.' Is this what she meant? Did she know of his tastes? She deserved better than this bastard. All it would take would be for me to draw my dagger and cut the cur's throat, and then Orlaith could be mine. But I knew Cerit was right. I heard Faelan curse as he rose to his feet and I spun on my heel.

Bjorgolf tried to stop me, but I was too quick as Cerit shouted words I did not hear. I thundered towards Faelan and aimed a kick at his manhood. His small, pig-like, eyes widened in pain as my foot connected squarely with his genitals. He screamed in pain as he cupped his groin and fell to the ground. I kicked him again, viciously, in the ribs and heard a crack.

I thought of drawing my knife and finishing him there and then but Cerit laid a calming hand on my shoulder and I relented. I knew Cerit had been correct; I could not risk Muirchertach's displeasure. I gazed at Faelan, who cut a pathetic figure as he groaned on the floor. I bent down and grabbed a fistful of his hair and stared into his face, tears escaped his eyes and I grinned menacingly. The drooping moustache quivered as he tried not to sob, he must have thought I would cut his throat. But instead I butted him and spat in his face; the man disgusted me.

I let his head fall and turned to my bodyguard. "Ruaidri and Oengus, secure the bastard. I want him shackled in chains." The two looked on in shock at what they had witnessed but soon recovered their senses. They advanced on the prostate figure and dragged him upright. I glanced at him, my expression full of distaste. "Secure him on *God's Wrath*, I want him tied to the mainmast. It shall be for Muirchertach to decide what punishment his crimes deserve."

I shook my head and left the building. The male thrall, scarce old enough to grow a beard, glanced nervously up at me. I aimed a kick at the lad and he cried out as I connected, I knew he had probably been forced into pleasuring Faelan but the whole thing disgusted me. God knows what that bastard had made the young slave do. I suddenly felt harsh for kicking the thrall but shook my head. If my campaign failed I would personally deliver Faelan, in his shackles, to Muirchertach and demand he be executed.

The townspeople formed a curious crowd as I marched down the street towards the quayside with my bodyguard. To my delight the crowd jeered the shackled Faelan, who shuffled in-between my bodyguard. I glanced

294

ahead and shook my head in disappointment, there stood Mac Ruaidri and a few of his men who had failed me.

As we neared *God's Wrath* I turned to Bjorgolf. "Secure that piece of shit round the mast. Gag him; I don't want to hear a sound out of the bastard."

Bjorgolf grinned. "Would be a pleasure, just hope the vile creature doesn't enjoy being manhandled." Bjorgolf chuckled at his own jest and Cerit joined in the laughter, but I was in no laughing mood.

I marched across to Mac Ruaidri, who eyed the scene nervously. The elderly warrior shook his head sadly. "So you know of his tastes, lord?"

I nodded and shook my head in disgust. "You didn't think to tell me?"

"No." The diminutive figure shook his head sternly, finding some of the backbone for which he had been famous in his youth. "King Muirchertach knows of his brother-by-marriage's tastes." I tried to hide my shock, but I was unsuccessful, as Mac Ruaidri's sad eyes fixed with mine. "Lord Faelan is very influential back home, so he is. You know that is true, so Muirchertach will not want him dishonoured."

"I know, but that will not hide the fact the idiot has ruined my campaign." Mac Ruaidri shrugged his shoulders in despair. "I will make sure the bastard is finished. Mark my words." I spoke forcefully and knew that, one way or another; I would see the end of Faelan.

The old Irishman nodded. "I am sorry, my lord, that I failed you."

I lowered my voice so only he would hear and I spoke menacingly. "Failed me? I think that is an understatement, you have been worthless on this campaign." The old warrior nodded his head and scratched his snowy beard. "Why Muirchertach sent you to keep that idiot in check I shall never know. You are redundant in your old age, my lord. You are no warrior, but an old woman."

The hurt in his eyes was clear but I did not care. Whatever the man's past exploits or reputation for bravery were they did not make up for the fact he had failed utterly throughout the campaign. He bowed his head silently and shrunk from my withering stare.

I turned my back on the old Irishman and called over my shoulder. "You and your men are to report to Sitric at Segontium before sun down." I barely registered the old man's acknowledgment and made for *God's Wrath.*

I clambered aboard the fine ship and looked ahead to Segontium, where my army waited. Now I would have to fix Faelan's mess and that thought did little to improve my mood.

You could feel the tension as my commanders waited patiently to hear my plans. The sun had set and they had all filtered into my tent in the centre of Segontium. The news of the rebellion led by Asser and the sons of Merwydd had filtered through the camp and they all looked on with apprehension. I knew that loyalties were beginning to be rethought and that fractures were appearing in the unity of my army.

Faelan's act of stupidity had earned me the mistrust of my countrymen, Tudur chief amongst them. Again I cursed the Irishman. He had been my representative in Lleyn and had acted with such stupidity he had created suspicion amongst my commanders. I knew some now suspected I had come to Gwynedd simply to plunder, but that was not true.

"My lords," I began. "It is with a heavy heart that I must order the army to advance to Clynnog Fawr. There we shall meet the sons of Merwydd and, God willing, it shall not come to battle."

Tudur puffed out his cheeks and chuckled at my hopefulness; all eyes turned to him. He seemed to bask in the attention he was getting and he cleared his throat. "It seems clear to me, Lord Gruffudd, that you only seek plunder in this land." Angry mutterings broke out from my supporters and Tudur's allies added their voices to the commotion.

I eyed the Lord of Cemais with distaste and the argument continued for a few moments until I gestured to Ronan, who stood guard behind me with Bjorgolf. The big Irishman stepped forward with his huge axe and hammered its base on the table in the corner of the tent. The commotion died down as the Irishman's thumping carried to them.

All eyes turned back to me. "If that is what you believe, Lord Tudur, you are nothing but a fool." Some of his allies found their voices and shouted that I lied. I raised my voice to drown out their bleating. "I am the true heir to the throne of Gwynedd, I, not Trahaearn and certainly not you Tudur!"

A chorus of approval rang out from my supporters and Tudur blushed. I pushed relentlessly on with my argument. "My family was unlawfully exiled and there are no others who have a more rightful claim than I." My supporters nodded their heads and Tudur's allies shifted uncomfortably. "As God is my witness, I only wish to see Gwynedd prosper under the rule of its rightful king." I stared at Tudur and his supporters. "If you do not wish for the same then you are no true men of Gwynedd. If I fail then you will be ruled by the King of Powys or, worse still, by the Frenchmen!"

I had made a convincing argument and Tudur nodded his head in acceptance, his allies silenced. He bowed his head respectfully. "Of course, my King, I too wish for Gwynedd's wellbeing."

Like hell you do, I thought, but I nodded my head respectfully at the man's words. I rose to my full height and eyed all those present with a hard expression. "It is time you made your loyalties plain, my lords. All those with me say aye."

A unanimous chorus of 'ayes' boomed out from the gathering of lords, I had expected nothing else. A few of Tudur's supporters glanced nervously at their leader and I knew I would have to keep a close eye on the man.

"Very good, my lords, we march on Clynnog Fawr at first light." I waited for any potential protest but none came. "I bid you all a good night, my lords, for tomorrow we shall resolve this misunderstanding."

As my commanders began to file out of the tent I turned my back and doubted my own words. 'Misunderstanding' indeed. There was no misunderstanding, the sons of Merwydd had rebelled following Faelan's opportunistic actions and rightly so. Were I in Asser's position I too would have attacked Faelan if he was sacking my own town.

A cough sounded behind me and I turned to face Sitric, Cerit and Maelgwn. Sitric spoke respectfully. "I have to announce that I suspect Lord Tudur's loyalty." Cerit and Maelgwn murmured their agreement and I knew my foster-father's doubts were well founded.

I sighed and raised an eyebrow, "Go on."

Sitric scratched his beard, an action I had become accustomed to when he was worried. "I had an interesting conversation with Lord Owain of Tegeingl." I nodded. The commander of Robert's Britons was a fine man and a good leader. "He believes that Robert the Frenchman may have held secret talks with Tudur."

I cursed. "You are sure?"

Sitric shifted uncomfortably. "Lord Owain believes that one of his men may be an agent acting under Robert's orders." I shook my head wearily; I did not want to believe what my foster-father was saying but knew I must listen. "Lord Owain saw his man coming from Tudur's tent; he believes treachery may well have been contemplated by Tudur."

Damn, I cursed again. "Has Owain questioned this man?"

Maelgwn stepped forward before Sitric could answer. "He delivered him to me." I could not believe I was only hearing of this now and said as much.

"We did not wish to burden you with this, brother." Cerit opined nervously and received a reassuring nod from Sitric. "We needed to be sure before we came to you."

Maelgwn nodded his agreement. "Unfortunately Owain's men had badly injured the man before they delivered him. He had received a rare beating and died before I could get much out of him." I groaned. "However, he did utter something interesting whilst my knife worked information from him."

I raised an inquisitive eyebrow and felt my interest rise. "What did he say?"

Maelgwn raised his hand to his face and itched under his nosepiece with a finger. "He said he knew of a plot against you. He claimed that someone close to you plotted your death." Maelgwn shrugged. "That was it, but we felt we must warn you."

I knew I could trust Bjorgolf and thought I could trust Ronan also. "I am aware of the plot." All three looked at me in surprise. I turned to Bjorgolf. "Care to fill them in, Bjorgolf?"

The Dane grumbled and moved a few paces forward. I knew he liked to tell a good story and so I thought he could explain. "After the fight with Gunnald, Gruffudd stumbled across a suspicious scene in some woodland close to the camp."

Cerit interrupted Bjorgolf and shot him an apologetic look. "I thought you had exhausted this theory, brother?" Sitric glanced at his son and plainly wondered why none of this had been brought to his attention. Perhaps I should have involved my foster-father but it was too late now.

Bjorgolf ploughed on with his story, plainly thinking Cerit's question did not deserve an answer. "As I was saying, Gruffudd stumbled across these two men in a clearing. He remained hidden and the two were talking in Briton, see. Now Gruffudd thought that was odd and crept closer for a better look." Bjorgolf was clearly enjoying telling the tale and smiled as he received the full attention of all present. "They kept saying 'tomorrow' but Gruffudd couldn't make much else out. The meeting was disturbed when a boar stumbled into the clearing and the two men took flight. One headed back to our camp and the other deeper into the woods."

Bjorgolf stopped for a second and coughed into his hands. "Next day, we come to Gunnald's old hall and what happens?" Maelgwn looked on intrigued as Sitric, Cerit and Ronan's eyes widened in recollection. "That's right, that old bugger tries to kill Gruffudd, saying Trahaearn sent him. Anyway the old goat died before we could get anything out of him. Then nothing happened 'til after Duibhlinn."

All eyes were on Bjorgolf and Cerit shot me a surprised look; this was news to them all. "We wintered over at Sord Cholmcille and one day we went for a walk in the woods. Next thing you know an arrow shoots out of nowhere and into a tree behind me. The bastard got a few shots off before he legged it. So, you see, it has to be someone close." He looked at Maelgwn, his distaste of the man forgotten, caught up in his own tale. "Now your mate that you questioned tells you that someone close to Gruffudd is working against him." Bjorgolf clapped his hands together. "Just one question to be answered. So, who the hell is it?"

The words lingered in the air and a memory jumped into my mind. Oengus was, seemingly, the only man who could speak Briton in my warband. It had to be someone who had been with me all the way from the fight with Gunnald to the present, but was I right? It could easily have been one of Sitric's men, but my suspicions were aroused. I had to be sure, I would have to set him a trap and see if he took the bait.

I smiled and all eyes turned to me. It would have to wait until after I had dealt with the sons of Merwydd, but I knew how Oengus' loyalty could be tested. "So this is how we'll do it……"

XXVI

Mac Ruaidri shifted uncomfortably as I glanced scathingly at him. We had reached Clynnog Fawr after half a day's march and the army milled about on the grassy land surrounding the monastery of Saint Beuno. The day was hot and I sweated under my mail as I sat atop Iago. I glanced up at the steep mountain which dominated the skyline above Clynnog Fawr. I needed to know the location of the rebels and Mac Ruaidri had insisted Asser had pursued his retreating forces as far as the monastery which lay before us.

"Well they're not bloody here now," I was in a foul mood. Less than a week ago it seemed nothing could go wrong as I strove to reclaim my birthright. But now all my hard won gains were slipping away due to the actions of others.

"No, my lord." I knew I was being hard on the old warrior, but I did not care that day. "They must have withdrawn at some point yesterday." Mac Ruaidri spoke quietly, knowing the worthlessness of his words.

I chuckled mockingly. "Well, now we have a firm grasp of the obvious." Mac Ruaidri looked down at his feet, trying to remain anonymous. Cerit and Maelgwn chuckled at my words as Sitric scratched his beard in thought.

Tudur cleared his throat and spoke insistently. "Lord King, allow me to send out riders to track the rebels." I was not the only one to be surprised by the words the Lord of Cemais spoke. Only a few days ago he had preached withdrawal and defence but now he seemed ready to pursue the sons of Merwydd.

Sitric grumbled his begrudging approval. "Lord Tudur talks sense. We must stamp out this rebellion before it grows in strength."

I could think of no other alternative. "Very well, Lord Tudur. Your horsemen shall leave with all haste and report the movements of the enemy at every opportunity. If Asser and his rebels so much as fart in this land, I want to know about it."

Tudur bowed his head respectfully. "Your will, my King." He turned on his heel and strode back towards his men. I watched him with interest; I was not sure I could trust him or his men but I had no choice.

Maelgwn snorted and spat out the phlegm before he scratched again, under his nosepiece. "I don't trust the little shit. Mark my words; he is playing a dangerous game. But to what end I am not certain." Sitric and Cerit mumbled their agreement.

Owain, the Lord of Tegeingl, had until now remained silent but chose to make his voice heard and pointed towards the steep mountain. "If I were Asser I would have taken my rebel scum up that mountain and forced you to march up it. There I would have bled your army badly and beaten you." I nodded at the truth of his words; it was the strategy I would have adopted. "Something draws the rebels south. And, whatever it is draws Tudur also."

I shook my head. "How can you be sure they go south, Owain?" It seemed likely that they had turned south yet I could not understand why.

"Where else?" He shrugged his shoulders before scratching a sore on his neck. "He may have withdrawn to take up a defensive position around Aberdaron or Carn

Madryn, but I doubt it. If he was going to fight you, on his own, he would have done so here."

Owain spoke with such conviction and I knew he was right. I cursed to myself, there could only be one reason Asser would go south. That would mean Trahaearn had resurfaced with Powysian help. Damn, events were moving too quickly and I made up my mind. "My lords, to your men. We take the road around the mountains to Deudraeth."

My commanders bowed their heads and returned to their men. If what I dreaded was indeed coming true then the fate of my campaign would be decided on the flat coastal plain of Traeth Mawr, under the shadow of the fortification at Deudraeth. I said the name out-loud to nobody in particular. "So Deudraeth is where it shall be decided."

Bjorgolf glanced up at me with a worried expression. "What? Do not say you are losing your mind and talking to yourself?"

I grinned. "No Bjorgolf. But all will be decided at Deudraeth, of that I am certain." My bodyguard reached the front of the column as Tudur's riders thundered up the dirt road which led south into Dunoding. Deudraeth was the logical place for the rebels of Lleyn to meet their Powysian allies, if indeed that was the case. I glanced at the blue sky and muttered silently, hoping that God willed victory. For soon I would either be the undisputed King of Gwynedd or be forced to return to Ireland in defeat. Defeat was not an option.

As night fell I cursed. Tudur's horsemen had fuelled my fears and as I sat atop Iago on the dark hill I knew luck had deserted me. I stared at the shadow of Deudraeth and shook my head as I tried to count the number of campfires that glowed on the floodplain below. As I had feared, Asser had indeed withdrawn to Deudraeth and his forces swelled the enemy army. Iorwerth, the King of Powys, had marched his army over the frontier and through Meirionydd to Deudraeth. The scouts had reported the Lord of Dunoding's banner as well as Trahaearn's were amongst the enemy and I cursed again.

I glanced at the camp fires of my army and compared the two sides. We were pitifully outnumbered, I estimated, by four to one. I knew armies often built more campfires than necessary to fool their enemies but I also knew that would make little difference. The King of Powys had marched in force and his army dwarfed those of Asser and Trahaearn, Iorwerth had seen an opportunity to expand his borders and had seized upon it. I wondered what deal had been brokered for Asser to join the Powysian ranks and, not for the first time, cursed Faelan's stupidity. Asser's rebellion had swung the balance of power away from me and handed the advantage back to Trahaearn and his ally, the King of Powys.

Bjorgolf could not count but he too knew my army was vastly outnumbered. He glanced around him at the battle-scarred and hardened faces of my warband and fixed me with a serious expression. "We are with you to the end, lad. We will kick their bastard arses all the way back to bloody Powys in the morning."

My bodyguard muttered their agreement with Bjorgolf's words, as did Sitric and Cerit. I looked from face to face, from Ruaidri's roguish grin to his brother's deformed bush of a head. I smiled to myself, we had been through so much together and I knew that tomorrow we might all die. I took strength from Gwcharki's confident air and knew the huge Pict would strike fear into the enemy. I glanced at Oengus, who grinned broadly back, all thoughts of treachery forgotten, as he clapped Ruaidri on the back. Ljot, his squat frame making him look tiny amongst the huge men opposite, added his agreement to Bjorgolf's words. Tyrnog crossed himself and launched into a long passage of Latin as he glanced up at the dark sky.

Cerit shrugged his shoulders. "I've put up with you for too long to give up now." He grinned happily and clapped me on the back.

"We will teach the bastards a lesson in war they will never forget." Sitric spoke confidently and I knew we still had a fighting chance. If the Powysians were anything like Trahaearn's army then we could defeat them.

I felt my chest swell with pride, we were all brothers of the sword and would share whatever fate God intended for us. "My friends, it has been an honour to fight at your side. Tomorrow we shall fight for our lives and, if God wills it, we shall win." A chorus of approval rang round my small group.

I glanced back at the enemy and shook my head ruefully. Whatever happened tomorrow, a lot of good men would die and history would be made. I turned my back on the enemy and descended the small hill back to my army.

My tent stood in the camp's centre and some of my commanders already waited for my council of war to begin. Would they all stand? I nodded to myself; they would, for they would have not come this far if they intended to run. I entered the musky interior of the canvas structure and stripped off my mail. Tyrnog and Bjorgolf had entered with me and the young monk began to clean the metal rings of the mail hauberk. Bjorgolf passed me the scarlet tunic with its grey lions made from the cloak of a warrior king.

Bjorgolf spoke quietly. "You can trust them?"

"We shall see soon enough, my friend." I could already hear the mutterings outside the tent as my commanders waited for the council of war to start. I glanced from the tent flaps to Bjorgolf. "I would like to pray for a moment, and then they may enter."

Bjorgolf nodded stiffly. He had not said anything but I knew I could read the man's thoughts. I had never prayed so much in my life as I had that day and the truth of it worried Bjorgolf. I knelt and bowed my head and began to pray.

I looked at each man in turn; a few looked confidently back at me but most glanced around the tent nervously. They knew we were outnumbered and were more likely to face defeat than victory. I cleared my throat and sounded calm and confident. "My lords, as you know we face a difficult task." A chorus of mutters broke out but I continued regardless. "We face the combined armies of Trahaearn, the King of Powys the Lord of Dunoding and the sons of Merwydd. Times are hard, my lords, but my courage shall never waver."

I had their attention and they hung upon my every word. "Our cause is just, lawful, and proper. We have beaten the enemy before and we shall damn well beat him again!" Sitric looked proudly on as most of my battle hardened commanders grinned at my words. "Discipline is the key that shall unlock victory, my lords. At Dyffryn Glyncul the enemy surged towards us in an ill-disciplined mob and broke themselves on our disciplined ranks.

Tomorrow, they will do the same. They will charge and we will hold our ground." I spoke passionately and took heart from the grins on the faces of my supporters.

I held my right hand over my heart. "So long as God is on our side, my lords, we cannot be beaten!" Sitric, Cerit, Maelgwn, Owain and Mac Ruaidri cheered. "Who is with me?"

A unanimous and hearty chorus of 'ayes' boomed out from all those present. My heart fluttered in my chest and I could not help but grin triumphantly. I had spoken from the heart and I knew I had spoken well. Even Tudur and his allies cheered my name. All thoughts of treachery had left my mind as every man present shouted their approval.

I silenced the commotion with a raised palm. "My lords, tomorrow we will defend the small hill to our front. We will form a shieldwall and let the enemy come to us. All men who carry a bow are to be entrusted to Maelgwn; we shall bleed the enemy and destroy them."

Maelgwn grinned happily as some of my countrymen eyed him warily. "My men, along with Sitric's and Mac Ruaidri's, will make up the centre. The right of the line shall be entrusted to Maelgwn and the left to Lord Owain and the men of Arfon." The men nodded and I glanced towards Tudur, who stared back. "Lord Tudur will have the honour of commanding the reserve." To my amazement I saw no disappointment on the young man's face and I smiled a friendly grin at him. He had at last realised the honour I gave him with such a role. "You will be needed to plug the gaps Lord Tudur. Your men shall see action and I expect you to be ready."

The Lord of Cemais bowed his head respectfully. "Of course, my King." His supporters followed suit and I smiled confidently at the men arrayed in front of me. How could I fail with such men as my allies?

"I bid you a good night, my lords. Tomorrow will be a fine day. We shall accept the enemy's challenge and we will rout them, by God we shall!" I enjoyed the support I was receiving and caught Bjorgolf's eye. The Dane nodded happily back, the pride evident in his expression. I had done well indeed. From this perilous situation victory might still be gained.

As my lords began to filter out of the tent in excited conversation only Sitric and Maelgwn lingered. I crossed to the two hardy warriors and embraced each in friendship. Sitric gestured for Maelgwn to speak first and the mercenary smiled happily. "We have come a long way, my friend. To think I caught your sorry arse in Duibhlinn and, had I made a different choice things could have been so different for both of us." The Powysian was not prone to talks of such emotion and he spoke awkwardly. "What I mean to say is, I am glad I didn't kill you."

I laughed at the jest and nodded my head respectfully. "I am glad you didn't kill me also. You have no qualms fighting your countrymen?"

The Powysian scoffed at the thought. "Of course not, I have no land, no home and no family that will accept me in Powys." I regretted asking the question, the strain so clear on the scarred face. "Those are the people who made me an outlaw. No, they are not my countrymen, I have no country. I fight for money or, more importantly, friends. I shall be honoured to fight and maybe die amongst friends tomorrow." The mercenary bowed his head awkwardly and turned on his heel. He strode out of the tent and into the darkness beyond. I could not help but smile.

Sitric cleared his throat and I turned my attention back to him. "Perhaps I have never made my feelings known to you, Gruffudd. But I am immensely proud of the man you have become." My heart swelled with emotion but I kept my feelings under control. "Your father would be so very proud, as would your dear mother."

"I know, father...."

Sitric held up a hand to silence me. "No, it is I that must do the talking." His grey eyes looked into mine. "Tomorrow we shall fight and it is likely we shall lose." He was right and I knew it, but there was still a slim chance we would win. "I am an old man now Gruffudd, I do not have long left in this world. If I fall tomorrow I want you to know just how proud of you I am. You have been a good son, Gruffudd, but you must promise me two things upon your honour?"

I was close to tears at the words but I fought them back. "Anything, father," I managed.

"If the battle goes badly, you are to flee to fight another day." He held up a hand to silence my protest. "You will not die tomorrow, my son, but I may. You shall live to continue the fight and if you must go back to Ireland, then so be it. One day you shall triumph, I know it." His face seemed to struggle to hold his emotions. "You must promise me these two things. If the battle is lost you must flee and return to Ireland. You must also promise me Wselfwulf's death will be avenged."

"Yes, father." I spoke reluctantly for I could not imagine enduring the shame of defeat and the cowardly act of escape.

"Good, you have made an old man happy. Now, I must retire for the night. I wish you well, my son."

I watched Sitric turn and leave the tent. Neither Bjorgolf nor Tyrnog broke the silence and, for that, I was grateful. I retired to my cot and could not believe what Sitric had said. It was impossible to imagine a world without the man who had raised me and loved me as if I were one of his own. I thought of my battle plan and hoped the enemy would be as foolhardy as they had been previously.

What had Tudur said the small hill was called? Bron yr Erw that was it. So tomorrow the small nondescript lump of rock would witness, one way or another, the outcome of my campaign. Tomorrow I would meet my enemies and, God willing; I would beat them back and pursue them to the borderlands of Powys. So then, in the morning my fate would be sealed upon the slopes of Bron yr Erw.

XXVII

Bjorgolf woke me shortly before dawn. He had stood guard over me all night and refused to have some rest before we met the enemy. The Dane could not wait to get into position on the slopes of Bron yr Erw and waited impatiently for me to don my war gear. Again I wore the scarlet tunic over my mail and made sure my blade was securely fastened on my hip along with the wicked dagger next to it. I grabbed my eating knife from the table in the corner of my tent and concealed it in my boot.

Bjorgolf grinned at the gesture. "Never know when you will need it, eh? Could be helpful." He chuckled softly to himself as I clipped my war helm in place and strode past him into the gloomy light of dawn.

All around me men moved into position and the camp was a hub of activity. Ljot and Gwcharki stood guard outside the tent and followed as I walked from the camp and up the gentle slopes of Bron yr Erw. As I crested the hill I surveyed my defensive position and cursed my lack of numbers. I regretted leaving Gwyncu and his men at Segontium, it was times like this when every man counted.

Mist covered the floodplain ahead and hid Deudraeth and the enemy army from view. My whole line was in position as the sun began to rise over the mountains, casting a ray of light over the landscape. The sky was clear and I guessed it would not be long before the mist burned away to reveal the enemy host.

Iago had been tethered by my tent, where a few thrall boys cared for the Irish stallion and the mounts of my commanders. Today I would share my men's dangers and stand in the front rank. My line stood half way up the slope

313

and above them stood the reserve below the copse which covered Bron yr Erw's crest.

Maelgwn's six *helwyr* had been joined by two dozen more men and the bowmen grinned as I walked down their line, clapping the gap-toothed *helwyr* on the shoulder. The bowmen had not strung their huge bows but were busy sticking their arrows in the ground. One of the bowmen pissed on his arrows, earning a disgusted look from Tyrnog. The archer laughed. "Do not worry monk. The piss poisons the arrows." He grinned wickedly before the young monk turned and scurried after me.

Everyone was in position and the banners of my army flew. It was a glorious sight. The banner of Aberffraw caught in the slight breeze as it stood in the centre of my line. I could make out Ronan's large profile and knew he would protect the banner with his life. Sitric's black raven on its white field hung next to mine. I glanced towards Maelgwn's men and noticed the banner of Mathrafal did not fly. Cynwrig's crow-pecked skull still topped the spear and I shuddered at the empty eye sockets and greying shreds of flesh.

The various banners of Arfon flew next to Owain's white cross on its red field and I glanced at the reserve. Lord Tudur's simple banner hung limply at the formation's centre, a black field with a thin white line running through its centre. The reserve would be pivotal today I thought.

My men grinned happily as I shouldered my way to the front rank to join Sitric and Cerit. Sitric was to my right with Cerit besides him; Bjorgolf shouldered his way through and took up position on my left. I glanced behind me to where Ljot and Tyrnog glanced reassuringly back.

Time seemed to slow as the mist began to clear and mid-morning approached. War horns sounded in the enemy camp, but still I could not see what was happening. It took another two long hours until the mist was almost entirely burnt off by the sun. The sun had reached its zenith and I could not believe it was only mid-day.

My army had been in position for hours and waited patiently for the first signs of enemy activity. The enemy host was slowly being cajoled into position and I, as well as most of my men, stared in wonderment. It seemed as though every man of Powys stood a mile ahead of us. The floodplain seemed crowded with the men as they swarmed under the banners of their lords.

As I glanced down the enemy's line I cursed. Like Trahaearn's army the enemy's ranks were swelled with peasant levies who jeered and shook their assorted weaponry with anger. They were not the men I worried about. The King of Powys had positioned his disciplined men at intervals down the line and I cursed as I counted the tightly packed ranks. I estimated Iorwerth had upwards of five hundred hardened warriors, who added the backbone to his horde of peasants. I had long since lost count of the peasants and wild men from the hills who, I guessed, numbered close to two thousand.

I swallowed hard as I looked down my well organised line and I could not help but notice how pitifully few my men were. I had just over five hundred men under my command and realised we must be outnumbered by nearly five to one. The enemy horde shuddered forward after a series of drones sounded from the vast collection of war horns and began to advance over the flat grassland to the front. A large troop of horsemen walked their mounts forward on the enemy's right flank to my left. I cursed again; the enemy horsemen would not risk their mounts by charging uphill but I knew they would butcher my army were we broken and I instantly feared for the camp and its followers at the foot of the reverse slope, as they were lightly protected. I counted the ranks quickly; almost two hundred horsemen and I noticed the yellow cloth with its burgundy lion catch in the wind. It was the banner of Mathrafal, the King of Powys marched his army towards me.

A troop of ten horsemen broke from the ranks and cantered towards the enemy centre, where a few lords pushed their mounts through the ranks. A war horn sounded and the enemy advance rippled to a halt around eight hundred paces away. A white cloth was tied to one of the horsemen's large spears and the troop of horsemen cantered forwards.

There must have been thirty riders in total with the enemy banners fluttering above them. Sitric turned to me. "Bastards have come to talk by the looks of it; I assume you won't give in to whatever they demand?"

I scoffed and Bjorgolf laughed. "Of course not. The question is, will they give in to my demands?"

All the men in earshot laughed at my words as the enemy horsemen thundered closer. They halted a hundred paces away and only four riders walked their mounts forwards. I broke clear of my line and strolled towards them, my shield feeling heavy on my left arm. I clasped my sword hilt for luck and glanced either side of me. Sitric, Cerit and Bjorgolf had come forward with me and Ronan carried my banner proudly behind us.

I halted thirty paces from my men and eyed the horsemen as they came to a stop and stared down at me. I recognised one of the men and nodded to him. Asser bowed his head respectfully and shot me an expressionless acknowledgment.

A finely dressed man in gleaming wargear sat atop a huge black horse, which reminded me of those that the Frenchmen used. He was in his early twenties and his brown moustache was interspersed with wisps of red as his brown eyes looked me up and down. He wore a finely crafted helm which sported the gleaming figure of a prancing horse, a symbol of Powys. A long plume of white horsehair fell to his shoulders from the rear of his helm and the plume seemed dazzling in the sunshine. His helm was expertly crafted with a golden crown. He spoke in an even tone. "I am Iorwerth, son of Bleddyn, King of Powys. I assume you are Gruffudd son of Cynan?"

I nodded my head respectfully. "I am he, lord. May I ask why your army marches through my lands?"

The king laughed and glanced at the two men either side of him. Asser smiled and chuckled nervously whilst the third man just stared at me. "Your lands? Ha!" Iorwerth spat to emphasise his point and the wad of phlegm landed at my feet. "My kinsman was killed by your un-Godly forces. The honourable Cynwrig's death must be answered."

I laughed bitterly. "Honourable? The man had no honour." Sitric chuckled as the King of Powys' eyes narrowed at the insult. "He died poorly, weeping and pleading for his life."

Asser swallowed hard as the third man went to draw his blade but Iorwerth laid a calming hand on his companion's sword arm. Bjorgolf eyed the third man and growled threateningly. Iorwerth's tone was laced with forced politeness. "Nevertheless he was a kinsman of mine and his death must be avenged. Unless you are willing to consider the proposal I put forwards?"

I cocked an eyebrow and spoke evenly. "I shall listen, but I warn you that you will be wasting your breath."

The king smiled to himself. "I expected nothing less, but formality dictates." I inclined my head at the truth of it. "You will surrender and your forces may return, unmolested, to their lands. However, you will surrender your mortal body to my safe keeping. The lands of Meirionydd and Dunoding shall become part of Powys." He gestured to his left, "The Lord Asser shall rule Lleyn independently as lord-protector." Iorwerth then gestured to his right. "And Trahaearn shall rule the northern provinces of this land."

I chuckled to myself. So this was Trahaearn the usurper, my enemy. The man I had never met but only seen the back of him as he fled a battlefield and ran to Powys. Trahaearn was in his late thirties and his blue eyes stared hatefully at me. A large blond moustache dominated his face, in the Celtic fashion, and he was of a strong build. He seemed formidable indeed.

I shot him a look of disgust. "Trahaearn has no right to the lands of Gwynedd and neither do either of you." Asser looked awkwardly away whilst Iorwerth fixed me with an amused expression.

"So you refuse?" The King of Powys spoke carelessly, as if he neither cared if I accepted or not.

"I refuse." I spoke firmly and smiled mockingly at the three men. "I have a counter-proposal though?"

Iorwerth rolled his eyes. "Yes, yes. Please go ahead."

I smirked. "I request that you and your forces surrender the field and return to Powys. Lord Asser will be forgiven and I request that Trahaearn be handed over to me so that he can answer for his crimes." The three men looked at me as though I was mad. Cerit, Bjorgolf and Ronan were clueless to the conversation, as none had mastered Briton yet, but Sitric chuckled approvingly at my words. I spoke mockingly. "So, lord, do you make the correct choice and surrender?"

The king shot me a scowl of utter derision and clapped his hands in mock applause. "Your confidence is to be applauded. In answer to your question, no I shall not surrender."

I smiled back at him; I had shown defiance that was all that mattered. "Then, lord, I wish you luck. For you will need it."

Iorwerth laughed and clicked his tongue before applying pressure with his knees, turning his mount back towards his army. Asser nodded awkwardly and spurred after his new master. Trahaearn did not follow and simply stared at me.

I raised an amused eyebrow. "Should you not scurry back to your master?" Before Trahaearn could respond I spoke forcefully in a voice filled with hate. "I shall look for you on the battlefield. One day, maybe not this day, but one day I shall see you dead."

Trahaearn sniggered to himself and turned his mount to follow the King of Powys. The riders reached their escort and galloped back to their host. I switched back to Irish and chuckled to myself. "Well they won't surrender."

We all laughed and turned to walk back to my waiting line, which looked so lacking in numbers on the slopes of Bron yr Erw compared to the vast host which plotted our deaths. As we took our places in the line horns sounded ahead and the vast enemy force shuddered forwards again.

The ground was dry and dust began to rise behind the enemy army. The sound was immense, no jeers could be made out clearly but they were hurled by the enemy nonetheless. The sound rose to the intensity of a storm as my line waited. The sun baked down and I began to sweat freely below my mail.

My hand gripped and un-gripped my sword hilt and I could feel the sweat moist in my palm. My legs began to weaken and my stomach sink as the enemy inched closer and closer. The enemy horsemen had taken up position on the far right of my line and waited patiently for their foot soldiers to break my small army.

All around I heard men muttering prayers to God and even a few to their Pagan gods. Gwcharki babbled in his strange language, driving himself into a frenzy. The huge Pict's presence strengthened the resolve of his fellows. The man mountain stopped his chanting and dropped his shield and fearsome weapons. He pulled the mail coat off his huge frame and flung it to the ground. His powerful fingers dug into his tunic and he ripped it from his body. The tightly muscled body tensed and his blue tattoos rippled as he bent to pick up his weapons. He brought the heavy shield up effortlessly and flexed his huge arm that held the most fearsome weapon I had ever seen. The Pict had discarded his axe in the camp and now held a new weapon, which he had crafted himself. He gripped the sturdy wooden handle in his giant hand and grinned as the chains clunked together as he tested the weapon's weight. Dangling from the chain was a large iron ball the size of a child's head; the ball was studded with metal spikes and I swallowed hard. I was not the only one who was thankful the huge Pict and his frightening weapon were on my side.

I glanced forward and looked up to the heavens. Again I saw a bird of prey, and wondered if it had been the same one I had seen days earlier. I admired the bird, one of nature's killers, as it circled high up in the air. I muttered a prayer to the heavens, hoping God or whoever was up there watched over me.

The enemy was closing and I felt my heart begin to quicken under my wargear. They were less than three hundred paces now. Please God, look favourably upon me. I drew my blade as others all the way down the line did the same. The enemy still jeered and a few ran forwards to brandish their arses or genitals. My men stared quietly on and I was proud of them, keeping their discipline against such overwhelming odds. Two hundred yards now and Sitric's men began to thump on their shields, making a fearsome racket. All down the line the men followed suit in the usual pre-battle ritual. The shields thumped and jeers were shouted. I closed my eyes and breathed deeply and I heard Maelgwn's voice bark across the battlefield.

"*Helwyr*, loose!" I heard the dull thump of the bowstrings snapping back and the humming of the arrows as they soared over our heads. I opened my eyes the moment the arrows hit home and the first screams began. The battle upon the slopes of Bron yr Erw had begun.

XXVIII

Volley after volley zipped overhead and cut into the enemy ranks. There were only two dozen bowmen in my ranks but their expertise created havoc amongst the leading ranks of the enemy. The poorly disciplined enemy levies and mountain men to my front took brutal punishment as more and more of their comrades went down, whilst the hardened warriors did their best to cover themselves with their small round-shields and hunched as if they walked into a violent storm.

The enemy were still over a hundred paces away and the screams of pain and anger carried clearly to my line as my men cheered the bowmen. I had ordered the fletchers amongst the camp followers to work long into the night using what ever wood and feathers they could find, to ensure my bowmen could bleed the enemy badly. As a result, each bowman had forty arrows studded in the ground about them but they were beginning to dwindle. And still the enemy came on under the relentless punishment.

A dark cloud suddenly appeared to shoot up from behind the enemy line. The dark cloud reached up into the sky and then began to plummet towards us. I cursed as I realised what the cloud was. Sitric shouted urgently at my side. "Prepare to receive missiles!" All along the line men raised their shields and did their best to shelter from the storm. Despite this some arrows managed to sneak through the gaps and the screams of pain began. My arm jarred as an arrow punched into my shield and I cursed at the stinging sensation that came with it. The arrow head had penetrated through the limewood shield and I cursed as I felt a warm trickle of blood run down my forearm; luckily the shield had served its purpose and absorbed the power of the missile, but it still hurt like hell. I heard a few more screams as more and more arrows began to hit home amongst my men. I dared not look as my ears were besieged by the sound, with each volley the noise seemed to intensify like a swarm of bees; buzzing sounded all around and I felt another thump on my shield and silently gave my thanks as the limewood held strong.

A huge roar erupted from my front and I heard the enemy bellow their war cries. I risked a glance over my shield and watched as the discipline of my enemy evaporated. The *hewer's* arrows had relentlessly found their targets and the peasants had had enough. They had soaked up their fill of death and let out a bloodcurdling scream and surged forwards. Eighty paces, seventy on they came. The leading men fell and sprawled in the turf as the arrows continued to find their targets. Some of the charging enemy caught their feet on the flailing limbs of their fallen comrades and crashed to the ground as chaos infected the enemy. The enemy bowmen still fired despite their charging allies and some of the poorly aimed missiles began to strike their own side.

Still they came. The peasants had surged forwards all the way down the enemy line and they laboured towards us. Sixty paces, fifty, forty. They had charged too soon and they were beginning to blow as they reached the foot of the slope. However I could feel no satisfaction as my eyes scanned the disciplined enemy hearth-troops, who marched steadily on, fifty paces behind their screaming countrymen who plodded up the slope. A reserve of peasants lingered behind the warbands of Powysian warriors and I noticed their lord gesturing to hold them back and recognised him instantly from his gleaming mail, Trahaearn.

The enemy levymen were blown as they climbed the last few feet and screamed their challenges. My shieldwall remained still and the peasants surged towards death. An elderly man with no teeth and wild greying hair thrust an ancient spear towards me. The spear glanced off my shield and the old shaft snapped with the pressure. The man's yellow eyes widened and he screamed in fear as Gwcharki's iron ball hurtled towards him. I felt the rush of air as the iron ball flew over me and grimaced as it made a sickly slapping noise followed by a dull crack as it obliterated the man's face. Another peasant took the old man's place and screamed as the momentum from behind pushed him into my shield. The hapless man was powerless to resist as my blade darted under my shield and into his guts. He screamed but was held up right by the press of men, blood spluttered out of his mouth as he drew his last breath. As he screamed warm droplets of blood and spittle landed on my cheeks and I thrust again with my blade, twisting it before pulling it free. The screams stopped and the dead man was gone.

The pressure was intense; all around men screamed and died. Gwcharki's iron ball hurtled backwards and forwards over my head, smashing skulls and creating panic. Blood spurted through the air from a peasant's neck after the iron ball removed his head. Tyrnog's short spear darted over my shoulder to take another man in the face, the tip cutting into the man's cheek before the young monk twisted it back.

Bjorgolf grunted at my side as he worked his blade in short, efficient, strokes. The ground was slick with enemy blood and I tried not to notice the stench of voided bladders and bowels as I cut forwards again. My blade scythed through a peasant's ribs and I twisted the blade before wrenching it back. I did not see the man fall as another thrust forwards and flailed wildly with a small axe towards me I ducked as his axe missed my helm by inches. Tyrnog's spear flashed back and the man was no longer there. A wildman of the hills, clad in filthy hides and furs screamed through his unkempt beard, spittle flying from his toothless mouth, as he was forced towards me by the press of men. He was pushed onto my shield and the man's cries of defiance turned into a shriek of pain as my blade punched through his groin.

Warm blood was slick on my hand as I cut forwards again taking yet another man above the crotch; his gut rope fell through the gaping wound and slithered around my feet like a blue-grey coiled serpent. The man screamed in despair and fell to the ground as yet another attacker summoned the courage to throw himself at my shieldwall. The man's sturdy wooden club hammered into my shield and again Tyrnog's short spear darted over my shoulder. The man saw it too late and he just had enough time to widen his eyes in surprise before the lethal point ripped away his sight forever.

I gritted my teeth against the pressure as the enemy threw away their lives on my shieldwall. "Is there no end to the bastards?" Bjorgolf heard my words above the din of battle and shouted an inaudible, no doubt sarcastic, response as he took another man's life. Suddenly the pressure eased as the casualties became too great and a shout of triumph went up from my line. A man swung his club at my shield in one last futile act of defiance and turned to run after his retreating brothers in arms. My muscles ached from the effort of killing and I ignored the beads of sweat running down my face as I watched the levymen and hillmen turn and hurtle down the slope towards their advancing comrades. The enemy warriors marched steadily on and pushed their way through their fleeing comrades, some even turning their blades on the broken rabble, forcing them away from the disciplined formations.

A wall of dead had built up in front of my shieldwall and Bron yr Erw's slopes were littered with the dead and dying and laced with blood. I glanced at the ground in front of me and shook my head at the slaughter; eight dead enemies were bunched before me and flies were already thick on the spilt gut ropes and gaping wounds. I watched as a wounded peasant dragged himself back down the slope, a half severed leg slithering behind him. The man wailed pitifully for help as he inched his way down the blood-laced hill.

I glanced either side of me, Bjorgolf screamed at the enemy through a blood splattered face and Sitric did likewise. I risked a look behind and cursed at the number of wounded men. Damn, but I could not afford to lose a single one. Maelgwn's *helwyr* had exhausted their arrows and now tended the wounded. Two monks from Clynnog Fawr had followed the army south and they too helped the wounded men. Tyrnog looked grimly on towards the enemy's second wave. I could not help but marvel at the young monk's bravery. The lad was clearly destined to be a warrior and I wondered why he had become a monk but I shook my head to stop my thoughts from wandering as this was no time to think of such things.

Ronan's bushy head nodded at me and I nodded reassuringly back at the big Irishman, who still flew my banner proudly, before turning my attention back to the enemy. The disciplined warriors of Iorwerth's army had reached the foot of the slope and began to labour up, shields ready. Some lords walked their mounts behind their men whilst some led from the front. I saw Trahaearn and Asser leading Iorwerth's reserve and cursed them. The two had halted their men and trotted their mounts forward. They slashed their blades through the air frantically and screamed at the frightened peasants and hillmen who had broken themselves on my defensive line. Some ran on beyond Iorwerth's reserve but most began to reform under the banners of Trahaearn and Asser.

A small number of men darted forwards from the warband approaching directly from the front as I shouted hoarsely; "Shields up!" The enemy hurled javelins towards us and I cursed as one thumped into my shield and dragged it down. Bjorgolf unceremoniously shoved me back and Ljot forced his way forwards and took my place. I cursed at my bad luck as I shouldered my way to the rear of my men. I dropped the useless shield to the ground before placing my foot on the damaged timber, wrenching the javelin free. The wood splintered as it came free and I judged the weapons weight as I held it in my hands. It was lighter than most spears and the point was wickedly sharp. I could see the enemy banners approaching twenty paces from my front rank. I drew back my arm and launched the wicked javelin over my men and watched it disappear amongst the approaching enemy, I thought I was rewarded with a scream but I could not be sure.

Ronan watched grimly on before turning his gaze on me. "The lads are doing well, so they are." The big Irishman nodded firmly at his own words before turning his gaze back to the advancing ranks of the enemy. He was right, we had broken their first attack and now had to hold firm again. If we could force back these men, who were the backbone of Iorwerth's army then the balance of power would swing in my favour.

With ten paces to go the enemy screamed and charged forwards, smashing into my tiring men. I crossed myself and muttered a silent prayer as my men grimly fought for their lives in front of me. I cursed my luck again, had that spear not ruined my shield I would be in that front rank; it was where I should be. There were screams all around and I cursed as one of my sword-brothers, Bjarni the old trader, staggered back from the line. The old Dane had been with me from the start and I grimaced as he fell on his back and waited for death. His face had been ruined by a strong blow that had cut across his eyes and the bridge of his nose. There was nothing to be done for him and I crossed myself as his chest rose and fell for the last time. I cursed loudly as I felt the tide of fortune turn against me for the enemy had the advantage. They could replace their tiring men with fresh warriors whereas I could not.

All along my line men fell back, wounded or dead. Ruaidri stumbled back through the rear rank and dropped his shield, clutching the wound on his left shoulder. The rogue had sheathed his blade and offered me an apology for being clumsy. I cuffed Ruaidri around the back of his head. "You owe me no apology, my friend. Help your brother protect the banner." With that I stooped and picked up his fallen shield.

I ran forwards and barged my way through until I was beside Tyrnog in the second rank. Gwcharki's iron ball hurtled overhead and crumpled through an enemy helmet, killing the man instantly. We were having the better of it here and I risked a glance down the line. Maelgwn's men were holding firm but I cursed as I noticed Owain's men and the men of Arfon faltering. The enemy had broken their shield wall and were amongst them. I saw the tip of Trahaearn's banner moving forwards to where my left flank faltered and I cursed as I realised what was happening, Trahaearn had led his reserve forward and was about to turn my flank.

I turned and shoved my way back through the line until I came to Oengus, who stood in the rear rank to

Ronan's front. "Oengus go to Lord Tudur now, he must bolster the left flank or all is lost. Now go!" Oengus nodded and trotted towards Tudur and my reserve who lingered in the copse fifty paces further up the slope.

I cursed as Trahaearn outflanked Owain's struggling men. I watched helplessly as Trahaearn waved his sword in the air, shouting words of encouragement to his men. Suddenly the sword was swept down and he dug in his heels. Trahaearn's mount surged forwards and all about him his men screamed their fury and followed him into my flank. Owain's men would break; there was nothing that could be done to stop that. The fate of the battle was in Tudur's hands and, if he did not act now, all would soon be lost.

I felt a blow on my helm and cursed as my ears rang with the impact. I glanced down to where a smooth pebble lay at my feet; more pebbles thumped into the ground around us and I petulantly picked one up and threw it back, cursing loudly. I glanced back at the left flank and felt the anger rise in my chest as Trahaearn's men drove further and further down my line. Where was Tudur?

I felt a rising sense of doubt and fear rising from my stomach, and looked back towards the tree line and could not believe it. Tudur and the reserve just stood there, Oengus secured between two burly guards. I glanced back towards Owain's men and despaired. Trahaearn's charge had smashed through Owain's final attempts of resistance. The Lord of Tegeingl and the men of Arfon knew all was lost and broke; the usurper had routed my flank.

Tears began to form in my eyes as I watched helplessly whilst the panic spread further and further down my line and I knew the battle was all but lost. I looked from the beginnings of defeat to the reserve. Tudur, calmly sitting atop his piebald mare, watched and did nothing as my left flank was turned. In that moment I knew I had been betrayed and the battle was lost.

I still clutched my blade and began to march up the hill, inconsolable with rage, towards the man who had betrayed me. I was vaguely aware of Ronan and a few others, still protecting my banner, at my side and Ruaidri awkwardly clutching his blade in his good arm. I ignored the chaos and sounds of defeat behind me as I continued up the slope my eyes vengefully fixed on Tudur. I heard a familiar voice and glanced behind me as Sitric pushed his way to my side. "What the hell is going on? Order the reserve forward or the battle is lost!"

Sitric looked from my mask of anger to the idle reserve and realised what was happening. Tudur had seen my advance and gestured to one of his men; the man passed him a long spear and Tudur took the weapon. The Lord of Cemais dug in his spurs and the mare charged forwards. His men followed suit and screamed their war cries as they surged after their master. Tudur picked me out and, even from forty paces, our eyes met and he smirked. Bastard, he had waited until the last moment to make his move and I knew the battle lost. Sitric glanced at my enraged expression and shouted orders frantically. "With me! Protect the King!"

I swear I could feel the vibrations as Tudur's piebald hurtled towards me. At the last moment I crouched and gripped my blade tightly, ready to strike, as the Lord of Cemais lowered his spear and braced himself for the impact. Time seemed to slow as the traitor thundered towards me. I could see all the fine detail as clumps of mud flew from the horse's hooves, the beast's nostrils widening

330

with the thrill of the charge and the glimmer of sunshine that glanced off the spear's point. Ten paces to go and I braced myself as Tudur licked his lips and his face contorted in the moment before impact.

I screamed in outrage as powerful hands pushed me aside. I shouted in anger as I hit the turf and realised what had happened. Sitric had shoved me aside and taken my place. I turned on the floor and watched in shock as Tudur's spear thumped into my foster-father's chest. Sitric grunted at the impact and died almost instantly on the shaft as the momentum lifted him off his feet. Tudur shouted a war cry as he abandoned the lance and drew his blade, continuing his charge into the rear rank of my line. His sword flashed brightly in the sunlight as he cut my men down, his mount kicked out and bit at my shocked men and I screamed my fury

Oblivious to Tudur's charging men I scrambled forwards on all fours to Sitric's side. The old warrior was dead, Tudur's treacherous lance had punched through his mail and smashed through Sitric's heart. I could no longer hold back the tears as I stared into my foster-father's blank grey eyes. I still wept as I rose and grabbed Sitric's sword, my fallen blade long forgotten. Bjorgolf's strong arms pulled me back, ripping my scarlet tunic. I tried to elbow the Dane away and struggled with all my might but the iron grip held me firm. In that moment I did not care for my own life, all I wanted was to charge at Tudur and kill the treacherous bastard.

Ronan shouted a warning and Bjorgolf released me. I turned to see the remnants of my warband and some of Sitric's men bracing themselves to receive the charge of Tudur's men. I rose to my feet, the blood-lust well upon me, and screamed my hatred as I sprinted forwards to meet their charge.

I swung Sitric's fine blade with all my might and hardly felt the impact as I hacked down the lead man and shouldered into the next. Bjorgolf and Gwcharki were screaming fury at my side as we cut into Tudur's disloyal men. They recoiled from our reckless charge and most darted past us in search of easier prey. I parried a spear thrust and reversed the blade so the tip sliced through the man's windpipe. All thoughts of caution were gone as I threw myself at another one of Tudur's men. The man's blade cut through my shield arm but I did not notice. I worked Sitric's blade in manic strokes, butchering the man down.

Bjorgolf grabbed my left arm and dragged me onwards. I paused in shock, it was only then the pain of the wound shot through me. A red-hot feeling surged through me and I screamed in pain as Bjorgolf shouted in my face. "We must go! The battle is lost." My vision began to blur as I looked around, my bodyguard were there and Bjorgolf pulled me forwards again. Gwcharki wheeled the iron ball above his head and screamed in his strange language as he held some of Tudur's men at bay, none daring to risk entering the arc of the menacing iron ball on its chain. Bjorgolf gestured at some of the men and began to run forwards to help Gwcharki before turning quickly back. He thrust me towards Ruaidri and Oengus. "Protect Gruffudd! Go!"

Oengus draped my good arm over his shoulders and, half carried, half dragged me upwards towards the trees as Ruaidri followed holding his wounded arm awkwardly. I glanced back and saw Tudur's men waver as Gwcharki's fearsome weapon crushed another head to oblivion. Bjorgolf was gathering as many fleeing men around my banner as he could. My vision continued to blur as tears escaped my eyes. Sitric was dead and I had lost the day to treachery. I looked up towards the sky, through the branches of the trees above, why? Why had God abandoned me now?

I cursed as Oengus quickly let go of me. I could not stop myself as I fell flat to the ground and flailed desperately to grab Sitric's blade as it skidded into the undergrowth. I spun round and my eyes widened in surprise as I bellowed in desperation. "No!"

Ruaidri gasped as Oengus' dagger plunged under his mail and into his side. Oengus pulled his dagger free and Ruaidri blinked in shock at the man he had considered a friend. Ruaidri's blade fell to the floor as he dropped to his knees, clutching his wound in silent horror. Oengus pushed him to the floor and loomed above his victim; his voice did not betray any regret. "Sorry, old friend."

The Irishman's brown eyes turned back to me as he gripped his blood covered dagger menacingly. I swallowed hard as my suspicions of the man's treachery flooded back, and I cursed my own stupidity. "Why?" That was all I could whisper as I glanced from him to Ruaidri's prone figure.

We were curiously alone on the wooded hilltop as the sound of battle raged behind us. "Why? For silver, why else?" The Irishman chuckled to himself as he bent down, putting a knee on my chest, forcing me still. He lowered his head close to mine and I could smell his foul breath as he looked into my eyes. "Nearly had you twice at Sord Cholmcille, I won't fail at the third attempt."

I fought the urge to beg for my life as the cold steel of his dagger pressed against my cheek. "Lord Robert wanted you to know that all you wished to gain will now be his." I gasped. Robert had planned all this? Oengus laughed as he took in my shocked expression. "Robert planned it all, Gruffudd, you stupid bastard. Paid me a shit load of silver to join you and your merry band. The man who so nearly had you at Sord Cholmcille the first time did not work for Trahaearn but for Robert."

I spoke harshly, all fear gone. "Bastard, I hope you rot in hell."

The Irishman chuckled. "I probably will, so I will. But I will have a rich life until then. Who knows, maybe I could bribe a priest and buy my way to heaven. A grand plan, so it was." He gestured behind him. "You think all that was Tudur acting on his own?" He laughed again. "The bastard is too thick to act on his own. Robert's bought him too. He will rule that shit hole, you call Ynys Môn, and Robert will have everything he wants. This whole thing was set up for you and Trahaearn to knock shit out of each other, then Robert could walk in and pick up all the pieces for himself. Clever man, so he is."

I shook my head. That slimy bastard of a Frenchman. I glanced behind Oengus then back at him, and smiled. "Not as clever as you, bastard." Oengus followed my gaze but was too late.

Bjorgolf rammed his blade up through the Irishman's back and into his chest. The blade ripped through Oengus' lungs and heart and the tip tried to escape through the studded leather on the bastard's shoulder. Blood streamed from his mouth and he gawped like a fish out of water, trying to take breaths that would not come. "See you in hell, you worthless piece of pig shit." Bjorgolf whispered in his ear before he withdrew the blade and kicked Oengus sideways, spitting on the limp body.

Bjorgolf held out a hand and I grabbed it. I looked at the prostate corpse and shook my head sadly. "I can not believe the bastard did this."

I glanced over to where Ronan gripped his brother's hand. The ugly Irishman looked back at me. "He still lives; I will carry him on my back."

I could do nothing other than nod my agreement as the big man put his unconscious brother over his shoulders and began to lumber on into the woods. Ljot picked up my fallen banner and followed with the rest.

I glanced again at Oengus' corpse and spat at it in disgust. Bjorgolf gripped my good arm. "No bloody time for that, we need to fucking move. Now!" The Dane steered me deeper into the wooded hilltop and then down the other side.

Bjorgolf cursed as we came to the tree line. The Powysian horsemen had ridden around Bron yr Erw and were running riot amongst the camp. Smoke rose in a straight black column and screams carried to us where the horsemen butchered fugitives and camp followers, doing what they pleased with the women.

I glanced to where my tent was ablaze and cursed as a Powysian led Iago away to where the other captured horses were tethered. The tent collapsed in a shower of sparks and I shook my head sadly; I had seen enough.

The sounds of a victorious army hunting fugitives through the trees sounded behind us and I looked back at my frightened men. We were well hidden amongst the trees that skirted my camp and I could see the road was clear ahead. I could not be sure that the horsemen would ignore us, but it was a risk we would have to take. I glanced at all the faces who stared back at me with a mixture of grim determination and fear.

I swallowed hard, trying my best to keep calm. "Men, we skirt through these trees until we come to the road. From there we go on to Segontium and then back to Ireland." I spoke bitterly for I knew the campaign to be lost and I remembered my final promise to Sitric. As much is it galled me, I would live to fight another day.

Thirty men were with me as we rustled through the undergrowth and trees of the woodland. The remnants of my bodyguard and Tyrnog were with me as was Cerit, who was inconsolable as tears streaked freely down his face, and Mac Ruaidri with five of his Irish. The rest were a mixture of what was left of my men and Sitric's warband. I did not know what had happened to Maelgwn or Owain, the Lord of Tegeingl, but now was not the time to think of such things.

My mind was fixed totally on survival as we crouched at the edge of the tree line and looked up the road. Scores of fugitives had tried to flee directly through the camp but the Powysian horsemen had caught them. The screams carried across to us as the men were butchered, I heard a few of my men mutter prayers for the souls of the trapped fugitives and I muttered one of my own. The Powysian horsemen were showing no quarter and I shook my head at their ruthlessness.

I glanced up the empty road which led to Segontium and at the landscape around it. The land was barren and windswept either side of the road, the tree cover ended and vast mountain peaks lay to either side. I could not risk the mountain passes or it could take days to reach the relative safety of Segontium. No, we must take the road. I knew it was a half a day's march and if we hurried we could be there under the cover of darkness. Or should I wait in the trees until dark and then attempt an escape?

Distant calls of alarm sounded deep in the woodland and that made up my mind. We would take the road, but would have to be quick and hope the horsemen were too distracted to see us before we disappeared from view.

I glanced back at my men. "Follow me and we shall be safe before the day is out. Trust me." Bjorgolf grumbled his agreement and most of the men nodded their consent. I swallowed hard and crept out of the tree cover and onto the dirt road. I beckoned for my men to follow and began to trot towards Segontium. Bjorgolf was soon beside me and I glanced behind to see all the men had followed. Ronan plodded grimly on with Ruaidri still on his back. Ruaidri had drifted in and out of consciousness and had gone worryingly pale before Ronan did his best to stop the bleeding. The big Irishman had learnt herbal remedies from his mother and he muttered a few words to himself as he had tended to his brother. The wound was bad and I hoped the journey would not kill him.

Ljot still carried my banner but did not hold it high. The cloth was ripped and blood splattered as it dragged in the dust of the road but that was the least of my concerns. Cerit caught up with me and met my gaze before his words failed him. We, like my banner, were all blood splattered and tired but we forced our aching limbs on. There had been no call of alarm or the sound of hooves of pursuing horsemen. I glanced behind and felt a twinge of relief.

Ahead the road lay open and we would have to push our bodies to the limit if we were to reach Segontium. I just hoped the enemy horsemen would be too preoccupied with plunder to launch a pursuit. I thought of Sitric lying dead

338

on the field and my eyes began to water again as I relived my foster-father's sacrifice. I held back my feelings and steadied myself to think only of how to keep these men alive. It must have been mid-afternoon as I glanced up at the sky and I prayed we would be unmolested, but I knew those chances were slim.

The sun was beginning to set as I glanced about me. The road to Segontium still lay open and there had been no signs of pursuit. The men were spent, but they knew they must push themselves again and soon. We rested amongst a small crop of boulders which shielded us from view.

I lay flat on a smooth boulder and peered over the top. I could make out the shapes of small groups of fugitives following in our footsteps and I could not help but wonder what had happened to Maelgwn. I was almost certain the scarred mercenary lived; if anyone would be able to extricate themselves from this mess I was certain it would be him.

I slithered back down the boulder and glanced at Cerit. His eyes were red and no more tears would come as he sat with his head in his hands. Now was not the time to talk of what had happened, I hoped he would not blame me for Sitric's death. My heart had been deeply torn by my foster-father's death and I knew all too well how Cerit felt, but I could not afford to give way to my feelings for lives depended upon me remaining level headed.

A pitifully weak whimper of pain caught my attention and I glanced across to where Bjorgolf and Ronan held Ruaidri still whilst Tyrnog stitched the wound. The monk's tongue stuck out of the corner of his mouth as he concentrated on stitching the wound. Tyrnog finished and tied a knot in the sinew, or whatever it was he had used. Ruaidri whimpered in pain as Bjorgolf and Ronan did their best to comfort him.

The monk caught my eye and quickly scuttled over to where I sat and began to inspect my wounded arm. I glanced again at Ruaidri. "Will he live?"

Tyrnog considered my question for a moment and then shrugged his shoulders. "He is in the hands of God, my King." I winced as the monk prodded my wound and he made soft soothing noises as he inspected it further. Tyrnog held up his needle to the dwindling light and threaded the sinew through the small loop at the top of the metal needle.

I tried not to show the pain as the needle worked its way through my flesh, but it was hard not to grimace. I closed my eyes and gritted my teeth against the pain but I was in good hands and it was soon over. I opened my eyes as Tyrnog finished his work and muttered a prayer for my wound to heal well and avoid infection.

Mac Ruaidri waited until the monk had finished before moving over to me. The old warrior knelt beside me. "What next, Lord?"

I glanced about me and could see the entrance to the straits as the sun began to set. I judged that it was not much further to Segontium and could afford the men a few moments more rest. "We will rest a few moments longer and then push on to Segontium. From there we shall sail to Abermenai and do our best to save as many of our men from this disaster as we can."

Mac Ruaidri turned his head quickly towards the road and I sensed it at the same moment. Calls of alarm sounded in the distance and the unmistakable growing rumble of approaching horsemen. My men had heard it too and all clutched their weapons as Bjorgolf began to work his way over to me. I ignored the pain in my arm and shuffled my way back up the big boulder and peered over the top. We were hidden from the road and, for that, I was grateful.

Mac Ruaidri had joined me and he whistled softly to himself. "Poor buggers, they will have to form up or the bloody horsemen will make mincemeat of them." Bjorgolf murmured his agreement with the old Irishman but I stared straight ahead whilst my mind worked.

A bedraggled band of fugitives had made their way round a turn in the road and urgently glanced about them as they searched for an escape. The thunder of approaching hooves grew but I still could not see them.

There were close to fifty men in the panicked band and they formed up desperately as their leader screamed at them. From that distance I could not tell who the men were or who led them but I knew they would need help.

I glanced back down and spoke sharply. "Men, to arms!" A few groaned but must muttered silent prayers or crossed themselves as they crouched, ready to surge from cover to the aid of their stranded comrades.

Mac Ruaidri cursed as the horsemen came into view and closed on the group of desperate men. I estimated close to forty horsemen were there and they formed into two ranks as their prey desperately formed up into a tight huddle around their leader, shields raised and weapons ready; the last desperate formation when all was lost.

The horsemen kicked their mounts into a canter as they closed the gap on the huddle of fugitives, less than fifty paces from my position. The front rank lowered their lances and urged their mounts on as the fugitive leader called encouragement to his men.

I glanced back down at Bjorgolf and nodded; the time was now. I dropped back down the boulder and drew my blade, ignoring the deep throbbing in my shield arm. "Now men. Show the bastards no mercy!"

I led my thirty or so men out of the rocky outcrop and screamed my war cry as the horsemen closed on the compact huddle of fugitives who, at that moment, braced to receive the charge. Bjorgolf and Mac Ruaidri panted either side of me and I felt my heart rate quicken as the enemy horsemen desperately tried to halt their beasts.

They were trapped and their leader knew it. The horses reared and the riders called desperately as they tried to turn their mounts. The fugitives knew it too and screamed their war cries before charging at the panicked horsemen.

The gap closed quickly and the horses screamed in fear as their legs were hacked from beneath them and their masters pulled from the saddle. The riders at the rear of the formation were beginning to break clear as my men reached the road. A riderless horse bolted down the road as we closed the trap. Just short of half the horsemen had escaped but the remnants were trapped.

A horse tried to kick out at me and screamed as I chopped Sitric's blade into the beast's leg. The animal crumpled to the floor and fell sideways, crushing its rider beneath its bulk. Mac Ruaidri thrust his blade down and into the trapped rider's throat as we surged on. A terrified horse turned to face me and reared as I slammed my blade into its ugly teeth. They were done, most of the enemy had fled and those who had not been killed tried to surrender.

The memory of defeat and the slaughter of my camp followers was still fresh in mind so I had no wish to stop the inevitable slaughter. Horsemen pleaded for their lives and screamed as vengeful weapons butchered them. A blood covered figure appeared before me and embraced me enthusiastically before I could react. The nosepiece had been lost and the man's left cheek cut open, but there was no mistaking him. Maelgwn lived and the mercenary clapped me fondly on the shoulder.

"We live to fight another day, eh?" He glanced down the road at the horsemen, who had stayed to watch as we looted their dead. "Piss off home, you bastards!" He jeered at the horsemen before looking about him. Nineteen horsemen had been killed and two left horseless as they sprinted towards their countrymen.

I glanced up at the setting sun and back to Maelgwn. "No time to linger, my friend. We must push on." The scarred face mumbled its acceptance and the Powysian began to shout at his weary men to get moving.

We had bought ourselves some time by ambushing the enemy horsemen. I just hoped it would be enough. I waited a few moments as Ronan retrieved his wounded brother and carried him forward onto the road.

Bjorgolf fell-in alongside me. "Nicely done, bastards didn't know what hit them." The Dane looked weary, as did we all, and I remembered he had not had any rest at all the night before. Bjorgolf cracked into a smile. "Don't you worry, lad, there is plenty of energy left in my limbs."

I hoped he was right as we started to move up the road. Not long until Segontium I told myself and mouthed the same words over and over; one foot in front of the other. I just hoped we had bought enough time and the horsemen would not reappear, for Segontium was not far.

The glow of the camp fires around Segontium had been our goal for the last few miles as we hurried as fast as our tired limbs would allow. My whole body ached and I wondered if we had lost anyone through exhaustion. A few enemy scouts had shadowed us for almost the entire way after we had ambushed the horsemen earlier. I glanced over my shoulder and saw the scouts had disappeared and that worried me.

Bjorgolf and Mac Ruaidri were at my side and marched grimly on as each step brought us closer to safety. My small column numbered little over eighty and I knew we would be no match for the horsemen if they returned in strength. My men were spent and only the prospect of an end to the nightmare pushed them on.

As we began to climb the small slope to the old Roman fort I heard a war horn blast its notes, quickly followed by a call of alarm from the rear. I turned but could not see anything in the gloom, but I knew what it was. I screamed at my men. "Run, for God's sake run!"

I forced my heavy legs forward and felt them begin to cramp as the incline worked my weary muscles. My feet had long since become a dull pain and I could feel the blisters burst and mingle with blood as I forced each foot down again and again.

Terrified shouts began to sound as the thunder of hooves grew in intensity. Two of Gwyncu's men stood guard behind the old Roman foundations and they both pointed down the slope at our approach. They threw their weapons to one side and ran. I cursed; they must have thought we were attacking them. The whole ground seemed to shudder as we fled as fast as we could up the grassy slope and in to the narrow passageways of Segontium.

The stone foundations narrowed into a small street and my men ran down it. I stopped and turned, beckoning my men on. Maelgwn trudged past as Bjorgolf pushed himself to my side. The Powysian made towards me but I shouted back at him. "Maelgwn, the ships! Secure the ships!" The mercenary nodded and plodded after his men.

The sound of hooves thumping into the turf was like a constant thunder as Mac Ruaidri came into view with a few stragglers. Then the first horseman appeared behind the limping fugitives. I called a warning but it was too late for one of the men as the horseman's lance punched through his back. The man screamed as he fell and the horseman abandoned his lance as he tried to draw a blade but he was too slow. Mac Ruaidri grabbed hold of the horse's bridle and punched the horse in its eye.

The beast reared and the rider toppled out of the saddle. With frightening speed the old warrior stamped down with his boot on the man's face until he was still. The horse bolted and hampered the advance of the other riders. Mac Ruaidri screamed at the stragglers to form up and he turned to face me. "Run you fool! Run!"

Bjorgolf grabbed my sword arm and dragged me further down the dark street of Segontium. I had been hard on the old Irishman and suddenly felt guilty as the sounds of battle began to grow behind me. Mac Ruaidri had failed in his task to control Faelan and he intended to put things right by sacrificing himself.

I risked a backwards glance and saw the old warrior fall. A horse trampled his fallen body and the rider kicked it forwards. Mac Ruaidri's sacrifice had bought us a few moments and I planned to take full advantage. I followed Bjorgolf as quickly as I could down the hill from Segontium and towards the ships.

It seemed all of Gwyncu's men had abandoned their positions around Segontium and followed my fleeing band back towards the ships. Campfires burned on the shingle beach ahead and I could make out the dark shadows of the ships' hulls as men clambered aboard.

Urgent shouts sounded ahead as men clambered to safety and then helped haul their comrades aboard. I had ordered five ships to remain below Segontium in the mouth of the Seiont and I knew they would be sufficient. Behind the thunder of hooves grew louder and louder and the horsemen whooped with the thrill of the chase as they caught sight of Bjorgolf and myself.

I dared not look back and only concentrated ahead as we sprinted towards the ships. My legs pounded and my chest heaved with the exertion. Bjorgolf panted next to me as we both ran grimly on. I heard a bow string snap and a horse screech in pain a few paces behind me and then we were there. We had reached safety.

Hands reached down from the dark hull and pulled us up. A familiar face came into view and I recognised the lazy eyed gaze instantly, Briain. "Never so glad to be aboard *God's Wrath* I wager. Desperate stuff, so it is."

I laughed with relief as the ship's master helped me up. The men who had clambered aboard the vessel had joined the crew on the oar benches and the men heaved the long wooden oars with all their might. *God's Wrath* inched away from the shoreline and I glanced back at the horsemen who jeered at us.

I saw firelight reflect off shining mail and a man edged his horse as close to the water as he could. I knew instantly who he was as his voice carried on the wind. "This time it is you who flees, young pretender. We shall meet again!" Trahaearn raised his blade in salute and stared for a few moments at the retreating shadow of my ship before turning his mount and spurring away up the beach.

"Bastard." Bjorgolf grunted through gritted teeth. "He has a lot to answer for, so many good men dead because of him." The Dane punched a fist into an outstretched palm and spat over the side of *God's Wrath*.

"Not just him, my friend. Oengus told me everything before he died." I shook my head as a sudden flash of anger surged through my veins, in memory of the betrayal. "Oh, we shall meet again Trahaearn. Mark my words, we will be back."

I stared at the black smudge of land until it disappeared from view. I would be back. Not just for my birthright, but for all the bastards who would pay. I had failed and the shame of it burned inside, fuelled by a deep feeling of anger at the betrayals I had suffered. I thought of Sitric, Wselfwulf, Mac Ruaidri and all the other good men who had died through the betrayal and greed of others. I knew that this was not the end. In that moment I made an oath to myself that scores would be settled and my destiny realised.

I stared at the dark smudge of land one last time and then, finally, turned my back. My birthright had slipped through my fingers but I would be back for my vengeance.

Author's Note

Firstly, I sincerely hope you enjoyed reading the book as much as I enjoyed writing it! I firmly believe that Gruffudd ap Cynan is one of the most interesting individuals to have lived in the early-Medieval period and I hope my book has done Gruffudd's story justice. Gruffudd's life was unusually long and highly eventful, so he and Bjorgolf will set out on more adventures in the future!

I chose to write about this topic, not just because it is the period that I find the most interesting but because I believe the history of the Welsh kingdoms is almost completely unknown - except to those who have a specific interest in the subject. The history of not just Gwynedd but of all the Welsh kingdoms is extremely bloody and filled with political intrigue. If you have an interest in the Medieval period then I urge you to take a look at the history of the Welsh kingdoms during this time. It was rare for a Welsh king, or nobleman for that matter, to meet a natural death and the level of sibling rivalry and betrayal will both fascinate and shock you in equal measure. It is not just the violence and warfare that make Medieval Wales interesting but also Welsh law (the laws of Hywel Dda - which were very advanced for the period, especially regarding women's rights). If you wish to expand your knowledge of the period then I recommend John Davies' "A History of Wales" for a general overview and Giraldus Cambrensis' "The Journey Through Wales and The Description of Wales" for a first hand account.

I feel I must point out that my book is a work of historical fiction based on "Vita Griffini Filii Conani: The Life of Gruffudd ap Cynan." the text of which is a near-contemporary biography of Gruffudd's life, almost certainly written during the reign of his son Owain Gwynedd (1137-1170) as a piece of dynastic propaganda. The text's accuracy is a subject of historical debate and is widely accepted not to be one hundred percent accurate. This gave me somewhat more of a creative licence to write my story. I used D.Simon Evans' translation "A Medieval Prince of Wales: The Life of Gruffudd ap Cynan" as my main point of reference - and I thoroughly recommend it to anybody who wishes to research further into Gruffudd's life.

I chose not to use some aspects of Welsh terminology, which those who are familiar with the topic will know and who may well be annoyed that I did not include them within the novel, and for that I can only apologise. This decision was made for ease of reading, so that all could understand. Thus cantref and cantrefi became province and provinces and ap became son of etc...

Things did not end well for Gruffudd in "Birthright" but do not worry, he lives to fight another day. He may be down on his luck but Gruffudd has scores to settle, a kingdom to win and a woman he loves. Gruffudd will march again!

If you enjoyed the read I would be extremely grateful if you could take a couple of minutes to write a positive review on Amazon. Good reviews really are the lifeblood of independent authors.

I would like to thank my family, for without their support, patience and wisdom none of this would have been possible. Also my editor for her valuable insights, suggestions and advice and the talented Soheil Toosi who designed my book cover, making it a book that stands out and one of which I can be truly proud. Finally, I would like to thank my proof readers Vicky Cortvriend, Gillian Jones, Maisie Lazarus, Daniel and Michael Ward for their valuable thoughts and positive feedback.

Ethan Jones

www.ethan-jones.com

Twitter: https://twitter.com/EthanJones1990

Facebook: https://www.facebook.com/pages/Ethan-Jones/177131622460198

Printed in Great Britain
by Amazon.co.uk, Ltd.,
Marston Gate.